BERTIE PLAYS THE BLUES

Praise for Alexander McCall Smith's
44 Scotland Street series

"Sweet. . . . Graceful. . . . Wonderful. . . . Gentle but powerfully addicting fiction." —*Entertainment Weekly*

"McCall Smith's assessments of fellow humans are piercing and profound. . . . [His] depictions of Edinburgh are vivid and seamless." —*San Francisco Chronicle*

"Irresistible. . . . Packed with the charming characters, piercing perceptions and shrewd yet generous humor that have become McCall Smith's cachet."
—*Chicago Sun-Times*

"McCall Smith's plots offer wit, charm, and intrigue in equal doses." —*Richmond Times-Dispatch*

"Readers will relish McCall Smith's depiction of this place . . . and enjoy his tolerant, good-humored company."
—*...ok Review*

ALEXANDER McCALL SMITH

BERTIE PLAYS THE BLUES

Alexander McCall Smith is the author of the international phenomenon The No. 1 Ladies' Detective Agency
series, the Isabel Dalhousie series, the Portuguese Irregular Verbs series, the 44 Scotland Street series, and the
Corduroy Mansions series. He is professor emeritus of
medical law at the University of Edinburgh in Scotland
and has served with many national and international
organizations concerned with bioethics.

www.alexandermccallsmith.com

BOOKS BY ALEXANDER McCALL SMITH

In the 44 Scotland Street Series

44 Scotland Street

Espresso Tales

Love over Scotland

The World According to Bertie

The Unbearable Lightness of Scones

The Importance of Being Seven

Bertie Plays the Blues

In the No. 1 Ladies' Detective Agency Series

The No. 1 Ladies' Detective Agency

Tears of the Giraffe

Morality for Beautiful Girls

The Kalahari Typing School for Men

The Full Cupboard of Life

In the Company of Cheerful Ladies

Blue Shoes and Happiness

The Good Husband of Zebra Drive

The Miracle at Speedy Motors

Tea Time for the Traditionally Built

The Double Comfort Safari Club

The Saturday Big Tent Wedding Party

The Limpopo Academy of Private Detection

The Minor Adjustment Beauty Salon

For Young Readers

The Great Cake Mystery

The Mystery of Meerkat Hill

In the Isabel Dalhousie Series

The Sunday Philosophy Club

Friends, Lovers, Chocolate

The Right Attitude to Rain

The Careful Use of Compliments

The Comforts of a Muddy Saturday

The Lost Art of Gratitude

The Charming Quirks of Others

The Forgotten Affairs of Youth

The Uncommon Appeal of Clouds

The Perils of Morning Coffee
(eBook only)

BERTIE PLAYS THE BLUES

A 44 Scotland Street Novel

ALEXANDER McCALL SMITH

Illustrations by Iain McIntosh

Vintage Canada

Published in Canada by Vintage Canada, a division of Random House
of Canada Limited, Toronto, in 2013, and simultaneously in the United
States by Anchor Books, a division of Random House LLC, a Penguin
Random House Company, New York. Distributed by Random House of
Canada Limited.

Vintage Canada with colophon is a registered trademark.

www.randomhouse.ca

Library and Archives Canada Cataloguing in Publication

McCall Smith, Alexander, 1948–
Bertie plays the blues : the new 44 Scotland Street novel / Alexander
McCall Smith.

(The 44 Scotland Street series ; 7)
Issued also in electronic format.

ISBN 978-0-307-36194-3

I. Title. II. Series: McCall Smith, Alexander, 1948– . 44 Scotland Street
series ; 7.

PR6063.C326B47 2013   823'.914   C2013-901563-9

Author illustration © Iain McIntosh
Cover design by Iain McIntosh

Printed and bound in the United States of America

2 4 6 8 9 7 5 3 1

This book is for
Mary Davidson

1. *The Question of Birth Order*

Elspeth Harmony's triplets arrived in the order that was to dog them for the rest of their lives: first, second, and third. They could not do otherwise, of course, but this was to determine so much for the three boys: emotional development, confidence, academic achievement, marriage, and ultimately – with that extraordinary synchronicity that nature can sometimes muster – the leaving of this world. Had the hospital not noted their order of appearance, and recorded it on the tiny bracelets fixed round the ankle of each by a nurse, then it would have been chance, rather than seniority, that governed how they fared in relation to one another. But these bracelets were put on, and the die, so to speak, was cast.

Matthew had some inkling about the significance of birth order within a family. As an only child, he had no sibling with whom to develop rivalries and other passions, but he knew so many who did. One friend, the youngest of five boys, had once opened up to him in a maudlin moment in the Cumberland Bar. "They've never taken me seriously," he said. "Never. And everything I had at home – everything – was fifthhand. Fifthhand clothes, shoes, handkerchiefs – the lot."

Matthew thought about this for a moment. "Fourth," he said.

His friend, absorbed in self-pity, had said, rather peevishly, "Fourth? Fourth what?"

"Hand," said Matthew. "It's been through four hands by the time it reaches the fifth child. Therefore – fourthhand."

Self-pity does not appreciate pedantry. "Fifth," said Matthew's friend. "Five owners – fifthhand."

Matthew had stuck to his guns. "No. It depends on the number of hands it has been through. And something that's secondhand has been through two sets of hands: the original owner's and the new owner's."

"That means you have to count the fifth owner too," said the friend. "My clothes were fifthhand. Five owners, including me."

Matthew had lost the point. "You're probably right. But anyway . . ."

"Well, it was awful, I can tell you. And it's carried on all my life. Do you know my oldest brother? You've met him, haven't you? He still treats me as if I'm six. He expresses surprise if he phones and my wife says I'm in the pub. He thinks I'm not old enough. He still thinks that."

"It could be worse," said Matthew. "You could have no siblings – like me. Nobody to compete with. Nobody to think you're too young. Nobody to dilute parental attention."

He was determined, of course, that he and Elspeth should make as few mistakes as possible in bringing up their triplets. A whole library of books had been purchased – each claiming to be the definitive guide to the raising of infants and young children. They had gone to a special talk put on for the parents of twins – prospective multiples had been the term used – and had listened intently to the advice that one should seek to achieve a balance between economy of scale and recognition of individuality.

"Your twin is a person, and not just a twin," said the lecturer. "I call this the paradox of the shared self. We are all ourselves, but we are, at the same time, something other than an isolated self. We are a social self – a self defined by those with whom we live; a self that has imposed upon it a number of roles – the role of sibling, the role of child, the role of lover, the role of employee and so on. The self has so many facets."

This required further thought. More immediate were the various questions raised by those attending, among them that of the effect on the child himself or herself of being a twin or, as the questioner somewhat untactfully put it, worse. This led to a discussion of the usual behavioural issues, and, significantly, to the issue of birth order.

"The experience of the multiple is different from other children," explained the lecturer. "The twin or triplet does not have to deal with existing rights – unless there are already older brothers and sisters. So there will not be a brother or sister who can do things better, who has an established position in the family: the playing field is level in that sense. Unless, of course, you tell the children who is oldest. And, frankly, I don't recommend that. Why create any sense of entitlement?"

"My father was a twin," whispered Elspeth. "He knew that he was younger than his brother. By a couple of minutes, apparently."

"Why did they tell him?" asked Matthew.

"They must have told them when they were very young. He said that he always knew."

"We won't tell," said Matthew. "We don't want to create any sense of entitlement, do we?"

"No."

They might not have wanted to, and yet they did. Five years later, in the face of persistent questioning, the parental position on birth order began to change and the official position that all three boys had been born at exactly the same time began to change. Yes, it was conceded, one had arrived first, but they claimed that they had forgotten who it was. That satisfied curiosity for a year or two, but the questions returned, and with the same determination as Mr. Tam Dalyell had shown in trying to winkle admissions out of Mrs. Thatcher on the sinking of the *Belgrano*, the boys managed to find out who was the oldest and who was the youngest. And so the fateful work was done, and the lottery of birth began to make its effects felt.

The first to be born was Rognvald, named after the Norse founder of the Earldom of Orkney, Matthew being Orcadian on his grandmother's side. The tiny baby, so small to be burdened with so great a name, was taken from his mother's arms, swaddled in a cloth, and given to his father, who wept with pride, with joy, as he looked down into the puckered little face. "Rognvald," he muttered. "Hello, my darling."

So moved was Matthew by this encounter that he quite forgot that Elspeth, still in the travails of labour, had two more babies to bring into the world. Matthew wanted to play with Rognvald, and had he brought with him to the hospital a Hornby Dublo train set – as some excessively keen fathers have been known to do – he would no doubt have set it up there and then and introduced his son to the pleasure of model railways. But all too soon, the nurse who had handed him Rognvald asked for him back. "You've got another one now," she said. "Look."

Matthew spent a moment placing the nurse's accent. It had a touch of the Hebrides to it – Stornoway, perhaps. He said, "Where are you from?"

She said, "Mull. Tobermory."

He was filled with gratitude. "We'll call the next one Tobermory," said Matthew. "As a thank you."

2. The Naming of Boys

Tobermory's tiny lungs, once filled with air, lost no time in expelling it in the form of a cry of protest. If birth – our first eviction – is a deeply unsettling trauma, and we are told by those who claim to remember it that it is, then this child was not going to let the experience go unremarked upon. Red with rage, he vented his anger as Matthew cradled him. "Hush, Tobermory," the new father crooned. "Hush, hush."

On her pillow of pain, already exhausted by the effort of giving birth to two boys, Elspeth half-turned her head. "Tobermory?"

"Just a working title," said Matthew, above the sound of Tobermory's screams. "It suits him, don't you think?"

Elspeth nodded wearily. They had agreed in advance upon the name Rognvald, and had more or less decided on Angus and Fergus for the others, but Elspeth, being wary of having children who rhymed, was less enthusiastic about these last two names. Tobermory sounded rather attractive to her; she had been there once, on a boat from Oban, and had loved the brightly painted line of houses that followed the curve of the bay. Why were Scottish buildings grey, when they could be pink, blue, ochre? Moray Place, where they lived, could be transformed if only they would paint it that pink that one finds in houses in Suffolk, or the warm sienna of one or two buildings in East Lothian.

"Tobermory," she muttered. "Yes, I rather like that."

She returned to the task at hand, and a few minutes later gave birth to Fergus, who was markedly more silent than Tobermory, at whom he appeared to look reproachfully, as if censuring him for creating such a fuss.

The family of five was now complete. Matthew stayed

in the hospital for a further hour, comforting Elspeth, who had become a bit weepy. Then, blowing a proud kiss to his three sons, he went back to the flat in Moray Place that the couple had moved into on the sale of their first matrimonial home in India Street. Once back, Matthew made his telephone calls – to his father, to Elspeth's mother in Comrie, and to a list of more distant relatives whom he had promised to keep informed.

Then there were friends to contact, including Big Lou, who had been touchingly concerned over Elspeth's condition during her pregnancy.

"You're going to have to be really strong, Matthew," she warned. "It's not an easy thing for a lass to have triplets. You have to be there for her."

You have to be there for her. Matthew had not expected that expression from Big Lou, whose turn of phrase reflected rural Angus rather than the psychobabble-speaking hills of California.

"I'll be there for her, Lou," he said, following her lead. "In whatever space she's in, I'll be there."

"Good," said Lou. "She'll be fair trachled with three bairns. You too. You'll be trachled, Matthew. It's a sair fecht."

"Aye," said Matthew, lapsing into Scots. "I ken. I'll hae my haunds fu."

But now there was no word of caution from Big Lou. "They're all right, are they, Matthew?" she said over the telephone.

He assured her that they were, and she let out a whoop of delight. This show of spontaneous shared joy moved Matthew deeply. That another person should feel joy for him, should be proud when he felt proud, should share his heady, intoxicating elation, struck him as remarkable. Most people, he suspected, did not want others to be happy, not deep down. However we pretended otherwise, we resented the success of our friends; not that we did not want them to meet with success at all – it's just that we did not want them to be markedly more successful than we were. Matthew remembered reading somewhere that somebody had written – waspishly, but truly – *every time a friend succeeds, I die a little*. Gore Vidal: yes, he had said it. The problem, though, with witty people, thought Matthew, was working out whether they meant what they said.

And it was the same with money. If somebody knew you had money – and Matthew had, when all was said and done, slightly more than four million pounds, transferred to him by his father – if a friend knew that sort of thing, then his face would cloud over, just for a moment, as the emotion of envy registered itself. We do not want our friends to be poor, but by and large we prefer them to be slightly poorer than we are – just a fraction.

Big Lou meant what she said. She was delighted that Elspeth and the triplets were well; she was thrilled that Matthew was so happy; she was, moreover, very pleased that the population of Scotland had gone up by three at a time when demographic trends pointed the other way.

"I'm going to celebrate," she said to Matthew.

"That's great, Lou. How?"

"I'll work something out," she said.

Matthew realised that his enquiry had been tactless. Big Lou lived on her own, and the thought of her celebrating by herself, opening a bottle of wine, perhaps, in her flat in Canonmills and then drinking a toast that would be echoed by nobody else, saddened him. Life could be a lonely affair, and there was no justice in allocation of company. There were many selfish and unmeritorious people who were surrounded by more friends than they could manage; there were many good and generous people who were alone, who would love to have somebody to go home to, but who did not.

Big Lou was one of those. Matthew had met some of her male friends, and had taken a thorough dislike to them. There was that cook who had gone off to Mobile, Alabama, and who had shown excessive interest in young waitresses – Matthew had not liked him at all. Then there had been the Jacobite plasterer, who had gone on about the Stuarts and their restoration and who had, in Matthew's view, been certifiably insane. No, Big Lou had not had the luck she deserved, but could anything be done about it? Should she wait until some man wandered into her life – if that was ever going to happen – or should her friends perhaps speak to her about a dating agency? Why not? Dating agencies worked – sometimes – and Matthew had read of one that allowed you to get as many men as you liked – seriatim, of course – for three hundred and fifty pounds. Matthew had three hundred and fifty pounds; perhaps he would speak to Big Lou – tactfully of course. Big Lou came from Arbroath, and people who came from Arbroath were fine people in so many ways, but could be unexpectedly touchy-touchy, not touchy-feely.

3. Sons of Auchtermuchty

Domenica Macdonald heard of the birth of Rognvald, Tobermory, and Fergus from her fiancé, Angus Lordie, who had in turn heard it from Big Lou. Matthew had tried to reach Angus by telephone to give him the news, but Angus had not been in and his answering machine was full. That answering machine, in fact, had been full for three and a half years – ever since Angus had bought the phone – not having been listened to because Angus did not know that it existed. Some human messages never reach their destination, but remain in electronic limbo, waiting for some future archivist, centuries hence, some archaeologist of quotidian things, to unearth them and reconstruct a distant social past. *Meet me at three – usual place* could have the same fascination as some Pictish or Linear-B inscription over which scholars of our own time have scratched their heads.

"They've arrived," said Angus, himself arriving at Domenica's flat in Scotland Street. "Three boys. Rognvald, Tobermory, and Fergus. Royal Infirmary."

Domenica shook her head. "Poor woman," she said. "I suppose they have everything ready, though. Three babies. And then imagine having three toddlers about the place. Three sets of temper tantrums. Three everything."

"She'll cope, I expect," said Angus. "She seems a very placid type. I always thought her name rather suited her. Elspeth Harmony – the Harmony bit is very reassuring."

Domenica was interested in the names chosen for the triplets. "We can be grateful that they've chosen real names," she said. "You can't go wrong if you name a child after a prominent geographical feature. Tobermory is very nice."

"I read about somebody called Glasgow the other day," said Angus.

"Not bad," said Domenica. "It has a certain friendliness to it. One could be . . . well, I suppose, a pop singer with a name like that. You know, one of these people who seem to think that the only way one can sing is in an American accent, even if one is markedly not American. Very peculiar.

Give me The Proclaimers any day. There's no doubt they come from Auchtermuchty, rather than the middle of the Atlantic somewhere. Along with Jimmy Shand – what a great man he was! These are honest people."

"Names," Angus reminded her. "We were talking about names."

"So we were," said Domenica. "Glasgow as a name. Yes, I rather like it. Glasgow Maclean. Glasgow Wilson. Glasgow seems to go with any surname, doesn't it?"

Angus agreed. "Tobermory is a comfortable name. It's redolent, I think, of Toby, which is very easygoing. He's destined for a happy life, that boy."

They were in Domenica's kitchen when Angus made that remark, he sitting at the table, she standing in front of the newly acquired espresso machine, waiting for the coffee to start dripping into the tiny jug. Angus had given her the machine shortly after they had returned from Italy as a newly engaged couple. Now Domenica looked up as Angus referred to happiness; she looked up at her ceiling and thought of the words he had used. Were there really people who were destined for a happy life right from the beginning, or did we embark on that course – or its opposite – only a little bit later? Were there still people, she wondered, who embraced predestination in the stern, old-fashioned sense; who believed that some of us were damned whatever we did? Burns had pilloried that so beautifully in "Holy Willie's Prayer" which went . . .

"'Holy Willie's Prayer,' Angus? How does it go again? The bit about predestination?"

Angus had been watching the espresso machine huff and puff itself into action, and had been wondering whether a new aphorism was required to accommodate contemporary coffee culture – people today not watching kettles perhaps as much as they used to. A watched espresso machine never . . . never what? Never expresses. That was it.

"'Holy Willie's Prayer'? Now then: let me think."

"Remember to put on your Burns face." Domenica had discovered that Angus, and indeed many others, assumed a particular facial expression when reciting Burns. It was a very curious expression: one of reverence mixed with a look of satisfaction that comes from finding that one can remember the lines. Perhaps it had its equivalent elsewhere, she thought; perhaps there was a universal face that people put on when they quoted their national poets – if they had them. Some nations had no national poet, of course; they had an airline, perhaps, but not a poet.

Angus looked out of the window, subconsciously, perhaps, turning to Ayrshire as some may turn to Mecca. "O Thou that in the heavens does dwell / Wha as it pleases best Thysel / Sends ane to Heaven and ten to Hell / A for Thy glory / And no for any guid or ill / They've done before Thee."

Domenica smiled. "That says it perfectly. Just perfectly."

"Yes," said Angus. "It does, doesn't it? And he's still with us, you know."

"Holy Willie?"

Angus nodded. "In a different guise. Not perhaps in predestination terms, but in terms of disapproval of others. There are any number of people who take real pleasure in lecturing and hectoring us."

Domenica frowned. "Is it the same thing? Is that what Holy Willie is about?"

"Yes, I think it is. But of course Burns is having a go at hypocrisy too."

Domenica said that she found hypocrisy rather complicated. "Is it just a question of saying one thing and doing another? Or saying something that you don't mean?"

"That's insincerity," said Angus.

"But a hypocrite is insincere too, isn't he?"

"No," said Angus. "He may really believe what he goes on about. It's just that his actions don't match his words." He paused. "You know the best example of sincerity? The absolute gold standard?"

"Who?"

Angus pointed to the door, outside which Cyril was waiting patiently. "A dog. Have you ever met an insincere dog – a dog who hides his true feelings?"

Domenica looked thoughtful. "And cats?"

"Dreadfully insincere," said Angus. "Psychopaths – every one of them. Show me a cat, Domenica, and I'll show you a psychopath. Textbook examples."

4. *Where, Then, Shall We Live?*

The conversation between Angus and Domenica about triplets, hypocrisy, and national poets – all of them subjects of undoubtedly great interest – now became concerned with that topic of even greater profundity in the minds of any newly engaged couple: where to live. While this topic tends to be fraught for the young, who will generally have to scrimp and save to find a place of their own, for those at a later stage of life the problem can be quite otherwise – that of surplus. Both Domenica and Angus were owners of the flats in which they lived: Domenica's flat being in 44 Scotland Street, directly above the Pollock family, and Angus's being several hundred yards away in Drummond Place. On the face of it, Drummond Place seemed more desirable than Scotland Street, at least in financial terms. But neither party to this engagement was hard up, and so there was no need for either of them to sell his or her flat. So the decision about where to live became one based entirely on domestic preference. Where would they be more comfortable and therefore happier: in the more intimate setting of Scotland Street accommodation, or in the distinctly larger premises in Drummond Place?

In the early days of the engagement, nothing had been said about a move. Angus had assumed that he would move into Scotland Street, as it seemed to him that Domenica was the senior party in the arrangement; he was being admitted to her life rather than she to his. For her part, Domenica had made a similar assumption; indeed, one of the main issues for her had been the question of what to do about Cyril. Marrying Angus meant acquiring Cyril, and that was not something that could be lightly undertaken. However, she had found that her feelings had mollified, and now the prospect of having Angus's dog actually living in the flat was not as appalling as it had seemed before. In fact, although she would not have admitted this to Angus, Domenica had begun to relish the prospect of having Cyril in the flat and being able to take him for walks in the

Drummond Place Gardens or, at weekends, along the road that led from Flotterstone into the Pentland Hills. She looked forward to the conversation that dog owners have amongst themselves on such walks, the dogs breaking the ice for their owners.

Of the two flats, Angus's was by far the bigger. He was on the south side of the square, in a flat that occupied the top two floors of a converted Georgian terraced house. The house had been undivided until the nineteen-fifties, when an Edinburgh architect had sliced it into three flats: one in the basement, one occupying the ground and drawing room floors, and one incorporating the top and attic storeys.

Although they were not as high as those on the drawing room floor, where they were a good fourteen feet, Angus's ceilings were nonetheless twelve feet on his main floor and ten in the attic. The other dimensions of the rooms were appropriately generous, with the result that Angus had a studio with the necessary feeling of space. Here he kept his easels, his drawers of paints and thinners, his spattered ground sheets. Here he kept the chair he used for portrait sittings, an antiquated Edwardian library chair covered in green velvet through which the horsehair stuffing protruded at points.

The rest of the flat consisted of four bedrooms; a study filled with papers, well-thumbed art magazines and books; an echoing, cold bathroom with an ancient tub; and a kitchen dominated by a massive scrubbed pine table used for the preparation of food and the entertainment of guests. It was a comfortable flat in the sense that it had a lived-in feel and contained nothing that was aesthetically offensive, but it was irretrievably masculine and no woman could reasonably be expected to live in it, no matter how much she was in love with its owner.

Angus imagined that once he and Domenica married, he would keep the Drummond Place flat as his studio. That would mean that the only impedimenta he would have to move down to Scotland Street would be his clothes, his shaving bag, and a selection of paintings that he thought Domenica would like too: a pencil sketch by James Cowie of a child with prominent front teeth, a Philipson nude (with cathedral background), an Alberto Morrocco study of a melon, and a snowy Scottish landscape by Anne Redpath. There would be Cyril's modest possessions too: the basket in which he slept, his bowl, and the collection of bright bandannas which Angus tied to the dog's collar when he took him for walks along Queen Street or Heriot Row.

"I've been thinking about flats," said Domenica. "We'll need to do something about that."

Angus continued to look out of the window. "Do we?"

"Yes. You see, there's not much point in having two flats – especially two that are so close together."

"I don't know," he said casually. "My flat is not just a flat – it's my studio."

"Of course," said Domenica. "But I thought that perhaps the spare bedroom here would do for that. It's quite large, after all. And the light's quite good."

Angus was silent. He could not imagine painting in a spare bedroom. "I'm not sure," he began. "I'm very fond of . . ."

Domenica held up a hand. "I don't want to put you under any pressure, Angus, but I really think we should consider something."

He turned away from the window and looked directly at her. "Consider what?"

"I've had a letter from Antonia," said Domenica. "And what she says has a bearing on what we might do."

Angus's curiosity was aroused. "How is she? Has she fully recovered?"

Antonia Collie, who owned the flat next to Domenica's, had accompanied them on their trip to Italy. Unfortunately, she had succumbed to Stendhal Syndrome, a rare condition that affects a small proportion of visitors to the great art cities of Italy. She had been referred to a psychiatric hospital in Florence and from there had been transferred to the care of a group of nuns in the Tuscan countryside.

"She's doing very well," said Domenica. "And she's asked me to do something for her that affects us very significantly, Angus."

"Tell all," he said.

5. A Request from Italy

Domenica went to the Welsh dresser and took an envelope from a fruit bowl. "This arrived yesterday," she said, holding up the letter. "I recognised her handwriting immediately even if it has become a bit more – how shall I put it? – disciplined than it used to be."

"The result of being looked after by nuns, perhaps," said Angus. "I should imagine that nuns are fairly quick to spot one's faults if one's staying with them. They'd be polite about it, of course."

"Of course," said Domenica. "I believe that nuns can communicate a great deal just with looks. There will be a certain sort of look that says, quite clearly, 'You must improve your handwriting' or, rather, 'We must improve our handwriting.'" She paused. "Have you noticed how useful the first person plural is for criticism, Angus? If I say to you 'We must do a little better' I may mean you need to do a little better, but somehow saying 'we' makes the criticism a little less blunt. Is it because it suggests that I share the fault?"

Angus did not agree. "No. It's just condescending. It's as if you're talking to a child. If you want to suggest that you share the problem, then you can say things like 'I'm not one to talk, but . . .' Or, 'I have exactly the same failing and I find that . . .' That's much better."

"Oh well," said Domenica, slipping the folded notepaper from the envelope. "Listen to what she has to say."

They both sat down. Angus watched Domenica as she prepared to read; she has such a peaceful, resolved face, he thought; I must ask her to sit for me. *Portrait of My Wife.* He found the simple title oddly moving, and he felt grateful, and proud too: my wife. Thank you, thank . . . whatever divinity has brought me this good fortune. Thank you.

Domenica put on a pair of reading glasses. Looking at Angus over the rim of these, she began to read.

"My dear Domenica . . ." She paused. "It's interesting, Angus, that she should say my dear rather than dear."

"Some people do," said Angus. "I quite like it, actually. It somehow suggests greater affection."

"Yes," said Domenica. "Perhaps it does."

She looked down at the letter and continued, "I am writing to you from Italy." She looked up at Angus. "Well, we know that, don't we?"

"Carry on."

"I am writing to you from Italy," Domenica continued, "where the sisters with whom I am staying have been so kind to me and helped me through this difficult period. I have very little recollection of what happened in the Uffizi . . ."

Domenica looked up. "I have," she said. "She started to

moan in a most embarrassing way. The entire gallery resounded to her moans."

"She was not herself," said Angus.

"No, indeed, but there we are. Shall I continue?"

"You must."

"Fortunately," she went on, "the human memory has powers to commit to oblivion many things that would otherwise distress us. I have recovered from whatever affliction it was that seized me in the Uffizi and have put all that behind me. I have discovered, I am happy to tell you, a whole new purpose in life. I have been helping the sisters with the running of the small farm that they have here. Sister Celestina is the beekeeper and she has been giving me some training in apiculture. It is most satisfying, I feel, to see the bees doing the Lord's work with such energy and determination! An inspiration for the rest of us, says Sister Celestina, and I believe she is right.

"My early Scottish saints would have been happy here, I think, and I like to believe that the life that I am leading now is not all that different from the life they themselves led in their rude dwellings in Whithorn. Indeed, I cannot help but feel that Saint Ninian himself is at my elbow here, and that my own journey is not entirely dissimilar to his."

Domenica paused, looking up at Angus. "Well! That's a bit steep – even for Antonia. Ninian must have travelled to Rome by boat and horseback – she went to Italy by Ryanair. Quite different, if you ask me."

Angus smiled. "Oh, I don't know. It's pretty basic on some of these cheap airlines. I think Saint Ninian might have felt quite at home."

"We digress," said Domenica, returning to the letter. "This is what she goes on to say: 'And now, my dear Domenica, I must ask a favour of you. I have decided that my vocation is here, and I am to be accepted into the community of sisters here as a lay member with a view to becoming a nun in the fullness of time. This is the work I am called to do. That means I am unlikely to return to Scotland and shall not therefore need a home there any more.'"

Domenica paused again. The last sentence hung in the air, almost visible to the naked eye.

"I continue," she said, taking up Antonia's letter once more. "I have decided therefore to sell the Scotland Street flat and I should be grateful if you would approach McKay Norwell to sell it for me. Lesley Kerr, whom I believe you know, will do that – please ask her to send me a power of attorney to sign so that I can authorise you to act on my behalf in this sale."

Domenica put the letter on the table. "So!" she exclaimed. "The deed is to be virtually done, Angus. We are to get new neighbours unless . . ."

Angus looked at her expectantly. "Unless?"

"Unless we buy the flat ourselves, Angus. Unless we buy it and then knock through that wall over there and make a much bigger flat for all of us – you, me, and Cyril. Cyril could even have his own room – if dogs like that sort of thing."

Angus looked at the wall, trying to envisage the space that lay beyond. He had been in Antonia's flat on one or two occasions before – once uninvited, when he had slipped in to retrieve the blue Spode cup that Domenica believed Antonia had stolen from her.

"But it would cost an awful lot," he said. "Flats these days . . ."

Domenica brushed his objection aside. "We sell yours," she said. "Then we use the money – or part of it – to buy Antonia's place. Simple."

6. *Paysage Moralisé*

For Bertie Pollock, Saturday brought few surprises. The day began, as Saturdays always did, with a walk to Valvona & Crolla with his mother and Ulysses, his younger brother, whose pushchair Bertie was allowed to propel along London Street as far as the Broughton Street roundabout. Then his mother took over for the ascent towards Albany Street.

"A *paysage moralisé*, Bertie," said Irene. "One's journey is easy at the beginning but becomes more arduous as time goes by. Thus Drummond Place and London Street are not particularly challenging, but then one encounters Broughton Street and it becomes more taxing. It is exactly the same with life: it's simple at the beginning, Bertie, but it gets steadily more complex."

Bertie, who had been gazing into the window of Crombie's butchery, with its display of famous sausages, was not quite sure what his mother meant. She often made opaque remarks, and this, he thought, was one of them.

"Do you think we could get some of Mr. Crombie's sausages, Mummy?" he asked. "It says in the window that they're world-famous."

Irene glanced over her shoulder at the butcher's window. "They're quite possibly world-famous amongst people who think a great deal about sausages, Bertie. Just like Macsween's haggises. But we are not amongst those who dwell upon sausages and haggises, you see."

Bertie knew that the cause was lost, but persisted nonetheless. "I've heard that they're very good," he said. "We could fry them, Mummy. In a frying pan. We've got a frying pan, haven't we?"

Irene hurried him along. "Come along, Bertie. Our diet does not include sausages, I'm afraid. We have a Mediterranean diet, as you know. It's far healthier."

"Don't they eat sausages in the Mediterranean?" asked Bertie.

"They do not, Bertie," said Irene. "They eat a great deal of sun-dried tomatoes and olives. They also eat fish and pasta. They do not eat sausages."

"What about salami?" asked Bertie. "I've seen salami in Valvona & Crolla. There was a great big salami there last time – it was much bigger than Mr. Crombie's sausages."

"Salami is quite another matter," said Irene. "We must allow the Neapolitans the occasional slice of salami, but my point stands. Now we must hurry, Bertie, or we shall be late for psychotherapy."

Bertie sighed. He enjoyed going to Valvona & Crolla, but he was considerably less enthusiastic about what followed their visit to the delicatessen. His weekly appointment with his psychotherapist, Dr. St. Clair, was something that he had tried to persuade his mother to abandon – to no avail – and he was now resigned to sitting through it, he imagined, until his eighteenth birthday. He was not sure why he had to do it, but all attempts to elicit an explanation from his mother had so far failed, and Dr. St. Clair's explanation had been distinctly less than satisfactory when he had taken the matter up with him.

"We sometimes have to do things we may not see the point of, Bertie," the psychotherapist had said. "And yet they may be very helpful. Perhaps psychotherapy is one of those things." He had paused. "It's all about growing up. Psychotherapy can help you to deal with things that worry you. It's like taking the sting out of a bee. If you take the sting out of a bee, it can't hurt you."

"It dies," said Bertie. "My friend Tofu told me. He said he took the sting out of one of those big round bees and it died just like that."

Dr. St. Clair looked out of the window. "Perhaps," he said. He had heard Bertie speak of Tofu before, and it seemed to him that extracting the stings of bees was very much the sort of thing that Tofu would do.

But that would come later; for the moment there was the anticipation of the delicatessen and the possibility that they might be serving samples. Bertie enjoyed those, especially if the sample trays contained something sweet such as panforte di Siena, or a tiny amaretto biscuit wrapped in delicate white tissue paper. Bertie had been given a tin of these biscuits once by Mary Contini, who ran the shop, and her husband, Phillip, had demonstrated to him how if one lit these wrappers they would float delicately up to the ceiling.

"A little airship," he explained. "Look, there it goes."

Bertie had watched the small square of paper, the flame

rising from its edges, waft up in a self-created current of hot air. It had seemed to him to be an almost magical sight – a miraculous defiance of gravity. He wanted to fly, too, and wondered whether one might be able to set fire to a much larger square of paper, sit in the middle of it, and gently be lifted up to the ceiling. Would it work with one of his father's copies of the *Guardian*? If one sat in the middle of the arts pages, perhaps, and then set fire to the edges, would it behave in the same way as an amaretto wrapper? He saw no reason why not, and yet surely if it were possible then it would be quite a common sight and he had never seen anybody attempting it successfully – not even once.

Bertie had gone on to psychotherapy clutching his tin of amaretti. He had offered one to Dr. St. Clair, who had smiled and accepted the biscuit.

"You can set fire to the paper," said Bertie. "That's what I'm going to do."

Dr. St. Clair, who had been on the point of biting into the amaretto, had paused. He stared at Bertie, and then, discreetly putting the biscuit down on his desk, had scribbled something on his notepad. *Fire*. This had, after all, been the reason for the initial referral for psychotherapy, as noted down by Dr. Fairbairn. Bertie had set fire to his father's copy of the *Guardian* – while he was reading it. It had been a couple of years ago, when Bertie had barely turned five, but it was significant, he thought, that the ideation had persisted.

"Bertie," began Dr. St. Clair, trying to sound casual. "May I ask you something? You'd like to set fire to these wrappers, would you?"

"Yes," said Bertie. "I'll show you if you like, Dr. St. Clair."

7. An Interest in Fire

At the end of Bertie's hour with Dr. St. Clair he usually went straight home with his mother. During the session itself, she often took Ulysses round the corner to Eteaket, a small tea room in Frederick Street, where she would read the paper or the book her book group was planning to discuss. Irene was not sure about her book group; she had been a member of it for several years now, but she did not enjoy it as much as she had hoped, largely because of the choice of books made by other members. She also disliked the way several of those in the group behaved when she was expressing her opinion on a book. One of them, in particular, had a habit of rolling her eyes up whenever Irene spoke – an unintentional mannerism, perhaps, but very annoying nonetheless.

On this occasion, when she returned from the tea room to pick up Bertie, Dr. St. Clair indicated that he wanted to have a private word with her.

"You read one of the magazines, Bertie," said Irene. "And keep an eye on Ulysses. Mummy is just going to have a quick word with Dr. St. Clair."

With Bertie's nose buried in the waiting room's copy of *Scottish Field*, Dr. St. Clair invited Irene into his consulting room and closed the door behind them. Irene, who enjoyed the company of psychotherapists, settled herself in a chair in front of his desk.

"Everything all right?" she asked.

Dr. St. Clair frowned. "Well, yes and no. I was actually going to suggest to you that we give Bertie a bit of a break from therapy at present – in fact, I was fairly sure that this would be appropriate. However . . ."

Irene took the opportunity to interject. "I'm not so sure.

As you know, I'm concerned about developmental issues, and . . ."

Dr. St. Clair shook his head. "I'm not going to suggest that any more. Rather to the contrary, I was going to recommend a certain degree of vigilance."

"Vigilance?"

"Yes. You see, Bertie revealed today a somewhat alarming set of ideas."

Irene's eyes widened.

"If I may ask you something," Dr. St. Clair continued. "Has Bertie expressed any interest in fire recently – beyond the occasion when I understand he set fire to your husband's copy of the *Guardian* while he was reading it?" He paused. "That was some time ago, wasn't it? He was very young, of course."

"It was attention-seeking, I think," said Irene. "Although I think that there was some latent hostility behind it."

Dr. St. Clair nodded. "There's a very interesting case in the literature. A young boy set fire to the *Guardian* and went on to become a Conservative. It was one of the first signs."

"Very disturbing," said Irene.

"Yes. But returning to Bertie, he mentioned some fantasy about doing it again."

Irene was silent for a moment. "He mentioned setting fire to the *Guardian*?"

Dr. St. Clair nodded. "Of course, an interest in fire is perfectly normal in childhood. Between the ages of three and five there occurs what we call fire interest. The child shows an interest in what fire is – how it starts and so on. And that, of course, is quite understandable – after all, fire is quite dramatic. Then there may be actual episodes of setting. Again that's normal. The vast majority of children start fires in the preadolescent years. Boys in particular."

Irene nodded. "And men," she said. "They continue, don't they? They may do it in an organised context, but they do it nonetheless with their bombs and blasts."

Dr. St. Clair shifted uncomfortably in his seat.

"Not that we must be too hard on men," Irene continued, allowing herself a smile. "They have their uses."

Again Dr. St. Clair moved in his seat. "Young Bertie is probably going through the normal interest phase," he said. "But I think that we should watch the situation. Just in case he does anything dangerous."

Irene said that she would keep a watchful eye. "I suppose it's a timely reminder," she said. "If it is, as I suspect it might be, an appeal for my attention, then I must be ready to respond. Perhaps I'm not spending enough time with Bertie. Perhaps I need to become more involved in his life."

"That could be," said Dr. St. Clair. "Attention usually solves childhood issues."

"And adult issues too," said Irene. "We all crave attention."

Dr. St. Clair said that this was undoubtedly true. "The desire to be loved," he said. "That is what lies at the heart of so many of our endeavours and stratagems."

She looked at the psychotherapist. What did he do for love, she wondered. "We all need a friend," she said.

Dr. St. Clair glanced out of the window. "Yes, that's right. And we spend so much of our time searching for that friend. All of us."

Irene hesitated. Then she said, "You must find it difficult, what with your family being so far away in Australia."

He turned to look at her. "Yes," he said. "It sometimes is."

"Are your parents still alive?" she asked.

"Yes, they are. My mother is not particularly well, I'm

afraid. My father copes. He's kept going by cricket, I think. He lives for it."

"We all need something, don't we? Religion. Cricket. Football. It's much the same thing, isn't it? Things that confer meaning upon our lives." She paused. "Love too. For most people that's what gives their lives some meaning."

Dr. St. Clair inclined his head, in a gesture of agreement. "It does," he said.

Irene was emboldened. "Do you . . . do you have somebody?"

She wondered whether he would be offended; whether her question was too intrusive, but he answered equably. "Not at present," he said. "But . . ."

The *but* was so eloquent, and his answer was exactly what she wanted. There are few greater pleasures than finding out that the person we are interested in is available.

"I'm sorry to hear that," she said. "Perhaps that'll change."

He smiled. "Perhaps. Who knows?"

For a few moments there was complete silence. Then, from the waiting room, there came the sound of Ulysses beginning to cry and, unmistakably, the smell of burning paper.

8. *The Holy Grail*

Matthew drove Elspeth and the triplets home in the mud-coloured estate car he had bought when they first became aware of the fact that there would be three babies, rather than one. The vehicle had been acquired through his father's motor-broker, George Mackay, whom Matthew had approached for something that was cheap, reliable, and capable of carrying three babies and their impedimenta.

"The Holy Grail," said George, as Matthew explained his requirements. "Cheapness and reliability don't always go hand in hand in the motor world. But I'll see what I can do."

A few days later he had telephoned to tell Matthew to come up to Colinton Road to examine a car. "It's nothing to look at, I'm afraid," said George. "But it'll work – I promise you that. And there's bags of room for all those children. You can put the back seat down for that."

The station wagon was perfect, and Matthew had bought it then and there, christening it the Holy Grail, after George's striking comment. "It's not very beautiful," he explained to Elspeth. "It's a sort of . . . well, it's essentially mud-coloured. But it has all the gizmos – satellite navigation and . . ." He thought of the buttons and switches that George had shown him and to which he had not paid adequate attention, "and temperature control," he added weakly.

Elspeth smiled. Dear Matthew! He was not very good when it came to machines and appliances – unlike her father, who had been able to fix virtually anything and who had always been assembling and disassembling pieces of machinery in his garden workshop in Comrie. Enthusiasm for things mechanical had proved his downfall eventually – his failing sight had been incompatible with his continued interest in biking, and his use of his guide dog on the motor-cycle had been so unfortunate. But it was easy to be wise after the event . . . At least Matthew did nothing dangerous – as far as she knew. He was, by contrast, always rather cautious, anticipating problems before they arose and warning her to be careful about this, that, and the next thing.

His enthusiasm for safety had resulted in his purchase of

three expensive new infant car seats, complete with padded carrying handles. These he had brought to the hospital, where they were inspected by a somewhat officious social worker.

"We have to check up that you can transport your babies safely," she had said. "Let me see these seats of yours."

Matthew frowned. He had not expected to be quizzed before being allowed to take his own children home. "They're my sons," he said testily, adding, "They don't belong to the Royal Infirmary."

The social worker's eyes narrowed. "We can't allow children to be taken home inappropriately," she said.

"So what's the alternative? Some have to stay? Is that what you're telling me?" He suppressed a smile, thinking of a tribe of children who were born in the Infirmary, but never allowed to leave, because their parents were deemed unsuitable. They would grow up in the hospital, playing in the corridors, perhaps being allowed to fetch and carry things for the nursing staff, eventually graduating to the kitchens, where they could help with the washing up.

The social worker sighed. "Of course not. We're simply following good practice guidelines. You see, the problem with your seats – as I can see from here – is that they are the wrong type. Children under twenty-nine pounds need to travel facing backwards. Your babies, we can safely assume, are under twenty-nine pounds. So they need backwards-facing seats, and these seats face the direction of travel."

Matthew looked at the car seats in mute desperation. It was already after six o'clock in the evening, and the shop where he had bought the seats would be closed; he could not take them back until the following morning. Yet it would be psychologically impossible for him to leave Elspeth and the babies in the hospital for a further night;

he had been looking forward to this moment so much and he had been waiting since ten that morning for his wife to be discharged by the doctors.

An idea occurred to him. "All right," he said. "If I put these seats in the car and then reverse, then the babies will be travelling with their backs to the direction of travel. Is that correct?"

The social worker nodded. "I suppose so."

"Then the problem's solved," said Matthew. "I'm going to reverse home."

He looked challengingly at the social worker, daring her to contradict him. She did not, and he took the seats through to the ward where Elspeth was waiting for him. Then, with some help from obliging ward assistants, they carried their newly minted family out of the hospital to the car park where the mud-coloured car was parked.

When Matthew set off, Elspeth turned to him and asked why he was reversing. "It's to do with the car seats," he said. "They face the wrong way. I was told that I had to . . ."

"Oh, don't be ridiculous, Matthew!" snapped Elspeth. "We can't reverse all the way back to the flat. It won't matter, just this time. Get the right sort of seat tomorrow."

The journey back was safely accomplished and the Holy Grail parked directly outside their front door in Moray Place. Then the babies were carried in and transferred to the cots that awaited them. Matthew handled each child as a museum curator might handle a priceless Chinese vase – tenderly and with reverence. But no curator ever felt such love and pride as he felt for each tiny scrap of humanity, each of his sons; nor would any curator have stood so still, so clearly transported, gazing with such awe at the cherished possession as Matthew did, silent, his expression of utter satisfaction, of unalloyed joy.

Elspeth came to stand beside him. Slipping her hand into his, she nestled her head against his shoulder. "Our little boys," she said. "Ours."

"I'm so proud of you," whispered Matthew.

She squeezed his hand. "And I'm so proud of you," she said. "Not every man can make triplets."

He laughed. "My darling, you're the one who did it. It was you who did all that pushing and shoving. And now, here they are – our lovely boys."

They gazed at the three babies, who were all sleeping soundly, their breathing sounding like the snuffles of some small animal, their tiny red faces in repose; so vulnerable, so utterly precious.

9. Remember to Expand

His new paternal duties uppermost in his mind – and what father of triplets would have anything else in his thoughts? – Matthew nonetheless remembered that he had a business to run. His work at the gallery could hardly be described as onerous, but it did require his presence at set hours, which were nine in the morning until six in the evening. During this period he had to be there, except for half an hour in the morning, when he had coffee at Big Lou's, or on the odd occasion went he went off to an auction or to see a painting in somebody's house. During these absences, he simply put a sign on the door saying, Back Soon, and hoped that any client, or potential client, who called while he was out would return in due course. But no businessman would want to do this too often.

From time to time Matthew engaged an assistant. These were usually temporary, or part-time, although he had taken the decision that he would at some point get some-body permanent. After all, there was no financial reason not to do this: the gallery was now making a reasonable profit and Matthew was emboldened to expand. "Remember to expand," was one piece of advice his father had given him, and Matthew had never forgotten this. He had been counselled about other things – about the importance of making provision for tax, about the importance of main-taining cash flow, and so on – but he found it difficult to recall the precise terms of these admonitions. Yet he had remembered this curious comment of his father's: remember to expand.

The advice itself had a vaguely comical ring to it, as if it could be taken to urge people who were somehow small, or thin, perhaps, to expand their girth. And would one expand in all directions, or confine oneself to a single area of expansion? Matthew felt, too, that the advice sounded vaguely megalomaniac – like the mantra of a dictators' training course: Remember to invade, gentlemen.

Appointing an assistant would count as expansion, he thought, but he suspected that he would have to do some-thing else as well. Expansion must mean more sales, and more sales meant that more pictures would have to be bought, and sold on to more clients. But what if one had the same number of clients – as Matthew did – and no ideas as to how to increase that number?

Of course it really did not matter all that much – at least to Matthew. The funds passed on by his generous father had been well managed by the Adam Bank and Matthew had no reason to worry financially, but he was still conscious of the fact that the reason for creating businesses was, after all, to make money, rather than to sit around. So in so far as an assistant represented at least one plank in a strategy of expansion, then such a person should be appointed. And now, with the birth of the triplets and the need for paternity leave, an assistant's presence was even more necessary.

His first response had been to contact an employment agency past whose door he walked each morning if he took the Howe Street route. A few weeks before the birth of the triplets, Matthew had gone to this agency one morning and made an enquiry. The man he spoke to had noted down the particulars of the job. "We won't send you anybody challenging," he said. "We don't do challenging, you know."

Matthew tried not to smile. "I don't really want to be challenged," he reassured him.

They were not for him, he decided, and he took his leave, promising to think about it. Later that week he placed an advertisement on a local employment website, which brought not much more than a trickle of unsuitable responses. Matthew began to despair. He had been under the impression that there was any number of graduates in the history of art who would jump at the chance of employment in a gallery. Where were these people?

History of art . . . He began to think. Pat Macgregor was still at university, he believed, and she had been a perfectly competent assistant. Why had he not thought of her in the first place? The reason was clear enough, and he intuitively understood exactly what it was, once he confronted it. Pat had been his girlfriend and he had gone through that process of quarantining that one goes through when one marries somebody else. The old girlfriend, the old boyfriend, had to be kept at arm's length in those circumstances. But if one had triplets, surely things were different: a man in that unusual position would hardly be stoking the flame of old passion if he were to ask an old girlfriend to help him out.

He found Pat's telephone number in his old diary, where he had written it when they had first got to know one another. Telephone numbers jotted down in bars or clubs have a certain poignancy to them: pencilled figures written in hope that maybe this will be the grand passion, the new and exciting friend, the person whose lively offers will somehow change one's life. And then, as often as not, the telephone number in question becomes a reminder of what was not to be, and reverts to being just another jumble of figures along with all the other figures that clutter our lives: codes, PINs, postcodes, registration numbers, and so on. And somewhere, Matthew suddenly thought, there was that number we all dread so much and do not really want to know: the number of days we have left to live – a number as yet unquantified, but which, like all such numbers, must be there precisely because it is going to be there. That number is n.

Pat sounded pleased to hear from Matthew.

"I was going to phone you," she said. "This is amazing."

"Were you?"

"Yes," she replied. "I was going to . . ." She paused, and Matthew detected a note of awkwardness in her tone.

Suddenly a disturbing, ridiculous possibility crossed his mind. Pat had become pregnant, by him, all that time ago and not told him. She had gone off and had the baby and had now decided to break the news. He had four children rather than three.

10. A Distressed Oatmeal Sweater

Matthew's voice took on a strained note. "You were going to what?"

"I was going to phone you about . . . well, about a job. The uni is on vacation now and I wondered whether you needed anybody for the next month or so."

He laughed, with some relief. It was ridiculous to think that he was responsible for another, non-existent child; such a fear struck him as rather like worrying about being hit by a meteorite. "As it happens, that's what I was phoning about. When can you start?"

"Any time," she said. "But how are things with you? Anything new?"

Matthew paused before he answered. Anything new? "I have three sons," he announced.

He explained to an astonished Pat about the triplets, and heard her gasps of surprise. "It's still sinking in," he said. "Three, Pat. Three boys. Imagine."

There was silence as Pat imagined. "Well . . ." she said.

"Exactly," said Matthew. "But I'm really thrilled, you know. I always wanted a son. Or not always, I suppose, but for the last couple of years I've thought about it. Now I've got three."

He brought the conversation back to its original purpose,

telling Pat what he had in mind. He would come into the gallery every day, he said, but would not stay long. She could phone him if anything came up that needed his attention, and he would always be able to drop back in if there was a crisis. Not that he thought this was likely, he assured her; nothing had ever really happened in the gallery that could be remotely described as a crisis.

Pat offered to start the following day – an offer that Matthew accepted with relief.

"You've saved the day, Pat," he said. "You're always doing that."

Am I? she asked herself. She was unaware of ever having saved Matthew from anything, but it pleased her that he should think this of her. She liked Matthew – even if he had one or two habits that irritated her. There was his tendency to be too kind to people – which meant that he was walked over by anybody unscrupulous who came into contact with him; there was his habit of leaving tea bags in cups and then putting the cups back on the shelf; there was that distressed oatmeal sweater of his and his crushed strawberry cords . . . Somebody had said that Elspeth had sorted his wardrobe out, but that remained to be seen. And, oh, there was another thing: his Macgregor tartan underpants. That was a ridiculous thing to be annoyed by, but it had made Pat feel quite cross when she had seen Matthew's underpants and had noticed that they were in her family tartan. Somehow this seemed disrespectful: there was no reason why people should not wear tartan underpants, but to take somebody else's tartan was definitely objectionable. It was rather like blowing one's nose on a handkerchief printed with the national flag; there were countries where that would not only be considered bad taste, but be deemed a calculated insult.

But these quirks were very small things when viewed beside Matthew's undoubted good points. He was generous to a fault; he had an even temper and never raised his voice; he was polite in an old-fashioned way that people really appreciated. These qualities far outweighed those other traits, all of which might be corrected if Matthew had them pointed out to him. The problem, as Pat knew, was that nobody would do the pointing out. She could have complained about his underpants, for instance, but had not – we do not like to criticise the underwear of others; at least not in Edinburgh.

Such thoughts were far from her mind when she met Matthew at the gallery the next morning. There was an odd embrace – a brotherly and sisterly affair, as meetings between former lovers can be – followed by a prolonged and gossipy exchange of personal news. They had not seen one another for some time, and there was much catching up to be done. How was Pat's course going? What was her new flat like? And her flatmates?

From Pat's point of view, there were questions about the triplets. Were they sleeping? Did they wake up at different times, or would one wake up the other two? How did you tell them apart? Did you need to have one of those little identity bracelets?

Matthew answered as best he could. He thought that he was beginning to be able to distinguish them from one another – more on the basis of personality than appearance.

"I think, though, that I can detect some differences in their character," he said. "Rognvald, for example – he's the oldest – has a really serious expression. I think he's more intellectual than his brothers. Tobermory is sensitive, if you ask me. He's probably going to turn out to be artistic."

Pat concealed her amusement. "It's amazing that you can tell all that this early," she said.

"Yes," said Matthew. "It's extraordinary. But you very quickly get used to having babies, you know."

He spoke with such authority that she almost believed him. It was touching, she felt, to see Matthew assume the mantle of fatherhood. And he would be a good father, in her view. One wanted a father to be decent, and that was exactly what Matthew was: he was profoundly decent. And that, she reflected with some alarm, was why it would never have worked between Matthew and her. Pat, for all her own normality, wanted danger. Or if not danger, she wanted spice.

As a psychiatrist, her father had sensed this and had sought to warn her. "It's a good thing," Dr. Macgregor said, "to be aware of who you are. You don't want to dwell too long on it – therein lies a direct route to neurosis – but it's useful to know your weak points. And one of yours, my dear, might be to search for . . . how shall we put it? Excitement? Perhaps that's it."

She had shrugged. "Maybe it's something to do with coming from the Grange."

The Grange, which was the area of Edinburgh in which Pat had been raised, and in which her father still lived, was synonymous with settled, haut-bourgeois existence; the Grange was no Left Bank.

He had smiled at the reference. "We're very sedate," he said. "But what's wrong with that?" He paused. "Sedate people of the world . . ."

"Sit down!" said Pat. "You have nothing to gain . . ."

"But your chairs."

They both laughed, father and daughter, together. There were very few real Marxists in the Grange.

11. *Flowers and Submarines*

Matthew needed to explain very little to Pat when he met her in the gallery that morning.

"Everything's the same as when I worked here last time," she said. "Same paintings, almost . . . no, not really."

Matthew struggled to smile at the joke. "It's not that bad," he said. "I really have sold quite a lot. Maybe it's because we have a lot of the same artists."

"Of course," said Pat. She regretted the attempt at humour; Matthew was so easily hurt, and she did not want that. "Mind you . . ."

"Mind you what?"

"Remember how we talked about themed exhibitions?" she asked. "It was a long time ago, but we discussed having shows with titles like The Scottish Landscape or Through Kirkcudbright Eyes – that sort of thing."

Matthew frowned. "Vaguely. Of course, Kirkcudbright might be quite a good idea. There was Hornel, and lots of others. There was quite a colony of artists down there. Still is, I think."

"Exactly. Although I can only take Hornel in very small doses. All those flowers. And all those Japanese girls picking them."

Matthew agreed. "Yet people buy them, don't they? People like flowers." He stared out of the window for a moment before turning to Pat again. "Perhaps somewhere other than Kirkcudbright. What about Pittenweem? There are bags of good artists there. Tim Cockburn, for instance. And that man who does those rather haunting paintings of Arctic scenes. What's his name again?"

Pat knew. "Reinhard Behrens. Yes. I did an essay on his work in my second year. It's beautiful. He paints these amazing pictures and puts a tiny toy submarine in them. He found the toy on a beach in Turkey years ago and he's constructed a landscape for it ever since then."

This gave Matthew an idea. "Flowers and Submarines," he said. "How about that for an exhibition?"

Pat smiled. "Should I work on it? Just a bit of Hornel and rather more submarines." She looked at Matthew. She was serious. In her view Matthew needed something unusual like that to raise the profile of the gallery. And it would make her time there so much more interesting, rather than simply sitting there, waiting for the occasional customer to wander in and buy a painting at random.

Matthew looked thoughtful. "Why not? We'll have to buy the paintings, of course, but you could go online and see what's available. The dealers all put their stuff on Artprice these days. You'll find things there. And there are sales coming up soon at Lyon & Turnbull, and Bonhams too. We could see what turns up."

She nodded enthusiastically. "I'll be careful."

"Don't buy without asking me first," said Matthew. "I want to see everything."

"Even the flowers?"

"Yes, even the flowers. And the submarines."

They both laughed. Then Matthew asked, "There are very few paintings of submarines, you know. Why is that, do you think?"

"Because we can't see them," said Pat.

"So they might be there in a seascape? It's just that the artists can't show them when they're submerged?"

Pat was grinning. "I've had the most fantastic idea. Let's call the show Flowers and Submarines, as you suggested, but it'll be mostly seascapes. Well, flowers too, but the seascapes will be normal – but with the possibility of a submarine under the waves."

"Are you joking?"

Pat was not. "I'm serious. It's the angle, Matthew. You need an angle to get attention. People will love it."

Matthew shrugged. "I suppose it can't do any harm. Seascapes sell. I had two of those old Dutch paintings of sailing boats being tossed about on the waves. I sold them both in three days."

"Well, there you are," said Pat. "Agreed?"

"Sort of," said Matthew. He looked at his watch. "Let's go over for coffee. Big Lou will be pleased to have you around again." He reached for the Back Soon sign and hung it on the door.

"I feel so nostalgic," said Pat. "Going for coffee at Big Lou's – just like the old days."

For a moment Mathew felt a pang of regret. Life had been simpler in those days, when he and Pat were together. Now here he was a married man with three sons. No, he should put those days out of his mind; everything had changed – changed completely.

As they made their way over the road to the coffee bar,

Pat asked Matthew how Big Lou was. "Same as ever," he replied. "She looks the same. She says the same things . . . As all of us do, of course. I'm not suggesting that I've got anything new to say."

"That's good," said Pat. "Too many things are different. If Big Lou is the same, then that's good as far as I'm concerned."

"But not necessarily from her point of view," said Matthew. "Maybe it's a mistake to think that people who don't have much change in their lives are happy with that. Big Lou would like to have a boyfriend, I think. In fact, I was wondering about treating her to a dating agency."

Pat looked at him sideways. "Be careful. Big Lou may be more vulnerable than you think."

"She's strong," said Matthew. "Remember where she comes from. Arbroath. They're strong in Arbroath."

"Strong people are just as vulnerable as the rest of us, Matthew."

They began to descend the steps that led down to Big Lou's basement café. Halfway down this stone staircase, it was possible to see through one of the windows into the café's interior. As Pat glanced in, she saw the familiar figure of Big Lou leaning over her counter writing something on a sheet of paper. At that precise moment, Big Lou looked up, alerted, perhaps, by the shadows cast by Pat and Matthew. She looked up, saw Pat, and waved.

Pat felt a sudden surge of emotion, and she realised that she loved this woman, with her matter-of-fact manner and her no-nonsense approach to life. And she realised that there was something missing in her life: something absolutely basic and essential. A mother. Big Lou is my mother, she thought. And she's Matthew's mother too. And Angus

Lordie's. And, in an odd, anthropomorphic way, Cyril's mother as well.

Matthew noticed that something had crossed Pat's mind. "What are you thinking of?" he asked. "You look very serious."

She reached for the handle. "My mother," she said.

Matthew raised an eyebrow. "I thought you never saw her."

Pat was silent. Then she said, "She's in a submarine." And added, "Metaphorically."

12. *The Ceilings of Edinburgh*

Angus did not say much about Domenica's plan to buy Antonia's flat and join it to hers. He knew that Domenica came up with impractical ideas from time to time, and his policy had always been to ignore them; sooner or later they would be forgotten, to be replaced by some other scheme that would also get nowhere. Domenica was a wise woman, he felt – far more intellectually accomplished than he was himself – but not all her ideas had the ring of practicality about them.

His lukewarm response was the result of his unwillingness to abandon his flat and studio in Drummond Place – something he thought would be necessary if they were to buy out Antonia. It was all very well for Domenica to reassure him that he would be able to paint just as well in Scotland Street – she did not understand that an artist needed space to work properly, and space was a question of ceiling height as much as it was one of the length and breadth of a room.

He had explained this to her once, but she had probably not been listening, or had forgotten. "Edinburgh is uniquely well suited to artists because of its high ceilings," he said. "We need that height; we just do. Look at James Pryde. Look at his wonderful paintings of Edinburgh interiors with their great high ceilings and curtains of a length and grandeur that would do La Scala proud."

To make his point, he had shown Domenica a picture of one of Pryde's paintings, but she had simply shuddered, and said, "How gloomy! How could anybody sleep in a bedroom like that, Angus?"

No, she did not understand that need for ceiling height, and that was why she thought he would have no difficulty in adjusting to painting in her flat, or its planned extension, with its considerably more modest headroom.

Of course he could simply refuse; the flat was in his name and could not be sold without his consent. He could tell Domenica that he needed it and that was that, but he thought this would not be a particularly good start to their marriage. But then her trying to sell Drummond Place from under his feet was equally uncollegiate – if one could think of the married state in collegiate terms.

These thoughts gave rise to the issue of the form of words to be used in their marriage ceremony. Angus was Episcopalian and hoped that Domenica would agree to the use of the Scottish Book of Common Prayer for their wedding service. He liked the language, which was beautifully resonant, and even if Charles I – still regarded by some, but not many of them in Scotland, as a martyr – had been a little pushy in expecting his Scottish subjects to embrace a prayer book that gave an order on its first page, that lack of political tact should not have obscured the essential linguistic merit of the Book of Common Prayer, and also, Angus felt, that of the Authorised Version of Jamie Saxt.

Angus knew that the wording of the traditional marriage vows was not to everyone's taste. There was nothing wrong with promising to love the other and to endow him or her with all one's worldly goods – including, in a modern context, one assumed, all necessary passwords and PINs. That was very much in the spirit of modern marriage, but one strayed onto controversial ground once one started to talk about honouring and obeying. No modern woman would promise to "love, honour and obey" her husband, and these words were being deleted from most wedding services. But if one threw out obedience, as the metaphorical bathwater, did one also throw out loving and honouring? Honouring one's husband sounded a bit servile, and would be objected to on those grounds, but surely one could still promise to love him? That raised the interesting question of whether one could really promise to love somebody: Could love be called up, commanded, as a matter of will?

Angus wondered about this: there were people, he supposed, who loved others because they knew it was their Christian duty to do so, but the love one was talking about in that context was a different matter. It was a sort of agape – a form of brotherly love that was quite capable of being willed into existence. Romantic love – the love that one might expect between lovers – was something different. It was an emotion rather than an intellectual idea; it was a disposition that the person experiencing it could not control. One did not decide to be in love – rather, one realised that one had fallen into the state.

If Angus thought that Domenica would browbeat him into selling his flat, then his fears were misplaced. That had never been Domenica's intention. She hoped that he would sell it, as a result of her putting a persuasive case for that to happen; she would never have forced him to do so, and would certainly have withdrawn the suggestion had she known of his unhappiness with it. Having been in one marriage where she had encountered overbearing attitudes – on the part of her in-laws, her late husband's co-owners of the family's small electricity factory in Kerala – she had no wish to start her second marriage on such a footing. And if Angus did not wish to sell Drummond Place, it would still be possible to buy Antonia's flat by realising some investments of her own. It would not be the best place for the money, as it would provide no income, but the investments in question showed no signs of doing that anyway and would not be missed if they were to be transformed into bricks and mortar – or, in the case of Scotland Street, into stone and pointing.

So it was that Domenica found herself telephoning McKay Norwell and arranging for her solicitor, Lesley Kerr, to come round to Scotland Street with her measuring tape, her notebook, and her unsurpassed expertise in the marketing and selling of flats. They would look at Antonia's flat together and then Domenica would ask the question that had been worrying her since the idea had been conceived. If the owner of a flat asks you to sell it for her, could you sell it to yourself? It was a question worthy of the Lord Chancellor in *Iolanthe*, she thought, a suitable subject for a chorus of assorted fairies and peers to debate in song. She wanted the answer to be yes – and an unambiguous yes at that – as this was something that Domenica now wanted with some intensity. She had to have it; she just had to.

13. *Facility and Circumvention*

"What I would advise," said Lesley Kerr, "is this. You should tell Antonia that you are interested in purchasing her flat. You should then suggest that she consults another solicitor and asks him to act for her. You can then approach her lawyer with an offer for the flat, and he will advise her as to whether to accept. That would all be quite proper."

The three of them – Domenica, Lesley, and Angus – were sitting in Domenica's kitchen, a cup of tea on the table before them. Next to her cup of tea, Lesley's tape measure and black Moleskine notebook were laid; the tools of her trade of buying and selling houses.

Domenica listened to this advice. Although she did not say so, she was secretly rather disappointed that it would not be possible to act as both seller and buyer at the same time. She would have offered Antonia a fair price, and she would have been spared the stress of having to participate in blind bidding for the property – something that made the business of buying a house or flat in Scotland an exercise in nerves and inflationary zeal. Lesley's compromise seemed very attractive: she could make an offer, but it would not be an offer that was competing with numerous others, and surely it would be attractive from Antonia's point of view to have an arrangement that would obviate the need for a great deal of showing of the property. Of course Antonia did not have to worry about any of that, as she had delegated the selling of the house to Domenica, but she should at least consider Domenica's convenience, now that she was a nun, or almost a nun, and should be thinking of others perhaps a little bit more than she used to.

Perhaps the most appropriate thing for Antonia to do – one view at least – would be for her to give the flat away. If one was going into a convent, as Antonia was on the verge of doing, then surely one did not want to be encumbered by material possessions, and great spiritual credit was surely obtained if one divested oneself of those things that tie us most to the outside world. One should give things to the deserving poor, and even if Domenica could hardly be described as poor, she could still be said to be deserving . . .

The deserving poor: she thought of this patronising concept and wondered, for a moment, who they were, these deserving recipients of charity. Presumably there was some notion of desert at work in the phrase: the deserving poor were deserving because they had done nothing to merit their indigence – at least in the view of the smug middle classes who had coined the expression. And if the deserving poor existed there must be those who were, by contrast, clearly undeserving. These must be those who had brought their situation upon themselves by a failure to work, those who were feckless or extravagant, or, more simply, those who had it coming to them all along.

And the deserving rich – what about them, or were all rich people undeserving? What about these bankers with their inflated, provocative bonuses – if anybody could be called the undeserving rich, then surely it was them. Yet there must be rich people who had earned what they had, and had done it in such a way as not to trample over others. Would their good fortune be recognised, or were we so accustomed in Scotland to resenting people with money that they simply could never be accepted as deserving of their financial good fortune?

"I wish that Antonia would just give me the flat," sighed Domenica. "She says she doesn't need it – then why not make a gift of it?" She turned to Angus. "Should we suggest that to her, do you think?"

"It's not a bad idea . . ." Angus began. "She's half away with the fairies, anyway. She'd probably say yes."

Lesley held up a hand. "Please! Please! You can't do that sort of thing. Even if Antonia agreed, there would be a major question mark over the transaction and I wouldn't be in the slightest bit surprised if her relatives were to challenge it. And if they did, then I'm afraid there could be a strong case for having the contract reduced on the grounds of facility and circumvention."

"Facility and what?" asked Angus.

"Facility and circumvention is a doctrine in Scots law that means that a contract with somebody who is weak and vulnerable can be set aside on the grounds that the weak and vulnerable person would never have entered into it had he been stronger."

"But that's ridiculous," protested Domenica. "Of course you have to help people who don't know what on earth's going on. You have to help them make up their minds, otherwise they'd never be able to do anything."

"I'm afraid not," said Lesley. "You simply can't make up somebody's mind for them."

Domenica was not prepared to concede this point. Antonia was impossible – she had no idea of what was good for her, and probably never had. "Well, I must say that I feel I know exactly what Antonia's best interests are. They're for her to stay with those Italian sisters and pursue her interest in beekeeping. She's perfectly happy out there, and she can write to her heart's content about those early Scottish saints of hers. She does not need this flat and she can hardly claim that she needs the money from its sale. I think she should be assisted in whatever way possible to make a decision that reflects well on her new-found vocation. And anyway, she's not right in the head – that's been obvious for years now, and this bout of Stendhal Syndrome merely underlines all that. Perhaps we should just have her committed – maybe that would be simplest."

Angus thought this was going a bit far. "Antonia may go on a bit," he said. "But she's not round the bend." He looked at Domenica reproachfully. "You can't have people committed just because they live next door to you and won't sell you their flat. You really can't do that, Domenica."

"Well, we could argue at some length about that," said Domenica. "And we might never reach a resolution. I suggest that we go in there, measure up, and then consider how best to proceed once we know the dimensions of the rooms."

14. *Senior Moments*

"Now pay attention for a moment, boys and girls," said Bertie's teacher, Miss Maclaren Hope. "I would like to tell you about a very special project we are about to embark upon. It's a very exciting one, and I want to see everybody looking at me and listening to every word I have to say! And that includes you, Tofu dear. And you, Hiawatha, while we're about it. I want every little face turned this way, every brow wrinkled in concentration, just as Somerled's brave warriors listened to him as he explained the dangers that lurked along the perilous shores of Morvern, or those courageous and noble Highlanders hung on every word of Prince Charlie as he explained to them the route they would follow to Victory!"

Miss Maclaren Hope, a Highlander herself, had a habit of making such references at odd moments, and the children had become accustomed to the West Highlands being brought into most of the subjects they studied, including mathematics. "Bonnie Prince Charlie never made a mistake in calculating the number of miles he had walked," she announced, "just as we ourselves must never make a mistake in the wee sums we do!" And in addition to these historical asides, the members of Bertie's class were now all word-perfect in Gaelic and other Highland classics, in "Fear a' Bhàta," in "The Eriskay Love Lilt," and in "Ho Ro, My Nut-Brown Maiden." They had also performed a two-hour play, written by Miss Maclaren Hope, entitled *The Leaving of Lochaber*. That performance, which had been presented to the rest of the school in fifteen-minute instalments over a period of eight days, had been compared by Bertie to the Oberammergau Passion Play, which he had read about in the *Encyclopaedia Britannica*. "It goes on for hours," he said. "And it's made the little village where they perform it really famous."

Olive, who had been standing nearby when Bertie made this remark, did not take kindly to the mention of the *Encyclopaedia Britannica*. She was aware that Bertie's reading ability was considerably better than hers, just as she was aware that Bertie seemed to know far more about the world than she did. And she resented both of these facts deeply. "You think you know everything," she said. "Well you don't, Bertie Pollock. You know hardly anything."

"I've never said I know everything," protested Bertie. "And I don't, Olive. There are still lots of encyclopaedias I haven't read – bags of them."

Olive ignored this. "And here's another thing," she said. "Your mother forgot to fetch you yesterday, didn't she? It's no good denying it, Bertie. My mummy said it was quite shocking seeing you standing at the school gate for twenty minutes like that. She said that next time it happened she was going to phone the social services and have you taken into care!"

"It wasn't really my mummy's fault," said Bertie mildly. "Ulysses was sick all over her just as they got into the bus. She had to go home and change."

Olive looked at Bertie with pity. "A likely story, Bertie," she said. "No, Bertie, your mother's problem is far more serious than that, you know. You do know that, don't you, Bertie? You seem to know everything else, don't you? Well, you do know about your mother, I take it?"

Bertie hesitated. He was accustomed to Olive's vague taunts, which he normally accepted quite philosophically, but it seemed now that she had special knowledge of some sort. He was defensive of his mother too: a loyal little boy, he did not like to hear her disparaged by others, especially by Olive, or even by his friend Tofu, who regularly reminded Bertie that his mother was, in Tofu's view, a cow.

"She's just a cow, Bertie," said Tofu. "I know it's not your fault, but there it is. She's a real cow. Everybody in Edinburgh thinks that. It's official."

"I don't think so," said Bertie. "I really don't think she is."

"Oh, but she is, Bertie. It's just one of those things. Some people have mothers who are really good at tennis or make brilliant cakes, but some people have mothers who are cows. That's the way it is."

Now Olive, it seemed, was making an even more serious suggestion about his mother, and Bertie felt a tinge of anxiety.

"Ulysses really does bring up over my mother," he pointed out. "It's really very hard for my mummy, Olive. Whenever she picks him up he's sick all over her."

"That's because even Ulysses thinks she's a cow," interjected Tofu, who had come to hear what Olive had to say on the subject.

Olive was not to be deflected. "We needn't go into any of that, Bertie," she said primly. "The point is this: your mummy is forgetting things, isn't she? She forgot to collect you yesterday and then made up some excuse for it. That's exactly what happens, Bertie. That's one of the signs you have to look out for."

Bertie looked puzzled. "Signs of what, Olive?"

Olive drew Bertie aside. Lowering her voice, she explained. "You know that people's memories get worse when they get older: You know that, don't you, Bertie?"

"Maybe," said Bertie guardedly.

"Well, they do," Olive went on. "They get so bad that they can't even remember their own names. Then they have to tie labels on them to prevent them wandering off. My mummy told me that there's a club called the New Club where just about everybody's got a label tied on to them to remind them who they are. Did you know that, Bertie? You think you know everything – did you know that?"

Bertie shook his head.

"Well," said Olive. "It's true." She paused. "Yes, it's really sad about your mummy, Bertie. I think that you're going to have to be quite watchful. Just look out for the signs. Check up on whether she remembers things. Ask her questions and see if she gets the answers right. You'll see what I mean soon enough."

"But she's not all that old," said Bertie.

Olive smiled tolerantly. "All grown-ups are old, Bertie. And any of them – any of them at all – can go like that. One moment they're fine, and then the next moment, they've forgotten just about everything. Just be watchful, Bertie, that's all I have to say to you. Just watch out! And look for the signs, Bertie – that's the thing to do – look for the signs!"

The attention of the class now focused firmly on her, Miss Maclaren Hope went on to reveal her project. "We are going to be creative, boys and girls," she announced. "We are all going to write a novel!"

She looked at the faces before her. Tofu looked blank, but that, she thought, was to be expected; that child knew so little and yet was so opinionated.

"A novel, boys and girls," Miss Maclaren Hope explained, "is a story – quite a lengthy one. Sometimes it tells the tale of a whole life; sometimes it just tells all about one particular thing that has happened to a person. There are many sorts of novels and there are many different sorts of novelists." She paused. "Can anybody give me the name of a novelist? Anyone at all?"

Nobody said anything. Bertie looked down at the floor. He knew a number of names, of course, but he did not want to draw attention to himself.

Tofu broke the silence. "Jeffrey Archer," he said. "My dad reads those books all the time. He's got hundreds of them. A big stack. This high."

Miss Maclaren Hope suppressed a smile. "Well, yes, Mr. Archer is indeed a writer. And I'm sure that there are many people who love reading Mr. Archer's books and get great comfort from them. But I wonder if there is anybody else?"

"Irvine Welsh," said Bertie.

Miss Maclaren Hope smiled. "Well, yes, Bertie. There is Mr. Welsh who writes about Edinburgh, or perhaps we should say Leith, so . . . so vividly. His books are perhaps not for children, but that's very good, Bertie."

"And Ian Rankin," said Bertie. "He's a novelist."

"Indeed he is," said Miss Maclaren Hope. "Dear Mr.

Rankin has a very active imagination and writes very good books indeed. I often curl up with a book by Mr. Rankin and a mug of hot chocolate! I freely admit that."

"You can buy his books in Oxfam shops," Bertie went on. "There are loads of them there."

"That's very nice, Bertie," said Miss Maclaren Hope. "It's so nice that people don't just throw his books away but give them to these charity shops! That's very kind of them, boys and girls."

The discussion moved on. Bertie pointed out that Walter Scott was a novelist, and Miss Maclaren Hope agreed that this was so, and spent some time extolling the virtues of *Waverley* and *Rob Roy*.

"So there we are, boys and girls," she continued. "We have had some examples of famous novelists and now we are all going to have our opportunity to try our own hand at writing a novel. Not that we need to write something as long as one of Sir Walter Scott's books – oh no, we should just aim for three or four pages, very neatly written, please! And you can put in pictures too, if you like."

The class sat in silence. Hiawatha stared up at the ceiling while Olive looked thoughtfully out of the window.

"Any questions?" asked Miss Maclaren Hope.

Olive put up her hand.

"Yes, Olive, dear?" said the teacher.

"Can it be romantic, Miss Maclaren Hope?"

The teacher smiled. "Of course it can, Olive. There is nothing wrong with romantic fiction, children. Love is one of the great noble emotions of which people are capable. There are many very fine romantic novels."

Now Bertie put up his hand. "*Madame Bovary*, for example, Miss Maclaren Hope."

Miss Maclaren Hope took a moment to compose herself.

Bertie really was a most extraordinary little boy, she thought; the depth of his reading was quite amazing for one who was still not quite seven. She had never encountered anything like it before, but did not want to talk too much about it, lest Bertie be spoiled. At present he was entirely composed of innocence and the last thing she would want would be for *The Scotsman* to get wind of the presence of a real prodigy in the school.

"Yes, Bertie," she said at last. "*Madame Bovary* is indeed an example of a romance. She was, however, a little bit unhappy."

"What did she do?" asked Tofu. "Was she rude?"

Miss Maclaren Hope blushed. "It's rather complicated, Tofu, and I don't think we should go into it just yet. It all happened in France and there are many things that happen in France that do not necessarily happen in Edinburgh."

"Such as?" asked Tofu.

"They eat snails in France," said Olive. "They put lots of garlic in them and they eat them. Can you imagine that, Miss Maclaren Hope? Eating snails that crawl around your mouth and leave trails of slime on your teeth? That's why the French have slimy teeth. I saw all about it on YouTube."

"Not nearly as slimy as your teeth," said Tofu under his breath. "Girls have really slimy teeth."

Olive's hand shot up. "Did you hear that, Miss Maclaren Hope? Did you hear what Tofu said about girls' teeth?"

"I am grateful that I did not hear it," said the teacher. "But Tofu, you may care to stand outside the door and reflect on the importance of not criticising other people's teeth. Then, when you have thought about it for ten minutes, you may come back in."

Bertie sighed as he watched Tofu get up from his desk and leave the room, sending dagger-like glances at Olive as he did so. It was such a waste of time all this bickering; if only Tofu and Olive could love one another as everybody was supposed to do . . .

"I shall definitely write a romance, Miss Maclaren Hope," said Olive. "It will be about a girl called . . . called Tracey Bovary who has a boyfriend called . . . Bertie Pollock who loves her very much but can't bring himself to admit it and who doesn't know that he will eventually marry her on the last page and live happily ever after in Morningside. It will be very romantic."

She glanced at Bertie as she related this, and Bertie, mortified, looked away. He had his own story to think about and a very interesting idea had come to mind. Yes, he would write a story called *The Secret Baby*, which would be all about a woman who has a baby who looks really like a psychotherapist she knows. She will discover that the psychotherapist is really the baby's father, by a miracle. It would be quite exciting, he thought, as the baby himself would know – again by a miracle – that the psychotherapist was his real father and would eventually go to live with him, although he would still write regularly to his mother every week – once he learned how to write. Bertie had noticed that novels had dedications in them, and he thought that he would dedicate *The Secret Baby* to his mother, which would make her really proud of him, he thought.

16. *Matthew Speaks Out of Turn*

Big Lou was extremely pleased by the arrival of Matthew and Pat. It was not Matthew's presence that gave her pleasure – although she was on perfectly good terms with him – rather it was the prospect of talking to Pat, whom she had not seen for some time. From Big Lou's point of view, conversations with Matthew and Angus Lordie were all very well, as conversations with men went, but talking with another woman was different – in ways which it was sometimes difficult to explain. She was not sure whether it was the subject matter of such exchanges or whether it was the tone that counted. Men talked about things that happened in the world, about events; women, by contrast, talked amongst themselves about being in the world. The difference was crucial.

"Well, well," said Big Lou. "This is a very pleasant surprise. When I saw Matthew's legs through the window I thought it would be just him; then I saw yours and I thought . . ." She stopped. She did not want to be rude to Matthew, and she realised that what she had said made him sound second best.

Matthew did not mind. "That's all right, Lou," he said. "I'd far prefer to talk to Pat than to me – if you see what I mean."

"I didn't mean that," said Big Lou. "I meant . . . Oh well, it doesn't really matter."

They took a seat at one of the tables near the counter; this would enable Big Lou to talk to them while she prepared their coffees.

Matthew explained about employing Pat. "It'll give me time to help Elspeth with the boys," he said.

"Good," said Big Lou, wiping the steam nozzle of her large, gleaming espresso machine. "She'll need all the help she can get, poor lass."

"That's what paternity leave is for," said Matthew.

When this remark was greeted by silence on Big Lou's part, Matthew looked at her sideways. "Well it is," he said defensively. "Paternity leave is a great idea. And I think that men should get exactly the same amount of leave as women."

Big Lou snorted. "Rubbish," she said.

Matthew prickled. "Why not?"

"Because it would cost far too much," said Big Lou. "And, anyway, it's a woman's job to look after children. That's just the way it is."

Matthew smiled. "You're very old-fashioned, Lou. Nobody thinks like that any more, you know."

"Do they not? Well, they're wrong, Matthew. You can't wish biology out of existence, you know."

"Men feel the urge to look after children every bit as much as women do, Lou. Men feel protective too."

"Protective, yes," said Big Lou. "Nurturing, no. Men don't nurture."

"I'm not so sure about that," ventured Pat. "I know lots of men who . . . well, who are into nurturing."

Matthew, who was normally very calm, now bristled. "Yes," he said. "You can't go making those . . . those utterly sexist remarks, Lou. You're not back on the farm, you know. You're in Edinburgh. Things have moved on."

"Sexist?" Big Lou retorted. "To point out what's obviously true? Let me tell you something, Matthew, one advantage of being brought up on a farm is that you know how things are. You get to know that in any animal it's the female, Matthew – the female – that does the looking after of the young. Cattle. Horses. Pigs. Sheep. Hens. You name it. The female, Matthew. The male pushes off or even attacks the young." She glared at Matthew. "Biology, ken, Matthew. Biology."

"Well, we're not animals," snapped Matthew. "We're a cooperative species that can decide what's best based on thinking things through." He paused. He felt a strong surge of resentment that Big Lou should have questioned the depth of his paternal instincts. And she was being sexist in her assumptions, no matter how she tried to dress it up in biological terms. That language was used, he felt, by all sorts of people who wanted to clad their reactionary prejudices in scientific clothing: as if it was inevitable that we should be greedy, or uncharitable, or suspicious of others because it was part of our immutable human nature. It was not! Human nature was malleable, and men could be as soft, as caring, and as concerned about feelings as women – and often were, thought Matthew.

He drew in his breath. His heart was beating hard within him; beating at the sheer injustice of what Big Lou had just said. How dare she suggest that he did not want to care for his young sons; how dare she imply that he would not be rolling up his sleeves to play an equal part in the messy business of their day-to-day care. He had already changed several nappies; he had already helped Elspeth with the feeding – in so far as he was able, of course; he was doing everything he could.

He looked at Big Lou, who stared back at him with that slightly bemused expression he had noticed she often used when speaking to him. She treats me as if I'm a little boy, he thought. I've had enough.

"And anyway," he said impulsively. "What do you know about looking after children, Lou? What gives you the right to lecture me about that, when I've got three and you've got none?"

The words came out quickly, but there was no doubt but that they were meant.

"Matthew!" Pat hissed.

He looked at Pat. "What? She told me that . . ."

"That's a very cruel, insensitive thing to say," Pat said. "How could you?"

"She said . . ." he stuttered.

"It doesn't matter what Lou said. You had no right to make such a hurtful remark."

It was clear that Big Lou was shaken. Even so, she attempted to brush off the slight. "It disnae matter," she said. "If that's what he thinks . . ."

"It does matter, Lou," said Pat. Then, turning to Matthew, she whispered, "Are you going to apologise to Lou, Matthew?"

Matthew rose to his feet. "No," he said. "Not until she apologises to me . . . and to all men."

"Don't be so ridiculous," said Pat.

"I'm not being ridiculous at all," said Matthew. "If she thinks she can go about insulting men like that, then she can think again." He turned, and began to walk out. "I'm going back to Moray Place," he called over his shoulder to Pat. "To look after the children."

"Aye, and don't come back," Big Lou shouted out after him.

17. A Letter from Arbroath

Pat felt distinctly uncomfortable when she returned to the gallery after coffee at Big Lou's. She did not like conflict – she never had – and the unpleasant row between Matthew and Big Lou had left her feeling raw. It had all blown up so quickly, so unexpectedly, and yet she could see how she might well have anticipated something like that. Matthew should not have spoken to Big Lou in such a way, she said to herself – it was thoughtless, intemperate, and, most of all, unkind; but she was not entirely surprised by what had happened.

The problem was that Big Lou had a long history of goading – admittedly in a gentle way – both Matthew and Angus Lordie, treating them as errant youths who need not be taken too seriously. Pat could understand how Matthew would have resented Big Lou's assumption that he would be a fair-weather father, prepared to help with the triplets until such time as the novelty wore off or something more interesting turned up. There were undoubtedly fathers who would behave in that way, but not, she thought, Matthew; it was very much in his nature to fuss, and attending to triplets was surely something he would relish.

Pat sighed as she unlocked the door of the gallery and took down the Back Soon notice. She had done her best to apologise to Big Lou on Matthew's behalf, but she was not sure how successful her efforts had been. Big Lou had dismissed the contretemps with a curt remark about Matthew's childishness, but she had not indicated that he was forgiven.

"You aren't going to ban him, are you?" Pat said.

Big Lou hesitated for a moment. "I think so," she said.

"Isn't that a bit . . . extreme? I don't think that he really wanted to hurt you."

"Aye, mebbe. But he's banned anyway. From now on, he's the only person in Edinburgh who's banned from entering these premises."

Pat had not pressed the point, and the conversation had drifted off in other directions. Big Lou, Pat noticed, had attempted some redecoration of her coffee bar, which now had a freshly painted ceiling as well as a new oak skirting board.

"Very effective," said Pat.

"Yes," said Lou. "I thought things needed brightening up."

"And what's that over there?" asked Pat, pointing to a large framed document hanging on the wall above the espresso machine.

"The Declaration of Arbroath," said Lou.

Pat peered at the framed picture of the ancient document, with its line of dangling seals. For a few moments she was transported back to a warm classroom at school, on a summer day some years ago – ten, possibly a dozen – when her teacher, Miss Fraser, cruelly called Miss Frazzle – which children are not innately cruel when they sense adult vulnerability? – taught them about that crucial moment in Scottish history.

"The Scots were in despair over the depredations of the English," she intoned. "And who would not be – in the circumstances? Our nobles – and unfortunately, girls, we cannot be unduly proud of them, scheming and malodorous lot that they were – nonetheless spoke from the heart when they signed this letter to Pope John XXII, luxuriating away in his distant Vatican – but that is another matter that we shall return to when we turn our attention to the stirring events that were to come over two centuries later, in 1560, and not a moment too soon. These nobles were fed up, girls, utterly fed up, that Edward I and his equally unsavoury successor, most objectionable men, should seek to engorge themselves upon our poor wee country. And so they wrote to His Holiness and asked him to give recognition to our struggling land and to remove that most uncharitable and unmerited excommunication of the courageous Bruce for some minor offence involving the alleged murder of some meddlesome personage."

That was Miss Fraser, who lived for Scottish history; who paid an annual pilgrimage to the Wallace Monument; who wept for the Covenanters; and whose voice and manner were imitated by generations of small girls until she retired to a small flat in Musselburgh – "I shall be so close to the site of the Battle of Pinkie Cleugh – remember the Rough Wooing, girls? – and not far from the scene of that resounding victory at Prestonpans: I shall be very happy, girls." She gave us so much, thought Pat as she looked at the Declaration, so much love – in her way – and we repaid her with so little. I shall go and see her.

Big Lou was watching Pat and wondering what she was thinking. Was she trying to remember exactly what the Declaration of Arbroath was? Was it possible that nobody taught anybody about it any more? Was it possible that Scottish history was being ignored by a nation that was encouraged to forget who it was and where it had come from?

"They wrote to the Pope . . ." she began.

"I know," Pat reassured her. "I don't suppose he received many letters from Arbroath . . ."

Big Lou continued. "When I was at school we learned the words by heart. I could recite it from start to finish. I was eleven."

Pat looked at her and smiled. "I knew a boy who could recite 'Tam O'Shanter' word-perfect when he was eight."

Big Lou nodded. "There used to be lots of boys like that," she said. "But still . . . Do you remember this bit?" She pointed to a section of the Declaration. "May it please you to admonish and exhort the King of the English, who ought to be satisfied with what belongs to him . . . to leave us Scots in peace, who live in this poor little Scotland, beyond which there is no dwelling place at all, and covet nothing but our own."

Pat nodded. "I remember that. It always seemed to me to be such a sad plea. Poor little Scotland."

"We have had our sorrows," said Big Lou. "Edward I. Flodden. The Darien Disaster. The near collapse of the Royal Bank of Scotland."

"Some of those were our own fault," said Pat. "Don't you think so, Lou?"

Lou thought for a moment. "Yes, perhaps; except for Edward I. He was bad luck." She thought further. "Of the other three, one was caused by bad judgement, one by me-too-ism, and another by either pride or greed, I'm not sure which."

"Both?" suggested Pat.

18. Measuring Up

While Big Lou and Pat were contemplating the Declaration of Arbroath, Domenica Macdonald was standing with her fiancé, Angus Lordie, and her lawyer, Lesley Kerr, outside the door of Antonia Collie's Scotland Street flat, key in hand.

"I must confess I feel somewhat furtive," said Domenica. "I know that I'm fully entitled to go inside – indeed Antonia asked me to go in as often as I could to see that all was well, but somehow . . ."

"You need not reproach yourself," said Lesley. "We are merely going in to measure up for the sale. That's all. And what we see inside will, of course, be kept confidential."

"Of course," said Domenica.

"Of course," added Angus hurriedly. He doubted that there would be anything of any great interest in Antonia's flat anyway; piles of books about Scottish saints and those unfortunate Russell Flint prints she insisted on displaying. It was extraordinary what people hung on their walls, he thought; perfectly reasonable people who should know better put dreadful things up: pictures of matadors by late French expressionists, for example, that induced nausea and, in some cases, even more severe symptoms; pictures by prolific Russian artists of well-padded female nudes that were enough to discourage even the most hetero-normatively compliant of men; there were so many crimes against art, Angus thought – and not all of them committed by the judges of the Turner Prize.

"Of course, it's really a question of what you like, Angus," Big Lou had once said to him. "Some people like one thing and others don't. That's what it boils down to."

"Oh no, it does not!" Angus retorted. "There is good art, Lou, and there is bad art. And there are aesthetic and even moral criteria for distinguishing between the two."

This fragment of conversation – the beginnings of a heated debate that had gone nowhere – came into his mind as Domenica began to unlock Antonia's door; and went right out of his mind as they stepped into the hall. Closing the door behind them, Domenica suggested that Lesley might wish to start there and work out into the surrounding rooms.

The lawyer looked about her. "It's a very charming hall," she said. "Some flats have very poky entrances, but this one has all this light." She pointed to the skylight, through which could be seen a slice of Edinburgh sky – high, blue, with only traces of wispy cirrus.

She moved to examine one of the walls more closely. "It could perhaps do with a coat of paint, but I think we should leave it. The new owners may have their own ideas as to colour schemes, and I always recommend that it should be left up to them, if possible. Of course, if things are really shabby, then there's a case for freshening a property up before it goes on the market. But most buyers can see beyond the immediate state of things."

"Exactly," said Angus. "And what about baking bread?"

Domenica looked at him curiously. "Baking bread?"

Lesley Kerr laughed. "Oh yes. People often ask about that. They've read somewhere that the smell of baking bread in the background makes prospective buyers feel more positive about a house or flat."

"And flowers?" asked Domenica.

"They might help," said Lesley. "But you're never going to impress a surveyor. A surveyor will probably be suspicious if he smells too much baking bread."

She extracted her electronic tape measure and took a few readings. "Very nice," she said, writing in her Moleskine notebook.

They went into the sitting room. There was a slight fustiness in the air – the result, Domenica explained, of the flat being closed up for so long. "I open the windows whenever I come in," she said. "I air the place as much as I can, but air goes off, doesn't it? It gets stale."

While Lesley busied herself with measurements, Angus sidled up to look at a framed print of a Highland ghillie standing with his dogs; behind him a cloud-wreathed mountain; a distant loch. His gaze moved on: there was that Russell Flint to which he had so strenuously objected; and then . . . a small oil of a woman arranging flowers. He had not seen this before and he wondered how it could have escaped his notice. He moved forward and peered more closely at the painting.

"Something interesting you?" asked Domenica from the other side of the room.

Angus continued to scrutinise the painting. "I'm not at all sure, but I think that this might be . . ."

"A Cadell?" asked Domenica. "It looks a bit like it."

Angus nodded. "Exactly what I was thinking."

He moved away from the painting, as Lesley was now ready to measure the kitchen. "It's a charming little flat," she said. "I imagine it will sell quite well. This light is a great feature – there's something to be said for living on the top floor. It's so airy."

At first Domenica was silent. If she was going to try to buy the flat, then she was not at all keen for its better points to push the price up. "And an awful lot of stairs," she said. "That will put off a lot of people – even people who are fit don't like the thought of trudging all that way up. And cupolas leak, I believe."

"That's true," said Lesley. "But remember that Scotland Street is a very popular street. Convenience and atmosphere may well outweigh any drawbacks."

Domenica said nothing. She was beginning to accept that she was going to have to compete for the flat; well, she would do that, and she would be cheerful about it. After all, it was only money, and there was no point, she felt, in leaving money to her distant heirs. She stopped. After she married, she would have a very close heir indeed – her husband. And yet she was sure that she would outlast Angus: it was the lot of women to survive their husbands – as actuaries were only too ready to point out. Those were morbid thoughts, though, and she did not want to think them when she should be enjoying herself snooping round her neighbour's flat. Who wouldn't enjoy such a heaven-sent opportunity – to go round a neighbour's place, seeing a life laid bare?

"Antonia has very poor taste," muttered Angus.

"Poor woman," said Domenica. "She . . ."

She did not finish. She had spotted a postcard lying on the floor where it had fluttered down from the letterbox. She reached down and picked it up.

19. *The Privacy, or Otherwise, of Postcards*

"What does it say?" asked Angus.

"It's addressed to Antonia," said Domenica.

"Of course it is. It's her flat, after all."

Domenica shot him a disapproving glance. "I know that. The point is: Should I read something addressed to another?"

Angus hesitated. "A postcard . . . I thought that postcards were more or less in the public domain. If you want to write something confidential, you write a letter."

"I'm not so sure," said Domenica. "You don't imagine that anybody else is going to read a postcard. You assume that the card will be delivered to the person it's addressed to – not passed around the neighbourhood for inspection and comment."

Angus peered at the card. Domenica's thumb was obscuring the message and he could make nothing out. She noticed his interest, and moved her thumb further down so as to obscure the message more completely.

"But what if it's something important?" he protested. "What if it's something we have to act on?"

"Unlikely," said Domenica. "It's probably something entirely personal. A card from a friend on holiday, or something like that." She paused. "It could even be from one of her lovers. Who knows?"

"Here's an idea," he said. "Let's give the card to Lesley and ask her to read it. She's a lawyer, after all, and can read it in her professional capacity. Then, if she thinks that we need to know the contents, she can authorise us to look at it. How about that?"

Domenica could find no fault with this suggestion. Lesley, having taken all the necessary measurements, was now inspecting the basin and shower in the bathroom. Domenica took the postcard through to her there and asked her to read it. "Not aloud," she said. "Read it as . . . as a lawyer to see if it's personal or whether it says something we should act on or tell Antonia about."

Lesley nodded. "I think I can do that quite properly," she said. "There's a doctrine in Scots law called *negotiorum gestio*. It comes from Roman law."

"There you are," said Angus. "I told you."

"You didn't," said Domenica. "You didn't say anything about *negoti* . . ."

"*Negotiorum gestio*," supplied Lesley. Being an Edinburgh lawyer, her command of Latin was naturally better than average.

"Yes," said Domenica. "*Negotio* . . ."

". . . *rum gestio*," prompted Lesley.

"Exactly."

"Same thing," said Angus. "Just because one doesn't know the Latin for a rule doesn't mean that one doesn't understand the rule itself." He looked enquiringly at Lesley. "What does this . . . this *neg* . . ."

Once again Lesley came to the rescue. ". . . *otiorum gestio* mean?"

Lesley closed her eyes momentarily, and was back in the lecture theatre at the University of Edinburgh listening to the late Professor T.B. Smith – Professor Sir Thomas Smith, as he became – talking about *negotiorum gestio* in Scots law. "If a man sees that his neighbour's house is flooding and he engages a plumber to deal with it – his neighbour being absent abroad – then it's surely right, ladies and gentlemen, that he should be able to claim from the neighbour such expenses as he necessarily expends in dealing with the emergency."

This had been greeted with a general nodding of heads, at least in the forward, more engaged rows of the lecture theatre. Yes, it was quite in accord with our sense of justice that such a public-spirited person should be compensated. And now, faced with the postcard, she reasoned that if an obligation could come into existence under the principles of *negotiorum gestio*, then there must be a right to determine in the first place whether action needs to be taken.

She looked at the postcard. The handwriting was easy to interpret; a firm, rather elegant script that a graphologist would have readily identified as belonging to a person of aesthetic sensibility. The message itself was brief – and not at all confidential.

"I don't think there's anything in the slightest bit private about this," she said. "Indeed, I think that you need to read it, Domenica. I think that it requires action."

Domenica took the card and read it quickly before handing it on to Angus.

"Dear Ant," he read. He looked at Domenica and smiled. "I don't see her as an Ant, do you? A term of endearment?"

"Short for Antonia," said Domenica. "Carry on."

"This is *pour memoire*," Angus read. "My visit is coming up – at long last. Thank you so much for agreeing to put me up. I have great hopes of being able to achieve a considerable amount in the month I'm in Edinburgh, which is just what I need. I have so much work to do, I can't tell you, but I know that I shall get through it like a . . . what is the correct metaphor? My metaphors seem to be deserting me these days – do you think that's a feature of where we all are *anno domini*, or is it just because one gets tired of the metaphorical as one goes through life? Perhaps we can discuss this when I arrive next Wednesday. Eleven thirty in the morning. I can come straight from the Waverley." He looked at Domenica. "And then there's a signature I can't make out. Can you?"

Domenica had not looked at the signature. Now she strained to make it out. "Magnus something."

Angus took the card back. "Magnus . . . Is it Cameron? Campbell?" He held the card sideways and squinted at it. "Why do people not sign their names clearly? Is it because they're hiding something." He paused. "No, it's Campbell. Definitely Campbell."

Domenica frowned. "Are you sure?"

Angus shrugged. "I think so. Did she ever mention a Magnus Campbell to you?"

"No. Not that I recall."

"Obviously one of her friends," said Angus. "She knew a lot of men, didn't she? Do you think he was one of her old lovers?"

Domenica did not reply. She was looking out of the window. Magnus Campbell was one of *her* old lovers. That was the problem. If it was the same Magnus Campbell, of course; there were bound to be numerous Magnus Campbells and she could not be sure. And yet, in spite of the plurality of Magnus Campbells, the name still had the power to tug at her heart, a shibboleth to unlock secrets long concealed; a reminder of love once glimpsed and then lost. Such names never lose their power, their ability to make us stop in our emotional tracks and remember the vision Venus sends to lovers in, as Auden put it, their ordinary swoon.

20. *The Presence of the Sun*

Angus left Scotland Street to return to his studio. He was intrigued by the possibility that Antonia had a Cadell – and a rather charming one at that. She had never expressed any views on art, although she had obviously been susceptible to it, given that she had suffered an attack of Stendhal Syndrome in Florence. That was not a condition that affected philistines: one had to be open to beauty to be overcome by it. This meant that those who were indifferent to art were immune, as those who have been exposed to a virus may be spared infection on subsequent exposure. No, that was perhaps not the best analogy, he thought: exposure to art did not confer immunity to its power – rather, it made one all the more likely to be affected. The real philistine did not notice art, and would therefore never be a candidate for Stendhal Syndrome, no matter how long he stood in the middle of the Uffizi or the National

Gallery of Scotland, or anywhere else where great art was to be found.

Cyril had been left behind in the studio and was delighted when his master returned. No matter how deeply he was asleep, the sound of the key in the lock was sufficient to wake the dog from his slumbers and send him bounding to the front door, ready to greet Angus on his return. The initial welcome would then be followed by an enthusiastic headlong dash around the flat, during which the excited dog displaced rugs, bumped into furniture, and sustained such a yelping as would pass for the wailing of an Irish Banshee, only in a more cheerful note, as Banshees wail in a melancholy fashion about impending bad news, and the return of Angus was never that – in Cyril's view at least. For Cyril, the presence of Angus was like that of the sun in the sky: it was there, it was necessary, it was life-giving.

And when the sun went behind a cloud, just as human spirits might drop, so too would Cyril's world contract into a tight glove of solitude when Angus went out without him. He had no understanding of the fact that Angus went far; in his mind, Angus went to the door, the door closed, and Angus stood on the other side of the door until such time as he chose to open it and come back in. Why his master should stand for hours on the wrong side of the front door was a question beyond the scope of his canine intellect. There was no reason for things to happen in Cyril's universe; they just happened, and one reacted accordingly. Squirrels, for example, ran up trees when chased. There was no reason for them to do that – it's just what they did. And dogs chased squirrels in the same spirit: that is what they did.

Angus, for his part, had reflected on this and had come

to the conclusion that issues of habit arose in the human world too. There were those who led the examined life – who questioned themselves, who weighed up what to do, who developed and nurtured the self – or the soul, if they were inclined to such terminology. But then there were plenty of people who simply did what they did because that was what they had always done and would continue to do. They ate certain things because they liked them and had always eaten them; they voted for a particular political party because that was what their grandparents and parents had done before them; and so on into virtually all the corners of their lives – an unevaluated, unchanging pattern of behaviour that was rarely challenged or reviewed. Such people did not feel themselves to be in control of their lives: decisions were taken elsewhere; they were told what to do.

The thought depressed him. It was not the fault of those who thought this way: they lived in a system that had actively encouraged such passivity. Vote for us and we'll look after you; join us and we'll make sure you have a job; let us house you, feed you, look after your health, take care of your children. And yet all of these things were goals that seemed so enticing. The world was a cold, hard place, and if there was somebody offering to protect you from it, then independence of thought and action was not much to give up in return. And surely it was better that there should be somebody to clothe and nurture those who would otherwise be naked and vulnerable?

It was noon by the time Angus arrived home, and Cyril was feeling hungry. Angus opened a can of dog food and put half of the contents into the metal bowl labelled CYRIL. Then, leaving Cyril to enjoy his lunch, he went into his studio and put on his painting smock.

He was proud of this smock, which had been given to him by Nigel McIsaac, a fellow artist who had lived round the corner in Dundonald Street. Nigel had been the kindest of men, and had taken Angus under his wing when he had first come to Edinburgh. Not only had he given him an easel – Angus's own easel being a distinctly shaky third-hand affair, retired from the Art College on health and safety grounds – but he had also passed on this smock which, tradition had it, had been worn by John Duncan Fergusson himself before it had been auctioned at the Glasgow Arts Club in aid of the Scottish Artists' Benevolent Association. It gave Angus such pleasure to know that it was this very smock that Fergusson would have worn in his Paris studio in the late Twenties; that it might have been seen by Matisse and Picasso – perhaps even borrowed by them if their own smock was at the dry-cleaner (if dry-cleaning existed in those days). And if Matisse had worn it, then some of the small smudges of paint hardened on the fabric, tiny, ancient specks of colour, might equally well have been from his palette as from Fergusson's . . . To be so close to greatness, and yet not be great oneself; a bitter thought for some, but not for Angus. I still have time to produce a great painting, he told himself. And to get married. And to visit Sweden for my honeymoon.

He stopped. Why had he thought that their honeymoon would be in Sweden? Who went on honeymoon to Sweden? And why?

21. *An Evening with the Triplets*

That evening, Matthew and Elspeth experienced for the first time the full implications of having triplets. It was not their first night at home with their newly arrived brood, but it was the first night during which there was a complete failure of synchronised sleep on the part of Tobermory, Rognvald, and Fergus. This meant that from the early evening onwards, when the infants all appeared to be wide awake – and hungry – there was no moment in the night when at least one of them was not awake and making his feelings apparent. If Matthew and Elspeth had been on a small yacht, undertaking a night-crossing of some dangerous body of water – and all bodies of water are dangerous, as Matthew had discovered on his honeymoon in Western Australia – then they would have shared the watches of the night, with one sleeping below while one took the helm and kept an eye out for shipping.

This, though, was different. To begin with, there was no metaphorical below; the flat was not acoustically discreet – and a niggle or cry in one room seemed to penetrate quite easily into the reaches of other rooms, or at least a baby's cry, designed by nature to alert the hearer, seemed to do this. And then there was the psychological factor: Matthew found that he could not sleep if Elspeth was up attending to a girning child. He would lie there wondering what the problem was, and eventually, after a few minutes, would be up at her side, offering to assist. And when he was attending to one of the babies, Elspeth found that she could not sleep either, being far too unsure as to Matthew's ability to deal with the situation.

Matthew tried to put on a brave face. He was not a complainer by nature – a worrier, yes, but not one to moan. "Isn't this fun?" he cheerfully remarked. "Having the babies all to ourselves while the rest of Scotland is asleep!"

"Yes," muttered Elspeth, struggling with a nappy. She would get better at putting them on, she felt; they were awkward things when a pair of little legs was moving with such determination. And it was remarkable what pressure such tiny bladders must muster to project quite so far – and with such accuracy.

"Do be careful," said Matthew. "You don't want to get those sticky tapes on his skin. Some babies are allergic to those things, I read."

She glanced at him. "You should try to get some sleep, darling. There's no point in both of us being up, is there?"

"I want to help, my darling," Matthew replied. "I don't want you to be the only one up dealing with all these tiny babies!"

"It's perfectly all right, dearest sugar. I can cope."

"We don't need all that sleep," he said. "There are plenty of people who can get by with just an hour or two a night. Winston Churchill, for instance. I think he only had a couple of hours' sleep a night. Apparently he lay in bed, smoking cigars, and dictating letters at two or three in the morning. He also used to dictate in the bath. The secretaries would sit outside and take shorthand."

Elspeth grunted. Tobermory was now dropping off to sleep, but Rognvald seemed particularly wide awake. And Fergus was rather quiet, she thought: Was he all right? Matthew checked, but in so doing woke him, and had to pick him up in an attempt to calm him down.

"There's something annoying him," said Matthew. "I wonder what it is."

Elspeth paid little attention to this. She was now feeding Rognvald and was concentrating on that task. So she did not hear Matthew say, "It's the bracelets. I think we should take them off."

The babies had been discharged from hospital wearing small plastic bracelets on which their names were written in ink. These had been kept on by Elspeth as she realised that it was the only means, at this stage, of identifying which baby was which. Matthew may have claimed to detect different personalities, but she had made no such unrealistic claim, and for the time being was relying on the bracelet for identification.

Matthew now laid Fergus down while he went to find a pair of scissors. A quick snipping relieved Fergus of his bracelet, which was tossed into the bin, alongside assorted baby wipes. A similar operation was then performed on Tobermory, gently and discreetly, but not sufficiently so to prevent his waking up and joining Fergus in full-lunged crying.

Elspeth looked up. "What's going on?" she asked.

"Tobermory's just woken up," said Matthew. "Here, give me Rognvald while you try to calm him down."

"No, give me Fergus first," said Elspeth wearily. "You take Rognvald and put him in Fergus's crib. Then pick up Tobermory and shougle him about for a while. He usually stops crying if you do that."

Matthew took Rognvald from Elspeth. Reaching for the scissors he snipped off his bracelet and threw it in the bin. Laying Rognvald down in the crib next to Tobermory, he went into the bathroom to replace the scissors on the shelf where they were kept; Matthew did not like to leave things lying about, and household objects were always where they were meant to be. But not necessarily babies . . .

Coming back, he saw that Elspeth had lifted a baby up from the crib where Rognvald and Tobermory had been lying. But which one?

"Is that . . ." He broke off.

"Is that what?" asked Elspeth, now sounding rather testy.

"Is that . . . Tobermory?"

"No, it's Fergus," she said. "He was the one who was crying, wasn't he?"

Matthew stood quite still. "No, it was Tobermory. I put Rognvald down next to Tobermory . . . Which side was he on? Left or right?"

"Oh, for heaven's sake, Matthew, I don't know! The place is full of crying babies – I can't remember who was where. Just look at the bracelets . . ."

She became silent. Then, in a voice that seemed unnaturally quiet, she asked, "What's happened to the bracelets, Matthew?"

"I can easily fix them," said Matthew hurriedly, scrabbling in the bin. "Here we are. Tobermory. And here's Rognvald . . ."

Elspeth was looking at him wide-eyed. "Matthew," she hissed. "You've mixed them up. You've mixed the boys up! Now we don't know which is which!"

Matthew sat down, his head sunk in his hands. He was very tired. Did it matter whether Rognvald was really Tobermory, or even Fergus – or the other way round? He thought it might – it just might; but he was far too tired, far too tired . . .

22. *Sheer Exhaustion*

Matthew walked out into the garden. Summer, although not yet high, nor blazing – Scottish summers having ceased to blaze years before – was nonetheless making itself felt in a hint of warmth in the breeze coming up from Stockbridge. This breeze lapped at the Georgian cliffs of Moray Place, rolled half-heartedly across Charlotte Square, and then moved lazily up Lothian Road, disturbing as it did the carelessly abandoned litter of the previous night's revellers: discarded tickets, exhortatory fliers from dubious bars, scraps of this and that from the pockets and purses of the lank boys and scantily clad girls who flooded in and out of the city's night spots with all the regularity of a tide.

Matthew looked at his watch, and sighed. It was six o'clock, but he would have preferred it to be three, or even four – hours at which it was always possible to go back to bed and have at least some sleep before the day began. He was afraid that now he would never get to sleep; he had never been able to linger in bed in the morning, the legacy of a regime that his father had imposed on him as a small boy – a regime that began with a shower first thing in the morning followed by a series of vigorous exercises. "*Mens sana in corpore sano,*" his father intoned. "Never forget that, Matthew!"

The things that our parents tell us never to forget are often instinctively mocked and refuted, scorned as old-fashioned advice. But the uncomfortable truth is that we do not forget them – they lodge in the mind – until years later they emerge in our consciousness, and we find ourselves repeating those very aphorisms our parents expounded. And the same is true of habits. The things we are taught as children, if taught well, remain taught. "Give me the child until he is seven and I will give you the man" was not intended to sound sinister when first uttered, but rings perfectly chilling in modern ears: chilling, but probably true, as long as it is realised that the early influence may have exactly the opposite effect of what is intended. Matthew's father had sought to raise a boy who, if everything worked out well, would follow a conventional *cursus honorum* and become a keen rugby player, perhaps even – oh, wildest dream – appearing at Murrayfield in some heroic match against mud-bespattered squads of New Zealanders or Welshmen. He raised instead an art dealer, with a penchant for distressed oatmeal sweaters and crushed straw-berry cords. But in so far as he wanted to produce a son who would not, like most teenagers, spend half the morning in bed if given a chance, he had succeeded: Matthew could not lie in long without feeling guilty. And not only that; the shower he took in the morning, if not exactly cold, was nonetheless deliberately never more than tepid.

So now, after that sleepless night of attending to the triplets, Matthew found that he had no alternative but to begin the day. He sighed again, knowing what would happen:

by noon he would be exhausted, befuddled and aching from sleep deprivation, good for nothing but an unreceptive grunt or a weary shrug. He might be able to sleep then, but what if Elspeth were tired as well? What if both of them dropped from exhaustion – at precisely the time that the triplets needed attention? Would they lie there in their cribs, crying, hungry, in need of a change, while their parents slept? Not only would that be traumatic for them – it could be downright dangerous. What if a bee came in the window and stung one of the boys on his nose, and it swelled up and made it difficult for him to breathe, and . . .

As a new father, such dangers seemed very real to Matthew. The boys were so tiny, such perfect little miracles of nature, and yet they were at the same time completely helpless: infinitely more so, Matthew reminded himself, than their equivalents in the young of other species. Lambs may gambol and skip within hours, it seemed, of arrival; lion cubs walk, unsteadily, perhaps, but on all four feet, on their first day; a newborn whale calf is born with the ability to swim alongside its mother immediately; we, by contrast, can barely move for months, cannot fend for ourselves for years. That was why parents had to be awake, Matthew told himself.

He walked towards the end of the garden. The previous owners of the flat had been keen gardeners; weeds, though, had now begun to appear – another thing to worry about, he thought. He made a mental resolution to tidy some of the beds up that weekend; the boys could be brought out if it was sunny – they needed their vitamin D, and a little bit of sun would do them good. And what about vitamin C? Would they be getting enough of that? When could you start to give them orange juice? Or Coca-Cola? He smiled. There would be no Coca-Cola for his boys; not until they were . . . No, never. They would not get hooked on sugar, or carbon dioxide bubbles, unlike those unfortunate American children, who became so puffed up with all that sugar and palm oil, and yet who had . . . such regular teeth. Would his boys go to an orthodontist, he wondered. How old should they be for that?

And what about Watson's? What age did they have to be before they could start at Watson's? Four? But did you have to telephone when they were two, perhaps, and ask for their name to be put on a list? Or did the school itself scour the birth notices in *The Scotsman* and put them down automatically when they read that Watsonian babies had been born? Matthew thought that this might happen in Edinburgh, but was not sure.

He reached the end of his garden. Beyond a hedge composed of California lilac and mahonia, Lord Moray's Pleasure Gardens began, descending precipitously down the hill to the Water of Leith. Matthew found himself peering through this hedge.

He saw something.

23. *Help Needed*

When Matthew went back into the flat, he found Elspeth sitting on the drawing room sofa, cradling one of the boys in her arms, her eyes closed. Taking her to be asleep, he became immediately concerned for the safety of the baby; it would be so easy to drop one of the triplets if one nodded off, and if he rolled off the edge of the sofa he would fall almost his entire height to the floor below – the equivalent, Matthew calculated, of an adult's falling five or six feet. Babies, of course, landed more lightly, but even so . . .

Elspeth opened her eyes. "I wasn't asleep," she said.

Matthew nodded. "Good. You wouldn't want him to fall . . ."

"I told you: I wasn't asleep. He was in no danger of falling."

Matthew sat down. "I didn't sleep at all last night," he said. "Not one wink."

"Nor did I."

Matthew closed his eyes. He felt slightly dizzy, and he wondered whether sleep would now overtake him, there and then, on the sofa. But the thought of sleep merely served to wake him up and he opened his eyes again to see the baby – whichever one it was, staring at him from his mother's arms, as if trying to focus. It would be so easy, he thought, just to have one; you would hardly notice a single child, really, especially with the two of them available to share the work.

"Elspeth," he said, "is this how it's going to be?"

"How what's going to be?"

"Parenthood. Having triplets."

She looked away. "They warned us. Remember that talk we went to where that woman who had had triplets came and spoke. Remember how you said she looked fifty when she was only twenty-seven?"

Matthew did remember. "Poor woman. She looked completely shattered."

They were both silent for a moment as they remembered the talk. Had they taken her warning seriously enough? Matthew thought they had not; at that point it had all seemed so theoretical, so removed from the state of pleasant anticipation in which Elspeth's pregnancy had passed. Now everything seemed so different.

He reached out to touch Elspeth's arm. "I don't want you to start looking fifty," he said quietly. "Or not until you really are fifty."

Elspeth smiled at him. "Fifty. Can you imagine what it's like to be fifty?"

"I suspect that you feel exactly the same as you felt when you were . . . well, whatever age."

She thought about this. "My father told me that he always felt eighteen. Even when he was forty and beyond."

"I've heard that," said Matthew. "I've heard that there are lots and lots of eighteen-year-olds around – some of them really quite old now." He paused. "But I don't think we should be talking about that; I think we should be talking about how we're going to survive."

She nodded. "Yes. If every night is going to be like last night . . ."

Matthew shook his head. It could not be, he said; nobody could cope with prolonged sleep-deprivation. "You die if you get really sleep-deprived. You just die."

"So what do we do?"

"We get help. We get a . . ."

"Nanny?"

He swallowed. He reflected on the implications of this; to live in the New Town and to have a nanny as well! What, he wondered, would be the next step on from that?

"We can't have a nanny," he said. "Or rather, we can't have somebody who's called a nanny. It's just too . . ." He trailed off. He was not sure what the word for it was. "Too . . . Edinburgh . . ."

Elspeth said, "But should we be worried about what people think of us?"

Matthew conceded reluctantly. "No, maybe not." He wondered whether it would be better to have an au pair. "An au pair is not quite as grand as a nanny," he said. "Less pretentious."

"Do au pairs still exist?" asked Elspeth. "They used to, I know, but nowadays?"

Matthew was not sure; the arrival of the triplets had taken him into distinctly unfamiliar waters, had introduced him to all sorts of equipment that he had never handled before – sterilisers, wipes, carry-cots, and so on – au pairs were just another possible constituent of that world.

"I think we should find out," he said. "I noticed that there was a firm that called itself Domestic Solutions – I walked past it the other day. I think that's what they do."

Elspeth, although tired, smiled weakly. "Solutions? Have you noticed how everybody calls themselves solutions? There are kitchen solutions, office solutions, travel solutions, and so on. Lots of solutions."

She was right, thought Matthew. Perhaps his gallery could be called Art Solutions or even Wall Solutions. One did not associate solutions with the art world, but he saw no reason why one should not. Perhaps when they had decided to paint the Sistine Chapel roof they had called up Ceiling Solutions, or Renaissance Solutions. He allowed his thoughts to drift for a moment. We've got this ceiling, you see, and we were wondering . . . Could you give us a quote?

"Matthew?"

He gave a start. "I was thinking."

"Thinking about what?"

"The Sistine Chapel."

He knew that this sounded strange, but he was too tired – just too tried to bother about being coherent. And another thought had come into his mind. He had seen something in the gardens, and he wanted to mention it to Elspeth.

"I saw something odd," he mumbled. He was feeling drowsy now, and his words were beginning to slur. "Something odd in the gardens down below. Through the hedge."

Elspeth looked down at Rognvald – or was it Tobermory? "Oh yes?"

Matthew leaned back into the soft embrace of the sofa. When had he last slept? Thirty hours ago?

"I think I saw some people in the gardens without their . . ." His voice became faint. "Not wearing any . . ."

Elspeth herself was struggling to stay awake. What was Matthew going on about? People not wearing anything in the gardens? Did that make sense? Of course: the Moray Place nudists that people had spoken about. How very odd! How remarkable that Matthew should have . . .

She struggled back into wakefulness.

"Matthew," she said, reaching out to shake him. "Phone Domestic Solutions now. Now."

He looked at his watch. "Too early."

"Leave a message. Say it's an emergency. Ask them to send a solution. Now, Matthew, now."

24. *Stuart and Irene Discuss Freemasonry*

For a small boy, Bertie's life was remarkably full. Much of his time, of course, was taken up by commitments of his mother's making: saxophone lessons, yoga, Italian *conversazione,* and psychotherapy were all imposed by Irene, but there was still room in this crowded schedule for those things that Bertie himself wanted to do. Foremost of these was the cub scouts, an activity that his father had managed to arrange for him in the face of a scathing maternal response.

"You might as well sign him up for the masons," said Irene.

"Oh come now," said Stuart. "The cub scouts are hardly in the same league. And, anyway, I'm not sure that I see anything wrong in being a mason, if that's what one wants to be. It strikes me as being fairly harmless these days."

Irene glared at him. "Harmless? Am I hearing you correctly, Stuart? Is it harmless to belong to an exclusively male organisation? And one that encourages people to dress up in aprons?"

Stuart winced; he had never been able to stand up to his wife when she was at full volume. "The aprons are historical, I think. And I thought that you would have approved of men in aprons. Very new man."

Irene's eyes flashed. "Not very funny, Stuart. And I don't think one should joke about the masons."

Stuart looked at the floor. "All that I was saying was that I saw no reason to compare the cub scouts to the masons. And I was wondering – just wondering – whether there was any proof that the masons got up to . . . anything untoward. They might have in the past, but these days, as far as I can work out, it's a perfectly above-board fraternal organisation."

She stared at him. "A secret society, you mean."

Stuart continued to look at the floor. "I don't think they are, actually. You make it sound very sinister. They have private rituals, but they're not a secret society in the sense in which the Mafia is a secret society."

Irene was silent. When she eventually spoke, her voice was quiet. "You seem to know a lot about the Freemasons, Stuart."

His reply came quickly. "Not really. I read something about them the other day. Did you see it? That piece in the paper. They mentioned Rosslyn Chapel."

Irene shook her head. "That's another thing," she said. "All this fascination with Rosslyn Chapel. Utter nonsense."

Stuart shifted his feet. "I rather like Rosslyn Chapel. Those pillars are remarkable examples of the masons' skill."

"Masons?" said Irene sharply. "Oh yes? And you'll be suggesting that there are hidden messages next. Numbers in the stonework. A code perhaps . . . All that da Vinci nonsense."

Stuart laughed. "Of course not. But it is a lovely place, you know. We could take Bertie out there some weekend. It's right on our doorstep and I think he'd love to see it."

"Certainly not," said Irene. "We don't want to fill Bertie's head with reactionary mysticism. And getting back to the cub scouts, I still have my misgivings, you know."

"He loves it," said Stuart, becoming slightly firmer now. "He looks forward to Friday evenings all week. It's his big thing."

The uneasy truce on the question of the cub scouts meant that it was Stuart, rather than Irene, who took Bertie to the Episcopal church hall at Holy Corner each Friday evening and collected him at the end of the meeting. That week, as they travelled up from Dundas Street on the 23 bus, he sat with Bertie on the upper deck while his son chatted excitedly about what lay ahead.

"Mrs. Gold – she's Akela, you know – has promised that we can play British Bulldog," he said. "Did you ever play that, Daddy?"

Stuart smiled. "Of course I did, Bertie. I loved it."

Bertie began to discuss the rules with his father. "One boy stands in the middle and the others have to rush past him. He's the bulldog."

"That's right, Bertie," said Stuart.

"And then the boy in the middle – the bulldog – tries to grab hold of somebody and has to shout out British Bulldog, one, two, three! If he holds on to him for long enough to say this then the other boy becomes a bulldog too. Do you remember that bit, Daddy?"

"I certainly do, Bertie. It's pretty exciting, isn't it?"

Stuart might have answered his own question; it was, indeed, pretty exciting. But he had been reminded of something he had read recently about a campaign against the game. Yes, that was it. Schools had banned the game because of the risk of injury. And now they were being encouraged to allow it again because children were becoming more and more obese through lack of exercise. Banning British Bulldog! How ridiculous, thought Stuart. There were people who wanted to ban everything, or change it out of all recognition. British Bulldog was a red rag to such people, of course, and an outright ban was what they wanted; unless, of course, they could neuter the game in other ways. Calling it British, for example, was provocative and chauvinistic: European poodle would be far better in their eyes. The poodle could stand in the middle and the other players would try to run past – or walk, perhaps, which would be safer – until they were apprehended by the poodle, who

would simply touch them and invite them to become a
poodle too.

"Why are you smiling, Daddy?" asked Bertie.

"Just thinking, Bertie."

They arrived at their bus stop near Hughes Fish Shop
and alighted. Bertie noticed that his father was carrying a
small case that had, when they left the flat, been concealed
in a large plastic bag.

"What's in your case, Daddy?" he asked.

Stuart looked at his son. "Can you keep a secret, Bertie?"
he asked.

Bertie nodded solemnly. "I promise I won't tell anybody,
Daddy. Cross my heart and hope to die. Cub scout's honour."

Stuart lowered his voice. "While you're at cub scouts,
Bertie, I've been going to a . . . special club nearby. They're
making me a member. But you mustn't tell anybody . . .
even Mummy. Especially Mummy, in fact."

"I promise," said Bertie. He looked at the small leather
case. "Has that got the stuff you need for your club in it?"

Stuart nodded. "Yes, Bertie, it has."

"That's really exciting," said Bertie.

"Yes," said Stuart. "It is."

25. The People Out There

It had been agreed that on that particular evening, Bertie
would not be picked up as usual by his father, but would
go on for a sleepover at the house of one of his fellow cub
scouts, Ranald Braveheart Macpherson. The invitation to
do this had been issued some weeks previously by Ranald's
mother when she and Stuart were waiting to collect the

children at the end of the Friday meeting. Stuart, who had struck up several conversations over the months with Ida Macpherson, and who had also met Ranald's father, Ross, had readily accepted. He had long felt that Bertie needed more friends, and it seemed to him that Ranald Brave-heart Macpherson was rather more promising than Tofu, whom Bertie appeared to tolerate, rather than actually like, and Olive, whom Bertie – quite understandably in Stuart's view – could not stand.

"You mustn't let people push you around, Bertie," he had said to his son. "The world is full of people who want to push other people around. You have to stand up to them, you know."

Bertie listened gravely. "Especially girls," he said. "Why do they like to push boys around, Daddy?"

Stuart suppressed a smile. "Not all girls are like that, Bertie. You must remember that there are some very nice girls . . . out there." He hesitated over these last words: the expression out there was used far too much, he thought. People at work – in the Statistics and Public Awareness Department of the Scottish Government – were always talking about what was being thought out there. But where, Stuart wondered, was out there? Were the people who were out there the same as the electorate, or the community perhaps, or were they somehow a little bit further out, just as some of the fielders on a cricket pitch are further out than those who lurk close to the batsman, ready, like hovering vultures, to catch him out should he send the ball in their direction?

He had explored this line of thought further. When peo-ple in Edinburgh referred to what was being thought or done out there, were they referring to people who lived somewhere like Bathgate, or Linlithgow, perhaps, or did they really

mean Glasgow? No, thought Stuart; when Edinburgh people referred to people in Glasgow, they would surely say
people over there, not out there; just as Glaswegians – or
Weegies, as they were affectionately known – referred to
Edinburghers – or the Edinbourgeoisie as they were affectionately known – as people back there. And there was a
further complication: there was a slightly threatening aspect
to being out there. People out there were often dangerous,
unpredictable, or, frankly, ill-informed, sometimes taking it
into their minds to ignore official advice – even when
tendered by statisticians – to eat the wrong food, and, in a
remarkable show of perversity, to vote for the wrong political parties. There was no limit, in fact, to the general
awkwardness of people out there.

"No, Bertie," Stuart continued. "You mustn't get it into
your head that all girls like pushing boys about. There are
many who do not."

"Name one," said Bertie.

He said this not in any confrontational sense; he was
simply trying to find an example. In his own life, of course,
it seemed to him, there were many who illustrated his general
proposition rather well. To begin with, there was his mother,
who was in charge of music lessons, yoga, Italian *conversazione,* and psychotherapy, in all of which fields of
endeavour Bertie felt that he was, on balance, being pushed
around. And his mother, as far as he could see, pushed his
father around with equal, if not greater, determination. He
was not even allowed to choose his own purchases at
Valvona & Crolla, being given a list by Irene and made to
stick to it. And that list, Bertie could not help but observe,
very rarely contained any of the things that his father
expressed an interest in buying and eating.

Following hard on the heel of Irene came Olive. His

classmate and now – to Bertie's abiding despair – his fellow cub scout seemed to devote a great deal of her emotional and intellectual energy to finding ways in which to cajole and threaten the boy whom she had frequently announced she intended to marry in due course.

"Actually, Bertie's really my fiancé," he had heard her say to a group of other girls in the school playground. "I'd prefer you to call him that rather than call him my boyfriend. He is my boyfriend, of course, but ever since he asked me to marry him he has been my fiancé as well. It'll be announced in *The Scotsman* quite soon: I'm saving up the money for the advertisement. They aren't cheap, you know."

Bertie had listened to this with a growing sense of horror. He had told Olive that he had no intention of marrying her, but she had ignored his protests. "You can't change your mind just like that, Bertie Pollock," she said, wagging a finger in his face. "God will punish you really hard if you do that sort of thing. You'll see. You'll find yourself getting the same as Tofu, who's going to be dealt with really firmly when his time comes. God's going to pull Tofu's fingernails out one by one; that's what's going to happen to him. So you just be careful, Bertie. You remember that."

"God doesn't do that sort of thing," protested Bertie.

"That's what you think, Bertie," said Olive knowingly.

"Yes," said Olive's friend, Pansy. "Olive's right, Bertie. So you just watch your step!"

Bertie felt a certain despair that the level of theological and other debate in the playground was so low. He wished that Olive and Pansy would stop telling him what to think, and would occasionally listen to what he had to say. He wished that Tofu would stop spitting at Olive and threatening to cut off her pigtails. He wished that the world was different – not a whole lot different, but a little bit different;

that there was a bit more sharing and a few less tears. If he had a wish, he would ask for that, he thought. And more panforte di Siena, of course, if supplementary requests were to be allowed.

26. *Ranald Braveheart Macpherson's Revelation*

It proved to be a very successful cub scout meeting. The game of British Bulldog was every bit as thrilling as Bertie had anticipated, with relatively few injuries, and a wonderful denouement. This occurred when Tofu, finding himself to be the last to brave the bulldogs, fought his way through a throng of opponents with much the same tenacity as Horatius had shown defending the Pons Sublicius against the Etruscan hordes.

"That was very courageous, Tofu," said Rosemary Gold, the Akela. "An example to all of us, I think. Don't give up, boys and girls, just because there may be more of the others than there are of you. Stand up for what is right."

The strenuous exercise of British Bulldog had rather tired the pack, and so the final part of the meeting was spent practising knots.

"You never know when you're going to need a knot," said Akela. "Baden-Powell was always tying knots. He was prepared, you see."

Bertie found himself sitting next to Ranald Braveheart Macpherson, who was struggling to master a reef knot. "You're coming to my house after this," said Ranald. "It's all fixed up. You have to come."

Bertie assured Ranald that he was perfectly happy with these arrangements. "You don't have to force me," he said.

"Good," said Ranald. "You'll really like my place. My dad's got surround sound. Did you know that, Bertie?"

Bertie shook his head. "I bet it's good."

"It is," said Ranald. "And we've got a small billiard table. It's only got three legs now, but it's still good fun."

Bertie expressed an interest in billiards. "My dad said that he used to play when he was at university. But then he met my mummy."

Ranald nodded. "My dad stopped having fun round about that time too."

They went outside, where Ida Macpherson was waiting for them.

"Ranald is very pleased that you're coming to the house, Bertie," she said. "You've been talking about it all day, haven't you, Ranald?"

Ranald looked slightly embarrassed. "That, and other things," he muttered.

They walked back to Ranald's house, which was in a quiet street immediately behind the Church Hill Theatre. Bertie was impressed with the garden, which had several large trees from one of which a rope descended invitingly.

"I swing on that, Bertie," said Ranald. "Just like Tarzan. Would you like to see?"

While his mother went into the house to prepare their

supper, Ranald showed Bertie his expertise on the swinging rope. It was an impressive performance, even if, as Bertie noted afresh, Ranald's legs were extremely spindly. Tarzan, he thought, was somewhat more muscular, but this did not detract from the expertise of the performance.

"You're really good, Ranald," said Bertie.

"Yes," said Ranald. "I am. And when Tarzan swings on a vine, he goes like this."

He uttered a piercing shriek – a sort of strangulated yodel – and then let go of the rope, landing, standing up, at Bertie's side.

It was now Bertie's turn, and he spent several very exciting minutes swinging to and fro while Ranald tugged on his ankles. That done, they went into the house.

"My dad's quite rich," said Ranald, as they went into the entrance hall. "He keeps most of his money in a safe. Would you like to see it?"

He led Bertie to a small study off the hall. On one wall there were bookshelves, and against another stood a squat grey safe.

"I don't know the combination," said Ranald. "But I could ask my dad to open it if you'd like to see our money."

"Where did he find all the money?" asked Bertie.

Ranald shrugged. "He has a business," he said. "He puts advertisements in the papers and then people send him their savings. Then he puts it in the safe. He's allowed to keep some himself, but he has to give most of it back to them when they ask him."

Bertie listened to this explanation. "It must be nice to have a lot of money," he said. "You could buy anything you wanted. Any time."

Ranald thought about this. "We've got just about everything we need," he said. "But we may think of something else some time. You never know."

They left the study and went upstairs to inspect Ranald's room. There Bertie was shown Ranald's collection of model aeroplanes and the shells that he had found on the beach at Gullane.

"My granddad lives at Gullane," he said. "He calls it Gillan rather than Gullane. He says that's the way it should be pronounced and that anybody who pronounces it differently needs their head examined."

Bertie nodded. "I'm sure he knows."

Ranald agreed. "He's really clever, my granddad. When he dies the University of Edinburgh is going to take his brain and put it in the freezer and charge admission to look at it."

"A good idea," said Bertie.

They were now summoned by Ranald's father, Ross, a tall man wearing a cardigan and a pair of mustard-coloured corduroy trousers.

"A very nice tea has been prepared for you boys," he said. "Do you like chocolate cake, Bertie?" Bertie said that he did.

"You're allowed to have as much as you like, Bertie," said Ranald. "That's true, isn't it, Dad?"

Ross Macpherson winked at his son. "I don't see why not. After all, the purpose of chocolate cake is to be eaten by appreciative boys. That is its destiny, I believe."

Bertie marvelled at this. He was rarely allowed to eat chocolate cake, and certainly never permitted to eat as much as he wanted of anything, let alone something as delicious as chocolate cake.

"Right, boys," said Ross Macpherson." *À table!* as our Gallic cousins might say."

"That means let's go to the table in French," explained Ranald. "My dad's always saying that."

"Parents repeat themselves a lot," said Bertie.

They made their way downstairs. As they did so, Ranald turned to Bertie and said, "Do you know something, Bertie? I'm adopted. These people are not my real mum and dad. Did you know that?"

Bertie shook his head. The idea intrigued him, though: that somebody should arrive, a *deus ex machina*, and take one into a warm and friendly house, one distinguished for its chocolate cake, and give one a more congenial home. Could it happen, he wondered, to those who had a placement at present, but who might wish, secretly of course, for something better?

27. Dinner with Dr. Macgregor

While Bertie was dining in the house of Ranald Braveheart Macpherson – enjoying a meal of macaroni cheese followed by copious quantities of chocolate cake – Pat was making her way to dinner with her psychiatrist father at his house in the Grange. She often did this on a Sunday, a day noted for its melancholic potential, but on this occasion was going on a Friday. Dr. Macgregor, who normally went nowhere, had announced that on that particular Sunday he hoped to attend a concert in the Queen's Hall and would Pat mind coming for dinner on Friday instead? She would not mind at all, she assured him; in fact, it was quite convenient, as on Sunday there was a showing at Film House of *Casablanca* and she had been invited to go with friends.

"*Casablanca*," mused Dr. Macgregor, as they sat down together for a predinner glass of wine. "I remember the first time I saw that film. I was a student and it was on at the Cameo. It made such an impression on me. Rather like the first time I saw an opera. That was Cav and Pag in Glasgow. And the first time I had a glass of champagne – I was fourteen. At a wedding in Kelso." He smiled. "These are big milestones in one's life. First *Casablanca*, first opera, first taste of champagne. Middle-class milestones, of course, but you know something, my dear? We are middle class. We can't help it."

She looked at her father, returning his smile. You are so accustomed, she thought, to seeing parents as part of your own world, that you forget the world they had before you. BM should be the acronym for that, she decided: Before Me. Things happened BM, of course, but did not really happen.

"And what about you?" he said. "Have you seen it before?"

"Yes, of course. Everybody's seen *Casablanca*. It was at the Dominion in my case. I saw it when I was about fifteen, I think."

He looked thoughtful. "Why do we like that film so much?"

"Because it's really a play," said Pat. "There's that

formality about the dialogue. People address one another as if they're on the stage. They say important things, memorable things. It's Shakespearean."

He nodded. "Whereas they don't do that any more? They say superficial things?"

"Mostly."

Dr. Macgregor reflected on this. "We're losing the ability to converse in sentences, I think. We use phrases, a few words here and there. We don't think about the shape of a conversation."

"Maybe."

He warmed to the topic. "There's a lovely line in a poem by Michael Longley, you know. He talks about Emily Dickinson, the poet. He writes about her waking early each morning in her house in Amherst, Massachusetts . . ."

While he struggled to remember the line, Pat thought: but everybody awakes in their house; the observation that one does so is hardly earth-shattering. Folksingers, for instance, were always waking up one morning: Woke up one morning, feeling kind of blue . . . and so on.

He found what he was looking for. "Yes. He thinks of her waking up early in the morning and then – and this is the bit I love – dressing with care for the act of poetry. What do you think of that? Dressing with care for the act of poetry."

"Is poetry an act?"

"Yes, I think it is. The poet sits at his table, puts pen to paper."

She took a sip of her wine. "Or switches on his computer?"

"I don't think so. I don't think one could write poetry on a computer, do you?"

She was not sure. But he was probably right, she thought.

"Computers change the way we deal with words," Dr.

Macgregor continued. "They somehow unlock language in the mind. But they do so in a very particular way – they induce . . . well, I suppose we should call it logorrhoea, a sort of verbal diarrhoea. The words come tumbling out and people feel they can go on and on. And they do. Poetry has to be much more disciplined, much more concise."

Pat thought about this. Computers had always been around, it seemed to her, and she wondered how·people could possibly write with a pen any more. BM there were pens, of course, but now . . .

"There's another thing I've been thinking about," said Dr. Macgregor. "Have you noticed how rude people are in their exchanges on the Web? Have you seen that?"

"In the comments they make?"

"Yes. And generally in the things they write online. They insult people with gay abandon. They resort to personal abuse when discussing things in which personal abuse should have no place. It's astonishing."

It was true, she decided; so true that she had never thought about it.

"It's the same with driving," Dr. Macgregor continued. "When people are behind the wheel of a car their personality changes. They lose their temper with other drivers just like that – in an instant. They scowl at them, they shout, they insult them – all for some tiny mistake – turning left when indicating right, or something like that – or failing to let them overtake when they want. All that sort of thing." He paused. "If you were walking along the pavement and somebody bumped into you by mistake, would you yell at him? Would you shake your fist and swear? Or would you accept his apology and carry on?"

"I'd accept the apology."

"Of course you would, because that's the ordinary human

thing to do. The trouble with technology is that it's dehumanised us – it's removed the restraints of ordinary human interactions. So we lose the notion that the person with whom we're dealing is a person like us, with failings and feelings. It's exactly the same as in wartime. When people are engaged in conflict, they very easily lose sight of the humanity of the other. They become capable of doing things that they would never do in their ordinary lives."

"War crimes?" Pat asked.

"Yes, exactly. But war is an extreme example, of course. Politics provides perhaps a better illustration. Look at the dismissive way in which people treat one another in politics – slanging matches, abuse, refusal to accept that one's opponent might have a point, or at least be half-right. People adopt positions and the positions dictate their response to the other, dehumanizing everybody in the process."

"Oh well," said Pat. "Isn't it time for dinner?"

28. *Innocence Before Freud*

Dr. Macgregor had prepared an egg and potato pie for his daughter. Once they settled themselves at the table and the pie had been served out, he filled Pat's glass with wine.

"Chianti is perfect with egg and potato pie," he said. "Not many people know that. In fact, I don't."

Pat laughed. Her father's remarks frequently required close analysis. What did he mean by this? That Chianti did not go with egg and potato pie? Or was he simply being self-effacing? That was the problem with being the daughter of a psychiatrist: you never quite knew what was what – or was not.

She looked about the dining room. It was familiar enough, of course, but becoming less so. A painting had been moved from one wall to another; a vase on the sideboard had disappeared; the curtains, exposed to the sun in a south-facing room, were more faded than she remembered. The house had changed since she had gone off to university and there would come a time, she supposed, when it would seem quite alien. For the time being, though, it was still home.

Dr. Macgregor raised his glass in a toast. "To your happiness," he said.

It was what he always said, and Pat would have been concerned if he had said anything different, but for some reason that evening his words seemed rather more deliberate than usual.

"And to yours." She paused. "Because happiness is important, isn't it?"

He was slightly taken aback by this remark. "Of course it is," he said. "It's the most important thing there is. If you're happy, then everything else is irrelevant."

"And yet it does seem to elude rather a lot of people, don't you think? Those surveys you read about . . ."

Dr. Macgregor smiled. "Those surveys come up with some very surprising results. Most of us, it seems, are a bit unhappy about something."

"There'll always be something wrong with your life," suggested Pat. "It's unrealistic to think that everything can be perfect."

Dr. Macgregor agreed. "You know, darling, my work as a psychiatrist has taught me one thing. I know that people are immensely complicated – they just are – but in one respect they are quite simple. They have to get the major thing in their life right – if they do that, then they're happy.

But if they get that wrong . . ." He sighed. "Then they are condemned to Sisyphean unhappiness."

"What's the major thing?"

"It depends. For most people, though, it's love. We all need to give love and receive it in return. I suppose that's the main thing."

Pat frowned; she was remembering something. "I've just thought of something in the McEwan Hall. Do you remember it? Right up at the top there is an inscription: *Wisdom is the principal thing, therefore get wisdom.* We have exams in there and if you look up from your exam desk you see those words. There's a mural of ancient Greek philosophers talking to young men. Then those words."

He thought about this. "Yes, maybe wisdom is the principal thing. If you possess wisdom, then you're able to deal with the other important things in life. If you're wise, then you can't be hurt in love. If you're wise, you'll understand that you can't have everything you want materially. And so on."

They were both silent for a minute or two. Pat was thinking of her father and of the sadness that she knew he felt for his failed marriage; he deserved better, she felt, but she could never say that to him. She wanted to hug him, to tell him that she understood how he must feel, and had the silence continued, she might have done that. But now he spoke, and the moment passed.

"I had a friend at university," he said. "When I was about your age. He fell in love – really rather badly. She was at the physical education college – Dunfermline – and was Northern Irish. They can be such attractive people, you know, and she certainly was. He talked about her nonstop.

"The problem was that she had this boy back home,

somewhere in Fermanagh, I think it was. She had known him more or less all her life and there was an understanding between them. She was allowed to see other boys, but ultimately she was destined to marry him. My friend sensed this and felt it terribly.

"When he went to their home he met her sister. The girl whom he loved – the physical education one – had eyes only for this boy from Fermanagh and so my friend took up with her sister. Now I can see that you're surprised, but that happens more often than you imagine. People marry people who are close to the person they really want. They see it as a way of getting closer to the real object of their affection."

Pat looked incredulous. "Surely not."

Dr. Macgregor assured her that it was perfectly possible. "There have been some remarkable instances of this. Look at Siegfried Sassoon. By nature he found himself attracted to a series of younger men with whom he became infatuated, although he appeared to remain scrupulously chaste through these affairs. It was rather innocent, really – the love of the scholar poet for the hero athlete, in an age when we were not so worldly-wise, when such things could be seen as unsullied."

"Pre-Freud," said Pat.

"Before his ascendancy. Everything was more innocent before Freud. Innocent, but not really innocent, if you see what I mean. Anyway, Sassoon was in love with a young man who did not share his inclinations. So he became engaged to the young man's sister. Needless to say . . ."

"It didn't work out."

"No."

"How sad."

"Yes. How sad." He paused. "Don't forget, my dear,

how many and how varied are the permutations of unhappiness to which the human soul is susceptible."

"And the same can be said of happiness?"

He appeared to think about this, and Pat waited for his answer.

"No," he said. "Happiness is so much simpler. It's really just like the sun, and there's only one sort of sunlight, I would have thought."

29. *The Home Life of Ranald Braveheart Macpherson*

Half a mile away from Dr. Macgregor's house, where the gentle psychiatrist was having dinner with his student daughter, Bertie Pollock was sitting at the dining room table in the house of his friend, Ranald Braveheart Macpherson, licking the last crumbs of chocolate cake from his fingers.

"You enjoyed that, didn't you, Bertie?" asked Ida Macpherson.

"Very much, Mrs. Macpherson," said Bertie. "Thank you very much."

"Chocolate cake is so good for a growing boy," said Ross Macpherson. "You like it too, don't you, Ranald? It builds up the muscles."

Ranald nodded. "Tarzan ate it," he said. "That's why he was so strong."

Ross Macpherson winked at him. "Quite right, Ranald. Well done you!"

The plates were cleared away and Bertie and Ranald had a brief time to play together before it was time for bed.

"My dad always comes up to tell me a story, Bertie,"

said Ranald. "He's really good at that. True stories mostly. You'll like them, Bertie."

"He's really nice, your dad," said Bertie. "You're lucky that they chose you, aren't you?"

"Yes," said Ranald. "I was really small when they found me and took me to a children's home. Then my mum and dad came and picked me out and took me back here. I'm really pleased it was them."

Bertie asked Ranald where he had been found.

"It was on the banks of the Water of Leith," came the reply. "I was in a basket."

"They found you in a basket? In the water?"

Ranald's tone was matter-of-fact. "Yes. There were some bulrushes and my basket had drifted into them. A social worker came past. He must have been fishing, I think, and he picked my basket out of the river. That's how I came to be adopted."

"That's really amazing, Ranald," said Bertie. He paused. "Do you think that somebody who's a bit older – maybe seven – could get adopted?"

Ranald thought for a moment. "Yes, I don't see why not. It would have to be a bigger basket, of course. But as long as you didn't sink, it would be fine. Somebody would find you and take you to a children's home. Then you'd just have to wait a few days until some people came and said they wanted a boy. Then they'd take you. Are you talking about yourself, Bertie? Would you like to get adopted yourself? It's really good fun, you know."

Bertie hesitated. The story of Ranald's adoption had planted the idea in his mind that adoption might be the answer to his problems. He did not want to offend his parents, but he thought that they would probably get used to the situation quite quickly, especially if he was able to visit them from time to time.

"Yes," he said at last. "I was wondering whether I could be adopted by some nice people . . . just like your parents, Ranald."

Ranald frowned. "You can't come here, Bertie. There isn't any room for anybody else here. Sorry."

"I wasn't thinking of your mum and dad," Bertie reassured him. "I was thinking of somebody like them."

Ranald looked relieved. "Yes, I think that will work. Have you got a basket at home?"

"I don't think so," said Bertie.

Ranald stroked his chin. "How about eBay, Bertie? Have you heard of eBay? You could put yourself on it, you know."

Not having a computer, Bertie was unsure what eBay was, and listened attentively as Ranald explained it to him. "You can get anything on eBay, Bertie, I'm telling you. Trucks, model railways, even swords. Everything. If you've got something to sell, you put it on eBay and they have a sort of auction. You could choose two weeks maybe. That gives people time to decide how much they want to bid."

"Would they pay?" asked Bertie. "Did your mum and dad pay for you?"

Ranald nodded. "Yes. I think I was quite expensive, and that's how I got a dad who's got lots of money. He took some of the money out of the safe and used it to adopt me. He's still got lots left, though."

"I don't mind if they don't pay," said Bertie. "As long as they're nice."

"It would be jolly funny if your mummy was looking at eBay and adopted you without knowing that it was you!" said Ranald. He looked at Bertie. "It is your mummy, isn't it? She's the problem, isn't she?"

Bertie looked down at the floor. "Maybe," he said.

"Tofu says she's a cow," said Ranald. "Is that true, Bertie?"

Bertie kept his eyes fixed to the floor. "No," he said. "She isn't."

"Maybe she's almost a cow," suggested Ranald helpfully. "And do you know something, Bertie? We could put you on eBay right now. We've got a computer downstairs and it's always on. I know how to do it."

Bertie's heart gave a leap. "Do you think we could, Ranald?"

"Of course we can, Bertie. Let's go right now."

Ranald Braveheart Macpherson led Bertie downstairs. From the kitchen there came the sound of his parent's voices. "They always drink after dinner," said Ranald. "They drink loads of wine, Bertie. They won't trouble us."

They went into a room which seemed to be used as a workroom of some sort. In the corner was a computer, the screen glowing with a dancing screensaver made up of little bursts of light. Ranald sat himself at the keyboard and typed in a few words. Immediately the dancing lights disappeared and a page of text and graphics appeared. "That's eBay," said Ranald. "Now all I have to do is to type in my dad's password and we can put you on, Bertie. What would you like me to say?"

Bertie thought for a moment. It would be best, he decided, to be modest, as people could surely see through exaggerated claims. "Scottish boy available for adoption," he dictated. "Will behave well if adopted by nice people. Speaks Italian."

"You'd better say something about where you are," suggested Ranald. "And maybe a bit about where you'd like to live. That would be helpful."

"Edinburgh area," continued Bertie. "Would prefer Glasgow, especially Bearsden if at all possible, but not fussy."

"That's very wise," said Ranald, as he typed in the details. "They don't like fussy people trying to get themselves adopted."

"I won't be fussy," said Bertie.

"Good," said Ranald. "But I think I should also add nonsmoker. They put that sort of thing in these days."

"Good idea," said Bertie.

"And now," said Ranald Braveheart Macpherson, "I push the button! See – that's you, Bertie!"

30. Angus Lordie and Cyril Visit Moray Place

That Saturday morning Angus Lordie, accompanied by his dog, Cyril, went to visit Matthew and Elspeth in their lower ground floor flat in Moray Place. There were several reasons for this visit: Angus had not yet seen the new flat and was eager to see it, and another reason was that on a visit to Big Lou's he had picked up the feeling that not all was well.

"Any news of Matthew?" he had asked Big Lou as she steamed the milk for his coffee.

Big Lou had barely turned round. "Who?"

"Matthew," repeated Angus, raising his voice in case the hissing sound of the steam was preventing Big Lou from hearing.

"Oh him. No."

Big Lou's dismissive tone had warned him that something was not right.

"It must be hard for him," Angus persevered. "Having triplets can't be easy."

Big Lou made a snorting sound. "Aye, for women. Makes no difference for men."

Angus raised an eyebrow. "Even for men. I remember when Cyril's puppies arrived – there were six of them, dumped on my doorstep by that ridiculous woman – I could barely cope. And that's puppies. Babies are so much more difficult, I believe."

"Aye, for women," repeated Big Lou.

Angus pretended not to have heard. "He's a very hands-on father, I should imagine. A lot of fathers are hands-on these days."

Big Lou passed the cup of coffee across the counter. "Aye, the men are hands-on all right. That's what leads to bairns in the first place. Then they're pretty smartly hands-off when the bairns arrive."

Angus affected a laugh. "Steady on, Lou! That's a bit hard. Not all men . . ."

He was not allowed to finish. "Ninety-nine per cent of them," said Big Lou. "And you can tell that dug of yours to stop staring at me."

Angus looked down at Cyril, who was seated at his feet. It was true that Cyril was staring at Big Lou, but he was not staring in an aggressive way; it was more of an inquisitive, slightly surprised look. Cyril was very good at picking up human feelings – as many dogs are – and he could tell when there was tension in the air. That was what was happening now, Angus thought: Cyril could sense the hostility. And like children, who will blame themselves for what goes wrong in the adult world, dogs can think that it is something they have done that has led to ill-feeling.

Without bothering to sit down, Angus drained his coffee cup at the counter. "Well, I must dash, Lou. It's been very pleasant talking to you."

Big Lou said nothing.

Angus kept up the cheerful tone. "I thought I might just pop over to see how Matthew and Elspeth are doing. I'll give them your regards, shall I?"

"Her," muttered Big Lou.

Angus took a handkerchief out of his pocket and wiped a speck of cappuccino foam from his lip. "Well, there we are, Cyril. Time to hit the road."

Walking along Great King Street, Angus reflected on his unusual and rather uncomfortable encounter with Big Lou. As a bachelor – and I am still that, he thought, even if my bachelor days are numbered – he knew that women could have their moods, but he had never seen Big Lou in quite such a negative frame of mind. Had there been some disagreement between her and Matthew, and if so, what could it possibly be? Of course the two of them had never quite seen eye-to-eye on many subjects – Big Lou tended to the conservative view of things while Matthew was somewhat more liberal in his outlook – but they had always agreed to differ and the discussion between them had been good-natured. Perhaps there had been some particular disagreement – one that had gone beyond the bounds of banter; but it was still unusual, he thought, for Big Lou to nurse a grudge over something like that.

The situation was no clearer in his mind by the time he

reached Moray Place. Finding the right house, he pressed the bell, noting the elegant brass numerals screwed into the door. There was an expensive air to the houses here – something that went beyond the solidity and prosperity of the rest of the New Town.

Matthew greeted him warmly, bending down to pat Cyril, who licked his hand enthusiastically.

"Nice place this," said Angus as they made their way into the entrance hall. "These basement flats can be very comfortable, can't they?"

Matthew shook a finger. "Lower ground floor, please!"

Angus laughed. "Of course. Sorry."

From somewhere within the flat there came the sound of a crying baby. "Ah," said Angus. "That must be Tobermory . . . or Rognvald . . . or perhaps Fergus."

Angus expected his joke to be appreciated, but Matthew did not seem to find it amusing. "Oh, I wish I knew," he said. "You see, they had these bracelet things and I took them off and then . . ." He faltered, his voice breaking up.

Angus looked at him with alarm. "Are you all right, Matthew?"

Matthew shook his head. "Not really."

Angus laid a sympathetic hand on his shoulder. "Come on. Let's go and sit down. Then tell me what's going on."

They went into the kitchen, where Matthew gestured for Angus to sit on one of the high bar stools.

"I'm at the end of my tether," said Matthew. "We're finding it really hard to cope."

"I can imagine," said Angus. "You must be worked off your feet."

"We've got somebody coming," Matthew went on. "There's this outfit called Domestic Solutions and I've been in touch with them. We're getting an au pair – but she's got to come from Denmark and won't be here until next week. In the meantime the boys are staying awake and Elspeth and I are just really shattered . . . I mean so shattered that we don't really know what's going on. I'm not exaggerating . . ."

"Of course you're not," said Angus.

"And then there's been a row with Big Lou. I don't know how it started, but it was pretty bad, and I said . . . well, I said something rather unkind, but she'd driven me to it, I'm afraid – you know how she can say things that make you feel you have no choice but to respond in kind. Well, that's what happened." He paused. "And now I'm banned."

Angus shook his head in disbelief. "Banned? From Big Lou's? That's ridiculous."

"It's true."

"Then go and apologise. Simple."

31. *Forgiveness*

How do you forgive somebody who refuses to see you? Angus walked back along Heriot Row, thinking of Matthew's dilemma. Most Catch-22s, he decided, were not real Catch-22s, except, of course, for the one involved in the obtaining of an actor's union card. Angus had heard of this famous example from a friend who had a stage-struck son. This young man had graduated from drama school in Glasgow, hoping to work as an actor. For that he needed a union card, but in order to get the card he needed to have worked professionally in the theatre. And he could not do that without the card.

How did new actors begin? As the rear section of a

pantomime horse, perhaps, slipping onto the stage unseen? That was absurd. Sir Laurence Olivier and Sir Ian McKellen must have started somewhere in the theatre, but surely not in pantomime. They started as Hamlet, presumably.

Of course there was no such difficulty in Matthew's case. He may be banned from entering Big Lou's, but that did not mean that he was physically prevented from entering the premises. It would be different if he had been excluded from one of those bars on Lothian Road – those dives at the doors of which stood the tough-looking bouncers, body-builders to a man, with short haircuts and faces untroubled by metaphysical doubt. If they banned you from their bars they meant it, and it would be impossible to cross the threshold. But Big Lou's was hardly a Lothian Road bar, and all that Matthew had to do was to go in and make his apology. And that was what he had eventually persuaded Matthew to do – though not that day.

"I cannot leave Elspeth with all these babies," he had said. "Some other time soon. But please, Angus, will you speak to her first and make sure she doesn't bite my head off? You know what she's like."

Angus had agreed to do this and now turned off down Dundas Street to complete his mission of reconciliation. "Blessed are the peacemakers," he said to Cyril. "And that means us, I suppose."

Cyril looked up at his master and smiled, his single gold tooth flashing in the sunlight. Cyril had an extraordinary ability to convey agreement, and he always seemed to agree with what Angus said. The gold tooth, although highly unusual in a dog, was not an affectation; it had been placed in Cyril's mouth by one of Angus's fellow members of the Scottish Arts Club, a sociable dentist, who had been sufficiently proud of his achievement to send a photograph of it to the *British Dental Journal*. This generous gesture on his part had been rewarded with a letter threatening him with prosecution for illegally practising veterinary medicine.

"Such pomposity," he had complained to Angus. "These London types have absolutely no sense of humour. What do they expect people to do if their dog's got a sore tooth? You pull it out. I just filled in the gap with a bit of gold I had lying around. What a fuss about nothing!"

"The trouble with this country," Angus had replied, "is that we are utterly surrounded by busybodies trying to stop us doing things. Or telling us what to do." He had recently seen a large illuminated sign on the road between Edinburgh and Stirling urging motorists to drive carefully if visibility was bad. Of course people should do that, but did the State really need to tell them that? If you had a driving licence you would have learned this; and if you had a modicum of common sense you would remember it. But Big Brother, with his ubiquitous closed-circuit cameras – which now monitored, it seemed, every square inch of public space – and his condescending imprecations and warnings, was everywhere. And signs telling one to go slowly in the dark or in fog irritated Angus almost as much as the signs that warned people not to approach cliff edges. In his view, it was up to the individual whether or not to approach a cliff edge; it was not the Government's business.

Remembering this now, Angus put state paternalism out of his mind. Big Lou, he could see, was in, and she looked up sharply as he entered the café.

"You again," she said.

"Indeed," said Angus. "And what a warm welcome!"

Big Lou ignored this. "Coffee?"

Angus shook his head. "I come as a peacemaker. I come, therefore, in peace."

From behind her counter, Big Lou eyed him suspiciously.

"That's what they said to those poor North American Indians," she said. "And look what that led to."

Angus smiled. "It led to the United States," he said. "It led to a fairly comfortable life for their modern descendants. Pickup trucks and antibiotics."

Big Lou narrowed her eyes. "And the loss of their culture," she said.

"My people were Gaels," said Angus. "They knew all about that. But I don't know whether we should really go there, Lou. I've come to ask you to accept Matthew's apology."

Big Lou put down her cloth. "Couldn't he come himself?"

"He wanted to," said Angus. "And he will. It's just that he has his hands a bit tied with the triplets."

Big Lou looked down at the surface of her counter. It was always spotless, but she still polished it. "Why should I forgive him?" she asked.

Angus met her gaze. "Because it's your duty," he said.

"Why?"

He made an expansive gesture with his hands – one that implied the justification for forgiveness was just too large to be explained.

"We have to forgive people," he said, "because it's cruel not to do so. And you wouldn't want to be cruel, would you, Lou?"

She would not; he knew it.

"He said something very . . . very hurtful," said Lou.

"I know," said Angus. "People say things. But they don't always mean them. And even if they do, they can feel sorry. Matthew feels sorry."

"All right," said Lou. "I'll forgive him."

Angus, relieved, reached out across the counter to take Big Lou's hand. Nobody had done that before – and certainly not Angus – and she was taken aback. Angus was surprised too and held her hand only for a moment or two. Forgiveness, he remembered somebody remarking to him, is like a balm applied to a wound, and stops the pain in much the same way.

32. Matching Scots

Pat was late for morning coffee that day. A customer had come into the gallery and had spent an inordinate amount of time admiring – and eventually buying – a Bellany study of East Lothian fishing boats, seagulls, and what appeared to be a puffin. Or possibly buying: the red dot that had been put below the painting was only a half one, indicating serious interest but not actual commitment. It was the same as the dubious practice of houses being described as under offer: a half red dot on a house could be very quickly peeled off if somebody came along with a better offer.

Pat was pleased with her half-sale which, she suspected, would become firm later that day. She had already informed Matthew, who had congratulated her, and who had revealed that there were another four Bellanys of fishing boats in the storeroom.

"He's very productive," he said. "Which is remarkable, as there are so few fishing boats left. I've wondered whether Creative Scotland could buy a few and keep them afloat – not for fishing, of course, but for the sake of art."

Pat thought that this was a very helpful suggestion. "I gather that the civic authorities in Naples hang washing out of windows every morning for much the same reason. It's so important for artists."

Now, making her way across Dundas Street towards Big Lou's, Pat wondered what inspiration an artist might find in the attempts of twenty-first-century architects to impose their phallic triumphs on the cityscape. Had any artist ever painted a contemporary glass block, for instance, or any other product of the architectural brutalism that had laid its crude hands here and there upon the city? The question seemed ridiculous, and yet it raised a serious point. If a building did not lend itself to being painted, then surely that must be because it was inherently ugly, whatever its claims to utility. And if it was ugly, then what was it doing in this delicately beautiful city?

She was pondering this as she entered the café and heard Big Lou's friendly greeting. "I've had nobody in this morning," she said. "Unless one counts Angus and that dug of his. They've been in twice."

"Why?" asked Pat, settling herself on a stool in front of the counter.

Big Lou hesitated. "He came with an apology from Matthew."

Pat's smile showed her relief. "Well, I'm glad about that. And Matthew really should apologise."

Big Lou shrugged. "That's that then." She began to grind coffee for Pat's cappuccino.

Pat sniffed the air. "My absolutely favourite smell," she said. "Freshly ground coffee."

"Aye," said Lou. "Mine too." She paused, spooning the coffee into its receptacle. "I was wondering, Pat, whether you would be free this evening. I need to go to something and I wanted somebody to . . . well, to hold my hand. I'm a bit nervous . . ."

Pat was intrigued. "Of course. But what is it?"

Big Lou busied herself with the coffee machine. "It's a social evening," she said. "In fact, it's a date."

Pat frowned. "But if it's a date, then why do you want me tagging along?"

Big Lou turned to her. "I don't know the fellow, you see. It's something I arranged on the internet."

Pat grinned. "Internet dating! Lou, that's really . . . really exciting. I didn't know that you were into that sort of thing."

"Neither did I," said Lou. "But I decided to take the plunge. It's not that . . ."

Pat waited for Lou to finish. "Yes?"

"It's not that I'm unhappy by myself. I'm not desperate."

Pat reassured her. "Lou, nobody would ever think that. You're . . ." How could she put it? "You're your own person, Lou – we all know that. But it would be nice if you found some nice man – somebody who appreciated you."

Big Lou nodded. "Yes, it would be good. You see, I get

back from work in the evenings and sit in my flat down in Canonmills and sometimes it gets . . . well, I suppose I must say that it gets a wee bit lonely. I think back to the days when I was in Arbroath, or even in Aberdeen, and there were folk about." She paused. "It's funny how you can be in a city, where there are thousands of people, and yet be by yourself. I never felt lonely when I was on the farm, even if everybody was away. Sometimes they went up to Stonehaven, to my aunt's place, and left me by myself. But I never felt lonely, even if the nearest other person was three-quarters of a mile away."

"Cities can be very lonely," said Pat. "But tell me more about this man. What did it say about him?"

Pat's coffee was now ready, and Big Lou was busy steaming the milk. "It was a site called Matching Scots. Funny name for a dating service, but I suppose it says what it means. It matches people who . . . well, who match."

Pat encouraged her to continue. "And?"

"And there was a list of men with a few sentences about each of them – in their own words."

"I know the sort of thing," said Pat. "I read the *New York Review of Books* in the George Square Library and I always look at the personals towards the back. It's fascinating. Highly talented, multifaceted individual, into Freud, wishes to meet SJF with view to LTR. That sort of thing. It makes me wonder whether they're telling the truth."

Big Lou carefully poured the frothy milk into Pat's cup and passed it across the counter to her. "Yes. They don't seem very modest, do they? But, talking of abbreviations, they used them on Matching Scots too."

Pat looked interested. "Oh? And this man you're meeting – what abbreviation did he use?"

"SM," said Big Lou.

"Single male," said Pat. "I hope. Maybe, Scottish male. And what else?"

"GSH and EI," said Big Lou.

Pat frowned. "GSH I know about. Good sense of humour. But EI – do you know what that is, Lou?"

"No," said Big Lou. "That's why I wanted you to come with me. Just in case."

33. *The Meaning of EI*

It felt very strange for Pat to be meeting Big Lou on the corner of George Street and Hanover Street. As she waited, a few minutes before the appointed time that evening, Pat reflected on the fact that she had never seen Lou out of the context of her coffee bar; had never seen her, in fact, anywhere but behind her counter, where she seemed to be engaged in the endless task of wiping away non-existent dirt with her cloth, her cloot, as Lou called it. The use of Scots words was one of the things that Pat liked in the older woman; that and her directness. Big Lou came from a Scotland that had been diluted in Edinburgh, a Scotland of unfussy, hardworking people who had no time for artifice or pretension, as hard-wearing and weatherproof as the land that produced them. Such lives, though, were discreet – they often followed a path that was set for them rather than chosen; they did not look for salience, they did not seek any limelight; they did not crave the things of this world; they believed, by and large, in sharing, even if they disapproved of not pulling one's weight and complaining. Big Lou was like that; she was the woman who ran the coffee bar, and ran it with brisk efficiency; it seemed as if she had always been there and always would be. She was not, then, somebody Pat would have imagined herself waiting for on the corner of George Street, prior to going off to a bar together to meet a man identified only by the opaque acronyms of a dating site, a man endowed with a GSH, an SM, and, opaquely, an EI.

The town was busy. George Street, which had previously been a street of staid businesses – banks, insurance offices, gas appliance showrooms and the like – had been encroached upon by bars, the bankers' halls providing space for jostling crowds of twentysomethings. Some of these were Pat's fellow students, or those of them whose means enabled them to enjoy a sybaritic existence. She saw two of them now, turning the corner, heading for one of the more expensive bars – a boy in her year, accompanied by a long-limbed blonde who rarely came to lectures and who was rumoured to be the secretary of a sex-addiction support group. She turned away; momentarily concerned that they might see her waiting on the corner and would wonder what she was doing. She could imagine the comments in the George Square coffee room, "We saw her, you know, standing – yes, just standing – on the corner of George Street – heaven knows why – no idea at all. Rather sad, don't you think . . ." Those types were so condescending, thought Pat; and look at them, with their drawly voices and their arrogant ways. Come the revolution . . . But no, there was not going to be a revolution, or certainly not in Edinburgh.

"Sorry," said a voice. "I'm late."

Pat turned round to see Big Lou behind her. The transformation struck her immediately. She had not expected Big Lou to be wearing her working clothes – a sort of hodden skirt with an old-fashioned gingham blouse – but equally she had not expected black patterned tights, a suede pencil skirt, a slightly too tight red stretch top, and a wide belt round the waist. The shoes, she noticed, were scuffed cream kitten-heels. It was an outfit, she feared, that missed the mark.

"You look nice, Lou," she said. She did not think before she spoke; it was what one said, as meaningless as good morning or good day. Poor Lou, she thought, she could look better if she . . .

"Aye, but my top is too tight," said Big Lou. "So don't make me laugh or it'll split."

Pat smiled. "Worse things have happened on dates. I knew somebody whose skirt fell down on her first date with this guy. He must have thought her a bit fast . . ."

They began to walk back along George Street. "How are you going to know who he is?" asked Pat. "There are bags of men about."

"Most of them about sixteen," said Lou. "Darren's thirty-nine, same as me. He'll stand out in this crowd."

"Darren?"

"Yes, that's his name. Darren Gow."

"Gow means smith, doesn't it?"

Big Lou knew about names. "Yes. It comes from ghoba in Gaelic. A ghoba is a smith."

Pat savoured the name "Darren Gow. Yes, it's . . . it's a solid sort of name. It's nice." Hypocrite, she said to herself. It's not a nice combination at all.

"We'll see what he's like. Here, Pat, is my mascara all right? I don't want it running down my cheek."

Pat peered at Big Lou's face. "It's fine, Lou. And don't worry, hen. It's going to be fine."

They were nearly at the entrance to the bar, now, and

they could hear music coming from within, and the hubbub of conversation. Big Lou hesitated. "What if he doesn't like me, Pat? What then?"

"Of course he'll like you, Lou! Everybody likes you. I've never met anybody who didn't like you. Not one single person."

They entered the bar. There were groups of people standing talking to one another; couples at tables. Pat looked about quickly. There seemed to be only one man by himself, and he was sitting on a barstool. As they went in, he turned in his seat and looked at them.

"Did you tell him you'd be bringing somebody?" whispered Pat.

"Aye," said Big Lou. "I told him."

Darren Gow stood up and walked towards them. He held out his hand. "Lou?"

Lou reached out and they shook hands. She looked down at the floor. Pat, though, was staring at Darren Gow. He looked like Elvis. He dressed like Elvis too.

"And you're . . ." The voice was deep; the accent from somewhere in the west. Motherwell, perhaps.

"This is my friend, Pat," said Big Lou. "Pat, this is Darren."

"I'll get you ladies a drink," said Darren. "Let's sit down over there. That table. What'll you have?"

With Darren off to the bar, Pat turned to Big Lou and said, "Well, Lou, he's good-looking, isn't he?"

Big Lou nodded. "He's braw."

"And I think I know now what EI stands for," Pat went on. "Elvis Impersonator."

If Big Lou responded Pat did not hear her, her attention being suddenly distracted by the person who had just come into the bar: Bruce.

34. A Miracle Wrought by Nature

It is easy not to see somebody. But try not to notice them when you know they are there – that is infinitely more difficult. The gaze may be firmly averted, the eyes resolutely fixed on something else, but both have a nasty habit of turning in the forbidden direction, as surely and as inexorably as the needle of a compass swings back to magnetic north. And so although Pat looked intently at the floor, then at Big Lou, and then up at the ceiling – such a fascinating pattern, she told herself – her gaze swung back to the doorway through which Bruce Anderson, surveyor, perfect narcissist, user of clove-scented hair gel, Lothario – his honours were piled one upon the other, as Pelion was piled upon Ossa – had entered.

No field mouse can look away from the cobra; no startled deer, once transfixed, can drag itself away from the beam of the headlights. Pat struggled to look away but could not; her gaze stayed where it was, and, after the briefest moment, was picked up by Bruce. He looked momentarily surprised, but then broke into a smile and started to move across the floor towards the table where the two women sat.

"Oh no . . ." muttered Pat.

Big Lou, who was looking towards the bar, where the Elvis-like figure of Darren could be made out amongst a crowd of younger, smaller men, turned round. "Oh no what?"

Pat did not have time to answer, as Bruce had now reached them and was holding out both arms in a gesture of discovery. "My two favourite people!" he said. "Pat . . . and you, Lou. This is seriously cool."

Big Lou looked up. She had never had much time for Bruce, and her feelings had not changed. "Oh," she said. And then, whispering to Pat, "I see what you mean."

Bruce sat down in front of them. "Well, who would have thought it?"

"Aye," said Big Lou. "Where have you been, Bruce?"

"Where have I been? I've been right here. Action central. Where have you been? Same old, same old?"

"Same old, same old," echoed Big Lou.

"Busy, busy," said Bruce. "And you, Pat? Still at uni?"

Pat glanced at Big Lou. "Yes. But I'm working part-time for Matthew."

Bruce smiled. "Matthew? God, I haven't thought about him for yonks. Still there? I suppose he is. Same sweater? Remember that one? The beige number."

"Distressed oatmeal actually."

Bruce let out a snorting laugh. "That's seriously funny. Distressed oatmeal! Poor old Matthew. He didn't get it, did he?"

Neither Pat nor Big Lou said anything. After a moment or two, Bruce continued. "Not that everybody can."

"Can what?" asked Pat.

"Get it."

Big Lou flashed a disparaging look at Bruce. "Matthew gets it," she said. "He gets it fine."

"They've had triplets," said Pat.

Bruce looked wide-eyed. "Triplets? Matthew managed triplets? Amazing!"

"What are you doing these days, Bruce?" asked Pat.

Bruce touched the side of his nose. "Hush-hush."

"You're a spy?"

He laughed. "Hah, hah. No, sensitive commercial stuff. Development projects. Big time."

"Tell us," challenged Big Lou.

Bruce looked at her playfully. "Wouldn't you like to know . . ." he began, but was cut short by Darren's return to the table.

"Hello," said Bruce, getting up. "The King, no less."

"This is Darren," said Big Lou.

Darren put the tray of drinks down on the table and offered a hand for Bruce to shake. Pat watched: Darren was frowning; he was obviously unsure as to where Bruce fit in. And at this point Pat made up her mind. Big Lou's date with Darren was rapidly being ruined by Bruce's arrival, and the only thing that she could do to rescue the situation would be to take Bruce away. "Listen," she said. "I haven't seen Bruce for ages and we need to catch up. Would you mind if we left the two of you? It'd get pretty boring for you if we talked about friends all the time."

Pat could see that Big Lou was relieved, as was Darren, who, understandably, looked as if he had taken an immediate dislike to the new arrival. The King! What a rude thing, Pat thought, to say to somebody who looked like Elvis. What if he just happened to look like Elvis and had made no effort to do so?

Bruce approved of her suggestion. "That's cool with me," he said. "See you, Big Lou. And you too . . . El Darren."

They walked over towards the bar, where Bruce shouted an order to the barman.

"So, Pat," he said. "Here we are. After all that time. You're looking great."

"And you too." The compliment slipped out; she had not meant it, although she immediately realised, with sinking heart, that it was absolutely true. Bruce did look great. Bruce looked wonderful.

"Yeah, thanks. I've got this new body trainer. You know what a body trainer is, Pat?"

She shook her head.

"He's like a personal trainer. But while a personal trainer makes you work out in the gym to tone up the muscles." And here Bruce took Pat's hand and laid it on the biceps of his right arm. "No tone-up needed there! Anyway, a body trainer looks after your personal grooming. I read all about it in *GQ*. You know *GQ*, Pat? *Gentleman's Quarterly* – it's really cool. All the stuff. Cars. Personal grooming products. The works. There was this article about body trainers, and I thought Hey, that's for me!"

The barman pushed Bruce's drink across the counter and Bruce raised it in a toast to Pat. "Cheers, dears, here's to the queers!" He smiled. "Heard that one?"

Pat wanted to shudder, but did not. There was a strange fascination about Bruce – there always had been – and she found now that she wanted him to carry on.

"This body trainer?"

"Yes," said Bruce. "So I found one here in Edinburgh. Great guy. He's called Louis. I went to see him and he took one look at me, and you know what he said?"

Pat shook her head.

"He just whistled. Then he said, 'Tops.' Just that. 'Tops.' He was obviously impressed."

"And then?"

"He said, "I need to make an assessment, get your shirt off.""

Bruce winked; Pat looked down at the floor.

"So I get the shirt off and he says, 'Fantastic! We're going to start with depilation. Just a touch off the chest. Then we're going to attend to the hairstyle, moisturiser, tan, nails – but honestly, it's going to be hard to improve much on the miracle that nature has already wrought.' That's what he said."

35. *The Benefits of Brotherhood*

Stuart sat in an uncomfortable straight-backed chair, a small roundel of carved mahogany pressing into his back in just the wrong place. It reminded him of the chairs in his aunt's house in St. Andrews, chairs he had sat in as a boy when visiting her on the last Saturday of every month. She was the widow of a professor of mathematics, a specialist in non-linear partial differential equations who had come close, she claimed, to solving the Navier-Stokes problem. "He would have done it," she said, "had he survived a few years more, but it was not to be."

The house in which this aunt lived was filled with chairs of varying degrees of discomfort, none of them designed to let the human form, in any of its known configurations, relax. Had the chairs been more accommodating, Stuart felt, then it is possible that his late uncle might have been able to concentrate sufficiently to solve the mathematical problem with which he wrestled; as it was, having something digging into one, he thought, above or below – some prominence or protuberance – was inimical to focused thought.

Just as it was now, in this small room in a building tucked away in a discreet Southside street. From the outside, the building was unexceptional; a small nineteenth-century warehouse, the passer-by might think, a tiny Victorian school perhaps, or the office of some ancient printer, now defunct. Nothing on the building's façade would indicate otherwise except for a small stone device above the front door's fanlight – a set of callipers – that gave the game away.

Stuart was now in the anteroom of Lodge No. 345, Star of the Heavenly Firmament, a branch of the Antient Free and Accepted Masons of Scotland (founded 1736). He had been initially quite alone, left to contemplate in silence the step that he was about to take, but was now joined by another initiate, who sat down in the apparently equally uncomfortable chair next to his.

Stuart smiled at the new arrival. "You too?" he said.

The other man was considerably younger than Stuart. He smiled warmly and extended a hand. "My name's Keith, by the way. We aren't allowed to give the proper handshake just yet," he said. "But we shall be in . . . what, half an hour's time?"

Stuart introduced himself. "They said we'd have a bit of a wait. They have a lot to do in there." He nodded in the direction of the closed door on the other side of the room. From underneath this door, a light could be made out burning in the room beyond – a light that was suitably dim for the mysteries it illuminated.

"I've been meaning to join for the last three years," said Keith. "Ever since my twenty-first birthday. My grandfather was in this lodge, you see, and my father too. My father lives in Australia now and so he's in a lodge in Adelaide. But he kept nagging me to join here. So this is it."

Stuart was impressed by the connections. "Your grandfather?" he said. "Well, that's something."

"Yes," said Keith. "And it stood him in good stead in the war. He was taken prisoner by the Japanese in Singapore and held in Changi – you know that place where they have the airport these days. They were half-starved and the Japanese were terribly cruel. They executed prisoners by chopping their heads off with swords. They beat them mercilessly. Thousands of men died."

Stuart nodded. It was true.

"My grandfather was in a pretty bad way at one point, but there was this Australian officer who saw how things were going for him. He knew that anybody who became too ill to work or to look after himself would probably not make it. When they met, my grandfather gave him the handshake and so he knew that he was a fellow mason. The officer managed to get hold of some extra food for my grandfather by arranging to have it stolen from the Japanese officers' mess. If he had been found out, he would have been executed straight away. But he did it, and he saved my grandfather's life. The Aussies were very brave.

"Not that I'm joining in case I need to have my life saved," Keith went on. "But I'll tell you this, Stuart: my grandfather's life was saved a second time. Yes, I'm not making this up. After the war he went to Malaya, where he ran a rubber plantation for a firm in Dundee. There was a big communist uprising there – remember? – and a lot of these rubber plantations came under attack. It was pretty dangerous. Anyway, my grandfather went into town one day and on the way back his truck broke down. A vehicle came along after a while and this chap got out and they shook hands. Same handshake.

"My grandfather didn't want to leave his vehicle and so

the other man offered to drive off for help. But he didn't want to leave him unarmed, and so he left him a Sten gun he had with him. He – the man who had come along – was prepared to take the risk of travelling without it just so that my grandfather could have something to ward off attack, if he needed it. How about that? Thinking of the other fellow first – that's what this is all about."

Stuart nodded. "And what happened?"

"My grandfather came under attack, but he fired a few shots with his Sten gun and they skedaddled into the jungle. But his life had been saved a second time by the fraternal handshake."

"Amazing," said Stuart. He thought it unlikely that his own life would be saved by the handshake, but one never knew.

The young man became silent, and they both stared for a while at the facing wall, which was covered in photographs of men wearing ceremonial sashes and aprons. From where he was sitting, Stuart strained to make out the faces in some of the pictures. His statistician's eye, by ancient habit, calculated the age of each person in each photograph, and then stopped. He knew him, and, yes, he knew him too. And that man in the middle was surely . . . yes, it was. Well, no doubt he got at least some votes that way . . . and there, if he was not mistaken, was his bank manager.

"Are you married?" Keith asked suddenly.

"Yes," said Stuart. "And you?"

"No. I've got a long-term girlfriend, though. I've bought her a Masonic brooch. It's got some of the symbols on it. Enamelled. She's really pleased."

Stuart closed his eyes. He was imagining himself presenting Irene with a Masonic brooch, symbols and all. It was a difficult envisioning.

36. Stuart Is Initiated

The door on the opposite wall opened and an apron-wearing man, laden with regalia, stepped out.

"You're first, Pollock," he said.

Stuart stood up. He had been told what to expect, but now, as the Lodge officer helped him take off his shirt, he felt his heart thumping heavily within his exposed chest.

"Put this on," said the officer, handing him a curious one-sided garment, a half shirt of the sort that would have been perfectly fitting for Italo Calvino's bifurcated viscount. On one side it was complete, with a full and buttoned sleeve; on the other it simply did not exist, so that there was only half a collar, half a back, half a front – the division being entirely vertical. Stuart slipped into it and the officer tied the pieces of tape that would prevent the shirt from slipping off his right shoulder. Then the officer placed a loose piece of cord about his neck, rather like the lanyard of a military uniform.

"Please take off your left shoe and left sock," the officer said. "Then roll your trouser leg up to just below the knee."

Stuart complied. He felt rather like Robinson Crusoe, he decided – clad in clothing that had been half torn off by wind and wave, trouser leg prepared for a walk along a deserted beach.

"Now then," said the officer. "Are you ready to go ahead with this?"

Stuart nodded, and then swallowed. He tried to keep Irene out of his mind, but now, faced with this question, he heard her voice echoing within his head. You did what, Stuart? You rolled up your trouser leg? Am I hearing this correctly?

The officer moved towards the door, which now opened

as if under its own momentum. Stuart followed him, entering the room to find himself flanked by two supporters, armigers perhaps, who gently propelled him into the centre of the room. There, standing beside a table, was the Grand Master. His, at least, was a familiar face, as Stuart had been interviewed by him before his application to join the Lodge had been submitted.

There were lights behind the Grand Master, and these shone directly in Stuart's eyes, imparting a halo to the Grand Master himself and bathing his assistants with gold. Stuart blinked as the first and fundamental question of the oath was administered: Did he believe in the Great Architect of the Universe?

This was no time for theological debate, but even as he began to answer this question – to which, in these circumstances, there could be only one answer, or at least that was the case if an initiate wished to be admitted to the Lodge – he wondered whether his response would be entirely truthful. And would you really want to lie if you were faced with a Grand Master asking such a thing?

You could hardly say, "It depends on what you mean by a Great Architect." People who asked you whether or not you believed in x or y – especially with a light behind them – tended not to be interested in equivocation – in much the same way as customs officers are not interested in hearing their query as to quantities of whisky in one's suitcase answered with debates on what was meant by whisky. Was there a Great Architect? Was the notion of a great architect any different from the idea of God as explained in Sunday schools or catechism classes, or New College on the Mound for that matter? Calling him a great architect suggested a degree of purpose and a design sense, indeed, that a concept of a creator did not necessarily entail. One might have such a being who simply brought matter into existence but who did not plan the outcome in any way; any thoughtful consideration of the world, with its chaos and its suffering, perhaps lent a certain attractiveness to such a theory.

Stuart felt that he could believe in that, and did so, in a rather vague and unarticulated way. He thought that there could well be something other than that which we saw; some motivating force, some directing principle; he believed that to be so because he felt it; he felt it when he experienced love, or joy, or a sense of wonder. He felt it when he penetrated to the heart of a mathematical theorem – as he had done as a student at university – and saw in the figures and symbols an underlying beauty. Perhaps the Great Architect was really the Great Mathematician; that was an altogether easier concept for him.

"Yes," he said. "I believe in the Great Architect."

The Grand Master then said something that Stuart did not understand. It sounded rather like Bemofmpth, and when the word was repeated by the varying grand panjandrums

standing in a circle, by the masters in the third to twenty-sixth degree, by the grand this and the grand that, it also sounded rather like Bemofmph.

"Repeat after me: As surely as the sun sinks in the west," intoned the Grand Master, "and the great star of Jerusalem and all the Orient rises in the third quarter of the Great Arch, so shall my soul wither and fall from the vine should I reveal, to those not entitled to receive it, any word or whisper of these proceedings of the Grand Scottish Rite, including this initiation ceremony."

Stuart repeated the words, which had been helpfully printed out in a small manual thrust into his hands. Then there were further oaths, with many references to arches, quadrants, corners, and even U-bends. After these had been administered, there was a formal handshake with the Grand Master, in which the Master's forefinger was firmly pressed on an upper knuckle of Stuart's right hand, while Stuart placed his heels together and his toes sticking out – "on the square" as the position was described. This was followed by the ceremonial unrolling of his trouser leg, and the donning of his original shirt.

"Congratulations!" whispered one of the brothers as Stuart took his place in their ranks. "That wasn't too bad, was it?"

Stuart thanked him, and smiled. It had not been too bad at all, and for all the mumbo-jumbo of ritual, the essential point of it all seemed clear to him. He was being received into something that stood for honour and dedication to sound community values. These men were simply under-lining the fact that they all accepted and practised the same values, which were entirely defensible ones: that you should act with integrity; that you should be truthful; that you should strive to help others. What was wrong with that? Nothing, he thought.

37. *We Meet the Duke of Johannesburg*

At the end of the ceremony Stuart and Keith were given the opportunity to mingle with their newly acquired Masonic brothers. Stuart, relieved that the ordeal of initiation was over, felt a curious sense of exhilaration, an almost light-headed feeling of special accomplishment. He was now a mason – fully fledged and inducted. It was, moreover, something that he had done personally, without any reference to his wife; it was, he realised, something that was authentic to him and to him alone, and in fact the first authentic thing he had done for years – almost for the whole period of his marriage.

He looked about him. Most of these men had wives, he assumed, and these wives would know all about their husbands' Masonic involvement. He wondered whether they would be shocked if he were to reveal that he had not told Irene about this. Would they regard him as weak, or even dishonest, in not telling her? Would he be considered to have failed a Masonic standard of probity, even at this early stage of his career as a member?

He was thinking about this, sipping at a cup of tea, when a well-built man wearing an ornate green apron and matching sash came up to him.

"You're the new brother. Congratulations on joining. Well done!"

Stuart studied the other man while they shook hands. "Thank you. I'm very pleased." He noticed the large, confident moustache, the welcoming expression, and the confident bearing. This was a man best described as clubbable.

"I should introduce myself," said the stranger. "I'm the Duke of Johannesburg. Call me Johannesburg – it's simpler."

Stuart's eyes widened. He had not expected a duke – but then there was much that he had not expected that day.

"I've been a member for a long time," continued the Duke. "Can't remember exactly why I joined, but it's a good group of people and the objectives are fine. All we do, as far as I can work out, is raise money for charity. That, and dress up. And I don't see what's wrong with that. The way people go on about the masons, you'd think we were some sort of sinister society. Nothing could be further from the truth. Why do people criticise things they know nothing about? Can you throw any light on that?"

"None at all," said Stuart. "Unless it's resentment. Envy and resentment make people suspicious. They don't like people to have fun. They don't like people to enjoy themselves. These people want to stop things."

"My views exactly," said the Duke. "You'd think the press would have better things to do than drop dark hints about freemasonry. Nonsense – complete nonsense." He paused. "Unless it's the oaths they worry about. You know this business about not being able to stop being a mason. People go on about that. That, and the oaths, perhaps. I must say that oaths are a bit much, but then I followed a very simple expedient when I took mine."

Stuart was curious, and asked the Duke what it was.

"I crossed my fingers," said the Duke. "As I was taking the oath, I had the fingers of my left hand crossed. I've always done that – ever since I was in short trousers. I crossed my fingers if I had to make a promise I didn't want to keep, or if I had no alternative but to tell some fib. We all did that as children."

"That means you're not bound?"

The Duke smiled. "Morally, I suppose one is. Promises should be kept, as any moral philosopher will tell you. As anybody will tell you, I suppose. But if you cross your fingers it means that you have some sort of mental reservation, and therefore are not quite as bound as you otherwise might be." He looked apologetic; as if he were defending some dubious proposition and needed support.

"Mental reservation is an interesting concept," the Duke continued. "Rome uses it to give people annulments of marriage. If you can show that your spouse had a mental reservation about having children, then you can get the whole thing set aside by the Holy Roman Rota. It's frightfully useful.

"But they don't throw it around, you know. There are people who claim that you can get an annulment on the grounds of mental reservation simply by sending a postal order for ten and sixpence to Rome. That's quite untrue. They're very careful about that sort of thing."

Stuart began to say something, but the Duke had not finished.

"Speaking of marriage," he went on, "I've just heard the most wonderful story from a Sri Lankan friend of mine.

"Apparently there was a marriage registration officer who was taking down details from an engaged couple who were applying for a marriage licence. The official asked the young man his name and was given the reply 'da Silva.' So he solemnly wrote that down. Then he turned to the young woman and said, 'And what is your good name?' They love the expression good name. She replied 'da Silva.' So he started to write that down and then paused and looked at her. 'Any relation?' he asked." The Duke himself paused before continuing. "The young woman looked a bit embarrassed and then said, very coyly, 'Only once, sir!'"

"Hah!" said Stuart.

"Indeed," said the Duke, looking around him. "It's fascinating to see how ubiquitous our Masonic brethren are. Virtually everybody's one, you know." He leaned forward to address Stuart with the air of one imparting a particularly significant secret. "Did you know that if you look at the proportions of the Edinburgh New Town, they reveal pi, a very Masonic number? Did you know that?"

Stuart confessed that he did not.

"Well," said the Duke, "if you take the distance from the Royal Bank of Scotland building in St. Andrew Square to the corner of Charlotte Square and Glenfinlas Street – which I believe is a distance of 469.3 metres – and then divide it by the width of the New Town – from Princes Street to Queen Street – which I understand is 149.4 metres, then the result is 3.142, which is pretty much pi."

The Duke let this information sink in. Then, when it had, he whispered to Stuart, "My God, I could do with a whisky! All you get in this place is tea. It makes me really relieved that I crossed my fingers when I took the oath and that I'm therefore not a real Mason. You, by contrast, I'm afraid, are the real McCoy! Bad luck, my dear chap!"

"Not bad luck at all," retorted Stuart. "I'm proud of what I am . . . Your Grace!"

38. *On the Machair*

The following Wednesday, Domenica awoke early, and in a state of lightness of soul that she had not experienced for years; how one feels at twenty, she thought. She was normally a sound sleeper, awakening regularly each morning at six thirty, at least in the summer; in winter, when the sun did not reach Edinburgh until after nine o'clock – if it reached it at all – she was slower to emerge from her bedroom. What was the point in getting up early if it was only to survey the encircling gloom and to shiver?

Of course, many people did have to get up early in winter in order to get to work, but for Domenica that was no longer necessary. Her days were now largely her own – something that she occasionally had to remind herself was an immense luxury. That luxury, of course, was soon to be given up, now that she and Angus were about to marry. After that, she realised, her time would no longer be her own: she would have a husband to think about – another person to consider in planning the day, in shopping, in deciding what to do. Was she quite ready for that? She thought she was, but every so often there were moments of doubt, moments of anticipated nostalgia for the single state.

It was not thoughts of the marriage and its implications that made her feel elated that morning, but rather the dream that she had experienced immediately before waking. The memory of dreams is curiously fleeting; the vivid experiences of a few seconds earlier, so entrancing or frightening, are lost after a moment or two, or only vaguely remembered. It is as if daylight acts as a spotlight directed onto a play that had seemed so convincing but is now seen to be nothing; an absurd jumble unworthy of critical attention. But if the mind obliterates the cluttering, silly stuff of dreams, it can also deprive us of the insights that those same dreams provide, the moments of love; the friendly, revealing visions; the ability to fly. In our dreams we may find the friend we have yet to find in our waking life; in dreams we may be eloquent and witty, popular, appreciated in a way that otherwise eludes us; such dreams are surely worth keeping. But if they are to be retained, they need to be committed to memory as soon as possible after waking, so that they are laid down in a different, more retentive part of the brain. Don't pay any attention to this, the rational mind tells us as it begins its task of obliteration. No, I want to remember, one must say.

We cannot all have a dream as beautiful as Auden's – the dream he described in his *Bucolics*, the dream that brought him face-to-face with the god of mortal doting, the dispenser of love; not for us, but Domenica's dream that day seemed to her to be close enough to that. She sat up in bed, wide-eyed. She had been with Magnus Campbell again, and they were both as they had been when they had been together on Harris all those years ago. She closed her eyes in an effort to invoke again the setting of her dream. A burn, and a path by that burn, leading down to an expanse of machair. And he had suggested that they should take off their shoes and walk barefoot across the sand that stretched out beyond the machair – fine sand that the wind blew in tiny whirls of white.

Magnus Campbell, looking at her and smiling; Magnus Campbell telling her that he had once fished for herring in this very bay and caught a bucketful of what he called the silver darlings; and Magnus Campbell taking her hand; she in the arms of Magnus Campbell. She opened her eyes. That had all happened; they had followed the course of that burn; there had been machair with abundant tiny flowers; they had walked on the sand, holding their shoes. That had all happened and now, in her room in Edinburgh, it had happened again, on the day that Magnus Campbell was due to arrive at Antonia's flat and she would see him once more.

silver darlings

She got out of bed and went into the kitchen to put on the kettle for tea. She stopped, and thought, I have never dreamed of Angus in that way. Not once. And he is the man whom I am to marry.

She looked down at the floor. She had been in love with Magnus Campbell. He had been her first love, and it had been an utter revelation. How could one feel so intensely about another person? How could one want nothing but to see him, to be with him, to hear his voice, to touch him? She had been in no doubt at all but that this feeling, this raw, helpless sensation was love. It had all made sense – at last. Now she understood what the poets were driving at, where previously she had had only a theoretical, intellectual understanding of what they meant. Now she knew.

39. The Landscape of Dreams

Standing in her kitchen at barely five o'clock in the morning, a steaming cup of tea in her hand, Domenica looked out of the window over the roofs of Edinburgh. It was close to the summer solstice, and it had been light for over an hour –

a reminder of latitude. The early light was bright and opti-
mistic, kissing all that it touched. Not far away, circling
above some morsel in the street below, a couple of seagulls
mewed and cawed, the sun lighting up their wings against
the background of chimney pots and sky. She felt a moment
of pity for the screeching birds; we have eaten all their fish,
she thought, and reduced them to this: bickering clients of
our scraps, of the detritus of our lives.

The experience of her dream was vivid. Having being
recalled on waking, it was now committed to more permanent memory, and it had begun to trouble her. She felt
guilty, first and foremost, at the thought that she had
somehow allowed herself to dream of Magnus, and certainly
to dream of him in that carnal way. But then she reminded
herself that this was ridiculous: we had no control of our
dream life – even children understood that. What happened
to us in dreams was ultimately insignificant: the events of
a dream were merely things that happened in the same way
as rain, or earthquakes, or lightning happened and had
nothing to do with human agency. It was a reassuring
reminder, and she felt momentarily relieved. How terrible
it must be, she thought, to believe that one was in some
sense accountable for one's dreams. The loyal husband
dreams he is in the arms of another – some Siren – and
concludes that he is an adulterer. The dieter finds himself
enjoying a feast – and reproaches himself for his failure.
The timid one commits acts of insane bravado – and quakes
at the thought of his recklessness. All that would be a
terrible burden; would make one dread going to sleep at
night for fear of what one might do.

Domenica took a sip of her tea and then put her cup
down on the table, relieved at the thought that she could
forget her dream of Magnus. I am not in love with him,

she told herself; it's simply a matter of . . . And there she stopped. We may have no control over what we dream about, but that did not mean that dreams were meaningless. It was trite psychology, but were dreams not wish-fulfilment? Was that not the whole point of dream analysis – that dreams told us about what we really wanted? Magnus had come to her that night because she wanted him. He might have slipped back into her life under the barrier of consciousness, but that did not mean he was an unwelcome caller – he was a visitor she wanted and welcomed.

She sat down, appalled at the thought. She had accepted Angus Lordie's proposal of marriage. They were publicly engaged and had celebrated their engagement in the presence of a number of friends. There had been a notice in *The Scotsman*, the words having been chosen with great care: Domenica Macdonald and Angus Lordie, both of Edinburgh, have great pleasure in announcing their engagement . . . Not pleasure but great pleasure, which was significantly warmer, more joyful, than those stiff bulletins that begin: The engagement is announced . . . Of course there were social niceties at work: Both families are delighted to announce . . . was a form of words looked down upon by some. But that was nonsense, Domenica thought; a vestige of a social code that judged by secret shibboleths. If both families were delighted, then why should they not announce the fact publicly? It was surely better to say that both families were delighted than to say that both families regretted to announce the engagement. It is with great regret that we announce the engagement of our daughter . . . No doubt there were cases where that was exactly what the parents felt, but of course to say so would hardly be a good start to the marriage.

Thinking of engagement announcements, and families,

Domenica wondered what her parents would have made of Angus. Had they been alive, would they have wholeheartedly announced the engagement with great pleasure? She did not have to think about it for very long. Of course they would. They would have loved Angus, because he was a good and generous man. Her father, in particular, had had no time for meanness, and he would have seen that Angus shared this view. And as for her mother, she had been interested in art, had haunted the National Gallery of Scotland and knew every picture it contained; she loved the Ramsays and the Raeburns, and would have been so proud of the fact that Angus was a portrait painter.

And here am I, Domenica thought, their daughter, engaged to a man whom they would have been delighted to welcome into the family; here am I dreaming that I am in the arms of another man, a former boyfriend, and on the eve, as it were, of my wedding . . .

Domenica closed her eyes. I am not going to think these thoughts, she told herself. A ridiculous dream is just a ridiculous dream. It means nothing. Nothing. I love Angus Lordie and I am going to marry him. I love Angus Lordie . . .

She opened her eyes. Did she? Did she really love Angus, or was he merely a friend with whom she was now planning to share her life? If the latter were true, then should she not do something now, before it was too late? Should she not confess to Angus that she did not love him and that it was wrong that in such circumstances they should proceed with their marriage? Was that not the right, the sensible thing to do?

She sat down. A voice within her asked a question. How many marriages are based on love, at least in the beginning? How cynical, she thought. And the voice within retorted, Realistic, Domenica; realistic.

Domenica had a rough idea from the intercepted postcard when Magnus would arrive from Waverley Station. She had toyed with the idea of leaving her front door open so that she would hear him come up the steps to the landing, but had decided that this would seem a little overeager, perhaps even pushy. So instead she had fixed a notice on Antonia's door reading, Please ring the doorbell opposite when you arrive.

The hour before his arrival did not pass quickly. She was no longer thinking of her dream, nor of the unsettling doubts it had released – she would deal with all that later – but her mind now was occupied with anticipation, and the thoughts that prompted. Would Magnus be surprised to find that she was Antonia's neighbour, or had Antonia perhaps told him? Would he even recognise her? She had not weathered too badly, she told herself – although there was never any room for smugness in that respect – but how would the years have treated Magnus? He had been devastatingly good-looking when young, an effortless turner of heads (thankfully unaware of it), but that had been a long time ago. He would not be like that now: many men lost their looks in no time at all, became coarse, sagged. It could happen quite quickly, within the space of a few years indeed, when the boy became the man. And then only too quickly there came the indignities of the flesh – the thickening of the torso, the appearance of jowls, the dulling of the light in the eyes. It was different with women, whose beauty was softer and seemed to fade more slowly; a beautiful woman also had at her disposal more tricks than were available to a man, even in these days of male makeup, of man-liner and manscara.

Her thoughts turned to the sheer coincidence of Magnus's arrival. She wondered how Magnus and Antonia knew each other. Antonia, for all her sudden enthusiasm for the order of nuns that had taken her in, had always been a man-eater. It was a rather crude term, thought Domenica, but it was accurate enough, expressing the voraciousness of such appetites. She had on her shelf a book given to her by an aunt, *The Man-Eaters of Tsavo*, a curious old memoir by a hunter who had dealt with a plague of man-eating lions that had terrorised railway builders in colonial Kenya. That book had been about real lions, but could have been about a group of man-mad women, inhabitants of Tsavo, who could not resist any passing male . . . She imagined them, heavily made-up, wearing revealing dresses, lying in wait under a tree for a passing male. And Antonia would be the alpha-female of such a group, a man-eater's man-eater.

Man-Eater of Tsavo

That same aunt who had given her the book had been in Kenya in those days and had told her of what she called the fishing fleet.

"The fishing fleet, Domenica," she explained, "was made up of women who were determined to get a husband. They went off to Kenya with that in mind and by and large were successful. Those who were not made their way home like all unsuccessful anglers – talking about the one who got away."

Domenica had wanted to ask her aunt whether she too had angled.

Her question was anticipated. "Honestly requires me to say that I, too, could be said to have been a member of that fleet. I knew them all – all the other girls. I was just like them. And do you know who we all looked up to? The late Diana Delves Broughton, that's who. She was very, very good at keeping men exactly where she wanted them."

It was just the sort of story that Domenica liked. "Oh yes?"

"She went out to Kenya shortly after her first marriage," said the aunt. "They travelled out by steamer to Cape Town and Mombasa and do you know what? She was said to have had an affair on the way. On her honeymoon!"

"That takes some doing," said Domenica.

"Indeed it does. It indicates, if you'd like my view, a certain determination, would you not say?"

"Yes. And her poor husband?"

"She had a number of husbands," said the aunt. "They were generally long-suffering. The one who had real difficulty was Jock Delves Broughton. He was a complete gentleman. A real gentleman doesn't notice if his wife is having an affair – do you know that? The reason for that is that it would be ungentlemanly to speak critically of one's wife, whatever the circumstances. So poor Jock just accepted it and let her get on with it. He was tremendously forgiving."

"Tremendously." Domenica imagined the cuckolded

husband eventually confronting his wife, "I say, old thing, you seem frightfully friendly with that fellow . . ." They were so naïve in those days; so unworldly; whereas we . . . what were we? Suspicious, sneeringly cynical, disbelieving of innocence . . .

"And then she took up with the late Lord Erroll, the one who was shot. Remember? His motto, famously, was *To hell with husbands*! His car was found in a ditch with him slumped over the wheel. He had been at a dinner party at Jock and Diana's."

"Who shot him?"

"The matter remains unsolved. Jock was tried for it, you know. They said that during the trial he had on him a silver syringe and a large dose of morphine so that he could do the decent thing if he was convicted. It would never have done for a baronet to be hanged. The polite thing for a gentleman in those circumstances is to take action himself and save everybody the embarrassment."

"He was acquitted?"

"Yes."

"So who really shot Lord Erroll? Does anybody know?"

"Oh, everybody knows. I certainly know. But do you mind if I don't tell you who it was? I have this rather old-fashioned view, you see, that one does not speak ill of the dead, even if they richly deserve it. All I would say is this: what a gentleman Jock was. He would do anything for his wife."

"So he shot him?"

"Certainly not. My dear, you really have a tendency to draw the wrong conclusion. I do hope you grow out of it. Otherwise you might . . . well, you might go through life drawing the wrong conclusions about everything."

41. I Am Come from Copenhagen

Anna, the Danish au pair promised to Matthew and Elspeth by the helpful firm of Domestic Solutions, arrived from Copenhagen rather earlier than expected. Even so, her arrival was not a moment too soon; Elspeth, suffering from chronic sleep-deprivation, was awake to receive her, but only just. Matthew had not slept at all the previous evening and although Elspeth had managed an hour or two, this had been snatched at odd moments and had not come in one sequence. The two of them felt dizzy with fatigue and barely had the energy to answer the door when the bell went; in fact, Matthew nodded off even as the bell rang and it was Elspeth who went, and found herself faced with a fresh-faced young woman with a large rucksack on her back.

"My name is Anna," said the young woman. "And I am come from Copenhagen to help you."

It was an extraordinary introduction, and even in her drowsy state Elspeth was struck by its sheer poetry. I am come from Copenhagen to help you – not I have come but I am come. The archaic form was undoubtedly accidental, thought Elspeth, wondering whether Danish used the auxiliary verb to be to achieve the past tense of verbs of motion, as French did. And yet the effect in English was a fine one. I am come from Copenhagen to help you had such a strong ring to it; it was the sort of thing that an angel might say to some helpless mortal as he gazed up at great wings and strong arms. An angel cannot simply say hello, or, worse still, hi; nor can he reveal himself as emergency services; I am come to help you is altogether more appropriate.

Angel, thought Elspeth as she stood at the doorstep and stared at the young Dane before her. You angel!

She wanted to say so much; to embrace the young woman then and there; to hand everything over – Matthew, the flat, the triplets, the kitchen, the sterilising equipment for the babies' bottles, the babies' bottles themselves, that awful breast pump – everything. She wanted to hand all that over to Anna as the representative of Domestic Solutions, who had come, or was come, rather, from Copenhagen to help her. But she said nothing, as no words came; instead there were tears, copious, warm, utterly unscripted tears.

Anna stepped forward, slipping out of her rucksack as she did so. "Oh dear," she muttered. "Please don't cry, Mrs. . . ."

"Elspeth," sobbed Elspeth. "Call me Elspeth. And I can't help it, I'm sorry, I just can't . . ."

Anna put her arms around Elspeth, as naturally and spontaneously as one might embrace another on first meeting, but with gentleness and sympathy too.

"You cry, Elspeth," she said. "It is always best to cry."

"I feel so foolish. You've just arrived, and I'm crying . . ."

"Shh, shh. That doesn't matter."

Anna propelled Elspeth gently away from the open door and then closed it behind her. "You sit down, Elspeth. Then we can see what's what. I have done this before, you know."

Elspeth dabbed at her eyes with the handkerchief that Anna had produced from the pocket of her jeans. "Before?"

"Yes. I have worked as mother's help – is that the word? – twice before. Once in Germany and once in the United States. They were both very sad mothers, but I hope I made them happier."

"Sad?" sniffed Elspeth.

"Yes," said Anna. "A bit like you. The husband of one of them had gone off with another woman and the other had a baby with a hip problem. The poor baby had to have big splints and the mother was very upset as a result."

Elspeth wondered whether there was implicit criticism in this story. She had three healthy boys and a husband who had shown no signs of going off with another woman. Matthew couldn't, she decided: he was far too tired. If he decided to go off he would probably reach only as far as India Street or Ainslie Place before he dropped from exhaustion – that would be no good for another woman. Other women tended to have greater expectations of the men they seduced away from their proper station.

This meeting had taken place against a background of silence. Now this was disturbed by a sudden crying from the nursery.

"They've woken up," said Elspeth.

Anna frowned. "They? You have twins?"

Elspeth looked at the floor. She was suddenly afraid that this young woman – this angel – would now take flight. Had Domestic Solutions not revealed the true state of affairs to her? Had they expected her to refuse the assignment if told in advance that she was expected to look after triplets? She sighed. One could hardly conceal anything at this stage.

"Triplets," she said quietly.

Anna looked at her in disbelief, holding up three fingers. "Three babies? Three?"

Elspeth nodded miserably. "I didn't mean to have three," she said. "Nor did my husband . . ."

Anna burst out laughing. "Of course not. But that is very nice news! I have never helped with three babies before. I am very lucky."

Elspeth hesitated. Was this sarcasm? "You like the idea?"

"Of course I like the idea. I love babies! I love them very much. And if you have three babies to love then that means . . . well, it means that there is more to love. I am very lucky."

"Let me introduce them to you," said Elspeth. Suddenly she felt stronger.

"I'm sure they will be very sweet," said Anna. "And I'm sure that I will like your husband too. Four men in the house! Three tiny little ones and one big one. And they all need to be looked after. No wonder you were crying, Elspeth!"

Elspeth rose from the sofa onto which she had temporarily collapsed, aided by Anna, who had extended a hand to her. "They are all in the one nursery," she said. "Your room is next door. I must show that to you."

"There will be time later on," said Anna. "The important thing now is to make the acquaintance of these lovely little boys."

"Your English is very good," said Elspeth.

Anna accepted the compliment gravely. "I went to school for a year in England when I was sixteen. That helped my English a lot. It was a boarding school and many exciting things happened. May I tell you about them some time?"

Elspeth smiled. "I'd love to hear."

They were now at the nursery door. "What are the little boys called?" whispered Anna.

"Rognvald, Tobermory, and Fergus," Elspeth replied.

"So sweet!" said Anna. "Such fine Scottish names, for fine little Scottish boys."

42. *Anna Takes Command*

They went into the room that served as a nursery. It had been only half-prepared for its new inhabitants, with two of the walls decorated in the bright primary colours of childhood, with cheerful pictures to match, while the other two – unfinished projects of Matthew's – were still eggshell blue, with the framed pictures of the Trossachs that had been left behind by the flat's previous owners. Under the window, neatly lined up, were the three cribs in which the boys slept.

Two of the infants were now awake, one crying and the other lying on his back staring up at the ceiling. Anna made her way across the room and bent down to pick up the crying child.

"He's very beautiful," she said. "Don't cry, little one." She turned to Elspeth. "Which one is this?"

Elspeth sighed; even as they had stood at the nursery door she had begun to dread this moment. What would Anna think of a mother who did not even know which of her children was which? What would she think of Scotland? "I'm afraid I don't really know," she muttered. "Not for certain, anyway . . ."

Anna smiled. "You've mixed them up?"

There was no accusing tone to the question and Elspeth answered it openly, and with relief. "Matthew took off their identification bracelets," she said. "He didn't realise . . ."

Anna's smile broadened. "It must be so easy to do that," she said. "I hope that you didn't blame him."

"Of course not," said Elspeth quickly. And that was true, she thought; she had been too tired to blame Matthew for that, or for anything, for that matter.

"So what we need to do is to decide which is which," said Anna. "And then I know how to make sure that we don't mix them up again." She touched the baby gently on the cheek. "Which would you like this one to be?" she asked.

"Rognvald," said Elspeth. "Or maybe . . ."

She did not finish. "Rognvald suits him very well," said Anna. "Right, if you hold him for me, Elspeth, we shall make sure that he remains Rognvald."

Elspeth took the baby. It is very strange, she thought, but I don't dread holding him any more. She felt calmer, more in control of the situation now that Anna was there; Rognvald was no threat.

Anna left the room and returned a moment later with two small bottles in her hand. "These are from my rucksack," she explained. "Nail varnish."

She now opened a bottle of red varnish and unscrewed the small brush-top. "Right," she said. "Could you show me little Rognvald's toes? Just the right foot, I think."

Elspeth complied, removing the tiny bedsock in which Rognvald's right foot was sheathed. So small, she thought; so small and pink.

Anna touched the little boy's minute toes. "So perfect," she said. "And you made him, Elspeth. Isn't that a miracle?"

Elspeth looked at her son's toes. She wanted to cry again, and felt the first welling of tears. Gratitude. Relief. Love.

"There, my little darling," said Anna as she daubed a speck of red nail varnish on the exposed toenails. "Rognvald has red toes. R and R. Easy to remember. Now, what about this little man here? What should his name be?"

"That one, I think . . . maybe that one is Tobermory. Yes, let's make him Tobermory."

"Tobermory will have much paler varnish," said Anna. "This is the colour that my mother uses. She calls it mother-of-pearl. In fact, this bottle of varnish belongs to my mother but she said I could take it to Scotland. I use all her things, you see, and she has stopped complaining. She lets me now."

Elspeth thought of her own mother. She had done the same thing with her mother's clothes, as they were the same size. "It is always a problem for mothers," she said. "For mine too."

"Family possessions belong to everybody," said Anna. "That's the way it should be."

She unscrewed the top of the mother-of-pearl varnish and waited for Elspeth to replace Rognvald in his crib and to pick up Tobermory. Deftly wielding the nail varnish brush, Anna in due course painted his nails. "There," she said. "That's Tobermory. He has mother-of-pearl. And finally, little Fergus, he is the one who has nothing on his toes at all. He is as nature intended."

Elspeth sighed with relief. "Such a simple solution," she said. "And now all we have to do is to keep their toenails those colours."

Anna nodded. "Exactly. And now maybe you could show me my room. Then I can meet your husband, if he is in. Is he?"

"I think so," said Elspeth. "He was falling asleep when you rang the bell. We're very tired."

Anna touched her lightly on the arm. "Of course you are. That is why you sent for me."

Elspeth smiled at her. "I'm glad you're here."

Anna pointed to the door. "Shall we look at my room?"

The rucksack was moved in and placed at the end of the

bed. Anna then looked out of the window and approved the view. "Edinburgh is very beautiful. Just like Copenhagen. I have a feeling that I shall be very happy here."

There was a noise from behind them – the opening of a door. "I think that might be Matthew," said Elspeth.

They made their way into the drawing room, where Matthew, who had been asleep on the sofa, was standing scratching his head. "I dozed off, he mumbled. "I don't know how long I've been asleep . . ." He suddenly noticed Anna. "Oh . . ."

Elspeth effected the introduction.

"You look very tired," said Anna. "And have you had anything to eat?"

Matthew shrugged. "There was breakfast," he said. "Or maybe it was lunch . . . I don't know."

"You poor man," said Anna. "Let's go into the kitchen. Elspeth, please show me where everything is. Eggs. Have you got any eggs? And ham? Do you like ham in Scotland? Men like eggs and ham very much, I think."

"The babies," said Matthew. "They're crying . . ."

Anna took command of the situation. "Elspeth," she said, "you go and feed Rognvald. Matthew, you bring Tobermory and Fergus into the kitchen. We'll look after them there while the eggs and ham are cooking. Right, everybody?"

Matthew looked to Elspeth for guidance.

"Mother-of-pearl," she said. "And natural. Simple."

43. *Bertie Takes the Fifth*

Bertie had been collected from Ranald Braveheart Macpherson's house the following morning by Stuart, who had taken him back to the flat in Scotland Street before going off on some unexplained errand.

"Did Daddy say where he was going?" asked Irene, who was making ciabatta bread in the kitchen.

Bertie shook his head.

"Are you sure, Bertie?" Irene pressed.

Bertie looked out of the window. He had assumed that his father had some business with the club to which he had recently been admitted, but he had been asked quite specifically not to speak to his mother about that. "He may have gone shopping," he ventured. "Maybe he's gone to Valvona & Crolla. Maybe he's gone to buy some olive oil."

Irene shook her head. "We have plenty of olive oil, Bertie, as I'm sure your father knows quite well."

Bertie shrugged. "Well, he's gone somewhere else," he said. "Maybe he's gone to Glasgow."

"And what would Daddy be doing going to Glasgow on a Saturday morning?" asked Irene. "No, Bertie, I don't think that Daddy has gone to Glasgow."

Bertie said nothing. After a moment or two, Irene resumed her questioning. "Are you sure that he didn't say, Bertie?"

Bertie shook his head. He had recently watched a film on television – at Tofu's house, television being forbidden in Scotland Street – and there had been a scene in which a German officer had been interrogating a member of the French Resistance. The officer had told his prisoner that he would get the truth out of him one way or another. "And another will not be very pleasant," he had said. "You can count on that."

"He's going to tickle him," said Tofu. "That's what they did, Bertie. They tickled them and they talked."

"That's very unkind," said Bertie.

Tofu, more wordly-wise than Bertie, had shrugged.

"That's what happens in war, Bertie. I wouldn't tell, though, if they tickled me. I would refuse to talk."

"You're very brave, Tofu," said Bertie.

"Yes," said Tofu. "I am. You'd talk, I think, Bertie. You'd talk straight away if they tickled you. You'd tell them everything, I think."

Bertie remembered this conversation now as his mother asked him about his father. Tofu might have no faith in him, but he was determined not to let his father down. "He's not in a club," he said.

Irene paused with her kneading of the ciabatta dough. "What did you say, Bertie?"

Bertie swallowed. "He's not in a club," he repeated.

Irene dusted her hands on a tea-towel. "That's very interesting, Bertie," she said. "Why would you say that Daddy isn't in a club? Who said anything about a club?"

"I said he wasn't in one," said Bertie. He felt slightly miserable now. Had he inadvertently betrayed his father? The whole point about saying that he was not in a club was to throw his mother off the scent. But it seemed, for some reason, to be having the opposite effect.

Irene came and sat down next to Bertie. "Listen, Bertie," she said quietly. "Your mentioning a club when Mummy had said nothing about clubs makes Mummy think that maybe Daddy is in a club. You see what I mean?"

Bertie stared fixedly at the floor. "He's not," he said.

Irene took his hand. "Bertie, Mummy doesn't mind if Daddy is in a club. It really doesn't matter. She would just like to know what club it is. That's not unreasonable of Mummy, is it? If I were in a club, I'd tell you, wouldn't I? And if you were in a club, you'd want Mummy to know all about it, wouldn't you?"

Bertie thought about this. He would certainly not want

his mother to know if he was a member of a club. It was the last thing he would want, in fact.

He decided on diverting tactics. "Are you in a club, Mummy?"

Irene laughed airily. "Of course not, Bertie! Can you see Mummy in a club?"

"What about the Labour Party?" asked Bertie. "You're in that, aren't you, Mummy?"

Irene smiled. "The Labour Party isn't a club, Bertie. The Labour Party is a political party."

"But you have meetings, don't you?"

"Of course we have meetings, Bertie. But the fact that one has meetings doesn't make us a club." She paused. "Daddy would be able to confirm all that to you – if he were to get round to joining the Labour Party. Which I'm sure he will do one of these days."

"I don't think so," said Bertie.

"Oh? And why don't you think so, Bertie?"

"Because Daddy wouldn't want that," said Bertie. "Daddy doesn't like the Labour Party."

Irene drew in her breath. "That's absolute nonsense, Bertie. Of course Daddy likes the Labour Party. Of course he does. He voted for it."

Bertie shook his head. "He didn't, Mummy," he said. "He voted for the Conservatives. He told me."

For a few moments Irene was silent. Bertie was still looking down at the floor and did not dare look up. He was vaguely aware that he had said something that compromised his father, but he was not quite sure what it was.

At last Irene spoke. "I think that you must have mis-understood Daddy, Bertie," she said icily. "Daddy would never do a thing like that."

Bertie decided not to say anything more. So this, he thought, is what it was like to be in the French Resistance. He wondered what had happened to the man in the film he had watched with Tofu. They had not seen the end, as Tofu's father had turned the set off before the film was finished.

"To get back to this club," Irene now said. "It really would be best, Bertie, if you told me what club it is."

Bertie shook his head. "He isn't in a club. And he didn't vote for the Conservatives, Mummy. I was only joking."

Irene looked as if she was unsure whether to be angry or relieved. "You shouldn't joke about these things, Bertie."

Bertie nodded. "Sorry, Mummy."

"Now tell me, Bertie, how did your evening with Ranald go? Are his mummy and daddy nice people?"

"Very nice," said Bertie. There was so much else that he wanted to say, but he remained silent. Ranald had promised to phone him that night and tell him whether any adoption offers had come in on eBay. If they had, then this sort of conversation would become a thing of the past. That, at least, was something to look forward to.

44. *B.O.A.C.*

Bertie was in his room, engaged with a challenging model aeroplane kit, when his father came home. The model aeroplane had been a gift from a colleague of Stuart's, who had discovered it in the attic, untouched in its pristine box, the price – in old money – stamped on the outside: five shillings and sixpence. The colleague had three daughters and no son, and when the girls had turned up their noses at the model he had offered it to Stuart, to pass on to Bertie.

Bertie had been thrilled. The plane was a passenger one, Stuart explained – a Comet, in fact. "The Comet was a wonderful plane, Bertie," Stuart said. "It was very big and it really was the beginning of modern air transport. Very few people travelled by air in those days." He pointed to the plane's livery. "And look at that, Bertie. B.O.A.C. That meant British Overseas Airways Corporation. How's that for the name of an airline?"

Bertie looked at the illustration on the box. The aircraft stood prominently on the airport apron, the runway stretching out behind it. A large set of steps had been wheeled up to the plane's open door and several passengers were ascending this. Down below, standing about the base of the steps, were the passengers' friends, who had come to say goodbye. One of these had a dog on a leash – an Irish setter, Bertie thought – and the dog was looking up at the departing people as if it, too, was bidding them farewell. At the top of the steps the Captain was standing with a woman in uniform behind him. The Captain was shaking hands with the first of the passengers.

"I wonder where they were going?" Bertie asked his father. "Do you think it was Glasgow, Daddy?"

Stuart laughed. "I don't think so, Bertie. They would have been going somewhere much further away. Look down at the bottom of the picture. There's the luggage being loaded into the hold. If only we could read the labels!"

Bertie looked at the suitcases. The man who was loading them was neatly dressed in overalls and was wearing a tie. He was clearly enjoying his job, as he was smiling in a friendly way at the departing passengers.

He looked again at the Irish setter. "Are dogs allowed in planes, Daddy?"

Stuart frowned. "I think you can take a dog in a plane, Bertie. Big dogs have to go in the special cages; small dogs are sometimes allowed in the cabin, as long as they behave themselves." He pointed to the picture. "But I'm afraid you wouldn't be able to take a dog out to the steps like that. You wouldn't be able to go out there yourself these days. Changed times, Bertie!"

Bertie was puzzled. "Why not? How can you say goodbye?"

Stuart thought for a moment. This was a difficult question to answer. How can you say goodbye? He looked down at his son, and for a moment he felt a curious, unexpected pang of regret. What sort of world were we bequeathing to our children? A world of distrust and conflict? A world in which ordinary human practices – ordinary human feelings – were suppressed by fear and the rules that fear brought in its wake? A world in which even dogs were regarded as a security risk.

Bertie reminded him of his question. "How can you say goodbye, Daddy?"

"You drop people off outside the airport terminal,"

said Stuart. "Then you drive away. Once you've paid, of course."

"Do you have to pay to say goodbye?" asked Bertie.

"Not in most normal places," said Stuart. "Unfortunately you have to do that in Edinburgh, Bertie. It's hard to believe, isn't it? The airport people make you pay to drop somebody off and say goodbye. Isn't that the meanest thing you've ever heard of?"

"They should feel ashamed of themselves, Daddy. Even Tofu wouldn't do something like that."

"No," said Stuart. "He wouldn't. But this country, Bertie . . ." He paused. There was so much wrong, and he was not quite sure where to begin. He sighed. "You enjoy the model, Bertie, and if you get stuck making it, I can help you."

And now, still unaided, Bertie was struggling with the wings of the B.O.A.C. Comet when he heard the front door open. It was a Saturday afternoon, and Stuart usually watched sport on television on a Saturday afternoon. Bertie was not particularly interested in sport – other than rugby, which he longed to play – and he was certainly more interested in his plane than in the rather tedious golf competition that Stuart was currently following.

That afternoon, though, the familiar sound of the commentator's voice and the polite applause of the spectators was replaced by the sound of raised voices in the kitchen. Bertie listened; his mother was saying something to his father, and now his father was replying. They were arguing about something, Bertie decided. It was something to do with the Labour Party, he thought, as he heard a few names he recognised from the news. Then there was something about a club, and his heart stood still; if his father was in trouble over his club, then Bertie thought that this was his fault, and felt mortified.

He put down the Comet and made his way quietly down the corridor.

". . . what if my friends discovered you were one of them?" It was Irene's voice, and it was full of reproach.

Stuart replied with something that Bertie did not quite catch. All that he heard was the word freedom and then, jumbled up with something else, he heard the word emasculation. That brought a tirade from Irene, so voluble and so rapid that Bertie could make nothing of it.

He withdrew to his room. His parents did not argue with one another very frequently, but, like all children, Bertie was dismayed when signs of parental discord surfaced. He did not want his parents to fight; he wanted nobody to fight. But it seemed that this was a forlorn wish: people fought. Tofu fought with Olive, and Olive occasionally fought with Lakshmi, who in turn fought with Pansy, who was jealous of her friendship with Larch. And now his parents were fighting too, and all over whether Stuart should be allowed to join a club and vote, if he wished, for the Conservatives.

Bertie sighed. Adoption was the only answer. If he were to be adopted and went to live in Glasgow, then he could see his real parents at weekends. That would keep everybody happy, which is all that Bertie, from the depths of his seven-year-old soul, desired.

45. *The Male Menopause*

Bertie put the B.O.A.C. Comet to one side and lay down on his bed. From the sitting room on the far side of the flat drifted the monotonous commentary on the golf tournament his father was watching on television. It sounded very dull to him, and he could not understand why his father should be interested in such a boring spectacle; but it was better, he thought, than arguing with his mother.

The row between Stuart and Irene had been rather more heated than usual. In fact, their usual rows were very low-key affairs, consisting of no more than some barbed comment from Irene followed by a brief word or two from Stuart. The infrequency with which these occurred was connected, perhaps, with their one-sidedness. Stuart saw no reason to argue, because he inevitably lost the argument to his more forceful and opinionated wife. So rather than pursue the matter, he tended to shrug his shoulders and leave things where they stood. This had the result of making Irene feel that she had won – which of course she had. And that suited her very well.

The heated discussion that day had been different. Armed with the intelligence that she had gleaned from Bertie, Irene had confronted Stuart about two matters: his clandestine political affiliations and his membership of some mysterious club on the south side of the city.

"I've been talking to Bertie," she said, as he came into the house.

"Oh yes."

"And it was very revealing."

Stuart was silent. There was something in Irene's tone that made him feel wary.

"Yes," continued Irene. "A very interesting conversation indeed."

"Bertie's a great wee conversationalist," Stuart observed. "I've often thought he should have a chat show of his own. Not a late-night one, of course, because that would be beyond his bedtime – something a bit earlier – six o'clock maybe."

Irene glared at him. "Don't be flippant, Stuart. It ill becomes you."

"Whatever," said Stuart.

"And don't say whatever. That's teenage slang these days. It's a substitute for thought."

"What . . ." Stuart stopped himself just in time.

Irene, who had been consulting a recipe book in the kitchen, slammed the book shut. "Yes, Stuart, and what have you been telling Bertie about the Conservative Party?"

"Nothing," said Stuart. "I think Bertie's a bit young for politics, wouldn't you say? I know there's talk about bringing the voting age down, but seven . . ."

Irene continued to glare at him. "What did the Jesuits say, Stuart? Didn't they say something about having children up to seven and then having them in their intellectual grasp for life?"

Stuart laughed. "Well, I don't think the Conservatives take the same line on that. And if you listened to your Gilbert and Sullivan you'd remember their observation about how all children are born liberal or conservative. Remember that?"

"I have no interest in shallow operetta, Stuart, as you well know."

Stuart frowned. "Shallow operetta? That's a bit steep, isn't it?"

Irene made a dismissive gesture. "Let's not get distracted with all that, Stuart. The issue is this: Where were you at lunchtime?"

Stuart hesitated. "Today?"

Irene's voice was steely. "Yes."

"I had lunch with some chaps, actually."

"Oh yes, and who were they?"

Stuart hesitated. He looked up at the ceiling for a moment,

and then out of the window. This, he told himself, is a watershed moment. There was no reason for him to accept it any longer. He had endured it for so long and done nothing about it. He had put up with Irene's ways for years and now, he decided, he had quite simply had enough.

"Masons," he said. "I've joined the masons. I've got my regalia here, if you'd like to see it."

"Stuart!" Irene's voice was raised to a shriek. "Have you taken leave of your senses?"

He looked at her calmly. "No, not at all. It's entirely harmless – in fact, the main purpose – as far as I can see – is to do various bits of charitable work. And what's wrong with that, may I ask?"

Irene opened her mouth to speak, but could not. Wives discover things about their husbands – sometimes quite dark things – and for many their first reaction is: How can I have failed to see? Of course they do see – they may see quite well – but what we see we do not always accept.

"And I'll tell you something else," Stuart continued. "I have no intention of resigning. It's going to be my thing from now on." And to add emphasis, he concluded, "Whatever."

There then followed an exchange of views that was both forthright and heated. Stuart held his ground, and it was at some point in this exchange that he used the word emasculation. "That's what you want to do to men," he shouted. "You want to emasculate them. That's what you want!"

Irene's gaze moved to her kitchen scissors, but moved away again. I must be calm, she told herself. I must try to imagine what Melanie Klein would have done if her husband had accused her of contemplating emasculation. She would have reached for a notebook, she felt, and written it all down for subsequent analysis.

She closed her eyes. What age was the male menopause? Was this it? Stuart was surely a bit young for that, as she understood that men were afflicted by it in their fifties, and Stuart was in his early forties. Was it a midlife crisis then? The life expectancy of the average male in the east of Scotland must surely be approaching eighty now. Divide that by two and that gave you a midlife point of forty.

The brief arithmetical calculation gave Irene some comfort. The best policy, perhaps, would be to ignore all this. If he wanted to be a mason, then she should let him. It was no more than a much-delayed form of adolescent rebellion. Or it might just be a desire to engage in male bonding brought on by a sense of male powerlessness. That would also explain his ridiculous remark about emasculation; if he had fears of emasculation it was because he was aware of the disempowerment of the modern male. Poor men. They were so, so useless, and it must be an understanding of this uselessness that made them want to be masons or members of male-only golf clubs, or similarly ridiculous things. Yes. That was it. And she could afford to be understanding because, as the French had it, *tout comprendre c'est tout pardonner.*

"It's all right, Stuart," she said soothingly. "You be a mason. I understand. It's quite all right." And then she added, "There, there."

46. *Lives of Purpose*

Angus Lordie's day usually began with a walk in the Drummond Place Gardens with Cyril. This was an important event, not to be missed even in the most inclement weather, including snow. That, of course, was a distant memory in high summer, and an unpleasant one, at least from Cyril's point of view. Some dogs may enjoy snow, but he was not one of them, and he had a tendency to blame Angus for the uncomfortable white disaster that snow represented for him.

"Not my fault, Cyril," Angus would say under Cyril's reproachful gaze. "I can do nothing about the weather, I'm afraid. We must both bear it with as much patience as we can muster."

That, unfortunately, was no answer. Cyril regarded Angus as omnipotent, the author and controller of his life, and by natural extension, of the conditions under which it was lived. Angus was, in fact, God to Cyril: a simple metaphor that has not escaped the attentions of some theologians who see the man/dog relationship as a helpful cipher for our own relationship with a creator. But whereas the human notion of god allows the creator freedom to order the world in a way which we might not find to our taste – acts of God, it must be remembered, include typhoons, lightning, and pestilence, at least as far as the interpretation of insurance contracts is concerned – in Cyril's theology there was no room for such discretion. Snow was uncomfortable and should not be there: Why had Angus allowed it and what was he proposing to do about it?

Here was no such issue that day: the Drummond Place Gardens, their stately trees in full leaf, were illuminated by shafts of morning sun – conditions that were ideal for the canine investigation of grass and shrub and the analysis of the scents left behind by the night. Some of these were intriguing, some – especially those left by squirrels, or worse still, cats – were simply irritating, an affront to any dog whose ambition was the ethnic cleansing of all felines.

These matters settled, Cyril returned to his master and to his leash. Then the two of them left the gardens and returned to the flat for breakfast. For Cyril this was a small bowl of reconstituted dog meal; for Angus it was eggs and bacon and a croissant, consumed while reading the copy of *The Scotsman* pushed through the letterbox by the paper boy. Angus read the letters column first, and was always pleased to read the contributions of the regulars. For the most part, these were people with causes, who were always primed and ready to sound off about their favourite issue. The letters column, not only of *The Scotsman* but of the other papers too, was the true national conversation of Scotland, Angus thought. The *Oban Times* and the *Press and Journal* were exactly the same; throughout the country there were people who were of the strong view that things were not quite right, and that this was the fault of others, who were then identified and shamed. The solution, of course, was simple, but for some reason had not been grasped by the Scottish Parliament, Argyll and Bute Council, or Aberdeen City Council. Would these bodies never learn? And then there were the bankers. They were clearly incapable of learning, and were simply laughing at the rest of us on their way to the bank . . . No, they were already in the bank.

The letter column digested, Angus turned to the obituaries. This page gave him the greatest pleasure, but it was not out of Schadenfreude. Angus was not one of those who read the obituaries with satisfaction at having outlived their subjects; he read them with a sense of proper awe at what people managed to make of their lives. What impressed him most of all were those lives that demonstrated a sense of purpose. Most of us, he thought, led lives that happened to us. We drifted into what we did; we fumbled our way past the challenges and obstacles we encountered; we took up one thing, dropped another; and then, rather too suddenly for most of us, the realisation came that it was almost over, and what exactly had we done with our time? These people were not like that. They decided at a very young age what they wanted to do, and they then did it, step by step. They often met their spouse early, and then married her, or him, and the marriage itself had structure and purpose, and was happy – perhaps for these very reasons. They built a metaphorical house for themselves and then lived in it. It was undeniably impressive.

Of course purpose and pattern in a life did not have to be conscious. There were many lives, Angus thought, that revealed a pattern when one looked at them at the end, even if the people living those lives may not have seen that pattern while they were actually leading their lives. People did the things they were destined to do without having any real sense of that destiny. But when their lives were laid out it became apparent where they were heading; it became clear why they had made the choices they did. And then, at last, some dignity is given to what might have seemed to be an aimless or dull existence, to what might have been seen as not much of a life.

And of course we should remember, he told himself, that the small life, the humble life, is as wonderful, in its way, as any grand life of achievement and public recognition. He knew a man who had never been much of a success in his work, who had held a succession of small jobs and then no job at all, but who had been a great one for his doos, as he called them, his doves, and had raised dynasties of beautiful white birds in his patch of back garden in what had been an old mining village in East Lothian. That gave his life as much dignity as any of the public lives lauded in the bigger obituaries. He was appreciated by his friends, who came to see the doves and marvelled at their whiteness and their fluttering shyness, their gentle cooing, the way they flew up in the air, hovered, and then on silent wings were gone.

47. *A Letter from Italy*

Angus Lordie's reading of the paper was interrupted on some, but not all, mornings by the arrival of the post. There were days on which he received nothing; he wrote few letters and received hardly any in return – rough justice that he fully accepted. While there were those who complained about their uninteresting or slender mailbag, little under-standing that by and large we get the mailbag we deserve, Angus never blamed anybody but himself for the fact that nobody wrote to him. On this particular morning, though, be-sandalled Hermes smiled upon him: a few days earlier Angus had written to Antonia, and now here was a letter addressed to Angus Lordie DA (Edin), Drummond Place, Edinburgh, Scozia. Angus smiled at the formal inclusion of his ancient qualification; that was Italy already exerting its influence on Antonia – the Italians were punctilious about titles, with any graduate, or indeed anybody who wore glasses, being accorded the title dottore; while a professor was Chiarissimo (most renowned one) or, if the dean of a faculty, Amplissimo (most ample one). Angus was content that he should be a simple Diplomate in Art, enough, he thought, for any painter; further honours and distinctions, he felt, would merely clutter his work, weigh down his brush.

He slit open the envelope and extracted several pages of thick cream-coloured paper. Antonia's handwriting, a small neat script, covered these pages, and for a moment or two Angus felt daunted, almost to the point of being unable to read what she had written. Antonia could go on, especially on the subject of early Scottish saints, and he was not sure that he was quite in the mood for that. But then he reminded himself that he had initiated the correspondence and the least he could do was to read her reply.

The letter was headed The Convent of Sant' Annetta dei Fiori. Underneath this, Antonia had written the date in Roman numerals, followed by the salutation "My dear Angus." Me, thought Angus; and read on.

"Your letter was a very pleasant surprise, as I had not expected to hear from you, although, as you know, there has been correspondence between me and Domenica. It gives me the pretext to say one or two things that I should have said some time ago, and never said. I shall deal with these and then go on to answer your question about that painting in my flat. That will be later, though, at the end of this letter. I tell you this now so that you should not read what I have to say with the irritation of one who feels that his question will go unanswered. I shall answer, I assure you.

"What happened to me in Florence was, as you know, somewhat distressing, not the least for you, I imagine. I had no idea that visiting Tuscany was so dangerous – and who could be expected to anticipate the sudden onset of Stendhal Syndrome? Looking back on it, of course, I can now see the signs that were there well before I collapsed in the Uffizi Gallery and was taken away so ignominiously. On reflection I can recall feeling slightly queasy two days earlier when I was paging through Gombrich, or was it Kenneth Clark, or somebody else altogether, and saw that photograph of Donatello's *David*. At the time I thought it might have been the fig tart I had bought in Montalcino, but now I know that it was the first warning of Stendhal Syndrome.

"Since my diagnosis, I have done quite a bit of reading about the condition and I must say that I have been astonished to discover how distinguished is the company in which I find myself! If one has to have a medical condition, then I suppose it can be a comfort to know that it is a condition that has laid low such distinguished people! Of course, Stendhal Syndrome would not be expected to affect just anybody: one has to be attuned to the artistic possibilities of a situation before one can be overcome and suffer emotional collapse. A person with no imagination or with no interest in matters artistic or spiritual will hardly be expected to succumb to extreme emotion in the face of great art: such a person will usually be quite indifferent to these matters.

"It's a very curious thing, Angus, but I have no memory at all of being in the gallery. Oh yes, I know I was there – I was told by the doctors in the hospital that I had been brought in from the Uffizi, and that this fact was of immediate relevance to their diagnosis. But for me that day remains largely blank. I think I remember breakfast, and I do remember being in the Piazza della Signoria, but apart from that . . . well, I'm afraid my memory provides no promptings.

"One of the doctors had a special interest in Stendhal Syndrome and he told me that amnesia of this sort is relatively rare in this condition. He felt that this meant that I had been in some sort of dissociative state as well. That interested me, and I read a bit about that too. Apparently we all experience dissociative states of some degree or other, and may have no recollection of what we did in that state. That's interesting, isn't it? I suppose most of us have no special name for it – we just know that we haven't been there, so to speak. I sometimes found that when I was writing about my early Scottish saints; or when driving and my mind wandered. I also remember being in Jenners once and suddenly thinking, My goodness, how did I get here?

"They were very kind to me in the psychiatric hospital in Florence. I was put in a ward with three other women, two of whom had visits twice a day from various members of their family. One of the women was the wife of a farmer, and her people brought in great baskets of fruit and large salamis virtually every time they came in. They insisted on my sharing this – the Italians are naturally so generous – and so I was always well provided with treats of every description. This helped my recovery, I believe, and certainly the doctors took that view. I lay in bed, looking out of the window, grapes and olives and garlic salami on the table at my side. Why return to Scotland when one is in that position? Would one ever get that at home? Does the National Health Service ever do olives – even for clearly therapeutic purposes?"

48. *The Scottish Male Psyche Laid Bare*

Angus turned the page of the letter.

"As you know," Antonia continued, "I was not in hospital all that long, but I had plenty of time to think. I must admit – and I hope that you will not mind my mentioning this – that I felt quite resentful of both you and Domenica. The whole idea of going to Italy was mine, after all, and yet it seemed to me that you excluded me more or less from the time we left Edinburgh Airport. And then, whenever I said anything, Domenica pretended not to hear – have you any idea how painful that was for me? Men sometimes don't pick these things up; they pretend to themselves that everything is fine even when there is a real atmosphere. I'm not blaming you for that; you are a man and can't help being a man . . . No, I shouldn't say that because I'm not sure if that's what I really believe. We are not trapped by gender to the extent that some people say we are; we can transcend all that and be people, simpliciter. (I like that word by the way, Angus; we had a teacher at school who misused it all the time to prevent any discussion of a rule. You will not do that, simpliciter. It somehow worked, and cut off any talking back. Simpliciter.) So the fact that you are a man is no real excuse for insensitivity to the feelings of others; we must all work to develop awareness of others; it is part of our necessary moral effort that we should make ourselves capable of sympathy. Too many men luxuriate in being men; they deliberately exclude the possibility of sensitivity and strike superficial attitudes. They close themselves off.

"Poor men! Have you noticed, Angus, how this all goes very deep in Scotland? The Scottish male psyche is a poor wounded creature, made to pretend to be tough, to pretend not to have feelings that are perfectly natural, human feelings. Do you know something, Angus, I had an extraordinary moment of insight while I was in hospital and thinking of home. It suddenly occurred to me that the Scottish male was not really interested in football! Yes, I know it sounds absurd, almost counterintuitive, but I think it really may be true. Football is what they feel they must be interested in because it is expected of them. They become involved in football through fear: fear of being excluded from the male group, fear of being thought to be insufficiently masculine, fear of being thought to be too interested in any of the things that men are not meant to be interested in.

"And all the time, inside himself, the Scots male is crying, Angus. He's crying for the hard, demanding world he's created for himself; he's crying for the softness and love that he, like all of us poor vulnerable creatures, needs and craves; he's crying for the fact that he knows he has a soul – somewhere beneath all that unhealthy food and beer and cigarettes and hardness – somewhere there, under all those accretions of crippling toughness, he has a soul – and yet that soul is not allowed to blossom, is thwarted, is made to be something other than what it is.

"If I had the time and the energy, Angus, I would make it my mission to release the Scottish male from this awful prison he has made for himself. I would blow apart the walls that have been built around him; I would kiss him gently, I would try to bring him the comfort that he so desperately yearns for but that has been denied him, for generation upon generation. Oh, I would do that, Angus, I would take it as my holiest of duties to do that for Scotland.

"But I digress. You must have seen that I was upset by being excluded from the intimacy that you and Domenica appeared to have, and yet you did nothing about it. I felt real resentment that you did this, but I forgive you, Angus, and I shall not reproach you any more for that. As I lay there thinking, recovering from my episode of Stendhal Syndrome, I realised that I had no real reason to expect sympathy from others, including you and Domenica. What bound us together? What created any obligation on your part to do anything for me, let alone to feel anything for me? Friendship? Well, that raises interesting questions, doesn't it?" Is the mere fact of being the friend of somebody else sufficient to constitute the obligation to do something for her? I'm not sure that it does. And it certainly creates no duty to feel for the person who claims to be your friend. Friendship as an institution can hardly create feeling; that, surely has to come from within.

"I looked about me. There I was in that hospital ward with my fellow patients and the salami-bearing members of their families who drifted in and out. I had no bonds of any nature with those people, other than those created by the fact that I happened to be there in the same room as they were. But why should that create a bond? Do we have a bond with the people we find ourselves sitting in the same bus with, or in the same railway carriage? Having raised these examples, I realise that they rather work against what I was trying to say. I think we do have some sort of morally significant relationship with them, even if a very attenuated one. Imagine yourself in the train to Glasgow, Angus, and for some reason it stops. You look at the faces of your fellow passengers and you smile stoically. A man glances anxiously at his watch and you catch his eye. You

We're all in the same boat together

shrug your shoulders, as if to say, What can one do? And he smiles back. You have established contact; there is something between all of you in that carriage. It is there, just glimpsed – a sense of being connected in some way. And that, perhaps, is what lies behind the old adage, We're all in the same boat together. Exactly! We are, aren't we; we're all in the same boat together, even if for much of the time we don't want to admit it. We want to pretend, I suppose, that our own boat is not sinking quite as fast as the boats of others.

"But enough of boats and railway carriages, Angus: let me tell you about the nuns."

49. *On Being in the Right Place*

"The doctors were extremely kind," Antonia continued. "One of them had trained briefly in Glasgow and was full of questions about the Byres Road, for some reason, and about a family called Mactavish, with whom he had stayed and whom he assumed I knew. But he was well-meaning and did everything he could to ensure that I was looked after properly. He brought me books in English although he was careful not to bring anything to do with art; an understandable reticence, I suppose, bearing in mind the nature of my condition. Nor did he bring me anything by Stendhal – that would have been extremely tactless, don't you think?

"Eventually they decided that I was fit enough to be transferred into the country for a period of recuperation. I felt quite well enough to leave altogether, but they were insistent. I was told that there could be a relapse if I was not careful. They mentioned a patient, a German woman, who had been discharged from hospital after only two days, apparently quite recovered, but who had then unwisely visited the Pitti Palace and had created a terrible scene in front of *The Martyrdom of Saint Agatha* by Sebastiano del Piombo. She had to be readmitted to hospital and eventually spent a further three weeks there. They did not want this to happen to me, they said, even though it would be a positive delight, they assured me, to have me in their hospital for a longer period. They are so polite, the Italians.

"They proposed that I should go to a convent in the Sienese hills. This was run by nuns who had taken a number of women who had gone down with Stendhal Syndrome, and who had all recovered very well in the care of the sisters. I explained to them that I was not a Catholic, but they said that this did not matter at all. The nuns had never turned anybody away and I would not be expected to participate in their religious activities.

"I was given no choice, really. It's not that I was a prisoner – they made it quite clear that I was not a compulsorily detained patient, and that I was free to walk out at any time. But they did rather cajole me into accepting their offer, and I must say that I'm very glad that they did.

"So I packed my things and said goodbye to my fellow patients in the ward. One of the other women started to weep when I told her that I was leaving; she wept copiously until a nurse appeared and calmed her down. The others all gave me presents: more salami, more olives, more dried figs. Then I was led out and put into a small van driven by a man in a white coat. This man insisted on practising his English throughout the drive, and I heard all about his history. He was from a village in the south, he said, and he was very pleased to shake the dust of his birthplace off his heels. I know very little about places like that, I'm afraid, other than that wonderful Carlo Levi novel – you know the one, Angus, the one in which the doctor is exiled by the fascists and finds himself in some awful godforsaken place where the local brass band had marched over a cliff by mistake and could still be heard playing . . . They're terribly superstitious down there, I believe.

"Then I heard all about his mother-in-law who, he says, is an incorrigible fraudster but will never serve any time in prison because the justice system is so slow. He says that she is very aware of this and continues with her frauds in the sure and certain knowledge that by the time they start her trial the offences will be prescribed by some sort of limitation period. Very odd. But he simply shrugged and said, 'That is how this country is. You can do anything – anything – you like. And people do. All the time.'

"His English was very good, and I complimented him on it. He was pleased, and revealed that he was now learning German, so that he could go to Germany and get work as a driver. He had a cousin who had done just that; he had been the hospital driver in charge of driving the more dangerous and deluded patients. He was now back in Italy, and was driving a prominent Italian politician around. There is no difference, he said. The skills are the same.

"And so this conversation continued until we turned off the main road and started to make our way along a small local road. There were farmhouses dotted around here and there, and lines of trees on the brows of hills. You know those lines of cypresses that the Italians like so much? I always feel that they had been put there with an eye to their inclusion in a painting. And isn't that an attractive idea, Angus, that you, as an artist, should approve of wholeheartedly – that farmers should think of artists and design their landscape accordingly? Can you see that happening in contemporary Britain?

"Eventually we arrived at the convent. It is at the foot of a hill – one of those small hills that rise up in the Tuscan countryside like anthills. On the hilltop itself there is a village, a cluster of houses and a fourteenth-century church; down below there are fields, vineyards, groves of trees, thick tangles of brushwood. The convent itself is a large building, but not at all daunting. It looks like a very big farmhouse, in fact; a farmhouse that has been allowed to ramble over the centuries and has built additions to itself. It has ochre walls and a red-tiled roof. It sits in the countryside with that perfect assurance that good buildings have. You can tell a good building when you see it, can't you? It's in the right place – just the right place for it.

"And that, Angus, is the most important thing, don't you think? Whether for a building, or a person: to be in the right place."

50. A Trip to Glasgow Is Planned

Bertie received no telephone call from Ranald Braveheart Macpherson that Saturday, nor did he get one on Sunday. Ranald had promised to let him know whether there had been any response to the adoption advertisement he had placed on eBay, but either there had been none, or Ranald had forgotten his promise. Bertie thought the latter explanation more likely: people promised things freely and rarely, in his experience, delivered on these promises.

Tofu was the worst offender when it came to broken promises, Bertie thought, with Olive and Pansy close contenders for second place. Tofu also told lies, not only about himself, but about others, and took a particular delight in baiting Olive with reports he claimed to have heard on the imminent arrest of her father for theft and of her mother for speeding.

"My dad knows a policeman," he announced one day while the children were in the playground. "And he says they're just building up their case. They're almost there, but not quite."

Olive looked at him suspiciously. "The police know all about you," she said dismissively. "They're going to get you, Tofu. Everybody knows that, don't they?"

Pansy and Lakshmi nodded sagely, Pansy shaking her finger sternly at Tofu and adding her own prediction. "They're going to send you to Polmont, Tofu. Have you heard of it? It's the place they send boys like you. Really bad boys." She paused. "Many of them from Glasgow."

Tofu was not cowed. "Oh yes? Well let me tell you something, Olive. The police have been watching your mum and dad for ages. Ages. That's what my dad's friend said. He said they've seen your dad pinching things and they know where he keeps them. And they've got tons of photos from those camera things showing your mum driving through red lights and going really fast. They're going to send them both to prison really soon. And you know where? Glasgow! That means you'll never see them again."

Olive struggled to deal with this information. She bit her lip. "That's not true, Tofu, and you know it."

Tofu smirked. "But it is true, Olive. It's really sad, and I feel very sorry for you. But there are some things you can't hide from. And that's one of them. Sorry about that."

This was too much for Olive, who started to wail before she, Pansy, and Lakshmi all ran off to knock on the door of the staffroom and report the incident.

"You shouldn't tell fibs, Tofu," said Bertie. "Even to Olive."

Tofu laughed insouciantly. "Why not?" he said.

Bertie thought for a moment. Why should one not tell fibs? Because . . . because it was wrong. But why were things wrong? Was it because grown-ups told you that it was wrong? But then some grown-ups were themselves wrong about so many things – look at poor Dr. Fairbairn, who had had no idea at all about what was what. Because God told you? That provided better authority, perhaps, but if God felt so strongly about fibs, then why had he not punished Tofu for all the lies he had told? It would be easy for Tofu to be struck by lightning, but Bertie had never seen anybody struck by lightning, not once – not even close to it. And that was in the face of a whole lot of unpunished, unrepudiated fibs, told, it would seem, by everybody; a whole forest of mendacity, stretching out almost as far as Aberdeen – fib after fib . . .

Ranald Braveheart Macpherson was, Bertie believed, more reliable than Tofu, but Bertie was upset by his failure to phone and told him so when he next met him at cub scouts some days later.

"It's not my fault at all," said Ranald. "I can't reach the phone at home, Bertie. It's too high. Sorry."

Bertie was unimpressed with this explanation. "You could stand on a chair, Ranald."

Ranald Braveheart Macpherson shook his head. "No, I can't stand on chairs. Health and safety, Bertie. Sorry. But I did check on the computer. I did do that."

Bertie held his breath. "And had anybody replied?"

Ranald Braveheart Macpherson shook his head. "No. Bad luck, Bertie. They'd removed the advertisement."

Bertie frowned. "Why should they do that?"

Ranald explained that eBay watched the things that

people tried to sell. "You can't sell guns or tanks on eBay," he said. "There are loads of people who'd like to do that sort of thing, but they're not allowed. It's health and safety, Bertie."

Bertie sighed. "Well, thanks anyway, Ranald."

Ranald looked at his friend with sympathy. He was a helpful boy, and he did not like the idea of Bertie being disappointed. "But I did find something out for you, Bertie. I typed adoption and Scotland into the computer and it gave me an address. I wrote it down for you. Here."

Ranald Braveheart Macpherson was in the course of passing a slip of paper to Bertie when the cub scout leader, Akela, spotted him.

"And what have we here, Ranald?" she asked. "Is this a new game you and Bertie have invented?"

Olive, who had been hovering nearby, decided to intervene. "They must be planning something, Akela," she said. "You'd better take it off him and read it out."

Akela looked at Olive. "It might be private, Olive," she said.

"Yes," said Tofu. "You can't stick your nose into everything, Olive."

"Now, then, Tofu," said Akela. "There's no call to speak in quite that way. But Tofu does have a point, Olive." She turned to Bertie. "You do know, Bertie, that it's rude to whisper or pass notes when other people are around. You do know that, don't you?"

Bertie nodded. "It's not an important note, Akela."

"Well, we'll leave it at that," said Akela. "Come now, boys and girls, time for Kim's Game!"

Bertie, relieved at this turn of events, glanced at the contents of the note. Ranald had written an address, followed by a telephone number.

"I'll come with you, Bertie," whispered Ranald. "I've found out the combination to my dad's safe, so I can get the money for the train tickets from there. That place is in Glasgow. We'll go together."

Bertie nodded. "When?"

"Tomorrow," said Ranald. "We'll miss school and go tomorrow."

"Great," said Bertie. "But don't tell anybody."

"Cross my heart," said Ranald Braveheart Macpherson.

Olive was watching. They were up to something, she thought. You could always tell with boys. They were always up to something, as all girls knew – deep in their hearts, they knew it.

51. *Domenica's Visitor*

When he arrived at Antonia's door, Magnus Campbell had the look of a guest who was unlikely to outstay his welcome. Guests who arrive at the head of a camel-train of luggage cause a momentary sinking of the heart: Are they planning to stay for weeks; or months perhaps; or even years? Are they planning to move in permanently? That has been known to happen; some guests have married their hosts, or their host's sons or daughters, and never gone away again. That is rare, but it has happened. It is also very impolite. Any etiquette book will advise against making any form of romantic or sexual advance towards the people with whom you are staying, especially shortly after your arrival. It is not a question of bourgeois inhibition: it is definitely rude. It is also slightly bad form for the soldiers of occupying forces to marry local women during the course of the military occupation. This can be a problem in those countries where the men are so clearly undesirable that local women will marry anybody, even invading forces, rather than marry one of their compatriots.

Of course, people also change their plans and stay rather longer than they intended. There is a curious phenomenon, more or less restricted to Scotland, of football supporters going to an away match in a foreign country and never returning. This has happened a great deal in Spain, where there are thought to be several thousand Scottish football supporters who have lived there for years after following Scotland's football team to a match in Madrid or Barcelona, or some such place. These men marry Spanish women the day after the match, or sometimes on the day itself, and are immediately assumed into rambling Spanish families, to which they contribute the genes for red hair and a fondness for alcohol. Many of these men retain a vague memory of having come from somewhere else, and will occasionally refer, with a certain degree of nostalgic longing, to a dear, green place somewhere to the north, but that recollection will in due course fade.

dear, green place

Magnus Campbell's intention not to stay too long was made evident by the size of his case – a smallish weekend bag into which not much more than a single change of clothes might be packed. With this modest holdall in his hands, he peered at the notice that Domenica had pinned to Antonia's door. Hesitating for barely a moment, he turned round and crossed the landing to press the neighbouring doorbell. Domenica, who had heard his footsteps on the stair, stood well back in her hall: one never knew when people might take it upon themselves to peer through the letterbox and it would never do to be found standing on the other side in anticipation.

She counted to five before she moved forward to open the door. And then, with trembling hand it was done; the door was opened to the man she had loved so intensely – so giddily – all those years ago.

There was no doubt but that Magnus Campbell realised who she was. There was a split second – not much more than that – as his mind went through the process of recognition; a split second during which his expression moved from surprise to pleasure.

"Domenica!"

She smiled at him coyly. She was nineteen again. "I hope this isn't too much of a shock."

He shook his head. "A shock? Not at all . . ." He put down his bag and in a single movement, one that seemed utterly natural and appropriate, he leant forward to embrace and kiss her on both cheeks.

She felt his hands upon her shoulders, and she shivered. I hope he didn't feel that. She pulled herself together. "Come in. Don't stand there. Antonia's . . ."

He looked at her anxiously. "Antonia's all right, I take it?"

Domenica reassured him. "She's absolutely all right. Very all right, if that makes sense."

He looked relieved. "I wondered. She hadn't replied to my card and it crossed my mind that . . ."

"One always thinks the worst. But no, Antonia is perfectly fine." She added, "Now."

Magnus frowned. "She's been ill?"

Domenica nodded.

"Nothing serious, I hope."

Domenica hesitated. She was not sure if Antonia would want everybody to know about her condition, but Magnus must be a reasonably close friend of hers if he was coming to stay. "Stendhal Syndrome," she said.

His hand went to his mouth. "Oh no . . ."

"But she's made a good recovery," Domenica went on. "And now she's . . . well, she's in a nunnery."

Magnus stared at her. "Permanently?"

"I believe so." Domenica gestured for him to follow her into the kitchen, where she had prepared a cafetière of coffee. "Leave your bag in the hall," she said. "I'll unlock Antonia's place in a moment. Coffee?"

He accepted, and they sat down at the scrubbed pine table. Domenica took the opportunity to glance at Magnus appraisingly. He had not changed a great deal, or not so much that she would have failed to recognise him. If anything, she thought, he is more handsome. The years had added dignity, she decided, and that curious, almost undefinable quality – gravitas. It became him.

He was looking at her too, and smiling. "This is extraordinary," he mused. "That you and Antonia should live next door to one another. Two of my oldest friends."

I'm more than that, thought Domenica. Or am I? The status of a former lover may be complicated; some former lovers might be enemies, others could be friends, but, if they were friends, they were surely a special class of friends. And how long, she wondered, did friends remain friends if they barely saw one another for years? Was friendship something that lasted forever, as family relationships do, or could it wither on the vine?

She looked at his hands. The skin was brown, and smooth. They were not the hands of one who spent all his time indoors, she thought; and yet he worked in the City of London . . . London hands. It was a strange notion; hands that took on the characteristics of the place they lived.

He noticed the direction of her glance. "I've caught the sun."

She looked away guiltily.

"I'm not in London any more," he said. "I go there, of course, from time to time. Last week, in fact. But I'm back in Scotland now."

"Good." The word came out without her thinking about it.

He smiled. "And it's good that you're here too."

She caught her breath. They understood one another perfectly.

52. *What About You?*

Domenica poured a cup of coffee for Magnus Campbell and passed it to him across the table.

"So," she said, trying to sound as matter-of-fact as she could. "So you've finished with London?"

He reached out for the coffee. "Thank you. Yes, I did

twenty years there. It all went . . . well, I suppose I have to say it went rather well."

"You don't need to apologise for that."

He blew across the steaming surface of his coffee. "Don't I? I suppose not. It's just that doing well in the financial world is regarded as somewhat suspect these days, isn't it?"

"Possibly," said Domenica. "But not always."

"Some people think it's little better than being a confidence trickster." He saw her expression of amusement. "They do, you know. I had somebody spit on me in the street once."

"Actually spit?"

"Yes. There was some sort of demonstration in London and I happened to be walking past. A young man came up to me and spat at me. It smelled of tobacco."

Domenica wrinkled her nose in disgust. "Why did he pick on you?"

"The clothes I was wearing, I suppose. A suit. The City. He put two and two together."

"How unpleasant."

Magnus nodded. "It was. Though curiously enough, I didn't feel any anger towards him. I found myself imagining what I might have felt had I been in his position."

"How tolerant of you."

"Not really. It's a simple expedient, I think. Put yourself in the shoes of another and an awful lot makes sense. There he was with no money – I assume that he had no money. Living off others effectively – as a student, perhaps, or on benefits."

Domenica raised an eyebrow. To describe somebody else as living off others was extreme. Not everybody can work, she found herself thinking, and what did bankers or financiers do but live off the efforts of others?

Magnus smiled. "Don't draw the wrong conclusions," he said. "I don't use the expression living off others pejoratively. But it is a reality, isn't it? Lots of people live on the charity of others and do you know what they feel about it? Not gratitude, I can assure you. They feel hostility."

She was not sure about that. Living in India, as Domenica had done, taught one something about charity and giving. "I don't know," she said. "In India there are millions of people who survive on the gifts of others. It's quite normal, and they don't resent it."

Magnus thought for a moment. "India? Of course you lived there, didn't you? You were married – I'd forgotten that."

"I was. I was Mrs. Varghese, for a time. We lived in the south, in Kerala. That's where his family came from."

He hesitated. "Do you mind if I ask what happened?"

She assured him that she did not object to the question. "My husband's family had a small electricity generating station near what was then Cochin. They called it their electricity factory. I know that sounds odd, but that's how they made their living. They had one or two other things, of course: a spice plantation in the Western Ghats and a pepper trading firm – a small-scale business empire, I suppose."

He waited for her to continue.

"My husband had an accident," Domenica went on. "He was electrocuted in the factory."

"I'm terribly sorry to hear that."

Domenica nodded. "Thank you. It was a long time ago now and I hardly ever think about it any more. Although sometimes I must admit I dream that I'm back there and I'm standing in the garden of the electricity factory – it had a wonderful garden, you know. Courting couples used to use it for assignations. I didn't mind, although my mother-in-law became livid when she saw that happening and would set dogs on them." She paused. "How many romances that woman must have blighted."

"No love lost?"

Domenica shook her head. "She never accepted me. I was not what she had had in mind."

"Wrong religion?" Magnus asked.

"Not in broad terms. They were Thomist Christians. As you know, Kerala is a fairly Christian state. They have other faiths, of course – including Marxism: the state government is communist – and you find busts of Karl Marx along some of the roadsides, along with Hindu temples and Christian shrines."

"India is astonishing."

Domenica laughed. "That's putting it mildly. It's such a mixture. But alongside everything else – all those wonderful spiritual traditions – there are these people in the south who claim that Christianity started there before it took root in the west. They call themselves Syrians – nothing to do with modern Syria, of course. They used Syriac as their liturgical language, you see."

Magnus sipped at his coffee. "They were disappointed you weren't a Syrian?"

"Yes. Not that they said anything about it, but I knew that my mother-in-law would never accept me. Mind you, that's not unusual, is it? An awful lot of mothers-in-law don't take to the woman their son marries. D.H. Lawrence had something to say about that, I think."

"Did he?"

Domenica laughed. "Possibly. He loved those dark corners of human relationships. I can't be bothered to read him nowadays. I think his prose has dated a bit – rather like Hemingway's. Hemingway sounds positively Old Testament at times."

He sighed, and she asked him if there was something wrong.

"No," he said. "Nothing's wrong at all. It's just that this conversation – with you talking about Lawrence and Hemingway and so on – reminds me so much of how we used to talk . . . back then. We discussed exactly these things, didn't we?"

They did, and Domenica acknowledged it. But even that acknowledgment, she felt, was taking her into territory from which she felt she must at all costs keep clear. She wanted to reach across the table and take Magnus's hand, but she could not. One cannot touch a person one loved in that way; it was far too dangerous.

For a few moments neither spoke. Then Domenica said, "I've been talking about myself. Forgive me. What about you?" She wanted to ask him whether he was married, but she held herself back. He knew, though, that this is what she wanted to find out; he knew, and he answered.

53. *On Teak, and Boyfriends, etc.*

"I never married," Magnus Campbell said. "I'd fully intended to, but kept putting it off. I suppose I was too busy." He looked at Domenica apologetically. "That sounds dreadful, doesn't it? Being too busy to get married."

Domenica's expression gave nothing away. "It's not for everyone," she said evenly. "And as for being too busy to get married – there are plenty of people who are too busy to live, let alone get married. They spend their lives working and then suddenly . . . But as for marriage, it's not compulsory. Lots of people are content to live by themselves."

"Oh, I'm sure I would have enjoyed it," said Magnus. "I'm not one of those crusty bachelors who would never make all the compromises that marriage involves – you know the sort."

Domenica tried not to think of Angus, but he came to mind immediately. "Was there anybody in particular?"

"Oh yes. In London I was with somebody for six years. She was a lawyer with one of the big firms. She was very successful, as it happens, and was one of the youngest partners. But you know what those London legal firms are like . . . they take their pound of flesh, and then some. They wanted her to go to Hong Kong to take charge of their office there. It was a big job."

"And?"

"She went. She had to choose between me and her career, and, well, she chose the career."

Domenica thought: How could she? "You were probably better off without her." She stopped; Magnus was frowning.

"I was very much in love with her," he said. "But I suppose it was not entirely reciprocated. Had it been, then she wouldn't have gone to Hong Kong, don't you think?"

"I do," said Domenica quickly. "But you obviously survived."

He nodded. "Actually, I fell out of love with her remarkably quickly. It took about three weeks – an almost indecently short time. I suddenly realised that I no longer loved her. It happened just like that." He paused. "And I'm not even sure whether I even liked her after that."

Domenica was thinking of the lawyer. Had she been in love with Magnus? It was inconceivable to her that anybody could prefer a career to happiness with somebody they loved. But people did.

"This happened not all that long ago," Magnus continued. "In fact, it was last year – last March to be precise. It pushed me into making a decision."

"About?"

"About my own career. I had made quite a bit of money in the City. It isn't hard, you know. They try to tell us that they're so skilled – it allows them to justify their inflated salaries. A certain amount of intelligence is required – and a head for figures – but not much more than that. A skilled craftsman needs more ability than a financier, if you ask me. But we don't reward the craftsman or the engineer in quite the same way, do we?"

Domenica's interest was aroused. "Well, let's say that I'm an ambitious young person and I want to make a lot of money. Can I just traipse off to the City of London and get a job? How do they hand them out?"

"Connections," said Magnus. "Not in every case, but in a very large number of cases."

"Oh?"

"Yes. But that's all behind me. I shook the dust of the City from my heels and came back here. I bought a house near Mallaig. And a boat."

Domenica stared at him. "Mallaig. We . . ."

"Yes," he said simply. "Yes, Mallaig. I remember."

She looked down at the floor. Her heart was doing something peculiar within her; racing, or straining at its moorings, or simply trying to cope.

"Would you like to hear about the boat?"

She nodded. "I don't know much about boats. But I had a cousin who sailed . . ."

Magnus interrupted her. "She's a gorgeous piece of

work. Forty feet. Lots of teak. In fact, the whole deck is covered in teak. And she's fabulous down below. Wood everywhere. Modern yachts are full of plastic. This is very different."

"Wood gives character, doesn't it?" Domenica felt embarrassed to say such a thing; it was rather like saying that books did furnish a room. But they did, just as wood really did lend character.

"It does," agreed Magnus. "But it requires upkeep. And teak has very particular requirements. It goes a silvery colour if you leave it exposed to the elements. If you want it to remain brown, you have to put a special sort of sealant on it. That keeps it."

"I see."

He had more to say about teak. "The great enemy of teak is dirt, you know. If you let teak get dirty, it's the Devil's job to get it off. So you wash teak down with seawater: teak likes to be scrubbed with seawater."

"I see."

Domenica wondered whether she had anything to say about teak; it was not a subject that she had paid much attention to, and Magnus seemed to know so much about it.

Magnus was looking at her again. There was something in his gaze – a look of affectionate interest, perhaps – that she found difficult to pinpoint. It was not in the slightest bit threatening – quite the opposite, in fact.

"Would you like to learn how to crew?"

His question was unexpected, but she answered immediately. "I'd love to."

"You sure?"

"Yes, I'd love to. I'm not sure if I'd be much good, but I could try."

He laughed. "It's not rocket science. Very few things are. In fact, I think that even rocket science isn't rocket science."

Domenica would have been amused at that had she not suddenly felt an almost overwhelming pang of guilt. *I've just agreed to go sailing with him. I'm an engaged woman and I've agreed to go sailing with a former boyfriend.* She closed her eyes. She had ruined everything. Rubicons had been crossed, boats burned, geese cooked – and metaphors mixed with all the enthusiasm with which Betty Crocker or Jamie Oliver might throw together the ingredients of a cake. *Why am I behaving like this?* she asked herself. *This is absurd.* But saying that made no difference; she was too far gone to be capable of controlling herself. And had there been a Greek chorus, its refrain would have been obvious: a few well-chosen lines on the foolishness of middle-aged women, whatever their pretensions to self-control, in the presence of one who beguiled them in the past and still does.

54. *Domenica Comes Clean*

"I'm sorry," said Magnus Campbell. "I'm sorry, but I feel a bit . . . well, a bit uneasy about staying in Antonia's flat while she's not there."

He made this remark when Domenica said that she would unlock Antonia's door and get him settled next door.

"But she did invite you," said Domenica. "It's not as if you're staying there uninvited."

"Yes. But that was some time ago. She must have forgotten that I was coming."

Domenica felt that this did not negate the invitation. Antonia had had a lot on her mind and bearing in mind that she had been suffering from Stendhal Syndrome she might be forgiven for forgetting social arrangements made back home in Scotland. Quite apart from that, Antonia had specifically asked her to take charge of her flat, and surely this would include permission to admit guests, forgotten or otherwise.

Magnus listened to these arguments, but made it clear that he still felt awkward. "I just feel that it would be an intrusion," he said.

Domenica thought for a moment. There was her spare bedroom; she could invite him to occupy that. It was an attractive possibility, but she had already been rash in accepting his invitation to go sailing; now she was about to ask him to stay with her.

"You could stay here," she said slowly. "I've got a spare room."

It was very curious: the voice that spoke was not, she thought, her own. The words were uttered by her but they were not her words, or at least not the words of that rational and cautious self that should have been in control of what she said. Should have been in control . . .

Magnus hesitated, but only very briefly. "Are you sure? I wouldn't want to impose . . ."

She shook her head. "It would not be an imposition."

"Then let me take you out for dinner tonight," he said. "I'll feel better if you didn't have to cook. We could go out to one of those fish places in Leith. I've read all about them."

She looked away. There were lines going through her head – the lines of a simple childhood ditty with which she had been admonished as a girl. Oh, what a tangled web we weave, when first we practise to deceive. For deceive, she thought, substitute fail to reveal. It was absolutely right, she decided, as so much of that folk wisdom was. She drew in her breath. "Look, Magnus, there's something I haven't told you. I should have mentioned it at the outset."

He smiled. "You're on a diet? Is that it? Well, we can go to Henderson's Salad Table or somewhere like that."

He was not going to make it any easier. "No," she persisted. "It's more serious than that."

He looked suddenly concerned. "You're not ill, are you, Domenica?"

"No, I'm engaged."

The words hung in the air between them. He said nothing for a while, but then, somewhat tentatively: "Engaged?"

"Yes. Angus Lordie and I are engaged to marry. We became engaged in Italy. He's an artist – principally a portrait painter. He has a studio in Drummond Place." She added this last bit of information lamely, as if having a studio in Drummond Place might somehow soften the blow for a rival.

She could see that he was struggling with his emotions. "I see."

"I hope that the news doesn't disappoint you."

He looked up. "Why should I be disappointed?"

She felt flustered. Had she presumed too much? Had the suggestion that she should go on his yacht been no more than a casual social invitation? Perhaps he needed a crew, and that was all.

He did not wait for an answer. "I assure you, Domenica, I'm delighted for you. This is very good news indeed."

She looked at him, and she could tell that he did not mean what he said. He was upset; she was sure of it.

"When are you going to get married?"

She replied that they had not yet alighted on a date, but that it would be soon enough. It would not be a particularly large wedding: neither of them wanted much of a fuss. She hoped that he might come if he was within reach of Edinburgh at the time. Of course he would, he replied.

"Do you still want me to stay?"

She was not sure what to say. She wanted him to stay, but she wondered what Angus would think. Angus was not a jealous man by nature, but surely any man would resent the presence under his fiancée's roof of a former boyfriend, particularly one who was not married.

"Perhaps we should think about . . ." She did not finish. There was knock on the door: the characteristic three, rather peremptory knocks that Angus gave. And then there was the sound of barking – the three, gruff barks that Cyril gave to echo his master's knocking.

"That's Angus now," she said. "You'll have the chance to meet him."

"Very nice," said Magnus.

Domenica went to let Angus in. "Magnus Campbell's arrived," she said. "Antonia's guest."

Angus bent forward to kiss her on the cheek. "Good." His skin felt rough and she wondered if he had bothered to shave. For a brief moment she had to suppress the urge to pull back from him, to make the exchange of kisses perfunctory, as kisses are between strangers.

They went back into the kitchen, where Magnus had now risen to his feet. Domenica introduced them and they shook hands.

"I believe I should say congratulations," said Magnus. "Domenica has been telling me about your engagement."

Angus glanced at Domenica. "I'm a very fortunate man," he muttered. Domenica looked away.

They sat down. Angus asked Magnus how he had come to know Antonia and listened to the explanation that one of his colleagues in the firm in London had been her first cousin. "We met at a dinner party," he said. "Antonia was visiting her cousin and we invited her around to our place while she was down there. Then we saw her virtually every year when she came down to London. Sometimes she stayed with us. She became very friendly with my partner, Shirley."

Shirley, thought Domenica. She had not expected that – not of a high-powered London lawyer. Claire, perhaps, or Margaret. And what was the nickname of that very famous woman lawyer – the divorce specialist who acted for the wives in all those high-profile split-ups? The Steel Magnolia – that was it. A very good nickname, she thought. One would not argue with a steel magnolia; or with a lawyer called The Undertaker or The Great White. Such soubriquets were very good for a legal reputation, she imagined.

Steel Magnolia

Pat's morning had begun inauspiciously. She had discovered at breakfast that somebody had eaten the last egg that she had stored in the fridge and had intended to boil for breakfast. It could only be one of two people; Pat was sharing the flat over the summer months with two young women she barely knew, her regular flatmates being away while the university was on vacation. Her temporary flatmates, Catriona and Lizzie, were both members of a drama group from Aberdeen that was going to be appearing in the Festival Fringe. They had come down for a month in advance to make the set and had responded to Pat's advertisement offering accommodation to nonsmokers, and those happy to muck in. Us, they had assured her eagerly: that's us.

On the whole they had been easy enough to live with, but the stolen egg was the third such incident in the space of a week and Pat was becoming annoyed.

"I think we should be careful to keep our food separate," she had said pointedly. "That way we won't mix it up."

"Absolutely," said Catriona. "Good idea."

But then Pat had noticed her cheese diminishing by half and, a day or two later, a half pound of butter and a packet of tagliatelle miraculously disappearing. She had said nothing; she did not want to accuse them of theft, not directly, but what other explanation could there be?

The disappearance of the egg was just too much to take, and she knocked on Lizzie's door to remonstrate with her. "An egg has gone missing," she said. "It was in the fridge and now it isn't. It's missing."

Lizzie stared at her. "So?"

Pat felt her heart racing. "Somebody's eaten it," she said. Lizzie shrugged. "Obviously. But it wasn't me." She turned to address Catriona, lying sprawled on a bed behind her. "Did you eat an egg?"

"No. Did you?"

"No." She paused, holding Pat's gaze. "Did you eat it yourself?"

"Of course I didn't. That's why I'm asking you."

"What about a friend? Those friends of yours who were here the other day – did one of them eat it maybe?"

Pat felt the back of her neck becoming warm. "Why would my friends eat an egg? And they were here ages ago. That egg was in the fridge yesterday. I saw it."

Lizzie frowned. "You think you saw it."

"What?"

"I said, you think you saw it. Sometimes we see what we want to see." She turned to Catriona. "You study psychology, don't you, Catriona? The mind can see things that aren't there, can't it?"

From within the room there came the reply. "Yes, sure. It does that all the time."

Pat bit her lip. "I'm going to eat some of your food," she muttered. "You just wait."

Later that morning, when she went over the road to Big Lou's, she narrated the story of this extraordinary exchange. "She stood there and denied it," she told Big Lou. "She flatly denied it."

Big Lou shook her head. "Folk lie," she said. "Just about everybody lies these days. I've come to expect it."

"I can't believe it," said Pat. "Why lie when you know that the other person knows you're lying? What's the point?"

Big Lou could provide no answer to that. "There was a fellow in Arbroath," she said. "He was called Davey – I forget his other name. But he was a real liar right enough, right from the time he was a wee boy. Lied and lied.

Everybody knew fine, of course, that he lied. He became a fisherman. He had an inshore boat that he took off in and fished from. He made an emergency call one day and said that he was in trouble off some rocks. One of the other boats picked it up."

Pat thought she could see what was coming. "And they didn't believe him? And he hit the rocks?"

Big Lou shook her head. "The call was picked up by one of the other fishing boats. They just laughed and ignored it. But it wasn't true anyway. He was fine."

"Oh," said Pat. "I thought that it was going to be like the story of the boy who cried wolf."

"No, it wasn't like that at all," said Big Lou. "Davey was fine."

Big Lou had been preparing Pat's coffee and now she served it, in a final flourish sprinkling the foamy white top with powdered chocolate.

Pat thanked her. She had not seen Lou since she had left her in the bar with Darren, and now she wanted to find out how the evening had gone.

"Your date, Lou?" she asked. "How did it go with Darren?"

"Nae bad," said Lou.

That was not very informative, and Pat asked another question. "And are you going to see him again?"

Big Lou seemed to think for a moment before she answered. "Aye, I'll see him again."

"Well, that's very nice, Lou. I hope . . ."

Pat did not finish. "Aye, he's asked me to a convention." Big Lou paused. "At Crieff Hydro."

Pat smiled. "That's nice, Lou. Crieff Hydro – we went there when I was twelve. I won the under-fourteen carpet-bowls competition."

"Well, there you are," Big Lou said. "The things we win when we're small are pretty important, aren't they?"

A brief silence ensued between them. Somewhere down the hill towards Canonmills an ambulance siren wailed, echoing against the canyons of stone buildings. A private tragedy, thought Pat; a heart attack, a stroke, a person coming suddenly to an end, a whole story receiving its final full stop; except that for most of us it is not a full stop but an unforeseen ellipsis.

She had turned her head, but now looked back at Big Lou. "Convention, Lou?"

"Aye," said Lou. "An Elvis impersonator convention." She looked down at the counter, as if ashamed. "I know it's not something you'd go to. I know folk will laugh . . ."

"I'd never laugh, Lou," said Pat quickly. "Never."

She wanted to reach across the counter and embrace Lou. She wanted to comfort, to reassure this fine, kind, hard-working woman, who had experienced such hardship and endured such bad luck, especially with men: that awful cook, with his penchant for young waitresses; that ridiculous Jacobite with his fantasies and obsessions; and now, instead of a decent farmer or rugby player from the Borders, an Elvis impersonator, of all things.

"Oh, Lou," she said. She wanted to say more, but could think of nothing to add. Was there anything further to be said about Elvis, or those who, for some bizarre reason known only to themselves – or possibly not – insisted on impersonating him?

56. *Thoughts of Bruce: Bruce Thoughts*

Back in the gallery, Pat thought about her own situation. It was all very well for her to reflect on Big Lou's unfortunate choice of men, but what about her own emotional record? She ran through the boys in her life; it was not a long list – the fingers of one hand would suffice to count them: that boy at Watson's, the one who had broken her heart with such consummate ease and had thought nothing of it – what teenage boy, when all is said and done, does not show at least some signs of psychopathic selfishness? She had pined for him for six months and then decided that there would be no more boys, ever, a resolution that remained until she met Bruce, for whom every woman fell with complete predictability; not that that led anywhere. And then that boy who worked in Glass & Thompson's and who was writing a dissertation on some literary topic – another mistake; and Wolf . . . that was four; Matthew was the fifth, and he was decent and considerate and it could have worked out, except for the fact that she had never loved him.

Pat's father, Dr. Macgregor, had never enquired directly about any of these boys, but had made remarks about love in general. "Don't make the mistake of confusing love with infatuation," he said. "So many people do. They don't realise that love is something that takes time. It never, ever announces itself immediately."

Pat was not sure about this. Had the poets got it quite that wrong? "So love at first sight is an impossibility?"

He nodded. "I'm afraid so. People may feel a strong and sudden interest in somebody else, but that's almost always purely physical. It might transform itself into love, but you have to wait and see about that."

"So what makes people notice each other?"

Dr. Macgregor thought for a moment. "One of two things: beauty or the biological imperative to settle down."

She waited for him to explain. "Beauty triggers interest because we yearn for the beautiful. We want to possess it because it represents harmony and resolution – things that we all need, whether we know it or not." He paused. "We also feel that it rubs off on us. If we are in the company of a beautiful person we ourselves feel more beautiful. Yes, we do. Don't laugh, Pat. I assure you this is so."

She apologised. "I'm not laughing. Well, all right, I was. It was just the thought of beauty rubbing off on people – like mascara or blush. Can't you see it? A very unprepossessing man standing next to a beautiful woman with makeup smeared all over his shirt."

"Yes," he said. "I can see that. But look at the pictures in those magazines you read . . ."

"I don't buy them," said Pat defensively.

"Of course not."

"I see them in the hairdressers. Or people leave them in the flat."

"Of course. But look at the pictures of those rich middle-aged men with their younger wives or girlfriends."

"Trophies."

"Exactly. And every one of them – the women, that is – beautiful. In other cases, though, where money and status are not a factor, then have you noticed something else?"

She looked puzzled. "What?"

"That people choose people who look like them."

"Do they?"

"Yes. I've made a habit of comparing spouses and partners. It's quite extraordinary, you know, but so many people choose others who have roughly similar facial features. Blondes prefer blondes. People with high cheekbones marry people who have equally high cheekbones."

Pat laughed. "Surely not." She thought of her friends who were in relationships. Surely they were not . . . Her smile faded. She had thought of her friend Zoe, and her boyfriend, Zack. Zoe had a long, thin neck and Zack . . . had that too. And they both had names beginning with Z: Was that significant? Did people choose others whose names were similar? There might just be a connection – it was probably true that one met more people who shared the letter of one's surname, at least, because one met them in groups where membership was allocated alphabetically, or in queues where the As had it over the Bs, and so on.

She thought of Elspeth and Matthew. Yes, they looked remarkably similar; it was something to do with their eyes, Pat thought. They both had rather gentle eyes; eyes that could never be calculating or intimidating. Then she thought of Bruce, just as she was returning from her coffee with Big Lou, and the thought made her stop. Bruce. Did she look like Bruce? Was that it?

She went into the gallery and opened the door of the small kitchen that gave onto the storeroom. There was a mirror on the wall there, just above the sink, and she approached this and stared in at her reflection. Was this the female face of Bruce? She shuddered.

I'm going to be strong, she said to herself. I'm going to telephone him and call the date off. "I'm going to go and speak to Lou about it and get her to tell me that I'm doing the right thing. I'm going to . . . She looked away and sighed. It was not going to work. She was going to see Bruce, she knew it, because she simply could not resist the temptation that he represented. There was no point in her telling herself that she could resist him: she could not. He had suggested they meet again after the evening in George Street and she had agreed; she had not been able to help herself. She felt exactly as she imagined a drug addict must feel when he needs the next hit. No matter what the higher part of the self – the will, the conscience, call it what you will – no matter what that may say, the receptors in the pleasure centres of the brain demand the satisfaction, the union, they have been led to expect. It was a chemistry every bit as powerful as magnetism, and every bit as impervious to efforts of will.

She returned to the front of the gallery and sat morosely at her desk. Before her was a small pad of paper, virginal, with a sharpened pencil beside it. She picked up the pencil absentmindedly and began to sketch lightly on the paper. The pencil moved swiftly, unhesitantly, propelled by something within her but not of her. She looked down and gasped. Had she drawn Bruce as David? Were the almost automatic movements of the pencil a pointer to the truth – every bit as revealing as the needle of a polygraph?

She blushed, ripping the sheet of paper off the pad and crumpling it up in her fist. Then she tossed it into the wastepaper basket, with determination and accuracy, as an author will throw away a piece of paper that takes his plot in entirely the wrong direction, down shameful ways that he knows will lead to nothing but disaster.

57. *Anna Receives a Shock in Moray Place*

If Pat's private life was showing signs of deterioration, then the opposite was true of the life that Matthew and Elspeth were leading in Moray Place. Even if they had been previously heading for collapse under the pressure of gross sleep-deprivation brought about by looking after triplets, the arrival of the Danish au pair, Anna, had changed everything. Now they had both enjoyed long and refreshing periods of sleep – in Matthew's case for fourteen, blissful hours – and were feeling the benefits; and not at any apparent cost to Anna, who, in spite of having been on duty during this period, appeared fresh and untroubled by this long shift.

"I feel very reassured," Matthew remarked to Elspeth. "I was able to sleep like that because I knew that Anna was on duty. I suppose that's how a president or prime minister must feel when he has to have an anaesthetic and the vice-president or deputy prime minister officially takes over."

Elspeth thought about this. "That happens in the United States, doesn't it? But what about here? Do you even know who the deputy prime minister is? Do you think they'd know who to put in charge?"

Matthew thought for a moment. "We never used to have a deputy prime minister," he said. "Then we started to get one. That chap, the one who almost hit somebody . . . he was deputy prime minister, wasn't he?"

"He was responding to somebody who threw an egg

at him. You can hardly blame him for that. He didn't start it."

Matthew was thoughtful. "Maybe not entirely. But still . . ."

"So who's the deputy prime minister now?"

Matthew scratched his chin. "That other one – you know the one I mean. Him. He's the deputy prime minister, isn't he?"

"Could be," said Elspeth. "He looks unhappy enough these days. Maybe it's being in power. His party had a terrible shock when it discovered it was sharing power, didn't it? Power isn't really what they were for. They were more in the . . . in the advisory tradition, I thought."

"Nice people," said Matthew.

"Yes, they are."

"And they try to do the decent thing. They really do."

"The cares of office," mused Elspeth. "Do you think that the Prime Minister wakes up in the morning and realises immediately that he's running the country, or do you think he has to remind himself?"

"I expect he has to remind himself," said Matthew. "I sometimes forget about the gallery – at least before breakfast, and then I say to myself: oh no, I've got to go to work."

Elspeth smiled. "Do you think we could ever forget the boys?"

Matthew shook his head. "Parents never forget they have children. Never. And I've heard that it goes on forever. That you worry about them even when they're forty and you're . . . goodness knows how old."

"Thank heavens for Anna," Elspeth said. "Have you noticed how efficient she is?"

"I could hardly miss it. I opened the fridge earlier on today and there were three little bottles all lined up like skittles in a bowling alley. And the bathroom . . . she has all the changing stuff carefully laid out with spare bits and pieces and creams and so on. It's like a clinic. It's fantastic."

Elspeth agreed. Yes, Anna was fantastic – a heroine, a life saver, a . . . solution. "She's even been organising the shopping," she said. "She went through all the cupboards and made a list of things that looked as if they were about to run out. Then she went off to the supermarket and came back with a whole bag of supplies. She even asked me what your favourite marmalade was and whether I thought you might like Danish fish roe."

"Those little black fish eggs? The ersatz caviar? I love it. I love it on boiled egg. I could eat it all day."

"She bought some," said Elspeth. "And she bought some odd fish paste that she's going to use for smorgasbord. She's going to . . ."

They were interrupted by the sound of Anna coming back; she had taken the triplets in their triple-baby-buggy for a walk round the Moray Place Gardens, and was now struggling with the front door. Matthew went off to help her.

He could tell immediately that something was wrong.

"Are the boys all right?" he asked. "You look upset."

Anna shook her head. "The boys are fine. I'm going to put them in their cribs for their sleep. They're fine."

"But you . . ."

"There's nothing wrong with me. I am fine too."

Matthew could see that this was not so. "But you look . . ."

"Don't worry about me. I am strong."

It was a strange thing to say, thought Matthew. One did not say that one was strong unless there was a reason why one needed to be strong. He stepped forward to help her get the boys out of the buggy.

"It's just that I have seen something," said Anna. "I saw something in the gardens."

Matthew frowned. "What? What did you see?"

Anna busied herself with laying Rognvald down in the crib. "I saw some strange people," she said. "Ten people maybe. They were . . . they were in the bushes."

Matthew sighed. "Oh . . . Oh, I think I may know."

"Some of them were not wearing any clothes," she said. "And then, when they saw me they walked off quickly and went into a house nearby."

Matthew looked at Elspeth with a mixture of astonishment and resignation. "It's those people," he muttered.

Elspeth looked at Anna solicitously. "This is ridiculous. It really is." She turned to Matthew. "Matthew, you're going to have to do something about it. They're entitled to be the Association of Scottish Nudists, or whatever they call themselves, but they're not entitled to frighten people."

Matthew agreed. "Of course not. I'm so sorry, Anna."

Anna smiled weakly. "We have many nudists in Scandinavia, but they usually keep to the beaches."

"Yes, well our beaches are a bit wild," said Matthew. "They'd be swept away into the North Sea most likely."

"You're going to have to talk to them, Matthew," said Elspeth. "You really will."

Matthew was resolute. "I shall. Which house was it, Anna? I'll go there right away."

58. The Great Highland Midge

Anna had indicated that the nudists had disappeared into a front door three or four houses up.

"It was a very respectable-looking door," she said. "Who would have guessed that such things were going on behind it?"

Matthew shook his head. "Don't be fooled," he said. "You do know, don't you, that Robert Louis Stevenson was from Edinburgh."

Anna looked puzzled. "The author of *Kidnapped*?"

"Yes," said Matthew. "The very same. But he also wrote *The Strange Case of Dr. Jekyll and Mr. Hyde*. Have you heard of that?"

Anna had not. "I have read *Kidnapped*, in Danish, but I have not read this other book."

"Well," said Matthew, "I know it's a hoary old chestnut . . ."

"Excuse me? A hoary old chestnut . . ."

"An expression," said Matthew. "An expression used to describe an observation that is rather . . . well, overused. And this business about Jekyll and Hyde is often wheeled out to describe contrasts in Edinburgh. People say it is a city with two identities: one respectable, the other quite the opposite."

"And Mr. Jekyll?"

"Stevenson's story was about a man who had two identities. There was Dr. Jekyll and then there was Mr. Hyde. But they were both the same person."

Anna looked thoughtful. "So Edinburgh has a respectable exterior and a not-so-respectable interior?"

Matthew sighed. "I wish it were that simple. I think that the metaphor is somewhat overused. Most cities are like that – they have a conventional, cautious side to them, and then they have an underbelly – a bohemian, darker side. In Edinburgh's case, I suppose it's just a little more obvious than in other places. So where we live here is regarded as being very . . . well, respectable is perhaps the word. And yet there are clearly things going on which represent the opposite of that."

"Such as nudism?"

"Yes, I suppose so. Nudism involves removing the restraints of clothing, and yet Moray Place is full of restraint. People here are very conscious of who they are and where they live."

"I see."

"Which is fine," Matthew conceded. "But they really should keep their nudism to themselves. Not everybody wants to see people romping around unclothed."

"No," said Anna. "We do not like that sort of thing in Copenhagen either."

"So I'm going to go and see them," said Matthew. "I'm going to go and complain."

Now he stood before the door that Anna had identified earlier and he felt less confident than he had done when he had first announced his intention of complaining. The door looked almost forbidding, with its shiny lacquer black paint and its impressive brass numerals. The numerals were Roman, which seemed to make the task of complaint all the more daunting. It is easy to complain to a set of modern figures, he thought, or to a plastic sign; to complain to the sort of person who used Roman numerals, and brass ones at that, was a different matter altogether.

Matthew stared at the small brass nameplate beside the bell-push. The lettering had been dulled by the elements or by excessive polishing – as can sometimes happen to much-loved brass – and it was difficult to make out the name. The first two letters were clear enough – Je – but then they became unintelligible. He took a deep breath and pressed the bell. I'm in the right, he thought. I don't like to complain to neighbours, especially having moved in so recently, but I really am in the right.

He heard sounds within the flat, a subdued hubbub of voices, he thought. And then the bell rose shrilly above them and he heard footsteps on the other side of the door.

Matthew had seen several of the neighbours since moving in but he did not recognise the man who came to the door. He was a thin, rather ascetic-looking man in his forties, wearing a white linen suit and a pair of canvas deck shoes. He looked, Matthew thought, rather like a weekend sailor about to set off on his yacht.

"Ah," said the man. "Do come in."

The tone was welcoming, and Matthew was momentarily nonplussed. He had expected their exchange to be formal and to take place on the doorstep.

"Come on," encouraged the man. "I'm Bill Jekyll, by the way. Do come in. We're about to start through there."

Matthew opened his mouth to speak. "I was actually . . ."

"Come along," said the man. "Through here. There are still a few seats. Come and sit down."

Matthew followed his host into the drawing room. There were about twenty people already there, most of them sitting, but one or two standing. He was relieved to see that everybody was fully clothed, although one or two of the men had a few of the front buttons of their shirts undone, revealing glimpses of tanned chests.

"Sit down over there," said Bill Jekyll, pointing to an empty seat on a sofa.

Matthew realised that he had been admitted to a meeting of some sort, and it did not take long for the nature of the meeting to be revealed.

"We're very fortunate to have Tom MacNaught as our speaker tonight," announced Bill Jekyll. "Tom has kindly agreed to bring along pictures of the Glencoe expedition. I know a lot of you were there and have your own photos, but Tom is a particularly good photographer and we can look forward to some very fine shots tonight." He turned to a man in a casual shirt and jeans, who was standing in front of an open laptop computer. "All right, Tom, it's all yours."

The lights were dimmed and Tom began to project photographs onto a bare patch of wall. "Buachaille Etive Mhor," he said. "I always look on this mountain as one of the guardians to Glencoe. I've climbed it several times. The day of our outing to Glencoe, as you'll remember, was a peach of a day. Not a cloud in the sky – and how often can you say that of the Western Highlands?"

There were murmurs of agreement.

"Of course," Tom went on. "It was midge season, and the little devils were out in force, in spite of the sun. Midges are a particular hazard for members of our club, as I'm sure you all well know."

There followed a picture of an exposed arm, dotted with small, red spots. Midges, thought Matthew – they must really take the shine off being a nudist in Scotland.

59. Edinburgh's Bone-deep Modesty

Matthew returned to the flat, where Elspeth was waiting expectantly, holding Rognvald while Anna attended to Tobermory and Fergus.

"Well?" she said. "What happened?"

Matthew shrugged. "I spoke to them. Or at least to one of them. He's called Jekyll – Bill Jekyll."

"And?"

"He was perfectly pleasant," said Matthew. "It happened they were having a meeting, and I got rather caught up in it."

"So that's why it took you so long," said Elspeth. "But you did raise the subject with them, did you? You did complain?" Matthew had to be pinned down, she had found out – he had a tendency to utter generalities.

Matthew nodded. "Yes, I had a word with him. But I had to sit through the meeting first. I couldn't very well barge in and start complaining . . ."

She agreed that he could not.

"So there we were," he said. "They had a slide show."

Elspeth smiled. "And . . ."

"And the slides were pretty innocuous. They had all gone up to Glen Etive and there were a lot of pictures of Buachaille Etive Mhor. They had lunch in the King's House Hotel – you know that hotel up there – and the . . ."

She interrupted him. "This was the nudists?"

Matthew nodded. "Yes, but they were all clothed on the expedition. Some of the men had removed their shirts, but that's all. The problem was that the midges were out, and they had all been bitten. They looked rather uncomfortable."

Buachaille Etive Mhor

"Poor them," said Elspeth. "It can't be much fun being a Scottish nudist."

"No," said Matthew. "Anyway, afterwards they had some sort of election for the committee. They asked me if I'd like to vote – I think they assumed I wanted to join, but of course I didn't."

She looked at him. How well do I know my husband, she asked herself. Some women thought they knew their husbands and then discovered, as a bombshell, that they did not. Secret interests might be disclosed and the wife may have had no idea at all that her husband was really a . . . what? A nudist? Were there secret nudists – those who were too ashamed to inform their wives of their hobby? Of course there could be other, less dramatic disclosures – as when a man reveals that he nurtured a secret and unfulfilled passion for model railways, perhaps. Elspeth imagined what it would be like to discover that one's husband was a secret train-spotter. That could be devastating: to be travelling on the train from Waverley Station and then suddenly, as the train draws out of the platform, to see him standing there in his anorak, furiously scribbling down the numbers of the trains as they went past. And he would not look up and see the astonished face of his wife go past, so absorbing were the numbers, and she would crane her neck to confirm the sighting and then sit back in her seat, utterly overcome by the discovery. To be married to a train-spotter! It could be worse, of course; Elspeth had read an article about a wife who discovered that her forty-year-old husband had a skateboard. It was hidden behind a wardrobe, together with a baseball cap and a pair of cut-off jeans. The poor woman had written to the advice column of a magazine and had received sage advice about the late adolescence of some men and about the necessity of understanding the needs of the inner boy. "Men are boys," had written the agony aunt. "Women must be patient."

But Matthew? No, she decided: she knew him far too well, and he was so utterly transparent. He could have no hankerings after joining the Association of Scottish Nudists, or whatever it was, because there was a bone-deep Edinburgh modesty about him. Edinburgh people rarely went unclothed, even in the privacy of their homes, where they modestly donned dressing gowns for the short trip from bathroom to bedroom. No, it was impossible.

"So what happened then?" she asked.

Matthew explained that it had all gone rather well. "I told him that Anna had been shocked, and he was very apologetic. He said that it was only a small group of the members that had been in the gardens before the meeting and it certainly wouldn't have happened had he been there. He said that the movement is split between an official wing and a provisional wing. He said that these were probably the provisional nudists."

Elspeth waited for further explanation.

"So," continued Matthew, almost apologetically. "So, I accepted his explanation. He said that he would speak very strongly to these provisionals, and that he was sure it would not happen again. He said he would reiterate the rule that no clothes were to be taken off in Moray Place Gardens, and he would, if necessary, expel them from the movement."

Elspeth sighed. "I still don't like it," she said. "I'm . . ." She paused. "I'm unhappy, Matthew."

There was no mistaking Matthew's concern. "Darling! My darling! You mustn't say you're unhappy."

She turned away. Rognvald had gone to sleep in her arms, and she laid him down gently on the sofa, a small bundle of humanity, wrapped in a shawl, placed upon chintz – where he lay, his eyes closed, small mouth open in the tiniest of Os; my son, thought Matthew, my son, Fergus; no, Tobermory; no, Rognvald.

Elspeth sat quietly, her hands folded on her lap, as in some picture of composed motherhood. But it was a pose, Matthew thought, of defeat – of resignation.

"You're not really unhappy, are you?"

She nodded; a small movement of the head, but enough to make it clear. Yes, she was unhappy.

"But my darling, why are you unhappy? You have everything – the boys, me, our life together." Could it be, he wondered, that he should have left himself off that list?

He took her hand. "It's not me, is it? It's not something I've said or done?"

She shook her head. "It's not you." She gave his hand a squeeze. "Not you, my lovely darling. I'm really happy with you. You're wonderful; you really are."

His probing was gentle. "Then what is it? You aren't depressed, are you? Remember that people can get very low after they've had a baby."

She shook her head. It was not that.

"It's the flat," she said. "I don't like it here, Matthew. I want to go back to India Street."

60. For Sale – Again

That gave Matthew something to think about. Her disclosure had at first silenced him, but then, when the shock had subsided, he questioned her further. Had she felt this from the beginning, or had the feeling come over her only recently? She answered, but was not forthcoming. "It's just a feeling I have," she said. "I began to feel a bit uneasy about the move after you had signed. I thought about saying something, but . . ." She trailed off. "I feel very bad about this, you know. I didn't intend to tell you. It . . . well, it just slipped out."

Matthew took a deep breath. "I'm glad you told me," he said. "It would have been awful if you had had to bottle it up. Now we can talk about it."

She nodded, but it was a miserable nod. "I'm sure I'll get over it."

"It's nothing to do with Jekyll and his friends, is it?"

She was vigorous in her denial. "No, it really isn't. Those people don't really worry me." She looked up at the ceiling. "This place is . . . well, Matthew, I'm sorry to say this but I find it oppressive."

"What do you mean 'oppressive'?"

She sighed. "I mean just that. There's something about the atmosphere – the light, perhaps, or lack of it. Matthew, this is a basement."

He looked about the room. There was enough light, wasn't there? "I wouldn't call it a basement. It's at the bottom of the building, yes, but basements are below ground level. This is a ground floor."

Rognvald, on the sofa cushion beside her, stirred in his sleep. A small foot, sheathed in a blue knitted sock so small that it could double as an egg cosy, moved against Elspeth's thigh. She reached down and touched it gently.

"I feel so bad," she said. "I feel as if I'm complaining about something that so many people would love to have. Look at us: we're relatively newly married, and yet we have everything. We have four bedrooms. We have all the appliances and things we need. We have an employee, for heaven's sake. We have bags of room, central heating, a garden – everything, and yet I'm complaining. I'm so sorry."

Matthew felt a surge of sympathy for her. "My darling . . ."

"No, I really feel bad. You're so kind and helpful, Matthew. And I'm being so selfish." She paused. Her voice was choked; the voice of one on the verge of tears. "I'm sorry I even mentioned it. I'll get over it – I'm sure I will."

"Will you?"

She took a handkerchief from a pocket and blew her nose. "Yes. I will, I will. I'm sure of it."

Sensing that she did not wish to discuss it any further, Matthew changed the subject. The triplets were due to go for a checkup at the baby clinic the next day and he wanted to discuss the arrangements with her. That done, he looked at his watch. "Would you mind, my darling, if I went to the Cumberland Bar? I haven't been for ages and I thought I could catch up with the boys."

Of course she would not mind. She was not sure who the boys were – she thought they included Angus Lordie – but she did not mind.

"I won't be long," said Matthew hurriedly.

"You be as long as you like," she said, trying to smile.

He left a few minutes later.

"So you are going drinking," said Anna, as he passed her in the hall.

"I'm just going to the pub," he said defensively.

"That is drinking," she said. "But there is nothing wrong with that."

"Don't people drink in Denmark?" He felt vaguely irritated by her remark. What business was it of hers whether he went to the Cumberland Bar or not? None, he thought.

"Yes," she said. "People drink in Denmark. Maybe a bit too much. But I am sure you do not."

He opened his mouth to reply, but she had left the hall, and so he set off. The next time, he thought, the next time she says something like that I'm going to tell her that it is not for her to tell me what to do.

He made his way round the circle of Moray Place and into Darnaway Street feeling somewhat low. Elspeth's confession of her feelings had dispirited him. Why on earth had she not spoken to him about it before they bought the flat? She must have had some misgivings at that stage, as dislike of the place would hardly have overcome her after they had moved in. But there was no point in reproaching her over that; the essential point was that she was unhappy with the flat and that was something they would have to tackle. Would it be enough to redecorate? Perhaps he could get somebody in to advise on colours and lighting: simple changes in those areas could make a big difference to the feel of a place. Perhaps he could even engage one of those feng shui practitioners who would give an opinion on the direction of the chi forces.

He walked slowly along Darnaway Street, sunk in thought of his conversation with Elspeth. Reaching the top of India Street, he looked down the sloping cobbled road to the trees and railings at the end. How many times had he walked that way on his way home? How many times had he turned onto that small stone bridge that led to the door at the bottom of his common stair, and slipped his key into the lock and pushed the heavy black door ajar? How happy he had been here; how right it had seemed to him, as home always does: it feels right.

His eye was caught by a sign. It was one of those For Sale signs that were attached to the railings of a house or flat on the market, and it was . . . He hesitated. Yes, it was outside their old flat.

Matthew decided to investigate. Perhaps somebody else was selling up; his neighbour on the floor below had mentioned that he might put his flat on the market if conditions seemed right. Perhaps it was him.

It was not. When Matthew drew level with his old doorway, he saw immediately that the sign referred to the top flat, which was theirs. But the new owners had only taken possession of it a couple of months ago; why would they be selling it on so quickly? Had they, like Elspeth, had second thoughts?

61. *In the Cumberland Bar*

Matthew had not expected to find Pat in the Cumberland Bar and, for her part, Pat had not expected to meet him. Each was pleased, though in different ways, to come across the other. Pat, who had been sitting on her own in a corner, was relieved that she was now no longer by herself – an understandable feeling on the part of any young woman who finds herself unaccompanied in a pub: even the most salubrious of bars harbours those who will look with suspicion, or askance, on a woman sitting by herself, just as a solitary man in a bar will sometimes be viewed with pity by those who enjoy the ordinary human assurance of company. As for Matthew, his feeling of rawness after Elspeth's disturbing revelations meant that he wanted to talk to somebody – anybody – and who could be more suitable than an old girlfriend? Pat was a good listener – something rather rare and wonderful – and he thought: good, here's Pat, and I can ask her what I should do.

He made his way over to her table and bent down to plant a kiss on her cheek. He felt that she held back slightly, but it seemed to him that this was the right thing to do – to give, and receive, a chaste kiss, a kiss of long established and easy friendship. At the same time he thought, even if fleetingly, that it might seem odd that here he was, a married man and father of three, leaving his wife and family in the flat to go to a bar to meet a former girlfriend, herself unattached, and, what's more, to kiss her. But then he reminded himself that this was not a prearranged assignation. And people kissed one another with very little thought these days – there was, some felt, far too much kissing going on. Angus Lordie, Matthew knew, was very much of that view.

"I can't stand it," Angus had once said to him, "when people come to dinner at one's house – people you hardly know – and they think they have to kiss you on arrival and departure. Why? What's wrong with shaking hands, or just smiling at one another? Since when did Scottish people have to kiss one another like this?"

"But you never invite anybody to dinner," Matthew had pointed out.

This had interrupted the flow of the complaint, but only briefly.

"The principle remains the same," he said. "And the reason why I hold very few dinner parties . . ."

"None," said Matthew.

"Listen," said Angus. "You don't have to experience something directly yourself in order to have views. You should know that, Matthew."

Matthew had not been at all sure why he should be

thought to know this, but did not press Angus on the question and had left the matter where it was. Now, in the Cumberland Bar, the memory came back momentarily, as he gave Pat her kiss and picked up the familiar scent of her favourite shampoo. It was a curious smell, a mixture of vanilla and coconut, two vaguely incompatible smells, one would have thought, but he liked it because it brought back so many pleasant associations. He was fond of Pat; indeed once he had loved her, and had wanted to marry her – a premature and immature idea, he now accepted.

"What are you doing?" he asked as he sat down beside her.

"Sitting here," she said.

He smiled. "I meant to phone you at the gallery today, but didn't."

"That's all right. Nothing happened. There were two letters for you – I could have brought them if I had thought that I'd meet you here."

He would pick them up, he said. He thought that he was rather neglecting his business while he was on his self-granted paternity leave, but that was what leave was all about. A leave in which one did not neglect one's business would be no leave at all.

He glanced at her drink, which was barely touched. "You meeting somebody?"

She looked away, embarrassed. "Yes."

Matthew smiled conspiratorially. "New boyfriend?" He was never quite sure what Pat's status was; there were boys from time to time and he assumed that she had somebody, but she had not said anything to him.

Pat winced. It was an immediate, unintentional reaction but it made Matthew realise that his question was intrusive. "Sorry," he blustered. "It's nothing to do with me."

She shook her head. "No need to apologise. It's just that I'm meeting . . . well, I'm meeting Bruce."

Matthew could not conceal his surprise. "Him?"

She smiled. "I know not everybody likes him. But . . ."

But what? thought Matthew. He found it difficult to think of anything good to say about Bruce, although he knew that he should try. Morally sensitive people always found at least something worth praising in another, even if their praise sounded faint. A truly selfish monster, a calculating psychopath, might still be said in his obituary to have been a good dinner companion, or well informed on the topography of France, or able to divine water with bent twigs: at least something might be dredged up to ameliorate the otherwise awful story of his life. A sinister tyrant might like dogs – although admittedly only rather vulpine, aggressive-looking ones; a serial killer might play the piano rather well; but of Bruce, although he did not belong in that company, of course, what might one say? And even as he posed that question in his mind, Matthew answered it. Bruce was good-looking, devastatingly so – that was the only positive that could be said of him. Or was it? Was Bruce capable of kindness and generosity? He must have at least some such moments. Were there occasions when he had encouraging things to say of people? Surely there were.

"But you like him?" said Matthew.

Pat looked down at her hands. "I suppose I do."

"As a person?" asked Matthew. "Or . . ."

"Or what?" Pat snapped.

Matthew wondered how he could put it tactfully. What were the euphemisms, the polite terms for concupiscence? Come to think of it, what were the ordinary terms for concupiscence? Should one just say lust?

"It's physical?" ventured Matthew, his voice lowered.

62. *The Use of Nominees*

Matthew knew immediately that he had offended Pat.

"I didn't mean to say that," he blurted out. "I'm sorry."

She did not look at him as she replied. "Why is it that nobody comments if a man is attracted to a beautiful woman, but if a woman is attracted to a beautiful man, then she has somehow to apologise, to feel embarrassed about it?"

Matthew blushed. "I didn't mean to embarrass you," he said. "I really didn't."

Pat continued. "It's still that we expect women not to confess to . . . to their needs – that's it, isn't it? We're meant to pretend we don't have any feelings about . . ."

Matthew shook his head. "Not any more," he said. "That used to be the case, but not any more."

"Then why shouldn't I be attracted to Bruce?"

He was struggling. "I didn't say that you couldn't. I just felt that . . . well, he's not really your . . ." He waved a hand in the air. "Your equal. You're a nice person and he's . . . well, you know what Bruce is like, don't you? He's just so pleased with himself."

Pat was about to reply to this, but did not. A young man had come into the bar, and looked about him quickly before striding across to their table. Now he stood before them, his hair slightly dishevelled and wet, the rain having started up outside. He looked first at Matthew, and then at Pat.

"You're Pat?"

Pat frowned as she tried to place him. She had seen him before somewhere – she was sure of it – but could not recall where or when.

"Yes, I am."

The young man pulled up a chair and sat down.

"You're soaking," said Matthew. "I didn't realise it had started to rain."

"I missed a bus and so I started to walk," said the young man. "My name's Neil, by the way. I'm Bruce's flatmate in William Street."

Pat was still trying to remember where she had seen Neil before. If he was Bruce's flatmate, then she might have met him there, at the flat – except for the fact that she had never been in Bruce's flat.

Neil half-turned to glance in the direction of the bar. "I'll buy you a drink in a moment," he said. "But first, some bad news, I'm afraid." He paused. Pat noticed a bead of moisture running down his cheek: the result of the rain. She wanted to reach out and mop it up; she wanted to smooth down his hair.

"You see," Neil continued, "Bruce has had an accident. He can't meet you. He's been taken off to the Royal Infirmary and he asked me to pass the message on to you. I went with him to casualty, and then came straight here." He turned to Pat. "He didn't have your mobile number – otherwise we would have phoned."

"Is he all right?" Pat asked.

"He's broken a leg," said Neil. "And they're worried he's cracked his skull too."

Pat was silent. Matthew glanced at her. He felt sorry for Bruce – of course he did, but not as sorry as if this had happened to a hundred other people. And that, for a moment, made him feel guilty.

It was a freak accident, Neil explained. Bruce had been taking a shower and then, when he came out, he had trodden on a tube of hair gel that had fallen off the edge of the washbasin. This had expelled a pool of gel, on which he had then slipped.

"Any head injury seems to produce a lot of blood," Neil went on. "You know how it is? I cut my scalp once when I fell off my bike. There was blood all over the place. Same with Bruce. Blood and hair gel. All mixed up."

Pat shuddered. "I hope he's all right," she said.

"He's fine," said Neil. "He'll have a leg in plaster for a few months, I suppose, but worse things have happened." He smiled at Pat. "He said that he was going to take you out to dinner."

Pat nodded. "Yes. We were going down to Leith. To The Shore."

Neil glanced at Matthew briefly and then back at Pat. "That's a great place. I wonder if you'd like to go with me. I had nothing on and I'd rather like to go out tonight after all that business with Bruce. Hospitals depress me."

Pat hesitated.

"You should go," said Matthew. "Go on."

"All right," she said. "On one condition: I pay for myself."

Neil shrugged. "That's fine." Then he grinned. "Actually I was hoping you'd say that. Not that I wouldn't like to pay for you . . ."

Pat liked his grin. "I'm sure you would." She liked his voice too. And his eyes . . .

Neil was now looking at her with interest. "You know something?" he said. "I think we've met before. Maggie Henderson's party?"

Pat had been there. Maggie Henderson had been several years above her at school, but had been prepared to socialise with younger girls, and had been much admired for that.

She had had a twenty-first birthday party at Prestonfield, in the marquee, and Pat had been invited.

She stared at Neil. Had she danced with him, perhaps?

"I was the piper," said Neil. "You probably don't remember me. But I was there and you and I chatted outside while you were waiting for your taxi."

It came back to her. There had been a piper, and she had talked to him, and she had wanted to spend longer with him but her taxi had arrived. That was Neil.

"I remember now," she said.

Pat now realised that she had not introduced Matthew to Neil, and now did so. Neil nodded as she explained that Matthew owned the gallery she was temporarily working in. "Yes," he said. "I know about that. You're the person who sold Bruce that flat."

Matthew frowned. "Sorry, I don't follow you."

"Bruce bought your flat in India Street. He was telling me about it."

Matthew struggled to deal with this disclosure. Bruce! He had sold the flat to a woman from Kelso who wanted to live near her daughter in Edinburgh; he had not sold it to Bruce. He started to explain this, but Neil just shook his head.

"No, that's not the case. Bruce uses nominees. It's really him. He's going to sell it on – at a profit." He smiled. "And he will, you know."

63. Solastalgia Explained

Pat and Neil left for their dinner together, but Matthew was not long by himself. After five minutes or so, during which Matthew brooded on Neil's casual disclosure of Bruce's perfidy, Angus arrived with Cyril in tow. Spotting Matthew at his table, Angus gave a cheerful wave and came over to settle Cyril while he went to the bar to buy a pint of beer for himself and the small dish of Guinness that Cyril enjoyed.

"Well," said Angus, as he placed Cyril's dish under the table. "It's very good to see you. Paternal duties, I take it, are suspended pro tem."

"Elspeth is at home," said Matthew. "And we've got a helper now – an au pair from Denmark."

"Ah," said Angus, taking a sip of his beer. "Pulchritudinous?"

Matthew did not reply, but gave Angus a reproachful look.

Angus winced. "That was a joke, Matthew. Listen, are you feeling out of sorts? You look somewhat peely-wally, if I may say so."

This remark had the effect of making Matthew look even gloomier. "Everything's going wrong," he said.

Angus took a sip of his beer. "Absolutely everything?"

Matthew told him of Elspeth's announcement.

"Oh," said Angus. "So she's pining for India Street? I can't say that I don't understand and, to an extent, sympathise. One becomes very attached to one's familiar place. It's fundamentally unsettling to have to uproot oneself."

"But surely a move can be stimulating," objected Matthew. "New surroundings. Not the same old view out of the window every morning. Surely that should be positive."

Angus was not convinced. "I don't think so. In fact, most people, I'm convinced, want things to remain exactly the same. And when they don't, when things change at too rapid a pace, I believe that we can feel considerable distress." He paused, and took another sip of beer. At his feet, Cyril, who had been noisily lapping up the beer in his dish, looked up in expectation. Sometimes he was allowed a second helping, but the dog had noticed that this only happened when he and Angus were in the bar by themselves; Cyril had noticed that when his master had company – as he now did – he seemed to forget to serve seconds. Cyril glared at Matthew, willing him to leave. This glare gradually slipped until it was focused on Matthew's exposed ankles, which were only a foot or so from Cyril's snout. Cyril had long harboured a desire to bite Matthew's ankles, which were of an appearance and attractiveness that would tempt even the most iron-willed, self-controlled dog, let alone a dog who, emboldened by beer, was weighing up the pros and cons of allowing himself a nip. It would be easy, so easy, but Cyril had a keener sense of consequence than most dogs, and he knew that if he were to bite Matthew, he could expect to be walloped by Angus with a rolled up copy of *The Scotsman*.

"In fact," Angus continued, "there is a name for this condition of distress over change: solastalgia."

"Solas-what?"

"Solastalgia. It's a neologism," Angus explained. "But unlike many neologisms, this is a useful one. It was coined by an Australian professor who was convinced that rapid or dramatic change naturally leads to unhappiness. And of course he was spot-on. Of course it does."

Matthew stared into his glass of beer. "I thought it would be good for both of us," he said. "It could get us out of our rut."

"Nothing wrong with ruts," said Angus. "The happiest people I know are in deep, deep ruts."

Matthew sighed. "And now, I just don't know what to do . . ."

Angus returned to solastalgia. "I've found this whole idea very interesting. I've always felt that people who said that we should embrace change were arrogant in their assumptions. People can't cope with too much change, you see. Change can hurt. People like the familiar. They like the things they're used to."

"But things can't remain the same," said Matthew. "If you don't adapt to changing conditions, then . . ." He made a throat-cutting gesture. "Then you're done for."

"Why?" asked Angus.

"Because the world is competitive. We have to work out new strategies for survival. Things have to change."

Angus looked at Matthew. "Even if we end up being unhappy? Even if we end up losing any sense of who we are or where we come from? Even if we end up with a world about us that we feel uncomfortable with because it's alien and featureless and confusing?"

"Economic necessity . . ." Matthew began.

Angus spluttered. "Don't talk to me about economic necessity! Money has no conscience, Matthew! Surely you understand that. Capital doesn't care what it does to people – it's driven by greed. Look at how it's slaughtered industry in Scotland. And elsewhere too. Even the United States. Look at the ruination of places like Detroit because capital has gone off to cheaper places. It never cared about them – those car workers or steel-men or whatever – it never cared. Not really. It left them high and dry. And it's the same everywhere."

"So what do you propose?" asked Matthew.

Angus shrugged. "I don't know. I'm an artist, Matthew – and artists don't always have solutions. We can show people what the world is like, I suppose. We can encourage them to think about spiritual possibilities. We can paint the just city – but we can't necessarily show people how to get there."

Matthew looked at his hands. "I only wanted Elspeth to be happy," he muttered.

"Oh really!" said Angus. "Stop going on about it. Move back there. A flat's bound to come up in India Street sooner or later."

"It has," said Matthew.

"Then buy it," said Angus.

Suddenly Cyril growled, attracting the attention of both Matthew and Angus.

"What's wrong with him?" asked Matthew.

Angus looked down at the dog, who seemed to be staring at Matthew's ankles. "He can't stand self-pity," Angus said. "He picks these things up, you see."

"It's all very well for you," Matthew retorted. "Everything's going fine for you. And for Cyril too."

Angus shook his head. "Except it isn't," he said. "I've discovered something, you see. I've discovered something about Domenica." He paused, as if uncertain whether to continue. Then he went on, "I've discovered that she loves somebody else, Matthew. Not me. Somebody else."

64. A Prospect of Glasgow

It was Ranald Braveheart Macpherson who undertook the planning of the expedition to Glasgow. The briefing, as Ranald called it, took place during an interlude in a cub scout meeting.

"Now listen to me, Bertie," he whispered. "This is how we're going to do it. We're going to go tomorrow, right? When your mummy drops you off at school, don't go inside, understand? Hide in the bushes. I'll do the same at my school. Then run out the gate and meet me at the edge of the Meadows, near the Brunstfield Hotel. You know that place?"

Bertie shivered with fear at the thought of the deception. Ranald's plan, he thought, was fraught with danger, but it was now too late to withdraw. "I know it," he said. "And then what, Ranald?"

Ranald glanced around him. Not far away, surrounded by a small knot of girls, Olive could be seen watching them.

"Try to talk out of the side of your mouth, Bertie," said Ranald. "Like an American." He pointed discreetly in Olive's direction. "That way Olive won't think we're saying anything."

No sooner had Ranald said this than Olive, followed by Pansy and Pansy's friend, Angela, a small girl with round glasses, a snub nose, and plaits, approached the two boys.

"What are you talking about, Ranald Macpherson?" asked Olive peremptorily.

Ranald was silent.

"I could see that you were talking to Bertie," continued Olive. "We're not blind, are we, Pansy?"

"No, we're not," said Pansy. "I saw your lips moving, Ranald. You were talking to Bertie. Anybody could tell that."

Ranald glanced imploringly at Bertie. He might have been

a good planner of trips to Glasgow, but he did not relish confrontation, particularly with Olive, who was noted for her sharp tongue and forceful manner.

"It was a private conversation, Olive," Bertie said mildly. "I was talking to Ranald, which was our business, and you were talking to Pansy and Angela, which was your business. Fair's fair, Olive."

Olive turned on him sharply. "Oh yes? Fair's fair, is it? Well I've got news for you, Bertie Pollock. There are going to be more girls in the cub scouts than boys. Did you know that? Well, it's true, and that means it's going to be the end of the road for you boys!"

Angela now joined in, her small eyes bright with triumph. "Yes, Olive's right, Bertie. There are going to be so many girls that we'll be in the majority. And then you boys are finished, understand – finished."

"And not just in the cub scouts," interjected Pansy. "My mummy read an article from the paper that said that there are already bags more girls going to university than boys. That's a fact. So soon boys will just get the rubbish jobs. So you're going to have a rubbish job and Ranald you're going to have an even more rubbish job than Bertie. That's another fact."

"Exactly," said Olive.

Bertie looked at Ranald, who seemed crestfallen at this news. "Why should Ranald have a more rubbish job?" he asked. "How do you know that, Pansy?"

"It's because of his legs," announced Olive. "That's why, isn't it, Pansy?"

"Yes," said Pansy. "That's why."

"What have Ranald's legs got to do with it?" asked Bertie.

"They're very thin and spindly," said Olive, pointing at Ranald's legs. "And he calls himself Braveheart! The real

Braveheart had big, strong legs. That was in the days when men were men. That's what my mummy says. She says that those days are over now."

The girls continued in this vein for some time, but did not succeed in winkling out of the two boys the topic of their conversation. At length Olive and her cohort retreated, leaving Bertie and Ranald with a vague threat to watch them very closely and to inform the authorities if there was any sign of their doing anything.

This exchange dispirited both Bertie and Ranald, but it did not prevent their later agreeing on the finer details of the plan and resolving to put it all into operation the following morning. Bertie returned home in a state of considerable excitement – and trepidation. He had very rarely gone off on an expedition of his own, and in each case it had ended ignominiously. There had been the occasions when he had run away from the Steiner School in order to enroll himself in Watson's and to play rugby; that had ended in his being pushed to the ground and kicked by Jack, whom he had previously thought of as a friend. Then there had been his ill-fated attempt to cross Dundas Street by himself; that had come to an end when he had frozen in the middle of the street, transfixed by the sight of the traffic hurtling down the road towards him. Had it not been for the extraordinarily courageous intervention of the then First Minister of Scotland, Jack McConnell (later given a life peerage for this very act), who had dashed out into the traffic and had rescued him, then the result of that outing could well have been tragic. So this trip to Glasgow, although carefully planned by Ranald Braveheart Macpherson, was taking place against a not particularly propitious backdrop.

That night he lay in his bed, willing himself to sleep so that the morning would come more quickly, and yet unable to do so through sheer excitement. Glasgow! Even the name had a more exciting ring to it than Edinburgh's. Edinburgh sounded so ordered and dignified by comparison – Glasgow sounded so much noisier and more exuberant. And quite apart from the thrill of the journey, there was the excitement of going to the adoption agency and registering himself for adoption. He wondered whether it would take long, whether he would have to wait while they telephoned some new parents to come in and pick him up, or whether there would be some prospective parents sitting in a waiting room. Bertie knew all about waiting rooms, of course; he regularly sat in Dr. St. Clair's waiting room in Queen Street; that had copies of *Scottish Field* in it. Would there be *Scottish Field* in the adoption agency waiting room?

He became drowsy and sleep slowly came upon him. As he dropped off, he entered a dream, a vague half-conscious dream, in which he was in Glasgow and there was a man waiting for him at Queen Street Station and he was walking towards him; and it was Lard O'Connor, and Mr. O'Connor said to Bertie, "I'm not really dead, Bertie, that's just wishful thinking on the part of those dry, stuck-up people in Edinburgh who so hate all spontaneity and life . . ."

65. *The Girl Within*

Bertie journeyed to school the next morning in the company of Irene and his younger brother, Ulysses. Ulysses, who had discovered the power of his vocal chords to achieve his objectives, was in more than usually good voice, causing Bertie a certain amount of embarrassment on the bus.

"Can't you stop him making such a noise, Mummy?" Bertie asked. "People are looking at us."

Irene smiled tolerantly. "It's natural for babies and very young children to scream, Bertie. And I'm not sure that we should stop them."

"But couldn't you give him one of those dummy things? Babies like them, I think. It stops them crying."

Irene shook her head. "No, Bertie, that's not a good idea at all. Oral satiation may be all very well, but it retards the development of the personality. And we don't want Ulysses to be stuck, do we?" Irene paused. "Besides, dummies are awful things. The Americans call them soothers, which is a complete euphemism, Bertie. They do not soothe, they suppress. And the Germans, you may be interested to hear, Bertie, call them Schnullers. A terrible word for a terrible device."

Bertie looked out of the bus window. His mother often went on about people being stuck, and he had never worked out exactly what it meant. She said that all sorts of people, particularly people who lived in Edinburgh, were stuck, but he had never noticed that very much. Certainly people on the street outside, most of whom lived in Edinburgh, unless they were just in town for the day, did not seem to be stuck; in fact, most of them appeared to be walking quite freely and with none of the slowness with which people who were stuck might be expected to move.

Irene continued. "The point is, Bertie, that it is natural

for Ulysses to express his rage. There is so much about the world that triggers such a reaction, and he is merely giving vent to it. That's what's happening."

Bertie hesitated before replying. As a general rule, he did not encourage his mother to explain things, as this could lead to long debates in which his own views were usually overruled. But what was this about rage? Could Ulysses really be expressing rage?

"I don't think he notices very much, Mummy," Bertie said mildly. "I don't think that Ulysses actually knows what's going on. So surely he can't be expressing rage if he has no idea what's happening half the time . . ."

Irene's discouraging look made Bertie trail off. "You're so wrong, Bertie," she said. "Ulysses knows exactly what's happening. His little mind is very busy, Bertie – busy as a bee, darting here and there, soaking up impressions of the world. Even now, if you look at his expression, you'll see that he's thinking about something. See. Look at his little frown of concentration."

Bertie glanced at Ulysses, and then looked away quickly. The expression that he had seen was not so much that of one soaking up impressions of the world as of one engaged in a much more physical task.

"I think you're going to have to change him, Mummy," Bertie whispered. "And I really wish he wouldn't do it on the bus."

Irene smiled. "Hush, Bertie, you don't want to disturb him. This is all entirely natural and everybody understands these things."

The journey continued. Ulysses had now become quieter, being diverted by the sight of a large beard worn by a passenger across the aisle. This gave Irene the opportunity to raise with Bertie the prospect of a visit from Olive.

"I've spoken to Olive's mummy," she said as the 23 bus trundled past the Renaissance splendour of Heriot's School. "And she says that it will be perfectly all right for Olive to come and play some day next week, possibly Wednesday. That will be nice, won't it, Bertie?"

"No," said Bertie. "It won't."

"Come now, Bertie," said Irene. "Olive is a very nice little girl and she loves coming to play in Scotland Street. Her mummy says that she plans these little trips for days and talks about it all for a long time afterwards. Isn't it nice that she gets such pleasure from coming to see you?"

"I hate her," said Bertie. "And she hates me back. We both hate each other the same."

"Oh, Bertie, don't be so ridiculous! Olive doesn't hate you. If she hated you, why would she want to come and play?"

"She comes because she likes pushing me about," said Bertie. "Olive's very bossy, Mummy. She likes to push people around and she really likes doing that to me. When she brought her junior nurse's kit . . ."

Bertie had not told his mother of the incident in which Olive had extracted a real syringe from her junior nurse's kit and insisted on taking a sample of his blood. That had all been too traumatic, and had directly resulted in the subsequent contretemps between Olive and Elspeth Harmony, then their teacher, who had, in sheer frustration, pinched Olive's ear. Bertie had not previously revealed this to his mother but now he thought that he might do so. If Irene heard that Olive was in the habit of wielding real syringes with real needles, then she might be less enthusiastic about her coming to the house.

His efforts were in vain, as Irene interrupted him with an explanation as to why it was a good idea for Olive to come to play. "The reason why it's nice to have Olive coming to the house, Bertie, is that it gives you the opportunity to have some female company. That's very important, you know. If you have female company it will allow you to get in touch with your feminine side."

Bertie sat quite still. What was this feminine side?

Irene thoughtfully explained. "You see, Bertie, every boy has a girl inside him – an inner girl. It's the bit of him that has a feminine understanding of the world – the bit that is gentle and sensitive."

Bertie looked at his mother. "Are you sure, Mummy?" He was thinking of Tofu, and also of Larch, who was currently in disgrace for cutting down a tree without permission and for throwing a brick at a window.

"Yes," said Irene. "Yes, Bertie, I'm sure."

"Well," said Bertie, "does that mean that girls have boys inside them? Do they have inner boys?"

Irene frowned. "No, Bertie," she said. "Such a concept is quite unnecessary."

66. Oh, Promised Land of Glasgow!

They alighted from the 23 bus in Bruntsfield and made their way along Merchiston Crescent towards Spylaw

Road. Bertie walked several steps behind his mother, who was pushing Ulysses in his pushchair; his mind was full of his forthcoming adventure, which he viewed with a mixture of eager anticipation and dread. This, he thought, is the last time I walk this way to school. As from next week, or possibly even the next day, he would, he imagined, be attending school in Glasgow, perhaps even Hutchesons', or Hutchy, as he had heard it called. He liked the sound of Hutchy, and had decided that even if his adoptive parents in Glasgow did not mention it, he would raise the issue of his going there. They had rugby, he had heard, and there was a stamp-collecting club and a pipe band and . . . it would all be so different for him. Perhaps Lard O'Connor had a son who went there and Bertie would get to know him in due course and they could go doon the watter together, as people in Glasgow appeared to do. There were so many possibilities in Glasgow, and it was now all so close – only a forty-five minute train ride away.

"Do hurry up, Bertie," said Irene over her shoulder. "You're really dragging your feet today. Are you thinking about something?"

Bertie did not look at his mother. Oh yes, he thought. Oh yes, I'm definitely thinking about something: I'm thinking about my new life in Glasgow. Poor Mummy, I hope that you won't be too upset when I'm gone, but you'll still have Ulysses and you can do lots of things with him. You can take him to yoga classes and teach him the piano and speak Italian to him. He can have my psychotherapy appointments and go with you to the Floatarium and float in your flotation chamber as long as he doesn't go to the loo. There's so much you can do with Ulysses.

Now they were drawing near to the school gate, and Bertie's heart within him was beating like a drum. He stared at the scene ahead: he saw Tofu's father dropping him off and then driving away in the old car that Tofu said had been converted to run on olive oil. He saw Pansy's mother waving goodbye to her daughter and blowing a kiss – so embarrassing for all concerned! He saw Larch's father draw up in his truck and throw Larch out of the passenger door, as if pleased, quite understandably, to be getting rid of him for another day. It was all perfectly normal except . . . except for the fact that one of the actors in this little daily performance was planning a major deviation from the plot.

They approached the school gate.

"Don't bother to stay around, Mummy," said Bertie when they were still some distance away. "I'll manage the last bit by myself."

Irene looked down on him with amusement. "But it's no trouble, Bertie," she said. "And Mummy always likes to wave goodbye at the gate and watch you go in. It's very nice for Ulysses to see you going to school."

"I don't think he knows that I'm going to school," argued

Bertie. "And I think he sees most things upside down anyway."

"Nonsense, Bertie," snapped Irene. "Ulysses sees things in exactly the same way that you do."

Bertie thought quickly. "It's a matter of independence, Mummy," he blurted out. "I feel that there are some things I should try to do by myself. Walking the last few steps to school by myself helps me to feel independent."

Irene looked thoughtful. "Well, I certainly wouldn't want to inhibit you, Bertie. So if it means that much to you, I suppose that Ulysses and I can stand here and wave."

"Better still if you turned round and started walking back up Spylaw Road," Bertie countered. "That way I'd feel even more independent."

Rather to his surprise, Irene agreed, and bent down to kiss him goodbye. "*Sois sage, mon sausage*," she said.

Bertie blushed. It was not just that his mother insisted on speaking French now – having temporarily abandoned Italian – it was the curious mixture of French and English that embarrassed him. *Saucisson*, he muttered under his breath, but not loud enough for her to hear.

He walked off. After a few paces he half-turned, and saw that his mother had started to retrace her steps up Spylaw Road. She had her back turned to him and did not see her son staring at her. Nor did she see him suddenly run into the bushes just inside the gate and dive underneath them for cover.

From his hidden vantage point, Bertie took one last look at his mother. The enormity of what he was doing now came home to him and he gulped as he realised it. He had just said goodbye to the mother who had raised him for the last seven years. He would see her again, of course, when he came back on holiday from his new Glasgow family, but it would never be the same – for either of them.

He swallowed. It is not an easy thing to say goodbye to a mother, and when you are only seven, and still emotionally dependent on her, it is particularly difficult. He loved her – of course he did – but she had left him with no alternative but to seek adoption. It was not that she had been unkind; she had tried her best to give him what he wanted; it was not that she had been unfeeling; she had tried to see things from his perspective, but had simply failed. Now Bertie was left with no alternative but to seek a new life where there would simply be less interference.

As he watched Irene's retreating figure, Bertie almost relented, almost ran over to embrace his mother and confess that he had thought disloyal thoughts; but he did not. Biting his lip, he realised that he might never see her again; or, when he next saw her, he would have a new mother, who would be Glaswegian, and fun, and would never have read Melanie Klein and have not the slightest interest in ever reading her. Oh, promised land of Glasgow; spontaneous, cheerful, warmhearted; oh, dear green place!

67. *By Waverley Station I Sat Down And . . .*

In so far as clockwork goes like clockwork, that is how it went. As soon as he was confident that his mother was well on her way up Spylaw Road, Bertie looked about him, saw that nobody appeared to be looking, and ran into the bushes lining the drive behind the school gate. They were old rhododendrons, thick-trunked, and suitable for the covering of a variety of juvenile illicit activity. All that Bertie demanded of them was temporary cover until the last of the stragglers had made their way down the school drive.

Then he could slip out undetected and go as fast as possible – without running, as that might attract attention – to his planned rendezvous with Ranald Braveheart Macpherson outside the Bruntsfield Hotel.

There were only one or two points at which Bertie found himself holding his breath. One was when one of the teachers stopped directly opposite his bush and conducted a lengthy mobile telephone conversation with somebody about the arrival of a central heating engineer to service a domestic boiler; another was when Olive, having been dropped at the gate by her mother, happened to look in Bertie's direction. For a brief moment it seemed to Bertie that Olive was looking directly into his eyes, and indeed she did take a half step towards the bush, but then she turned away and continued down the drive. It was an awful, agonising moment, every bit as tense as that involving Nazis sweeping the churchyard for Maria and the sheltering von Trapps, and although the stakes were hardly that serious, they were bad enough. Had Olive seen him she would undoubtedly have run straight in to report him to the authorities. And then he would have had to explain what he was doing in the bushes. Birdwatching was the most obvious innocent explanation, but he was not sure whether he would be believed. And Bertie, being utterly truthful, had always found it well nigh impossible to lie, unlike Tofu, who lapsed into mendacity more or less whenever he opened his mouth; or Larch, who was similarly untruthful; or even Olive herself, to whom truth seemed at best a malleable concept. So he would have had to confess that he was hiding in order to run away, and that would have been brought to the attention of his mother and his plans would be ruined.

Once Olive had gone inside, Bertie gave a quick look about him and then scrambled out of the bushes and through the school gate. From there he walked with measured tread all the way up Spylaw Road and along Merchiston Crescent. Nobody stopped him; nobody appeared to be in the slightest bit interested in the sight of a small boy making his way purposefully along the pavement. And even in Bruntsfield Place, as he neared the Bruntsfield Hotel and the pavements became thronged with people on their way to work, nobody so much as looked at Bertie. This gave him confidence, with the result that by the time he reached the rendezvous point his step was light and carefree.

Ranald Braveheart Macpherson was waiting exactly where he had promised to be. "So, Bertie!" he said. "Everything is ready. Let's go."

Ranald claimed that he knew exactly how to get to Waverley Station, but Bertie had taken the precaution of bringing with him a small map of Edinburgh that he had found in the back of one of his father's magazines. This was a map of the bars and restaurants of the city, but the principal streets were clearly shown too, as was Waverley Station itself. Following the map, they made their way across the Meadows and along George IV Bridge. Now Bertie was on familiar territory, as this was the route that the 23 bus took every morning. "We can't go wrong now, Ranald," he said confidently. "Waverley Station is just over there – beyond the Scott Monument. Can you see it?"

Bertie pointed to the spiky edifice of blackened stone. Ranald nodded. "They keep Sir Walter Scott's bones in there," he said. "My dad told me about it. For ten pence you can have a look."

"I think that's really rude," said Bertie. "I wouldn't want anybody to look at my bones when I'm dead."

"Neither would I," said Ranald. "Bones are private. That's why you can't see them, except with an X-ray." He paused. "Have you heard about X-ray specs, Bertie?"

Bertie had, and had secretly wanted a pair ever since he had seen a small advertisement for them at the back of a comic.

"You put them on," Ranald Braveheart Macpherson continued, "and then when you look at people you can see through their clothes. It's really good fun. You see some very funny things."

Bertie nodded. "I think they're really expensive," he said. "Because otherwise everybody would have them."

They turned off the Mound and began the descent towards Waverley Station. Ranald now assured Bertie that he had enough money for their fares to Glasgow. "I'll need a return," he said. "But you will only need a one-way, won't you, Bertie? You're going to be adopted over there and so you won't need a ticket to come back."

Bertie nodded, trying not to show his anxiety at this arrangement. It was all very well to dream about being adopted in Glasgow, but now that the dream was becoming a reality he was beginning to have second thoughts. What if he did not like the adoptive parents suggested for him by the adoption agency? Would he be able to ask to meet other possible parents, or did he have to accept the people they chose for him? What if he liked them at first and then discovered that he was not so keen on them after a week or two? Could one ask to have another shot, and hope that the second lot would be better? He had not really thought about these questions, and now they were almost at Waverley Station, and the sound of trains could be heard quite clearly – the whistles, the grinding of metal wheels upon railway lines, the echoing announcements of trains leaving for impossibly exotic-sounding destinations: Dunfermline, Croy, Montrose . . .

68. *On the Shoulders of Another*

The great slippery concourse of Waverley Station was heavily populated with travellers, some watching the bulletins on the departure board, some hurrying for trains, some engaged in conversation, some standing uncertainly by piles of luggage as if unsure where to go, or perhaps whether to go at all. In this general thrang of Scottish humanity, two small boys hardly stood out, and would have been assumed by others, if they noticed them at all, to be attached in some way to some adult in the crowd. Fifty years ago, of course, they would simply have been boys – and boys were ubiquitous, unattached, mendicant even; scruffy urchins who frequented street corners, who sold papers, did errands, picked pockets, played ancient and obscure games of marbles. How different were things now, as the streets had been largely cleared of children, who were now sequestered indoors, attached to addictive electronic gizmos, as if led off by some ultra-effective pied piper.

"The ticket office is over there," said Ranald Braveheart Macpherson. "I've been here before, you see. I went in there with my dad and we bought some tickets."

Keen not to be outdone, Bertie nonchalantly mentioned his own trip to Glasgow some time before, when he and Stuart had taken the train to retrieve their car. "I went to Glasgow too," he said. "I went with my dad to fetch our car."

Ranald looked puzzled. "Why was your car in Glasgow, Bertie?" he asked.

Bertie explained about his father's having forgotten that he had driven over and then having taken the train back. "We met a very fat man over there," he went on. "He was called Lard O'Connor and he ate those deep-fried chocolate bars. That's what they eat in Glasgow – it's their staple diet, I think."

"I wish I lived in Glasgow then," said Ranald. "You're lucky, Bertie: you're going to be living there from this afternoon."

Bertie nodded, but said nothing. The idea of living in Glasgow still appealed, but not quite as much, perhaps, as earlier on. Even deep-fried chocolate bars could pall after a while, he imagined, and what if there were boys at Hutchies who turned out to be like that boy, Jack, who had pushed him over in the rugby match and then kicked him for good

measure? And what if there was nowhere like Valvona &
Crolla, which was perfectly possible, and consequently there
was no panforte di Siena and no opportunity to sample
small squares of salami on little wooden cocktail sticks?
And what if there was no One-O'Clock Gun fired from the
Castle, and even no castle at all? What then? What if there
was no National Gallery of Scotland and no picture of a
skating minister and no street like Princes Street with the
flags all flying and the band playing in the Ross Pavilion,
and no Ross Pavilion, and a river that was big and full of
floating bodies, unlike the Water of Leith, and boys who
said things to you that you couldn't understand and then
head-butted you for good measure when you asked them
to repeat themselves or asked them something in Italian
because that is what they might have been speaking? What
then?

But it was far too late for such thoughts. Like a pilot
who realises that he has used too much runway to change
his mind about taking off, Bertie felt that he could do
nothing about withdrawing from the expedition now.
He did not have many friends, after all – one could not
count Tofu as a real friend, since he was such a liar, and
so inveterately given to spitting at those who disagreed with
him on virtually anything – so Ranald Braveheart Macpherson
was really one of Bertie's few real intimates, and he did not
want to go down in Ranald's estimation; not that Ranald
was particularly brave – indeed, Bertie had always thought
that Ranald needed the support of others to do anything.
That came, he imagined, from the fact of having such spindly
legs: if one had such legs in life, then support was one thing
that one must constantly lack, at least in the physical sense.

They entered the ticket hall, where a few orderly lines of
people waited for their turn to purchase tickets from a long

counter. Ranald and Bertie joined the queue, with Ranald clutching in his hand a small wad of Royal Bank of Scotland twenty-pound notes. "I got these from my dad's safe, Bertie," Ranald whispered, showing him the money. "You should have seen how much money there was. We've got heaps of money at home, you know. Any time you need some, just ask me."

"Thanks, Ranald," said Bertie.

"Don't mention it," said Ranald. "Any time."

The queue moved forward slowly and as they approached the counter, Bertie became aware that they were about to be faced with a problem.

"He won't be able to see us," he whispered to Ranald.

"Who won't?"

"The man behind the counter. Look, it's way above our heads. He won't see us when we're standing right in front of it."

Ranald glanced in the direction of the counter. Bertie was right, he realised. He thought for a moment. "You sit on my shoulders," he said. "Then you'll be tall enough. And he'll also think you're much older – maybe even twelve – because you'll be so tall. He won't ask us then if we're allowed to go to Glasgow."

At first, Bertie thought this a very good idea, but then an objection came to mind. "But will you be able to support me, Ranald?" he asked.

"Of course I will," Ranald answered. "Why not?"

It was a delicate issue. "Your legs." Bertie began.

"What about my legs?"

"They're really good legs," Bertie said hurriedly. "But I think my legs are maybe a bit thicker, Ranald – just a bit. So why don't you get on my shoulders?"

Ranald shrugged. "I don't care," he said. "If that's what you want."

When their turn came to be served, Bertie bent down while Ranald Braveheart Macpherson climbed onto his shoulders. Then, holding firmly on to Ranald's knees, Bertie raised his friend up. Ranald was now quite tall enough to speak directly to the man behind the counter, who was looking at him in astonishment.

"Two tickets to Glasgow please," said Ranald, trying to make his voice sound as deep as possible.

The man smiled. "Single or return?"

Bertie realised the significance of the question and gave a slight shiver. "One single and one return," said Ranald.

"Halves?" asked the man, and then added, with a further smile, "Since you appear to consist of two halves anyway."

69. *Queen Street Station*

Their tickets grasped firmly in their hands, Bertie and Ranald Braveheart Macpherson made their way towards the relevant platform at Waverley Station.

"Mine say OUT and RTN, Bertie," commented Ranald. "I see that yours just says OUT. That's because you're not coming back."

Bertie glanced at the wording on his ticket and saw that this was so. He swallowed hard. There was something very ominous about the word OUT on a ticket, and it brought home to him the full implications of what he was doing: as far as his old life was concerned, he was, indeed, going out and was not going to be coming back in. Suddenly he thought of his room at home, and of his things. His model aeroplanes. His shelf of books. He thought of Valvona & Crolla. He thought of the cub scouts. He was leaving all that for a future that although it might be fun and exciting, was also quite uncertain.

"Ranald," he began, as they neared the platform from which their train was due to depart. "I've been thinking and . . ."

Ranald cut him short. "We've got to hurry, Bertie. That's our train."

"I've been thinking," Bertie said again, but just behind them, on a line that disappeared in the opposite direction under the cavernous roof of the station, a passing train let out a mournful whistle, completely masking Bertie's words.

"Come on, Bertie," urged Ranald. "We don't want it to go without us."

They entered a carriage and found two empty seats. Ranald glanced at his watch and then looked at Bertie. "The big hand is on . . ."

Bertie read the time for him and Ranald pointed out that they had only a minute more to wait. If that: the doors slammed shut and there was a whirring sound from a motor somewhere underneath the carriage floor. And then, with a gentle jolt, their journey began.

The train drew out of Waverley Station slowly, giving the boys a view of the towering cliffs of the Old Town's stone buildings. Bertie recognised the Bank of Scotland, with its fluttering Saltire flying alongside the flag of the ancient bank itself. He spotted the top of a bus as it made its way down the Mound, and he wondered whether it was the 23. The thought caused another pang: there might well be a 23 bus in Glasgow, but he would have no idea what its route would be and it could well be a very different bus from the Edinburgh 23. He looked away; it was just too painful. He was making a terrible mistake and he wanted to go back to Scotland Street. He wanted to go home and throw himself on the mercy of his mother, who would be so cross with him for trying to run away, and who would probably arrange even more psychotherapy for him as a result.

"Ranald . . ." he began, but the train had now entered the tunnel under the National Gallery and his words were once again lost. By the time that they emerged at the other end, to trundle through Princes Street Gardens, Ranald was making some remark about the Castle above them and Bertie was prevented from completing his sentence, which consisted of only five words anyway: I want to go home.

There was another tunnel and then within a very short time the train started to slow down.

"We're here," announced Ranald, getting out of his seat. "Come on, Bertie. This is Queen Street Station. We're in Glasgow."

Bertie thought that the trip had taken a remarkably short time, but he was now seized by a strange acceptance of his fate and he was not in a mood to argue with Ranald. The train now stopped to admit more passengers, and to allow Bertie and Ranald off.

"This way," said Ranald confidently, pointing to a set of covered stairs climbing up from the platform. "Hurry up, Bertie."

They joined a small crowd of passengers, disgorged from another train, and went out into the street.

"So this is Glasgow," said Ranald, gazing about him. "It looks different, doesn't it, Bertie?"

Bertie nodded. He had now decided on his course of action, which would be to go through with the visit to the adoption agency but then to reject the parents they offered. This would mean that he would not lose face with Ranald and could quite legitimately say that he would return to

Edinburgh with his friend, to think about coming through to Glasgow some other time; which of course he would not do, and it would all be forgotten about.

The making of this plan had cheered Bertie, and he was now able to face Glasgow without feeling too miserable.

"Let's just walk about a bit," said Ranald. "I'm sure that we'll eventually find the street we're looking for."

This suited Bertie: if they did not find the street, then it would be even easier to bring the expedition to an end.

"I think that looks like it," he said, pointing to street going off the main thoroughfare. "Let's try there."

"Good idea," said Ranald.

They walked along the street that Bertie had indicated, and then along another one. At each corner, where a sign indicated the name of the street, Bertie read this out to Ranald, who consulted his piece of paper and shook his head. They continued their search, wandering along streets and crescents until they came to a road that led sharply downhill. They followed this, and found themselves in a small cluster of buildings beside a river.

"Look, Bertie," shouted Ranald excitedly. "The Clyde!"

Bertie stared at the water flowing past them. "It's not very deep," remarked Bertie. "I can see the bottom. Look, those rocks are sticking out of the water."

"That's very dangerous for ships," said Ranald. "They have to sail very slowly on the Clyde in case they hit a rock."

Bertie continued to gaze at the river. "I can't see any ships," he said.

"That's because they've all gone out to sea," said Ranald knowingly. "They'll be back."

Bertie looked at the river again. The owner of a small dog out on a walk had thrown a stick to the other side of the river and the dog, although hesitant at first, had scampered across, hardly getting its feet wet. How could ships navigate such a river, he wondered? Was the mighty Clyde another of these myths, dreamed up by civic bureaucrats anxious to find something to boast about?

70. *Mains of Mochle*

While Bertie and Ranald Braveheart Macpherson contemplated their dubious river, Big Lou, her coffee bar closed for the day, was in Crieff, a pleasant Perthshire town known for its famous hydropathic institution, a large Victorian hotel, popular with generations of Scottish families. This hotel had been chosen by the South of Scotland Elvis Association for its annual Elvis impersonators' conference, and it was for this reason that Big Lou found herself there, having been invited to attend this event by her new friend, Darren Gow.

Big Lou had accepted the invitation, but stipulated that she would be returning to Edinburgh that evening after the commemorative dinner and subsequent Elvis karaoke competition. Darren would be staying on, he announced, and would not return to Edinburgh until the following day. "We could have dinner in Edinburgh, maybe," he said. "And I can tell you about what happened on day two."

Big Lou had made a non-committal response.

She had rather taken to Darren, but she wanted to be sure before matters went any further. The Elvis interest was unfamiliar to her and she was not sure about it. Was it really all that different from being a Jacobite – as her previous boyfriend had been? What was it about her, she asked herself, that seemed to attract men with issues? Big

Lou travelled up to Crieff on her own, Darren having gone up the previous evening. "Committee business," he said, giving these two words all the gravity they inherently had, even when applied to something like an Elvis impersonators' association. "We need to set the agenda the day before – the Elvises can be a bit bolshy if we don't have things very clearly set out. Prima donnas, many of them." Big Lou arrived at four in the afternoon, which was in time to see the cavalcade of Elvis-impersonating bikers ride up the driveway of the hydro, three abreast, the engines of their Harley-Davidsons roaring throatily under the cloudless Perthshire sky. Back towards the hotel, interrupted in mid-stroke on the lawn, a party of croquet players composed of retired Church of Scotland ministers and fund managers from North Berwick looked up in astonishment from their game and its polite incivility. Croquet and Elvis were not an obvious mixture, but the hydro staff had seen even more surprising combinations before and were quite capable of coping with such contradictions. For a hotel that had at the same time hosted a party of American morticians on a golfing tour of Scotland along with the North Sea Oil industry's Gay Barbershop Quartet Singing Competition, the juxtaposition of ministers and Elvises was but as nothing.

Big Lou met up with Darren near the reception desk. He seemed pleased to see her, and gave her an affectionate kiss on the cheek. "Things are pretty busy, Lou," he said, looking about him at the scenes of activity in the hall. "We've got a record attendance this year, you know. It's going to be vintage – real vintage."

"I'm glad, Darren," said Big Lou. "It must be awful if you hold a conference and you get no folk coming. Awful."

"Yes," said Darren. "But no danger of that today. Things are going to be popping, Lou. You'll see." He looked at his watch. "Would you mind if I went and spoke to some people? We have to make arrangements for the banquet tonight. There's a bit of competition about who's going to sing, and things are getting a bit complicated. I'll see you in the bar in an hour's time? Five thirty? Okay, Lou?" She told him that she did not mind, and she went off on a walk through the gardens. She had not been to the hydro before and she wanted to explore. Perhaps she would come back one day and spend a few days here, she thought, in the peace of these hills, with this wonderful crisp air. By a quarter past five she was back inside to be in good time for her meeting with her host fifteen minutes later.

By six o'clock there was still no sign of Darren, and Big Lou was becoming anxious. Had she heard him correctly? Had he said five thirty, or was it six thirty? She decided to wait. The banquet was at eight and she could always meet him then; presumably some tricky point of committee business had arisen and was keeping him from meeting her. Big Lou understood. It was never easy being on an organising committee, and a committee of Elvises must have challenges all of its own.

A man sitting at the table next to Big Lou's in the bar also appeared to be waiting for somebody. She noticed him glancing at her, and eventually she addressed him. "Fine day, isn't it?" she said, looking out of the window towards the strath.

The man looked at her quizzically. "Excuse me," he said. "You're from . . ."

She recognised his accent, just as he had hers. "Arbroath," she said.

He smiled. "My name's Alex MacPhail. And you're . . ."

He did not finish his question. "Alex MacPhail?" Big Lou asked.

"Aye," he said.

"I never thought I'd see you again," said Big Lou. "Mains of Mochle?"

The man nodded, breaking into a smile. "Aye. And I know fine who you are. Don't tell me. You're . . . You're Big Lou, aren't you?" The introductions made, he moved over to join Big Lou at her table.

"You waiting on somebody?" she asked.

He shook his head. "No, I'm here by myself." He hesitated. "I lost my wife about a year ago and sometimes I find that time . . . well, it hangs awful heavy on my hands."

"But what about the farm?" asked Big Lou.

"There's not much for me to do," said Alex. "I have a really good stockman who does everything. He prefers to have me out of the way, and so I get away a lot. Here, the Peebles Hydro, a hotel near Ballachulish. It fills the time."

Big Lou looked at him. She had last seen Alex MacPhail when they were both sixteen. He was about to leave school to go and work on his father's farm, Mains of Mochle, and she was about to start looking after her elderly uncle on his farm. Neither had had any great sense of a future, other than that which involved their doing what they had always done, which was hard work, in one place, until marriage or fate took them away from the land where their people had always been, living their life in a Scotland that they thought would be there forever.

71. *The Pros and Cons of Rare-breed Pigs*

Big Lou and Alex MacPhail had a great deal to talk about. There were reminiscences of well-known Arbroath characters; there was discussion of the difficulties of running a farm compared with those involved in running a coffee bar. Alex, it transpired, was thinking of raising rare-breed pigs, as a sideline to his Aberdeen Angus cattle, but was concerned at the growing cost of animal feed and the slow growth rate of some of the breeds.

"The standard production pig these days matures quickly but tastes of very little," he said. "Look at the bacon you get in your average supermarket. Look at what happens when you cook it. Water comes out. Water and salt."

Big Lou agreed with this. "Disgusting," she said.

"Yes," said Alex. "But let me tell you something, Lou. I had a nice piece of bacon the other day that Mrs. Forrester smoked herself. You remember her? Mains of Morriston? She had that wee dog that won all those prizes in Dundee one year. Remember? Best dog – dog of the year. Something like that. There was a full page spread in the *Courier*."

Big Lou remembered. "A great dog," she said.

"Anyway," Alex continued. "She gave me some of her bacon. It came from a Gloucester Old Spot and Tamworth cross. Nice-looking pig. And it couldn't have been more different from supermarket bacon. Fantastic, Lou. Thick rashers with real taste." He paused. "You should serve bacon rolls in your coffee bar, Lou. Real bacon. Those Edinburgh types would love it. Muckle great rolls with big bits of bacon in the middle. How about it, Lou?"

Big Lou thought for a moment, but only for a moment. "Great idea, Alex," she said.

"Mind you," Alex went on, "you have to be careful with some of these pigs. Some of them get quite vicious. Mike Stuart – remember him, Lou? – he was attacked by one of his pigs. Aye, a few years back. It was a nasty business. He slipped when he was dealing with one of his breeding sows

and she went for him. Bit his ear, and he was lucky not to lose it, Lou. A pig will easily take your ear off. Of course, some of them have very easy temperaments. The British Saddleback, for example. There's a great pig. Pretty, too. They're the black ones with that thick pink stripe round them. A bit like Belted Galloway cattle. Do you remember Willy Lawson, Lou? He had Belted Galloways. But that was after your time, I think."

"I think so," said Lou.

She suddenly looked at her watch, and gave a start as she realised that it was almost time for the banquet and there was still no sign of Darren.

"I'm meant to be going to a dinner," she said to Alex. "I'm with this fellow, you see, and there's a big meeting of these . . ." She did not say it; she did not want Alex to know about the Elvises.

He looked crestfallen. "Oh."

She reached her decision. "Look," she said. "I'm not really in the mood for a big, formal dinner. I think I'll just go and tell them that I'm not going to be there."

The disappointment on Alex's face lifted immediately. "I'll wait," he said. "I'll wait right here."

Big Lou got up and made her way to the reception desk, from where she was directed to the function room in which the Elvis dinner was being held. This was on the ground floor, not far away, and even as directions were being given she heard the sound of Elvis voices drifting down the corridor. And as she approached, this noise became louder, until she stood at the doorway of a large room thronged with Elvis impersonators and their wives, girlfriends, and boyfriends.

It seemed to Lou to be an impossible task to find Darren. She thought she saw him, and made her way purposively across the room to have a word with him, but when she came face-to-face with the person she had seen, she realised that she had been wrong. He looked like Darren from a distance, but then so did everybody else, because they all looked like Elvis, and deliberately, defiantly so.

She turned round and gazed over the sea of faces. There he was. No, that wasn't him. Was that him? No, that Elvis was too short. Darren was a tall Elvis, but so were fifty or sixty other Elvises in the room.

Big Lou turned round and walked out of the room. On her way out, she inadvertently bumped into an Elvis who was standing by the door, talking to another Elvis.

"Sorry," she said.

"Lou!" said Darren Gow. "Sorry, I've been talking to Harry here about the karaoke and . . ."

"I'm going home, Darren," said Lou. "Thanks for inviting me, but I have to go now. I hope you enjoy yourself." He opened his mouth to say something, but she was gone.

Back in the bar, Alex MacPhail had ordered himself a drink and asked Lou what she would have.

"I've been thinking about bacon," he said. "I wonder if there's much of a market for good bacon in Edinburgh. Or do you think people can't be bothered?"

Lou thought that it all depended. There were some people, she said, who would go out of their way to buy good bacon, as long as they had the time.

Alex nodded his agreement. "Time's the thing," he said. "You're right there, Lou. Time."

They sat in silence for a moment. Then he said, "You wouldn't want to have dinner with me, would you, Lou? They have a very good dining room here."

Big Lou smiled. "I'd love that, Alex."

They finished their drink in the bar and then went into the dining room, where they were found a table at the window. Outside, even in the dying light of the day, the hills of Perthshire were touched with soft gold. They looked at the menu, and Alex pointed out that the lamb probably came from a local farmer whom he had known for years. "He sells a lot of meat to these people," he said. "It's very good."

"I'm sure it is," said Lou.

She looked at Alex, and it was with fondness, and he looked back at her in much the same way. And she realised, as she sat there at the window, that each of us eventually comes home to the thing that we have always been, to the thing that we really are.

72. *Edinburgh for Phobics*

At the end of Antonia's letter to Angus, after loving and detailed descriptions of her new life in the Tuscan convent that had been so kind to her, there had come a paragraph that caused him not only an agony of indecision but also a considerable amount of lost sleep. It was not any particular ambiguity that gave rise to this; the message was simple. "As for that painting you mentioned," wrote Antonia, "I want you to have it even if it is valuable. I know that a Cadell can sell for goodness-knows-what at an auction these days, but that's not the point. Please have it and enjoy it or, if you will, sell it and buy something else. This is a gift to you, Angus. Material things no longer mean to me what they once meant. I am released from their tyranny, and quite frankly I can tell you: this feeling of freedom is quite exhilarating. And please do not come back to me and seek to persuade me otherwise. It is important, you know, to be able to accept gifts from the hands of others, and to do so graciously is an ability which I am sure you will find within you – if you look."

Angus had read and re-read these words and each time he had come to the same conclusion: Antonia wanted him to have the painting. But more than that, she wanted him to have the value that the painting represented, and this meant that he could, if he wished, sell it and use the money, as she had suggested, to buy something else. At first he had thought that he would have no wish to do this, but more recently, following the discouraging conclusion that Domenica's feelings for him had changed, a new thought had occurred. He would sell the painting and use the proceeds to buy Antonia's flat for Domenica. This could be a gift from him to show that however disappointed he might be by her change of mind – and he was certain that she had, indeed, changed her mind – he was not one to resent her nor to harbour a grudge. That is what he would do, and it would mean that he could retire from this whole engagement with Antonia feeling that he had behaved honourably and generously. And that was exactly how he had always wanted to behave.

By the time he reached the Scottish Gallery on Dundas Street he had worked out the exact terms of the letter he would write to Antonia. "I accept your generous gift, dear Antonia – and it is generous. You mentioned in your letter that the painting comes to me free of any restraint on what I might do with it. That, I suppose, is a paradigm of the gift: the thing that is given becomes the property of the recipient, free of any encumbrance as to purpose or destination. I note that you said that I could sell it myself, if I so desired. That is so thoughtful of you . . ." He stopped, and for a moment stood rooted to the spot in Great King Street where this thought had occurred.

From his customary position at his master's heel, Cyril looked up at Angus expectantly. The dog was used to walks that were punctuated with these unscheduled moments of reflection, and it would give Cyril the time to carry out a more in-depth sniff of their surroundings. Great King Street had a particular smell at dog-level, a smell that humans were completely unaware of but which to dogs meant a great deal. Indeed a canine map of Edinburgh, were such a thing possible, would have an entirely different look to it from any maps drawn up by human beings. Human maps referred only to the names of the streets, and gave little other information, apart from the recording of distances. Dog cartographers would be uninterested in such a concept, but would include so much else. The streets in the immediate surroundings of butcheries, for example, would be red-lined, triple red-lined perhaps, while those occupied by cats would be specially marked in some other prominent colour. Feline escape routes of cats – the paths taken by cats fleeing for their lives from pursuing dogs – would be carefully traced, allowing the more intelligent dogs to waylay their quarry further down the line. Lampposts would be individually illustrated, with attention being drawn to those that were more promising – a helpful guide to what canine argot, for some obscure reason, refers to as cottaging. The homes of those known to object to dogs, along with the houses of prominent cat-lovers, would be marked out with a symbol designed to encourage loud barking in that area. And so on . . .

Such a map is pure fantasy. Less fantastic are the obscure but non-apocryphal Burglars' Map of Edinburgh, the Social Climbers' Map of Edinburgh, and Edinburgh for Phobics, a map which sets out those spots which are best avoided by those suffering from various phobias. George IV Bridge,

for instance, is not recommended for those affected by vertigo, as is the Castle Esplanade. Princes Street is best given a wide berth by those with a fear of crowds, while the gardens that lie alongside it are marked on this map as having particular dangers for anthophobics (those afraid of flowers) and chorophobics (those afraid of dancing). A symbol for this latter phobia is printed next to the Ross Pavilion, because of its association with Scottish country dancing events during the summer, when the innocent passer-by, enjoying a walk through the upper levels of the gardens, may suddenly look down and see a group of otherwise rational people, bedecked in kilts and tartan skirts, weaving past one another in strange tribal rituals known as Strip the Willow or the Dashing White Sergeant. Nothing can guarantee that one will not suddenly come across public dancing – public dancing is in a sense like lightning, and must be accepted as such – but a glance at the phobics' map will at least enable the chorophobic to visit Edinburgh without running too great a risk of encountering the thing that he or she fears most. And if we can get through life without encountering the thing that we fear the most, then we are not doing too badly.

And for most of us, the thing that we fear the most is to find that nobody loves us. Which is what Angus felt at that moment, in Great King Street, in spite of the fact that his dog, who loved him so intensely and unconditionally, was directly at his feet and trying, wordlessly, to convey the length and depth and breadth of that love.

73. *A Venetian Interior*

When Angus arrived at the Scottish Gallery, Guy People was in the middle of a telephone call in his office. "Don't disturb him," said Angus to Elizabeth Wemyss, who was busy hanging a new exhibition. "I shall wait." He looked at the painting that the other assistant, Tommy Zyw, was holding in position for Elizabeth's approval. Tommy was the grandson of an artist, Aleksander Zyw, who had come to Edinburgh from Poland and whose paintings Angus had long admired; grandfather and grandson both had a good eye.

"Exactly right," said Angus. "Right where you've got it."

The painting was secured in position.

"Cyril likes it," said Elizabeth. "See the way he's staring at it."

Angus looked down at Cyril, who was looking intently at the recently hung painting, a street scene in what appeared to be Naples, or possibly Palermo.

"There must be a dog in it somewhere," said Angus. "Cyril loves to see pictures with dogs in them. He always finds the dog."

"Surely not," said Tommy, who had not met Cyril before and had no idea of his abilities.

Angus moved forward to inspect the painting at closer range. As he had suspected, there was a small dog making its way down the colourful Mediterranean street. "There," he said, pointing. "Do not underestimate Cyril's powers, Tommy. They are considerable."

Guy appeared from his office and suggested to Angus that they adjourn to Glass & Thompson up the road to talk. Once there, Angus ordered coffee for them both before extracting a small parcel from his briefcase and starting to unwrap it.

"I have a painting here, Guy," said Angus.

"So I see. I'm intrigued."

Angus paused in his task of unwrapping. "So you should be. Isn't it the most delightful moment – to be waiting for a painting to reveal itself?"

Guy looked at the parcel. "You've obviously found something very nice."

"Indeed I have," said Angus.

He began to remove the final layer of paper in which he had carefully wrapped Antonia's painting when he removed it from her flat.

"Here we are!" he whispered. "Just look at this."

Guy took the painting from Angus and held it at arm's length. For a few minutes he said nothing, but gazed at the painting, occasionally moving it slightly to allow the light to play on it from a different angle. When he spoke, it was in quiet, almost reverential tones.

"This is exquisite," he said. "Absolutely exquisite."

"Cadell?" asked Angus.

Guy did not hesitate. "Yes. Undoubtedly."

The word undoubtedly was exactly what Angus wanted to hear, and to hear it from Guy, the grandson of S.J. Peploe, made it mean all that more.

"I've never seen this before," said Guy. "Do you know anything about the provenance?"

"Domenica's neighbour," said Angus. "I think that she inherited her paintings from a distant relative. They were Glasgow ship-owners, I think."

Guy nodded. "Many of those people were great patrons of the arts, you know. Not just the Burrells of this world, but lesser families. They were very generous to artists."

"What do you think?" asked Angus.

Guy put the painting down on the table and took a sip of his coffee. "There's a very interesting thing here," he said, pointing to the right hand side of the painting. "This is an interior of a woman arranging flowers. A fairly popular subject, by the way. Vuillard did a number of them, as you probably know. Also very intimate interiors. But take a look at the view from the window behind her. Familiar?" Angus peered at the painting. Although the painting was painted in a very free, impressionist style, there was enough detail to make out . . . a canal. And not just any canal . . . "Venice?" he said.

Guy nodded. "I'd say so. And that ties in very nicely with Bunty Cadell's career. He went to Venice in 1910 at the behest of a patron of his, Sir Patrick Ford. He did some lovely Venetian paintings, and this, I think, is one of them. Look at the fluidity of it – the beautiful freedom of expression. After the War he changed . . ."

"Oh?"

"Yes. He served in the Argyll and Sutherland Highlanders. When he came out – and he was lucky to get out in one piece – he sought more structure in his work. His post-War paintings are much tighter."

"I love them all," said Angus.

"And so do I," said Guy. "And I love this painting, Angus. Does the owner want to sell it? Is that why you've brought it to me?"

Angus hesitated. He felt ashamed. "She wants to give it to me."

Guy inclined his head slightly. "Oh yes."

"And she said that I could sell it if I wanted to."

Guy was silent.

"She really does," said Angus. "And she knows it's

a Cadell. It's not as if she isn't aware of its value. I think . . ."

Guy interrupted him. "Which is really considerable, Angus. You are aware of that, are you? I mean, really considerable."

"How considerable?"

"It could be three or four hundred thousand," said Guy quietly. "One went for more than that not all that long ago. And this is something very special. It really is."

Angus nodded. "I know that."

"I would take a second opinion," said Guy. "I always suggest that. Take it up to Bonhams, if you like. Speak to Miranda Grant about arranging something. I expect they'll say much the same sort of thing as I've said."

Angus took the painting and began to wrap it up again.

"I'm going to try to persuade her not to give it to me," he said. "I can't accept it."

Guy studied his friend's expression. "You know something?" he said. "There are times when you have to accept things. People are generally rather bad at it – they feel bad about accepting things. But sometimes it's exactly the right thing to do." He paused. "The owner of this painting – what are her circumstances? Does she need the money?"

Angus shook his head. "She's joining a convent in Italy."

Guy shrugged his shoulders. "Then she won't need this. And if she really wants you to have it – or to have the money you could get from selling it – then perhaps you should accept graciously, even if you subsequently sell it."

"Or keep it," muttered Angus.

"If you love it," said Guy.

"I do," said Angus.

74. *Unhappiness Revealed*

Disappointed by the Clyde, Bertie suggested to Ranald Braveheart Macpherson that they make their way along the path that followed the river. He had now reached the conclusion – and it was a welcome one – that they would never find the street they were looking for. He had gone off the idea of adoption, for the time being at least, and he thought that the best thing to do would be to find somebody who could direct them back to Queen Street Station. Ranald had his return ticket to Edinburgh and he had enough money to buy Bertie one; with any luck, they would be back in Edinburgh in a couple of hours, possibly before the end of the school day, and therefore before their parents discovered that they were missing.

"I think that we should give up looking for this place," Bertie suggested as they began to walk along the riverside. "Glasgow's just too big, Ranald: we'll never find it."

Ranald took little persuading. He, too, was beginning to feel anxious, and was keen to get home. "That's a good idea, Bertie. Glasgow's not all it's cracked up to be, if you ask me. It's not all that different from Edinburgh, is it?"

They followed the path as it wound its way along the course followed by the Clyde. There were few people about, but after a while they saw a woman whom they thought they might ask to direct to them to Queen Street Station.

"Excuse me," said Bertie politely. "We're looking for Queen Street Station. Could you tell us the way, please?"

The woman stopped in her tracks. "What station did you say?"

"Queen Street," said Ranald Braveheart Macpherson, trying to sound authoritative.

The woman smiled. "Well, the best way of getting to Queen Street Station, I believe, is to get a train from Waverley."

"We did that," said Bertie.

"Well, then, what are you doing in Edinburgh? You must have come back again."

There was a silence. Bertie looked at Ranald Braveheart Macpherson, and Ranald stared down at the ground.

"You said it was Glasgow," whispered Bertie. "I thought that it was too quick. That was Haymarket Station we got off at, Ranald!"

The woman had overheard this, and laughed. "So you got off before you even left Edinburgh. Oh dear . . . And what were you boys doing going to Glasgow by yourselves, may I ask?"

Bertie looked away. "Business," he said. Bertie was a truthful boy and did not like to lie; this answer was, he felt, honest enough – adoption business was business.

"Oh yes," said the woman. "And what business would you boys be in?"

It was at this point that Ranald Braveheart Macpherson began to cry. The tears came suddenly, and Bertie was taken by surprise. "Don't cry, Ranald," he said, putting a protective arm about his friend's shoulder.

"I never wanted to go," sobbed Ranald. "Honest. I like Edinburgh. I never wanted to go to Glasgow. It was him. I promise. It was him."

The woman looked disapprovingly at Bertie. "Did you force this little boy to run away?"

Bertie blanched. "I didn't! I promise I didn't!"

"Well," said the woman. "Whatever may have happened, I think that I should get you two boys home. Where do you live?"

"44 Scotland Street," said Bertie. "But Ranald Braveheart Macpherson lives in Church Hill. He's got this house with a swing in a tree and . . ."

"And my dad's got surround sound," added Ranald, still sobbing. "And he's got a safe."

The woman seemed to recognise the Scotland Street address. "I have a friend who lives there," she said. "Well, well. Now it sounds as if you both have nice families who would be very worried if they heard that you had run away. And to Glasgow, of all places! What Edinburgh boys would ever think of running away to Glasgow? What could you be thinking of?"

"It's his mummy," said Ranald, pointing at Bertie. "She makes poor Bertie do all sorts of things. Yoga. Psychotherapy. Saxophone. Italian."

The woman listened gravely. "Is that true?"

Bertie nodded. "Yes, it is."

"And are you unhappy about all this?"

Bertie nodded silently.

The woman pursed her lips. "And have you ever told anybody that you're unhappy?"

"I tried to tell my psychotherapist," said Bertie. "But all he wants to do is to talk about my dreams."

They continued their walk, the woman holding hands with Ranald on one side and Bertie on the other. Before too long the path they had been following emerged in Stockbridge, and Bertie realised exactly where they were. "That's where I go for yoga," he pointed out. "And Mummy's floatarium is just round the corner. She went there once with the psychotherapist and Mummy showed him how to float."

"How interesting," said the woman.

"Yes," said Bertie, who was feeling more cheerful now.

"That was my first psychotherapist. He went to Aberdeen where they had found somewhere for him to sit down. My wee brother, Ulysses, looks just like him, you know. They've got the same sort of ears."

"Even more interesting," said the woman.

They reached Scotland Street and made their way up the several flights of stairs that led to the Pollock flat.

"I hope Mummy's in," said the woman.

"I hope she's not cross," said Bertie.

"I'm sure that she'll just be relieved that you're safe," said the woman. "Then we can get Ranald back home too."

Irene opened the door. For a few moments she was completely nonplussed, and nothing was said or done. Then Bertie rushed forward and threw his arms round her legs.

"I met the boys down by the Water of Leith," said the woman. "I brought them back, but I think perhaps we might have a word or two."

Irene recovered herself. "Bertie," she said. "You go and play with Ranald in your room. Show him your Italian books, maybe."

The two women went into the kitchen. "My name is Dilly Emslie," said the rescuer. "I happen to be a friend of your neighbour – Domenica Macdonald."

Irene nodded. "I see."

"Those boys were running away," said Dilly. "I found them."

Irene's expression was sceptical. "Highly unlikely. Why would Bertie run away?"

Dilly hesitated. "He tells me he's unhappy. Very unhappy."

Irene looked at her coldly. "Unhappy about what?" she asked.

"You," said Dilly.

75. Bertie Plays the Blues

Bertie did not hold it against Ranald Braveheart Macpherson that his friend had so quickly buckled under adult pressure and accused him of engineering the abortive Glasgow trip. Ranald was unreliable – he had long since come to understand that – and he was also not particularly courageous, in spite of his name, with its unlikely William Wallace associations. But for all that he was aware of these failings in Ranald, Bertie was tolerant of them. Ranald's bravery might by questionable, but Bertie thought that this was something to do with having spindly legs; it must be difficult to stand up to people when the slightest push, even a puff of breeze, might have one down on the ground. So when he and Ranald went off to his room while Dilly Emslie, their rescuer, engaged Irene in conversation in the kitchen, Bertie did not confront Ranald with his recent perfidy, studiously avoiding any mention of it. For his part, Ranald was interested in Bertie's saxophone, inviting him to play him something.

"I can do 'As Time Goes By,' if you like, Ranald," he offered.

"No thank you," said Ranald. "Can you do 'Nellie the Elephant,' Bertie?"

Bertie shook his head. "I can play blues, though, Ranald," he said. "Listen to this."

In the kitchen, Irene had made Dilly a cup of tea. She had not done so with particularly good grace, but had realised that she could hardly decline to acknowledge that her visitor had, after all, retrieved Bertie from the depths of Stockbridge somewhere.

"You say that he told you he was running away," said Irene, passing the cup to Dilly.

"Yes," said Dilly. "Actually it was the other boy who said that, but Bertie did not contradict him."

"Well, that's just a piece of childish nonsense," snapped Irene. "Children get these ridiculous ideas put into their heads by Enid Blyton and the like. Her absurd books are full of stories of children running away. She's a disgrace. And as for that Rowling woman and her wizards and what-not. How thoroughly ridiculous!"

"Do you really think so?" said Dilly, taking a sip of her tea. Tea bags, she thought. "I was under the impression those Harry Potter books brought great pleasure to millions of children."

"Bah!" said Irene icily. Adding, "Infantilism. Magical thinking."

"I suppose magic does involve magical thinking," said Dilly mildly. "Anyway, I do think that your son was serious about running away. Apparently he wanted to get himself adopted."

Irene, who was on the point of saying something about Melanie Klein, paused. "Adopted?"

"Yes," said Dilly. "The poor little boy was under the impression that children could arrange their own adoption if they were unhappy with . . ." She hesitated. This woman was insufferable, she thought, and she could well see how Bertie would want to be adopted by somebody else. But she was tactful. "If they were unhappy with their circumstances." For circumstances, she thought, read: overbearing, pushy mother.

Irene was silent.

"It has nothing to do with me, of course," said Dilly. "But I wondered whether you aren't perhaps arranging rather too much for that little boy of yours. He's obviously very talented – he seems to have an extraordinary knowledge of all sorts of things – but he's still a little boy, isn't he?"

Irene remained silent.

"Perhaps you might consider loosening up a bit," said Dilly. "Let him do the things a little boy wants to do."

Irene was looking at the floor. In the background, drifting through from Bertie's room, they heard the sound of the saxophone. The blues. Sad, haunting music – even when played by a small boy; but this was no average small boy, this was Bertie, who had had so much to worry about in

his short life; who wanted only to have fun, to explore the world, to do the things he had seen other boys do; who wanted to wear jeans rather than pink dungarees; who wanted a dog; who wanted to play rugby and cricket and have a bicycle with racing handlebars; who did not want to talk Italian and have psychotherapy; who wanted to drink Irn-Bru and go fishing in the Pentlands; who wanted so much and had, it seemed to him, so little.

"I love that little boy so much," muttered Irene.

Dilly put down her cup. Reaching out, she laid a hand gently on the other woman's forearm. "Of course you do. I can tell that. Of course you do."

"And I'm only trying to give him the best start in life," Irene went on.

"I can see that," said Dilly. "But sometimes you need

to let children make their own start. And sometimes you have to give them what they want, not what we want for them." She paused. "And it's never too late, you know. It's never too late to start afresh. In all sorts of circumstances."

Irene looked up at her. "What shall I do?"

Dilly smiled. "Take him out for . . . for an ice cream. Or fish and chips. Yes, what about fish and chips? There's that place down in Henderson Row – L'Alba D'Oro. They get awards for their fish and chips. Take them both down there and then Ranald can go home. Then take Bertie to buy some jeans on Princes Street. And some of those trainers with lights in the heels. How about that – for a start?"

Irene nodded. "I'll do it," she said. She looked at Dilly. "You must think I'm an awful mother."

Dilly shook her head. She did think that, but she knew that telling awful people that they are awful is never the way to change them. You should tell awful people that they are really rather nice, and that made them less awful. It worked every time – every time. And there were very few people, when one came to think of it, who were without some redeeming features. Irene was typical of the excessively pushy mother, but for all the complications that brought, it was infinitely preferable to the mother who did not love her children at all. Love sometimes needs to be redirected; love sometimes needs to be told that it is swamping or overwhelming its object, but it should never be locked out entirely, never be told to go away.

"Thank you," said Irene suddenly.

Dilly was modest. "I've done nothing," she said.

"You've done a great deal," said Irene. "Let me give you more tea."

Dilly hesitated. "Have you tried leaf tea?" she asked.

76. The Oleaginous Bruce

Bruce's accident – one of the few hair-gel related accidents to be reported in Scotland in recent years – had resulted in his having a leg in plaster and sporting a dramatic head bandage for a few days. Vanity kept him out of circulation for a few days – his bandage, he decided, looked vaguely comic – but once that was off, he was quite ready to accept Matthew's invitation to join him for a drink in the Cumberland Bar.

"Need my advice on something?" Bruce asked jauntily when Matthew telephoned him. "Always ready to dispense that."

"It's not advice," said Matthew. "It's a proposition."

Bruce laughed. "Sorry, Matthew. You're barking up the wrong tree. Can't oblige. I don't play for that team. They'd love me to, of course, but you know how it is."

Matthew bit his lip. "I didn't mean that. I meant a business proposition."

"Now you're talking," said Bruce.

They made the arrangement and Matthew was already sitting in the bar when Bruce hobbled in on his crutches.

"I've broken a leg," he said, waving a crutch. "Slipped on something. Last time I had a leg in plaster was yonks ago when I was playing rugby at Watson's."

"You're a Watsonian?" asked Matthew.

"Of course," said Bruce. "Who isn't?" He paused. "Anyway, what's this so-called proposition of yours?"

Matthew looked at his hands. He did not like Bruce – he never had – and he felt uncomfortable talking to him about this. But he had no real alternative, he had decided. "India Street," he said.

Bruce raised an eyebrow slightly. He seemed amused. "Nice street," he said. "I've always liked it. Broad. Slopes the right way – which is down. Of course if you live at the bottom end then you can only go up, which is not bad, after all. Some cool flats."

Matthew nodded. "As you know, I lived there."

Bruce affected surprise. "You lived in India Street? Really? Well, that shows that you've got good taste, Matthew."

"You knew I lived there," muttered Matthew.

Bruce said nothing.

"I sold my flat, as you know, and we moved to Moray Place, just round the corner. You surveyed the place for us, you may remember."

"Good address," said Bruce. "Now that you mention it, yes, I did look it over for you. I see so many places that I forget. No offence, of course. I remember it quite well, come to think of it. It had that big Chinese thingy that was holding up the ceiling, didn't it?"

Matthew ignored the question. "Then you bought India Street – through a nominee."

A smile flickered around Bruce's lips. "Maybe."

"Not maybe," said Matthew. "You definitely did. And the woman you used as the buyer implied that she wanted to live in it."

"She liked it," said Bruce. "She liked it a lot."

"Whereas in reality," Matthew continued, "you intended all along to develop it."

Bruce shrugged. "That's what I do. Property deals. Fair enough?"

Matthew looked directly at him. "I need to buy it back, Bruce. Elspeth is unhappy in Moray Place. She wants to go back to India Street. We were both happy there."

For a moment or two Bruce's composure was disturbed. But he recovered quickly enough. "So you want to go back? You have to be careful about going back to things, Matthew.

Often it's a mistake. You have to look forward in this life. Look forward. Let go. Keep on the move."

Matthew pressed on. "So I want to make you an offer."

Bruce sat back in his chair. "Well, that's fine, Matthew. I'm always open to offers."

They stared at one another. Matthew found himself looking at the cut on Bruce's scalp, just at the hairline. He saw the sutures and noticed that there were small globules of what looked like gel on the surface of the wound. He smelled cloves.

"I realise that you'll be forgoing your developer's profit if you sell at this stage," he said.

Bruce nodded. "Big time," he said.

"So what I intend to do," said Matthew, "is to offer you eighty thousand pounds above the price you paid for it – the price you effectively paid me. That's eighty thousand for a period of what is it? Two months. Two months in which you haven't had to do anything."

Bruce held Matthew's gaze. "Not nothing, Matthew. Two months of having my money in that property. That's money that could have been working elsewhere, Matthew. So that's two months of lost profit on some other venture – maybe something really big. Plus all the skill. Plus all the risk. Plus everything."

Matthew sighed. "All right. Two months of lost interest on the money. That's . . ."

"Not just interest," interjected Bruce. "Capital appreciation too. What if I'd invested in gold? Look at gold prices. I would have made far more. No, Matthew, it's not that simple."

Matthew looked defeated.

"But I'll tell you what I'll do," said Bruce. "I'll sell it back to you for the price paid and . . . and, let's say, three hundred thousand on top. How's that sound to you?"

Matthew closed his eyes. It was a ridiculous premium, but he realised that he was not in a position to argue. Bruce knew that he was desperate to get back into the flat, and he had pitched his price accordingly.

"Three hundred thousand on top," Bruce repeated. "And your wife."

Matthew gasped.

"Only joking. You can keep your delightful wife. No, just the price I paid plus three hundred grand." He paused. "And you pay the legal fees too. Agreed?"

"I don't seem to have much choice."

"You could carry on living in Moray Place," said Bruce. "Nobody's forcing you. You came to me, remember, not the other way round."

Matthew agreed, and Bruce leant forward to shake his hand. Matthew hesitated, but took the proffered hand and shook it. Bruce then offered to buy him a drink. "It's the least I can do," he said, smiling. "You've enriched me by three hundred grand, so I should be able to manage to stand you to a beer."

Matthew looked at his watch. He wanted to get home. He wanted to tell Elspeth the good news; he wanted to get away from Bruce.

"Do you mind if I don't stay?" he asked.

"Not at all," said Bruce. "Busy, busy."

77. Danish Pastries in the Pleasure Gardens

Matthew did not tell Elspeth that evening of his conversation with Bruce. There were several reasons for this, the main one being that he wanted to tie everything up before he spoke about it. Bruce was slippery, and he was quite capable, Matthew thought, of reneging on their agreement. The other reason why Matthew did not speak to Elspeth about it was that he was ashamed. He knew that he should have stood up to Bruce and yet he had not. Greed – in the shape of Bruce – had triumphed over need – in the shape of Matthew. That was a bleak conclusion, but it was an accurate one.

The next morning, Matthew made an early appointment to meet his lawyer, Lesley Kerr, at the offices of McKay Norwell. These were in Rutland Square, immediately behind the great Victorian edifice of the Caledonian Hotel, and were opposite the Scottish Arts Club, where Matthew had occasionally had lunch with Angus Lordie. It was in the Scottish Arts Club that Cyril, some years ago, had been given his gold tooth, an operation performed by another member, a dentist who had carried out the pioneering procedure – after a few generous glasses of whisky – in the Club's main drawing room, watched over by several other interested members, while another member, a talented pianist, played arrangements of Hamish MacCunn's "Land of the Mountain and the Flood," Marjory Kennedy-Fraser's "Eriskay Love Lilt," and Robert Burns's "Ca' the Yowes" on the grand piano.

Matthew explained to Lesley Kerr about the bargain he had struck with Bruce. She was sympathetic and made no comment on the one-sidedness of the arrangement. "I shall put in the offer as instructed," she said. "Now, you should stop worrying about it, Matthew. You're doing the right thing. Just leave everything to me."

When he left the offices and stepped out into Rutland Square, Matthew tried to put Lesley's advice into practice. I shall not think about Bruce, he said to himself, somewhat grimly, and through metaphorically gritted teeth. But the thought of Bruce, smiling with self-satisfaction at the advantageous deal he had struck, did not leave Matthew easily, and remained with him all the way through Charlotte Square and down the steep inclines of Glenfinlas Street. By the time he reached the flat in Moray Place, though, the cloud that was Bruce seemed to have lifted. And his spirits were to rise even further when Elspeth suggested that they take the triplets into the garden for a picnic.

"It's such a gorgeous day," she said. "We mustn't waste it."

Matthew could not contain himself. "And I have wonderful news for you," he said. "We're returning to India Street. I've bought the flat back."

She leant forward and kissed him. "You clever man," she whispered. "You're a worker of miracles!"

Matthew blushed. I am not clever, he thought. I am not a worker of miracles – not proper ones. I'm something of a failure, really, but . . . but I'm a fortunate man, leading a fortunate life. I have a loving wife; I have three sons, even if I occasionally find difficulty in remembering which is which; I have a job that I love doing; I live in a city that is exquisitely beautiful. The list of his blessings was long indeed, and he knew it.

The picnic was prepared by Elspeth and Anna jointly. Once again, Anna proved herself to be invaluable: buttering slices of bread with extraordinary speed and the cheerful energy that she brought to all her work. She had been busy baking too, and there were homemade Danish pastries, stuffed with slices of apple and small clusters of marzipan-surrounded raisins. There were small mussel and monkfish pies, with pastry decorations in the shape of anchors – a speciality, Anna explained, of a remote, entirely fish-eating corner of Denmark.

At the end of their lawn, a discreet wicker gate gave access to the communal Lord Moray's Pleasure Gardens. These gardens tumbled down the cliff to the Water of Leith far below. Carefully raked paths criss-crossed the gardens, and gave access to various small terraces. It was on one of these terraces that the blanket was set down and the picnic hamper opened. The tiny boys, well wrapped against the breezes that could sweep up from Stockbridge even on a warm day, were placed in three small baby chairs – miniature deck chairs, almost, that could be bounced up and down if the occupant became bored or began to girn.

"If you want to go for a walk," said Anna, as she sat down on the rug, "please do so. I shall look after the boys."

Matthew and Elspeth took her up on the offer, strolling off along one of the paths, arm in arm. Matthew felt a deep contentment: the pleasure one feels in going back to something that one knows one loves and should never have left in the first place. He had been happy in India Street, and he would be happy once again. It did not matter that he had been obliged to pay so much for the privilege of returning. What was money anyway? Nothing, compared with the happiness that comes from being with the right person – and she was at his side now – and in the right place – as he would be once they returned to India Street. You could die at any moment – even here in Lord Moray's Pleasure Gardens – and you would not be able to take a penny with you – not one. Why not spend it, if you were fortunate enough to have it, on the things that you loved? Or the things that other people might love?

They returned from their walk. Anna had moved to a nearby bench and was sitting with her back to them. They noticed that Tobermory – or was it Rognvald? – was seated on her knee and that she was talking to him.

"Many English verbs are irregular," she said to him.

"Extremely irregular," replied Tobermory. "It will be a long time before I can speak my native language, I think."

Matthew and Elspeth looked on with complete astonishment. Then Anna half-turned and, seeing them, smiled. "I didn't tell you that I'm a ventriloquist," she said. "I come from the best-known family of ventriloquists in Denmark. I was practising with Tobermory."

They sat down on the rug. Anna, abandoning her position on the bench, came back to join them, with Tobermory. The little boy was silent now.

They began the picnic. The Danish pastries were delicious, ·the fish pies equally so. The sun came out.

78. *Domenica Devastated and Then Undevastated*

Domenica Macdonald made her way slowly down the stair at 44 Scotland Street. Usually she did not linger, as she had never liked the smell of the stairway – a rather dusty smell – the smell of stone, if stone had a smell. But on this occasion she was deep in thought, and somehow speed of gait and thought seemed incompatible. A slow, deliberative walk aided deep reflection, and she needed to reflect very deeply indeed.

Here I am, she thought . . . And then she asked herself: how often do we start our thoughts with the expression Here I am . . .? Those three words were a powerful prelude to self-mockery – Here I am at my age (or my weight, or in my position, or dressed like this) doing this, of all things – or to a form of clear-eyed self-analysis – Here I am about to do something that will have profound implications (change my life, ruin everything, start a new chapter, etc.).

Here I am, she thought, a woman of a certain age who has agreed to marry a man I have known for years, a neighbour, more or less, a good, kind man, even if he has his little ways – and what man, anywhere, does not? – although admittedly some men have more little ways than others; here I am, then, having experienced one of those sudden visions sent by Venus, and having fallen, like a giddy schoolgirl, for a man from my past who wanders in and discloses that he has a yacht in the west of Scotland and wants me to go sailing with him! And instead of laughing or making one of those vague promises to think about it – as one accepts invitations that one will never be able to take up – instead of doing that I say that I would love to come, and mean it. You stupid, stupid woman! You false, foolish, ridiculous, absurd, venal, fickle . . . She ran out of adjectives and had to stop. One can only berate oneself for so much time before one's vocabulary of reproach fails, and hers had.

By the time she reached the front door, her mind was made up. Now walking up Scotland Street with a sense of purpose – having abandoned the gait of one sunk in thought – she began to make her way to Angus Lordie's studio in Drummond Place. She pressed the bell at the bottom of the stair, the bell under which a small brass plate announced Mr. Lordie (Portrait Painter). There was an intercom linked to a lock, but Angus never used it, complaining that it never got very good reception of Radio 3; she ignored it too and simply pushed the defective outer door open.

Angus, hearing the buzzer, had opened the inner door by the time she reached his landing. He smiled at her, and gestured for her to come in.

"I'm feeding Cyril," he said. "Do come in. You can watch."

She entered. There was the smell of turpentine that always seemed to hang in the air in Angus's flat; there was the smell of the dog meal that Angus fed Cyril, an earthy smell like the smell of . . . what was it? she wondered. The smell of the potato barn on her uncle's farm in East Lothian. She had played in it as a child, and had startled a great rat that had bared its teeth at her and sent her screaming back to the farmhouse, where her mother had said, "There is no rat, Domenica." But there was a rat, and mothers and all the authorities put together could not deny that there was a rat, and still was.

"Angus," she said. "I need to talk to you."

He laid Cyril's bowl on the floor and Cyril, looking up, gave one of his smiles.

"Yes," said Angus, not looking at her. "I know what you're going to say. You don't have to tell me."

She was momentarily taken aback. Had he suspected something? Was it that obvious? She felt the shame and embarrassment of one whose most private thoughts are exposed.

"I don't think you know what I was going to say."

He moved away, so that he was standing in front of his

kitchen window, looking out. On the table, his copy of *The Scotsman*, opened to the letters page, his notebook, a half-empty bottle of milk, his cracked china teapot. She thought of Lear's tragic, lonely figure, the Yonghy-Bonghy-Bò, who had lived on the coast of Coromandel and who had had possessions just like this: two old chairs, and half a candle, one old jug without a handle . . . A nonsense rhyme, but like so much of Lear, so poignantly true about human suffering.

*Two old chairs,
and half a candle,
One old jug
without a handle*
EDWARD LEAR

"I know very well what you're going to tell me, Domenica. And please, please don't worry about it. I'm not blaming you for one moment – not one moment. You cannot make people do things."

She was puzzled. "You cannot make people do what?"

"You can't make people love you. You can hope that they will; you can will it; you can delude yourself into thinking that they do. But you'll always know that there's nothing that you – or the other person – can do about it. So . . ."

She waited for him to continue. Below her, she heard Cyril wolfing down his food, a gobbling, slurping sound.

"So nothing," she said. "Angus, I haven't come here to lie to you. I've come here to say that I had a moment – and it really was just a moment – when an old passion was rekindled. But it was absurd, and it only lasted for a very short while. Barely a day. I've come to my senses. You are the one I love. You really are."

He was silent.

"It would be best if we didn't marry," he said. "I don't want to hold you to it."

"Then I shall be devastated," said Domenica.

He turned round. "Deforested?"

"What?"

"I thought you said you'd be deforested."

She laughed. "No! Devastated. I'd be devastated."

He laughed too, and Cyril, having finished his dog food, padded over to Domenica and licked her ankles. It was a gesture of acceptance and affection that was not lost on either of them.

"Look," said Angus.

"Yes," said Domenica, reaching down to pat Cyril's head.

Angus looked at his watch. "Let's go and have coffee at Big Lou's," he said.

"And make our plans," she said.

He did not contradict her.

79. *Wedding Plans*

The date of the wedding was soon fixed, as was the place, and the officiant. There then remained only the matter of the music, and since neither Angus nor Domenica would have described themselves as particularly expert in that area, this was left entirely to Peter Backhouse, an old friend of both of them, who had agreed to play the organ. "Wedding music is very straightforward," said Peter. "You want to play something calm while the guests are sitting there waiting – you do not want them getting excited. Then something fairly dramatic when the bride enters – that is, undoubtedly, the most theatrical moment – and finally, when all is said and done, you want something triumphant."

"Exactly what I had in mind," said Angus. "Act one, act two, act three."

They had two weeks to get ready. Some of this was taken up with the mundane issue of arranging for the merging of two households. Fortunately, Angus had little by way of furniture, kitchen equipment, or linen, and so Domenica would have to make no change in that respect. The possible sale of his flat in Drummond Place had been quietly and tactfully dropped; he would keep that as a studio, and Domenica would remain in her flat in Scotland Street, which would become the matrimonial home. The vexed issue of Antonia's flat was also neatly resolved by Lesley Kerr's suggestion that Antonia should be persuaded to let it. Domenica had written to her accordingly and had suggested that the rental be paid over to Sister Anne-Marie's mission to sailors in the west of Scotland. Antonia readily agreed to this, as she had long admired Sister Anne-Marie's work and was greatly supportive of it. As far as the gift of the Cadell was concerned, she could not be shifted. "You are to have that painting, Angus. There are so few chances we have to bring happiness in this life that we must not lose those that present themselves. You do love it, do you not?"

Angus could truthfully say that he did. "I shall so enjoy having it," he said. "I shall look at it every day and think of you." He did not mention that, when he looked at it each day, he would also think of the four hundred thousand pounds he was forgoing by not selling it. But we all have unworthy thoughts (some of us, it must be accepted, rather more than others).

The guest list was, as in the case of all weddings, a complicated matter. Both Angus and Domenica had a large number of friends, and the initial list came to eleven hundred people. "Is it necessary to invite the entire Scottish Arts Club?" asked Domenica. "I'm sure that they are most agreeable people, Angus, but the entire membership?"

There was radical pruning of that part of the list. "And the Duke of Johannesburg?" Domenica asked, looking further down the list. "And who are these? East Lothian, West Lothian, and Midlothian?"

"They are his sons," said Angus. "Very charming boys."

There were more hard decisions to make. "I'm not having her," said Domenica, pointing to one well-known name on the list. "You choose between having her at the wedding, Angus, or having me."

He hesitated, but only for a moment. "I have very little choice," he said.

"None," said Domenica.

"And what about her downstairs?" said Angus. "That awful woman – wee Bertie's mother?"

"Needs must," said Domenica. "And anyway, I get the distinct impression that she's changed. She greeted me very politely on the stair the other day and didn't immediately start lecturing me about some pet issue of hers. And Bertie looked a bit happier too. Do you think she might have seen the error of her ways?"

Angus thought for a moment. "I like to believe that people are capable of change," he said. "But I wonder if I delude myself. I wonder if people really do change their fundamental disposition."

Domenica sighed. "I fear that not many do. The die, I'm afraid, is cast very early."

"But you don't think it's impossible?"

"No, it's not impossible. Look at Antonia. Look at what she used to be – a rather calculating man-eater. And what is she now? A nun, or about to become a nun. What more of a change can one imagine?"

Angus looked out of the window. "Do you think she's happy?"

"Certainly," said Domenica. "Look at her letters. And you know something, Angus? It is undoubtedly the case that the practice of the virtues makes one happier. We've somewhat lost sight of that essential truth, now that we, as a society, admire selfishness and vanity so much. Look at this so-called celebrity culture. Look at what it's doing to the minds of our children. Did you see that item in the press about the survey of the career ambitions of contemporary children? You know what most of them say they want to be? Celebrities! Can you credit it? Where are all those little boys who wanted to be firemen and pilots and circus strongmen and the like? Or the girls who wanted to be nurses? Where are they?"

"Perhaps we're just getting away from stereotypes," ventured Angus. "Perhaps the boys want to be nurses now and the girls pilots."

"Possibly," said Domenica.

"And as for little Bertie, do you think he'll survive that mother of his?"

"Of course he will," said Domenica. "Bertie will be fine. That little boy has a heart, and a head, in the right place. He represents goodness, I think. He represents innocence, and innocence has taken such a profound battering in our times. We have mocked it. We have sullied it. We have put it in intensive care, and frankly, I don't see how it can survive. And yet here and there one sees flickers of its light – just flickers. And so we know that innocence isn't entirely dead."

Angus was silent as he thought about this. Domenica was undoubtedly right, as she was about so many things. And as he reflected upon this, he thought of his good fortune in having found somebody like her, prepared to take on somebody like him, and a dog like Cyril thrown in for good measure. The shoulders of women were broad indeed, and none broader, he felt, than this amusing, entertaining, and observant woman who had agreed to marry him and, in so doing, had agreed to reduce the sum total of this world's loneliness by a minute, but to him, inestimably important measure.

80. *Finale*

On the evening before the wedding, Domenica and Angus held a dinner party in Scotland Street. It was a largish affair by the standards of Domenica's dinner parties, but by creating two tables, one in the kitchen and one in the drawing room, they were able to fit everybody in.

"People will have their first course at one table and then the guests will change round and have their second course at the other table," Domenica announced to Angus. "That will ensure that everybody gets the chance to speak to everybody else. Or to at least to look at them, if they have nothing to say."

"A good idea," said Angus. But then, after a moment, he added, "Hold on, Domenica. If they all change tables, then they'll be with the same people all over again. In a different place, of course, and that might be important, but it will be the same dramatis personae."

"True," said Domenica. "You're very perceptive, Angus."

He acknowledged the compliment with an inclining of his head. "So what I suggest is that we get the men to change, and the women remain where they are."

Domenica thought about this. "But then that will mean that the men all have to listen to the same men, and the women all have to listen to the same women. That surely defeats the object of the exercise."

Then Angus raised another objection. "And there's always the problem of glasses with such arrangements. If you have two glasses – a water glass and a wine glass – then you should really take both with you. And your table napkin. Because otherwise you'll get the germs of the person who was sitting there before you."

"There are very few germs in Edinburgh," said Domenica. "But I see what you mean. So perhaps we shall just have two separate tables."

That issue was resolved, and by the time that the first guests arrived, the seating plans seemed so natural as to give no clue to the thought that had gone into them. Many of the guests were those who usually came to Domenica's dinner parties; one or two were newcomers, but everybody, of course, knew one another.

"It's so reassuring," said James Holloway, "to see no new faces."

"Precisely," said Susanna Kerr. "It would be a terrible shock if one went to a dinner party in Edinburgh and met people you didn't know."

The conversation before dinner was every bit as good as the conversation during the meal, and indeed after it. There was so much to discuss, and a great deal to provoke intense merriment. When the subject of the latest Turner Prize shortlist arose, the laughter almost made the windows rattle.

At the table, toasts were proposed, and drunk. David Robinson, who had known Domenica for years, spoke briefly, expressing the pleasure of all the guests at the satisfactory conclusion to the long friendship between host and hostess. On the other side of the table, opposite David, by coincidence sat Mhairi Collie, the surgeon who had been so kind to him, and to so many others. She nodded her head in agreement with the sentiments he expressed. Beside her, entertaining all around him with amusing stories, sat Harvey McGregor, who would, after the dinner, play several Noel Coward numbers on the piano. In the adjoining room, the guests who were at the table there could not, of course, hear any of this, but they received brief summaries of what was said, passed on by the one who sat nearest the door. This made them feel very much part of the evening and in no sense second class.

Halfway through, Angus slipped out to check up on Cyril, who was waiting outside on the landing. Cyril's personal hygiene issues made it impossible for him to attend dinner parties in person, but he had been given a bone, and was happy with that, as most dogs are – and people, too, when the bone is metaphorical.

Angus discovered that Bertie had heard Cyril barking and was sitting on the steps beside him, in his pyjamas and dressing gown.

Angus sat down on the steps.

"Are you having fun in there?" asked Bertie.

"Yes," said Angus. "And shortly I shall go back in and recite a poem. I always do that, Bertie."

"Could I hear it?"

"I don't see why not," said Angus.

He closed his eyes. The words came to him, and came so easily.

Dear friends, gathered again together in a place
That has become so familiar to all of us,
We might wish to forget the world outside,
Might wish to think that here, with our friends,
We are the world. Would that were true:
The world outside is not the world
We would like it to be; I don't need
To enumerate its woes – they are legion,
And greet us each time we open a newspaper.
But it would be wrong to become cynical,
Would be wrong to dismiss the possibility
Of making bearable the suffering of so many
By acts of love in our own lives,
By acts of friendship, by the simple cherishing
Of those who daily cross our path, and those who
   do not.
By these acts, I think, are we shown what might
   be;
By these acts can we transform that small corner
Of terra firma that is given to us,
In our case this little patch of earth
That we call Scotland, into a peaceable
Kingdom, a place where love and friendship
Are writ large not doubted, nor laughed at,
But embraced and proclaimed, made the tenor
Of our quotidian lives, made the register
In which we conduct ourselves.
How foolish I once thought I was
To believe in all this; how warmly
I now return to that earlier belief;
How fervently I hope that it is true,
How fervently I hope that this is so.

Angus opened his eyes. Bertie was staring at him.

"Sorry, Bertie," he said. "I got carried away."

"I understand, Mr. Lordie," said Bertie.

And he gave Angus his hand, and Angus held it briefly. Such a small thing, he thought: so fragile, so human, so precious.

THE 44 SCOTLAND STREET SERIES

"Will make you feel as though you live in Edinburgh. . . .
Long live the folks on Scotland Street."
—*The Times-Picayune* (New Orleans)

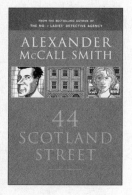

44 SCOTLAND STREET

All of Alexander McCall Smith's trademark
warmth and wit come into play in this novel
chronicling the lives of the residents of a
converted Georgian town house in Edinburgh.
Complete with colorful characters, love
triangles, and even a mysterious art caper,
this is an unforgettable portrait of Edinburgh
society.

Volume 1

ESPRESSO TALES

The eccentric residents of 44 Scotland Street
are back. From the talented six-year-old Bertie,
who is forced to arrive in pink overalls for his
first day of class, to the self-absorbed Bruce,
who contemplates a change of career in
between admiring glances in the mirror, there
is much in store as fall settles on Edinburgh.

Volume 2

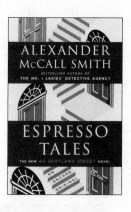

LOVE OVER SCOTLAND

From conducting perilous anthropological
studies of pirate households to being inadvertently left behind on a school trip to Paris, the
wonderful misadventures of the residents of
44 Scotland Street will charm and delight.

Volume 3

THE WORLD ACCORDING TO BERTIE

Pat is forced to deal with the reappearance of Bruce, which has her heart skipping—and not in the most pleasant way. Angus Lordie's dog, Cyril, has been taken away by the authorities, accused of being a serial biter, and Bertie, the beleaguered Italian-speaking prodigy and saxophonist, now has a little brother, Ulysses, who he hopes will distract his mother, Irene.

Volume 4

THE UNBEARABLE LIGHTNESS OF SCONES

The Unbearable Lightness of Scones finds Bertie still troubled by his rather overbearing mother, Irene, but seeking his escape in the cub scouts. Matthew is rising to the challenge of married life, while Domenica epitomizes the loneliness of the long-distance intellectual, and Cyril succumbs to the kind of romantic temptation that no dog can resist, creating a small problem, or rather six of them, for his friend and owner, Angus Lordie.

Volume 5

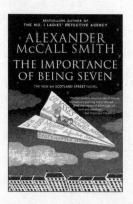

THE IMPORTANCE OF BEING SEVEN

Bertie is—finally!—about to turn seven. But one afternoon he mislays his meddling mother, Irene, and learns a valuable lesson. Angus and Domenica contemplate whether to give in to romance on holiday in Italy, and even usually down-to-earth Big Lou is overheard discussing cosmetic surgery.

Volume 6

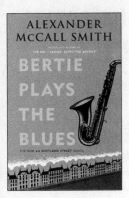

BERTIE PLAYS THE BLUES

New parents Matthew and Elspeth must muddle through the difficulties of raising their triplets—there's normal sleep deprivation, and then there's trying to tell the children apart from one another. Angus and Domenica are newly engaged, and now they must negotiate the complex merger of two households. And in Bertie's family, there's a shift in power as his father, Stuart, starts to stand up to overbearing mother, Irene—and then there's Bertie, who has been thinking that he might want to start over with a new family and so puts himself up for adoption on eBay. With his signature charm and gentle wit, Alexander McCall Smith vividly portrays the lives of Edinburgh's most unique and beloved characters.

Volume 7

THE CORDUROY MANSIONS SERIES

"A new cast of characters to love."
—*Entertainment Weekly*

CORDUROY MANSIONS

In London's hip Pimlico neighborhood, Corduroy Mansions, a block of crumbling brickwork and dormer windows is home to a delightfully eccentric cast of residents including, but not limited to: a wine merchant who desperately hopes his son will move out; a boutique caterer who has designs on the oenophile down the hall; a snarky member of Parliament; and Freddie de la Hay, a vegetarian Pimlico terrier.

Volume 1

THE DOG WHO CAME IN FROM THE COLD

Freddie de la Hay has been recruited by MI6 to infiltrate a Russian spy ring. A pair of New Age operators wants to use Terence Moongrove's estate as a center for cosmological studies. Literary agent Barbara Ragg represents a man who hangs out with the Abominable Snowman, and the rest of the denizens of the housing block have issues of their own.

Volume 2

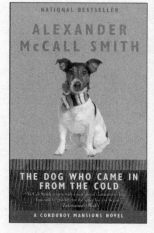

A CONSPIRACY OF FRIENDS

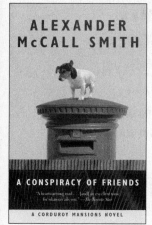

There's never a dull moment for the residents of Corduroy Mansions: Berthea Snark is still at work on her scathing biography of her own son; literary agents Rupert Porter and Barbara Ragg are still battling each other; fine-arts graduate Caroline Jarvis is busy blurring the line between friendship and romance; and William French is still worrying that his son, Eddie, may never leave home. But uppermost on everyone's mind is Freddie de la Hay— William's faithful terrier (and without a doubt the only dog clever enough to have been recruited by MI6)—who has disappeared while on a mystery tour around the Suffolk countryside.

Volume 3

THE NO. 1 LADIES' DETECTIVE AGENCY SERIES

Read them all....
"There is no end to the pleasure."
—*The New York Times Book Review*

The No. 1 Ladies' Detective
Agency—Volume 1

Tears of the Giraffe
—Volume 2

Morality for Beautiful Girls
—Volume 3

The Kalahari Typing School
for Men—Volume 4

The Full Cupboard of Life
—Volume 5

In the Company of Cheerful Ladies —Volume 6

Blue Shoes and Happiness —Volume 7

The Good Husband of Zebra Drive —Volume 8

The Miracle at Speedy Motors—Volume 9

Tea Time for the Traditionally Built —Volume 10

The Double Comfort Safari Club —Volume 11

The Saturday Big Tent Wedding Party —Volume 12

The Limpopo Academy of Private Detection—Volume 13

The Minor Adjustment Beauty Salon—Volume 14

FOR YOUNG READERS, INTRODUCING PRECIOUS AS A YOUNG GIRL

THE GREAT CAKE MYSTERY

"A detective is born! Lucky young readers will now be able to make the acquaintance of the one and only Precious—Alexander McCall Smith's beguiling and intrepid Botswanian sleuth, as she takes on her very first case."
—Mary Pope Osborne, bestselling author of *The Magic Tree House* series

THE MYSTERY OF MEERKAT HILL

Precious has a new mystery to solve! When her friend's family's most valuable cow vanishes, Precious must devise a plan to find the missing animal. But she needs the help of the family's pet meerkat to solve the case. Will she succeed and what obstacles will she face on her path?

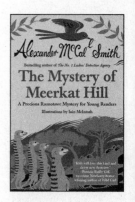

THE ISABEL DALHOUSIE NOVELS

"The literary equivalent of herbal tea and a cozy fire. . . .
McCall Smith's Scotland [is] well worth future visits."
—*The New York Times*

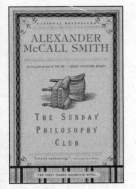

The Sunday Philosophy Club

Isabel Dalhousie is fond of problems, and sometimes she becomes interested in problems that are, quite frankly, none of her business—including some that are best left to the police. Filled with endearingly thorny characters and a Scottish atmosphere as thick as a highland mist, *The Sunday Philosophy Club* is an irresistible pleasure.

Volume 1

Friends, Lovers, Chocolate

While taking care of her niece Cat's deli, Isabel meets a heart transplant patient who has had some strange experiences in the wake of his surgery. Against the advice of her housekeeper, Isabel is intent on investigating. Matters are further complicated when Cat returns from vacation with a new boyfriend, and Isabel's fondness for him lands her in another muddle.

Volume 2

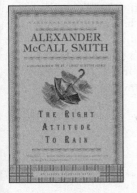

The Right Attitude to Rain

When Isabel's cousin from Dallas arrives in Edinburgh, she introduces Isabel to a bigwig Texan whose young fiancée may just be after his money. Then there's her niece, Cat, who's busy falling for a man whom Isabel suspects of being an incorrigible mama's boy. Isabel is advised to stay out of it all, but the philosophical issues of these matters of the heart prove too tempting for her to resist.

Volume 3

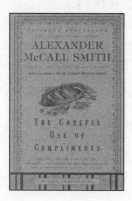

The Careful Use of Compliments

There's a new little Dalhousie on the scene, and while the arrival of Isabel's son presents her with the myriad wonders of life, it doesn't diminish her curiosity about other things. While attending an art auction, she discovers a mystery revealed in one of the paintings, launching her into yet another intriguing investigation.

Volume 4

The Comforts of a Muddy Saturday

A doctor's career has been ruined by allegations of medical fraud and Isabel cannot ignore what may be a miscarriage of justice. Meanwhile, there is her baby, Charlie, who needs looking after; her niece, Cat, who needs someone to mind her deli; and a mysterious composer who has latched on to Jamie, making Isabel decidedly uncomfortable.

Volume 5

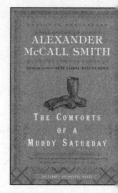

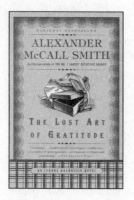

The Lost Art of Gratitude

When Minty Auchterlonie takes Isabel into her confidence about the complicated troubles at the investment bank she heads, Isabel finds herself going another round: Is Minty to be trusted? Or is she the perpetrator of an enormous financial fraud? As always, Isabel makes her way toward the heart of the problem.

Volume 6

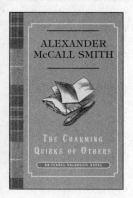

The Charming Quirks of Others

Old friends of Isabel's ask for her help in a rather tricky situation: A successor is being sought for the headmaster position at their alma mater and an anonymous letter has alleged that one of the candidates has a very serious skeleton in their closet. Could Isabel discreetly look into it?

Volume 7

The Forgotten Affairs of Youth

A visiting Australian philosopher asks Isabel's help to find her biological father. As usual, Isabel cannot help but oblige, even though she has concerns of her own. Her young son, Charlie, is now walking and talking, and her housekeeper, Grace, regularly attends a spiritualist who has taken to providing interesting advice. And could it finally be time for Jamie and Isabel to get married?

Volume 8

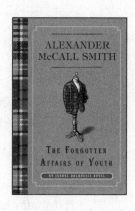

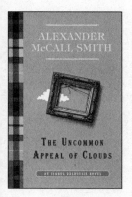

The Uncommon Appeal of Clouds

Isabel answers an unexpected appeal from a wealthy Scottish collector, Duncan Munrowe, who has been robbed of a valuable painting. Never one to refuse an appeal, she agrees, and discovers that the thieves may be closer to the owner than he ever would have expected. Isabel also copes with life's issues, large and small, and finds herself tested as a parent, a philosopher, and a friend.

Volume 9

THE PORTUGUESE IRREGULAR VERBS SERIES

"A deftly rendered trilogy . . . [with] endearingly eccentric characters."
—*Chicago Sun-Times*

Welcome to the insane and rarified world of Professor Dr Moritz-Maria von Igelfeld of the Institute of Romance Philology. Von Igelfeld is engaged in a never-ending quest to win the respect he feels certain he is due—a quest that has a way of going hilariously astray.

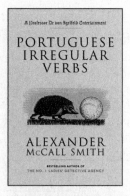

Portuguese Irregular Verbs

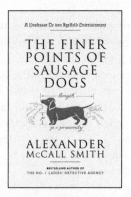

The Finer Points of Sausage Dogs

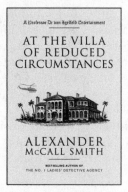

At the Villa of Reduced Circumstances

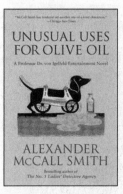

Unusual Uses for Olive Oil

ALSO BY ALEXANDER McCALL SMITH

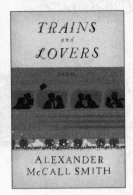

TRAINS AND LOVERS

A wonderful new novel that explores the nature of love—and trains—through a series of intertwined romantic tales told by four strangers who meet as they travel by rail from Edinburgh to London.

LA'S ORCHESTRA SAVES THE WORLD

A heartwarming novel about the life-affirming powers of music and companionship during a time of war.

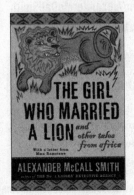

THE GIRL WHO MARRIED A LION AND OTHER TALES FROM AFRICA

"These are pithy, engaging tales, as habit-forming as peanuts."
—*Publishers Weekly*